Indulge all of your
two bra

Mills & Boon

A Very Special Mother's Day

These two rich and vivid stories are a real treat to
treasure – and brought to you by two stars of romance:

Secrets of the Outback
by bestselling Tender Romance™ author

Margaret Way

&

A Wicked Lady
by the winner of the 2004 Romantic Novelists'
Association ROMANCE PRIZE –
Historical Romance™ author

Anne Herries

Margaret Way takes great pleasure in her work and works hard at her pleasure. She enjoys tearing off to the beach with her family at weekends, loves haunting galleries and auctions and is completely given over to French champagne "for every possible joyous occasion". She was born and educated in the river city of Brisbane, Australia, and now lives within sight and sound of beautiful Moreton Bay.

Margaret Way is an international bestselling author who writes for Tender Romance™ and Silhouette Superromance™. Don't miss her brand-new duet coming soon in Tender Romance!

Anne Herries, winner of the Romantic Novelists' Association's Romance Prize 2004, lives in Cambridgeshire. After many happy years of having a holiday home in Spain she and her husband now have their second home in Norfolk. They are only just across the road from the sea, and can see it from their windows. At home and at the sea they enjoy watching the wildlife and have many visitors to their gardens, particularly squirrels. Anne loves watching their antics and spoils both them and her birds shamelessly. She also loves to see the flocks of geese and other birds flying in over the sea during the autumn, to winter in the milder climes of this country. Anne loves to write about the beauty of nature and sometimes puts a little into her books, though they are mostly about love and romance. She writes for her own enjoyment and to give pleasure to her readers.

Look out for Anne Herries' superb new medieval trilogy, *The Banewulf Dynasty*, starting next month with A PERFECT KNIGHT.

A Very Special Mother's Day

Margaret Way

Anne Herries

*MILLS & BOON and MILLS & BOON with the Rose Device
are registered trademarks of the publisher.*

*First published in Great Britain 2005
Harlequin Mills & Boon Limited,
Eton House, 18-24 Paradise Road, Richmond, Surrey, TW9 1SR*

A VERY SPECIAL MOTHER'S DAY
© by Harlequin Enterprises II B.V., 2005

The publisher acknowledges the copyright holders of the
individual works as follows:

Secrets of the Outback © Margaret Way, Pty., Ltd. 2005
A Wicked Lady © Anne Herries 2005

ISBN 0 263 84528 1

108-0305

*Printed and bound in Spain
by Litografia Rosés S.A., Barcelona*

CONTENTS

This book is dedicated to Diana Palmer, who once told me, "If I can do it, so can you!"
Thanks, Diana

Secrets of the Outback

by

Margaret Way

Dear Reader,

At some time we all have to grapple with the difficulties of family – as well as drawing strength and pleasure from its great joys. This story is about how one young woman tries to deal with her life when she discovers, at the age of twenty-five, that her true parentage had been kept secret from her. A monumental discovery and one that creates many new problems, invading every aspect of life. Think how those problems would be compounded if the "new" family considers itself under threat. Human beings aren't always understanding and tolerant, let alone ready to accept an "outsider" without suspicion. The best one can do is find the courage to reach out, find a way to link the past with the present.

I hope you enjoy Jewel's story. I enjoyed writing it. It has been a great pleasure and an exciting challenge for me. As always, I want to convey my great love for my unique homeland, Australia. Who knows, it might lure you to come Down Under!

Margaret Way

PROLOGUE

February, 1981

STEVE BISHOP, overseer of a remote Outback cattle station, sat in one of the back pews of the Anglican cathedral in the Queensland State capital, thinking he'd never had an experience like this. In fact, it had to be the most extraordinary occasion he had attended in his thirty-one years. Living the way he did in the vast, sparsely populated Outback, he was in awe of the crowd. Used to counting head of cattle, he estimated there had to be at least three thousand people packed into the church, all sitting bolt upright in the crush. Outside on the street, mourners who couldn't make it through the door stood twenty deep, prepared to smile if a camera came near. Inner-city traffic had ground to a halt. So had business.

Today was the funeral of one of the most powerful and influential men in the nation: Sir Julius Copeland, mining magnate, land baron, executive chairman of the giant mining firm Copeland Connellan Carpentaria. Self-confessed Titan.

Important as Sir Julius had been, Steve had had no idea the funeral would be so huge. Or so glittering. Most people, himself included—and it had set him back—had suited themselves in funeral black. But the women treated their somber gear as some sort of blessing in disguise. They wore jewelry. None of your costume jewelry stuff. Lots of extravagant yellow gold. Ropes of pearls and diamond brooches that sparkled brilliantly as they caught the light. He had the notion that just one of those brooches could feed an Outback family for a year. The hats were spectacular, too. Fit for the Melbourne Cup.

The cathedral with its miles of red carpet was redolent with not only the vaguely sickening scent of flowers, great banks of them, but the smell of *money*. Big money. Power. The milieu in which Sir Julius had lived and become a monolith of industry.

As expected, the dignitaries sat up front, striving to look lofty—the governor of the state, along with the roly-poly premier who was working hard to suppress his usual big vote-winning smile. The dour leader of the Opposition sat a pew behind, holding a snowy white handkerchief to his face as though he had a nosebleed or was grieving for the deceased. Steve recognized the federal senator sent to represent the prime minister. This was the same guy he and his cattleman friends had shouted down when the senator last came Outback to deliver more empty promises. Behind them sat the representatives of the legal and business communities, their expressions masked. Then there were the cattle barons, land owners and lesser mortals, all of whom had braved the scorching heat—heck, it was hotter in the capital than in his desert home!—to pay their respects to a giant among men. At least, that was how the press had described Sir Julius in his obituary.

Steve had read it that morning with a sense of mounting wonder and irony. Sir Julius had been all sorts of things, but no one in his right mind could've called him a nice guy. Julius Copeland had been an ogre. Six foot four, built like an armored tank. Voice like the rumble of thunder. Pale ice-blue eyes sharp enough to drill holes in cement. He might have been larger than life, cleverer, more determined, more ruthless than most, but he hadn't been liked, let alone revered. Maybe *loathed* would describe it. Steve had been surprised by his boss's sudden death of a massive heart attack, but he honestly couldn't say he felt any sorrow. With no provocation, Julius Copeland had made life difficult for many, many people, including him.

Now it was time for Sir Julius to meet up with his own Boss. Yet as villains went, Steve supposed Copeland had to be a long way down the list. After all, there was Hitler, Stalin, Nero, Genghis Khan…

Across the aisle, in the front pew, sat the widow, Lady Davina Copeland, a woman much respected for her dedication to public affairs. Fighting for equality for minority groups, that kind of thing. One could say she had set herself in direct conflict with her husband. God knows why she'd ever married the man. They couldn't have hit it off. Steve could only glimpse her from the back. She looked like a woman half her age. Of course, he'd seen grainy photographs of her in the newspapers over the years, but he'd never seen her in the flesh. She was supposed to be beautiful. Very glamorous. He was determined to get a good look at her before he went home. Her godawful son Travis sat beside her. Tall, dark, saturnine, a real personage in his own opinion. Some women might find him attractive, Steve reasoned, rubbing his chin, but Travis Copeland had always made him feel downright queasy. Though Travis always acted like a power to be reckoned with, he was in no way competent to step into his father's shoes. He wasn't a total dolt, either, Steve supposed. The business community would've figured *that* out. Travis's upper-crust wife sat beside him, spine straight, allowing his body to touch hers at the shoulder. She was good-looking, sure, but skinny enough to make a man weep. It couldn't be all sunshine for Travis. Steve had heard, too, that the wife was a bit of an ogress. Must've rubbed off from her father-in-law. Steve knew they had a child, Amelia, a few years older than his own little darling. Amelia wasn't in attendance. Probably she'd been judged to be too young. Funerals weren't very pleasant at the best of times, but especially if you were a friend of the family. Now, little Amelia's grandfather, the man who'd been so very important to the state and to so many lives, would shortly be laid to rest.

If they ever got through the eulogies, Steve thought, loosening his tie. Too many. Too long. Some of them *had* to be tongue-in-cheek. Especially the archbishop's. He had to have some knowledge of Copeland's true nature. The Sir Julius that Steve knew, his boss, owner of Mingaree Station, and a string of other pastoral properties adding up to some five million hectares, was a bastard in anyone's language, and you'd better believe it.

Forgive me, Lord. Steve momentarily bent his head, ashamed of his irreverence. Not that the good Lord wouldn't agree after He'd talked to the man, however briefly. Julius Copeland had been intimidating beyond belief, so rough of tongue he made the crudest station hand blush. A complete contrast to his partner of the old days, Sir Stafford Connellan. Steve had had the greatest respect for Sir Stafford, knighted, like Copeland for service to his country. The big difference was that Sir Stafford had been a great man, a bred-in-the-bone gentleman. A real thoroughbred, now sadly deceased. Sir Stafford's son, Earle, had succeeded his father in the firm. Steve could just see where Earle Connellan sat, his lean handsome face solemn, with his dark-haired wife, Rebecca and their only child, a son of around thirteen, Keefe. The boy was the image of his father which was to say strikingly handsome, but there was more to it. Like his father and grandfather before him, he had that aura of integrity and high intelligence. That special look of breeding. Industrial giant though he'd been, Sir Julius had never had that. No doubt, in time the boy Keefe would become a force in the firm. The Connellans were still major shareholders, despite Sir Julius's best efforts to outwit them after Sir Stafford's death. No sense of decency there.

The Connellans, too, were possessed of great wealth, but they'd always had virtually the opposite approach to it. Earle Connellan stood head and shoulders above the likes of Travis, whom Steve detested for a number of reasons. Earle was a great guy, a man you could talk with, no side to him for all his privileged background. Travis, though, was an arrogant son of a bitch. Pretty much thought himself a god. As did his old man. Not that Steve and Thea had to suffer Travis much these days. At one time, Travis had flown into the station regularly in his Beech Baron, but not for ages now. Come to that, Steve hadn't visited the city in years. Today he was part of a contingent of cattlemen who'd traveled a thousand miles and more to attend the great man's funeral. Damn near mandatory. It was easy to tell who the cattlemen were. Though suitably dark-suited, all of them to a man balanced their trademark akubras on their knees. As did Steve. He'd nodded to most of them as they made their bowlegged way in. Horsemen. And it showed.

Landowners were up front, as befitting the guys who owned the whole caboodle. Employees were at the back. Steve didn't mind. He wasn't part of this world of wealth and privilege. He didn't want to be. Steve considered himself blessed. He had a job he enjoyed. Plenty of back-breaking work, of course, but he was well-paid and he had security of tenure if only because he knew his job and had a good business head. He had the sweetest wife, too, his loyal Thea. She had given him such happiness since the moment he put his ring on her pretty finger. Above all, he had Jewel. God, he adored that child! She was his life. Six going on seven. The most adorable, the spunkiest, smartest, most affectionate daughter a father could want. Hair of spun gold. In total contrast, her delicate winged eyebrows were many shades darker than her hair, almost black. She had blue eyes of such radiance that he had bypassed the name she'd been christened, Eugenia after Thea's mother, to settle on the only name possible when one looked into those sparkling eyes—Jewel. Jewel Bishop. Nowadays no one on the station called her anything else. His little Jewel. His sweetheart. His treasure. He couldn't wait to get back to his "girls." He already knew what he was going to bring them as gifts. Every trip away, even a trip like this, Steve bought his girls surprises. He loved the moment they opened them, the way their eyes lit up with love for him. His girls. His life.

The service droned on to the point that he actually considered getting up and stretching his legs. About time things got moving. He couldn't bear being trussed up in this city gear. And the heat! Some guy choked up and had to be led off. Must've been an act. Still, this was no place for such an unChristian thought, Steve decided. He lowered his curly dark head to his hymn book, joining a choir of uniformed kids from one of the posh schools. Probably Sir Julius's alma mater. He tried to visualize Julius Copeland as a small boy. Couldn't. He'd always figured Sir Julius had sprung into this world fully grown—and had believed the old boy could never die. Now Sir Julius's final destination was waiting. Steve didn't know exactly where that would be, but he wouldn't be a bit surprised if Sir Julius was going straight to hell.

TEN MINUTES LATER, Steve got his first good view of Lady Copeland as she made her dignified way down the aisle. No one to support her. She probably felt as though a great weight had been lifted from her shoulders. She didn't look from side to side. She didn't look at anyone. Steve had to keep reminding himself of her age. She was Travis's mother, which had to put her well into her fifties, but behind the short black veil she wore over her face—he thought only royalty did that—she looked as youthful as her daughter-in-law.

Steve found the opportunity to study her again outside. He was tempted to go up and say hello to her. Explain he was overseer of one of the Copeland cattle stations. Of course he didn't. He hung around watching the VIPs go, instead. Her elegant beringed hand came up to push back the short veil. Now, for the first time, Steve saw her face exposed to the brilliant sunlight.

Lord God! He gulped as a terrible malevolent humming started up in his head. The clarity of shock and the pain almost felled him. In one soul-destroying moment of revelation, Steve knew his whole life had been stolen from him. He reeled with the impact. Slammed into something hard. A stone pillar. He knew beyond any doubt that he could never be happy again.

The face of this woman, Davina Copeland, was the same magical face as his own daughter's. The resemblance was startling. Here was the mould for the face of the child who had given him all the joy in the world. His daughter, Jewel. There was the hair, dressed differently, of course—maybe the woman's owed a little these days to artifice—but it was the same thick, gleaming gold. There were the distinctive winged black brows, the heavily fringed blue eyes that shone like jewels.

Now all those hazy questions he'd sealed away in his mind broke out of the vault. He turned in blind anguish, his feelings of betrayal so powerful that they were beyond words. He looked for and found Travis Copeland. The destroyer was standing by himself. Without hesitation Steve moved in. He would have liked to shout ''Adulterer!'' but his throat closed up. Travis was sweating and shaking, just standing there staring at him. Knowing what was coming.

Before anyone could stop him, Steve Bishop, superbly fit, launched himself at the man who had dishonored his wife, ruined his life. He grabbed him powerfully by the shoulder, then—as mourners turned, both aghast and agog—punched Travis so hard in the face that he was knocked clear off his feet. Copeland's patrician nose was most assuredly broken. Steve had felt the crunch, but without any satisfaction.

A woman in a chic black suit began to wail. Not the widow. Not the wife. Perhaps they realized this sort of display was bound to happen sooner or later. While Travis Copeland sprawled on the stone steps, his nose gushing blood, police descended on Steve Bishop. They overpowered him swiftly although he offered no resistance. He rocked back and forth on his feet, his face ashen, not a shadow of regret in his eyes. Steve Bishop was in an altered state from which he would never give himself time to recover.

It was impossible to hide things. In the end they always came out.

CHAPTER ONE

The present

MONDAY MORNING. Traffic was heavier than normal. Jewel swung a U-turn, not exactly sure if it was legal, and took a different route, only to find some of the lights were out on Station Road, which put her farther behind. Another couple of delays would precipitate a minor crisis. She would be late for her Monday morning "chat"—a quaint tradition—with her boss, Blair Skinner, a man she found extremely abrasive. Few in the prestigious law firm of Barton Skinner Beaumont didn't, but they all wanted to hang on to a career. Instead they made jokes about him behind his back.

A vacant parking space in the small basement of her office building almost caught her unaware. She drove into it nearly dizzy with relief. The only real way to secure basement parking was to arrive early. Which she always did. Except today…. Someone, bless him or her, had obviously called in sick.

Jewel grabbed her handbag, so expensive she really should insure it, then locked her car by remote. She made directly for the lifts, feeling reassured, despite her workouts at the gym, that there were a few fellow workers about. Must've been stalled by the same set of lights. A few weeks back, another young woman who worked in the building had had a bad scare when a man approached her, pulling a gun from an inside pocket. As it later turned out after a comparatively easy citizen's arrest—the young woman's rescuer was a prominent footballer—the gun was a fake and the man had a long history of psychiatric problems. Still, no one needed an experience like that. There really should be security, she thought for perhaps the hundredth time, knowing full well it wasn't going to happen.

In the handsomely appointed ladies' rest room— thank God Barton Skinner Beaumont hadn't gone unisex like they did on *Ally McBeal*—Jewel checked herself in the mirror. Skinner demanded that the three female associates of the prestigious law firm that bore his name—well, his grandfather's—be groomed to perfection. Impeccable himself in all matters of dress, manners and taste, Skinner was very severe about it. Up until recently, Barton Skinner Beaumont hadn't even allowed bright young women through their hallowed portals. All vacancies had been filled by bright young men. But Jewel, who held firmly to the belief that women could achieve anything, had become a prime target for Skinner's "wit." Not that the male associates were entirely spared. They, too, received a fair sprinkling of Skinner's sarcastic comments without a one of them game enough to tell him to mind his own business. Extraordinarily enough, Jewel had. That was what came of being born in the bush.

Skinner wasn't going to catch her out today, even if he tried an average of three times a week. Today she'd dressed in a brand-new suit, which had substantially set her back, fine-quality midnight-blue wool, austere but beautifully cut. Under it, to add flair, she wore a brilliant silk blouse, turquoise striped with fuchsia, matched exactly by her lipstick. Incredibly, Skinner noticed things like that. The turquoise intensified the blue of her eyes. She'd had her hair cut recently to just past chin length. It fell thick and heavy in a side-parted classic pageboy. She used to wear it much longer, the way the ex–man in her life liked it, but this was a fresh start. Why did women always cut their hair on such occasions? Perhaps she could find out with a few sessions on a psychiatrist's couch. Not that she trusted psychiatrists. Not after the way they'd sorted out her mother's problems—from depression to grand psychosis.

Just thinking about it was an agony, even though it had been going on for years and years. Determinedly Jewel redirected her attention to the mirror. With her suit she wore good daytime jewelry. Nothing tacky. So what if she could only afford 9-carat gold? It was tasteful, understated. Anyone might think she'd been hired as a clotheshorse instead of a pretty good corporate lawyer, she thought with a grin. No, not *pretty* good. She was underrating herself. She was darn good, and moving up the ladder. A welcome raise after the Stanbroke deal had allowed her to indulge her weakness for beautiful shoes—which might've had something to do with the fact that she'd had to go barefoot for much of her childhood.

OUTSIDE SKINNER'S DOOR, Jewel knocked, then stood back, certain Skinner would permit himself the pleasure of making her wait. She didn't think it was worth brooding about it; it made her laugh. Finally came his peremptory ''enter,'' as though he could ill afford the time to see her. Jewel opened the door and walked into Skinner's plush inner sanctum. It was furnished with an array of handsome Georgian bookcases holding weighty

legal tomes, several favorite paintings by maritime artists and too few chairs, clearly signaling that anyone
who wanted to visit him might have to stand up.

As expected, Skinner had his head down, perusing
some file he seemed to want to keep secret; he held one
arm around it, presumably to prevent Jewel from catching sight of the client's name. Blair Skinner, in Jewel's
opinion, was the sort of man who could sour a woman
on the entire male sex, but she had to concede that at
forty-five he could be rated handsome by the casual
observer. He oozed wealth. He loved fashion. He
dressed in expensive Italian suits that she knew for a
fact cost the best part of two thousand dollars; she'd
checked when she'd visited an exclusive men's store
with her ex. Skinner had never been known to make a
single mistake with his shirts, ties, shoes and socks. He
had good regular features that were always darkly
tanned, thanks to his yachting expeditions, and a fine
head of hair, but the close observer would have rejected
those eyes, small and set too close together. Then again,
other factors weighed in. He was a brilliant lawyer with
a career that went swimmingly and he was, of course,
grandson of one of the firm's founders. Nevertheless,
Jewel always thought he could have posed for a shot of
an upmarket Dirty Rotten Scoundrel. She never stood
forlornly in Skinner's office waiting for his attention.
She amused herself with thoughts such as this.

Finally Skinner looked up, favoring her with an all-
over glance that took in her appearance to the last detail.
Not offensive. Not overtly sexual. Just a quick rundown
of her appearance and grooming. "My, aren't we glamorous today?" he said with a languid wave of a well-
manicured hand.

"Delighted you think so, Blair." Jewel didn't make

the mistake of taking a seat before being invited to do so. That was exactly what Skinner wanted.

Skinner leaned back in his wonderfully comfortable-looking leather. "Yes, you've come on well under my tutelage," he said. "I nearly wept when I first saw you come through my door—what, all of three years ago."

Jewel nodded, not believing he was going to bring up her outfit again—white shirt, designer jeans, navy blazer. A bit on the informal side, but classy.

He was. "I know daggy dress is all the rage in the sticks, but I was frankly horrified to see someone so *scruffy* standing in my office."

As usual, he was exaggerating wildly, and on the strength of her recent achievements, Jewel tried a little taunt. "A good thing for the firm I wasn't marched off in shame."

"The only thing that saved you was your résumé," he reminded her.

"And the fact that I topped my law class, along with winning the University Medal." She would never have been so self-congratulatory with anyone else, but it was part of the routine with Skinner.

"Such revelations! And so many people to speak for you! Wonderful recommendations." He shook his head. "Generally speaking, our young males are the outright winners."

"Were," Jewel emphasized. "But if you look at the results, Blair, they've finally been overtaken."

"Not exactly," he said silkily, "but no sooner do we train them than they mooch off and get married. I hope you're not going to do that, Eugenie," he said as though contemplating a crime.

"Not for a good while," Jewel assured him. "I'm a

touch nervous about marriage. I have a friend who was married for an hour.''

Skinner, divorced himself, almost giggled. ''I take that to mean they were doing it for a stunt. I just love our Monday mornings, Eugenie. Even the run-ins. You seem to be one of the few courageous enough to speak your mind.'' Skinner leaned back. ''Sit down, Eugenie.'' He paused, his expression reflective. ''I simply can't bring myself to call you Jewel like the rest of the office. It's an over-decoration and you don't need it.''

''That's okay. Eugenie is fine. And I get a kick out of your French pronunciation. Besides, I haven't heard it in a long, long time.''

''So who started calling you Jewel?'' Skinner actually looked interested.

''My father,'' Jewel announced casually, although any mention of her father made her feel lonely and sick inside.

''I understand he was killed?'' Skinner stared at her.

Slammed his car into a power pole. ''You've already read my file, Blair,'' Jewel pointed out too sharply.

''My dear, please don't take offense.'' Unexpectedly he backed off. ''I have indeed studied your file. Smart and ambitious as you are, with an ability to write excellent briefs, you're still extremely lucky to be here. I have to hand it to you, Eugenie. For a little girl from the bush with absolutely no connections, you've turned yourself into a real achiever. A young lawyer with a future. Not easy.''

''But I have you on my side, Blair, rooting for me, showing me the way to professionalism, self-improvement, correct dress and behavior. As only someone born to life among the gentry can.''

He laughed. "Watch it!" His smooth cosmopolitan voice was mellow. "Snob, aren't I?"

"Sincerely, yes."

"For which you must be grateful." Skinner began to hunt through the files on his splendid partner's desk. "Don't imagine for one minute that my influence hasn't helped you impress the clients. No one who works here can afford to look like a loser—" He broke off. "Ah, here it is." He withdrew a thick file from the pack. "Remember the Quinn Corp. thing? We handled their takeover of Omega Enterprises?"

"The Copeland Connellan subsidiary?" Jewel asked. "I should. I put a lot of research into that. Around two-hundred pages."

"I wouldn't have let you do it if I didn't have confidence in you," Skinner said a little testily. "However…things don't appear to be working out. In fact, they're going bad."

"Really?" Jewel was surprised. "I would've thought it was airtight."

"Except some of Omega's top people didn't fully appreciate that their jobs were on the line. They're suing."

"You mean Copeland Connellan canned them after the buyout?" Jewel sat back, frowning.

Skinner nodded. "Exactly. Their argument was that Omega's top guns turned out to be duds."

"With their salaries, the Omega people can't have been pleased."

"Don't worry about them," Skinner, never a man to dwell on the misfortunes of others, said equably. "They're all millionaires. Copeland Connellan has a way of clearing out duds. Anyway, it looks like litigation—which, as we represent Copeland Connellan, we will win. Not saying it won't be tricky. So let's get started. Can't have our biggest client saying they're not getting our immediate attention. Then we've got Kussler Consolidated versus the ATA Group. Pull your chair up here. I'll be shoveling a lot of work onto your desk, so don't go making too many outside plans." He glanced up at her. "By the way, Keefe Connellan will be coming in this afternoon on an unrelated matter. He's accompanying Lady Copeland, which is somewhat surprising given the situation with Travis. I'd like to be able to tell him we're already onto the Omega thing at the same time— Haven't met Keefe, have you?" Skinner asked out of the blue.

"I haven't had that great honor," Jewel said, wondering if Skinner was doing his usual job of trying to confuse her.

"Of course you haven't." Skinner stared at her thoughtfully.

"Then, why ask?"

Skinner suddenly turned on a charming smile. "A clever young lady like you might find a way to contrive it."

Jewel had no idea what he was getting at, and merely shook her head.

"I thought every woman wanted to marry a millionaire," he murmured.

"Finding a millionaire would be the easy part. Marrying him and living happily ever after would be a lot harder," Jewel answered dryly.

"*You* could do it, I'm sure." Skinner narrowed his eyes as though thinking deeply. "Anyway, Keefe rarely comes in. He's a very busy man. Quite brilliant. Extraordinarily responsible."

"So they say." Jewel nodded her head with mock

solemnity. According to everyone in the know, Keefe Connellan was guaranteed to become the future executive chairman of Copeland Connellan.

"It's in the genes, of course," Skinner said, as though no one in *his* family had ever been accused of being an idiot. "My family's always mixed with theirs, socially and in business. There was no finer man than Keefe's grandfather, Sir Stafford Connellan. Compared to him, Julius Copeland was a very dodgy character."

"Who knew how to forge an empire," Jewel pointed out. Everyone had heard the saga of Julius Copeland and his great achievements, despite the dodgy bits.

Skinner widened his gray-blue eyes. "You don't hold any brief for the Copelands, do you."

"Blair, I don't *know* any of them. As you've frequently pointed out, I was a girl from the Deep North, and before that the bush. I don't mix in your... distinguished circles."

"Nooo...but you could," he said thoughtfully. "You've got what it takes. I'm absolutely sure there's an interesting story in your background. Something very unusual."

He made it sound as though she'd been switched at birth. "Sorry, Blair. Nothing to discover. I had a very ordinary childhood. My father was an overseer on one of the Copeland cattle stations, if you want to make something of that."

Skinner looked like a man who'd missed out on important information. "*Really?* This is news."

"Considering that Sir Julius left a legacy of nearly five-hundred thousand hectares in Outback Queensland, it's not so unusual. My father died when I was six, going on seven. My mother and I went to live with my aunt almost immediately after. My father's early death left my mother a very sad woman. There wasn't much money and she wasn't always able to work. My aunt half-supported me until I could support myself. As you know, I won a scholarship to a very good girls' school. And I worked my way through university.''

''From whence you graduated with top honors.'' He inclined his head in a gesture of exaggerated respect. ''I have to say I'm surprised to hear there was any connection to the Copelands. You kept that from me.''

''I didn't know you well enough then. You're not onto something here, Blair. Don't get excited. My father was an employee. A fairly lowly one at that. No real connection at all.''

''So where did you get your brains?'' Skinner asked, his tone suggesting her family had to be a bunch of morons.

''My father and mother helped out,'' she countered, her voice dry. ''In addition, my aunt isn't exactly stupid.''

''Which leaves me with one question—who do you *look* like?'' Skinner asked. ''Is your mother beautiful?''

''She is to me,'' Jewel said quietly, remembering her mother before grief and depression overtook her.

''Does she have that golden hair, the black brows and sapphire eyes?''

''Blair, this interest is bizarre,'' Jewel said. ''Not to mention inappropriate. No, my mother doesn't have my coloring. I believe I resemble my grandmother, Eugenie.'' Though she'd never actually seen a photograph of her grandmother.

Skinner brooded a while. ''I know you're considered a warm, attractive young woman, an excellent mixer, everyone seems to like you—and that's not always the case, believe me—but you tend to keep things to yourself.''

"Perhaps I picked that up from you,'' Jewel said smoothly, making him laugh.

"It might seem strange, but when I met you I wondered where I'd seen you before.''

"Maybe we met in another life?'' Jewel suggested flippantly. "Otherwise our paths would never have crossed. I lived and worked over a thousand miles away.''

"True,'' Skinner said, almost wryly. "All the same, something about you seems familiar. Anyway, if you're very good and handle all the work I give you—for which you know I'll get the credit—I'll take you along to a function or two. Lady Copeland doesn't do as much entertaining as she used to, but Travis loves to splash out. Since his divorce, his beautiful daughter, Amelia, acts as hostess for him. Leaves Travis free to pursue…other interests. He loves the ladies, does Travis. Makes no secret of it. The Connellans are far more private. So much tragedy there.''

Jewel looked up, liking Skinner a little better for the soft note in his voice. "Keefe Connellan's father was killed in a mining accident, wasn't he?''

"He wouldn't have been,'' Skinner answered somber, "except that he was a hero. He went back to save some of the men trapped underground. Freed quite a few, but in the end he was trapped himself. It was a tragedy. None of us really got over it.''

"How terrible.'' Jewel bowed her head, thinking events like that could never be forgotten.

"Rebecca—that's Earle's widow—was very nearly destroyed, but she had her son to think of. She and Lady Connellan, Keefe's grandmother, held the fort until

Keefe came of age. Splendid young man. It's an open
secret that he has his troubles with Travis—just as
everyone knows Travis is trying to land Keefe for a son-
in-law. A marriage of dynasties, so to speak."

"It usually works that way." Jewel shrugged. "It's
a tough life. I've seen photographs of Amelia Copeland
and Keefe Connellan in the papers. Both very glamorous people." Connellan was every woman's dream. A
young Sean Connery.

"My dear, you could brush her aside," Skinner surprised her by saying. "She *is* beautiful, as you say, but
there's not a lot of sparkle. I like sparkle in a woman.
So, I fancy, does Keefe. There's nothing doing so far,
despite Travis's best efforts. When I take you to one of
their parties, I'll go with you to pick out your dress. Or
I'll send you off to a friend of mine. She'll know exactly
what's required."

Jewel stared at him, a little dazed. "Blair, I'm overcome."

"That's nice." He smirked. "There *are* perks to being one of my protégées, my dear. Of course, it's not
my intention to marry again," he reassured her, quite
unnecessarily. Christy, one of her colleagues, had always thought Blair was borderline gay. "It's *glorious*
to be free. Now, enough of the chitchat. We must get
down to business. I'm expecting Keefe at three, although if something important crops up, he might have
to cancel. He has a law degree, did you know? Brilliant
legal skills he puts to good use, as well as being a mining engineer. At thirty-two he has more presence than
most of the big names in the state. And I believe he
intends to take over the whole group eventually. He's
developed a reputation as a man with a mission. That

mission, so far as I can see, is to get rid of Travis Copeland.''

"Sounds like you're a bit in awe of him, Blair," Jewel slipped in gently. Blair Skinner rarely spoke so highly of anyone.

"I consider it an honor to call Keefe my friend," Skinner admitted with a modest smile. "I like to think my maturity and experience has left its mark. I hope so. By the same token I often partner Travis at golf. He's an excellent player. So's Amelia. She could give most of the men a run for their money. Do you play yourself?"

"Nope." Jewel smiled. "Never had the time. Nor the money for expensive clubs. Tennis is my game."

"Don't be ashamed of tennis. If you're good enough, I'll give you a game. I can see you now!"

"Another Anna Kournikova?" Jewel asked blithely.

"Women's tennis was in the doldrums before her," Skinner said in a brisk voice. "I'm with Cash and McEnroe. The best woman player can't match a man. Couldn't come close. Now, you've got your legal pad, haven't you?"

"Open, ready and waiting," Jewel said and held up her pen. She didn't bother to tell him about her cupboard full of tennis trophies. That could wait.

ALMOST TWO HOURS LATER, Jewel made it back to her office, so small that some days she thought she'd faint from claustrophobia. She was about to enter, when Anthea, one of the receptionists, all but bolted down the corridor to speak to her.

"Jewel!"

"Hi, Anthea, anything up?" Jewel turned.

"I wanted to catch you." Anthea spoke a little

breathlessly. "They don't have an appointment or any-thing, but two teenage boys are out front asking for you."

"Are they respectable?" Jewel grinned. "No shaved heads or outrageous tattoos?"

Anthea laughed. "No, they're just kids. Nice-looking, actually. They say they know you."

"Names please, Anthea," Jewel said patiently, des-perately wanting to get on with her workload.

"Harry and Josh Hungerford."

"Good Lord," Jewel said. " I have to keep remind-ing myself that kids grow up. Show them through, Anthea. I grew up in Hungerford country. I can spare them a few minutes, though we'll all be knocking heads just trying to fit in my office."

A few minutes later she was shaking hands with two young men she could easily identify, even if they'd both outgrown her by many inches. "This is a wonderful surprise." She smiled at them warmly, as pleased to see them as they apparently were to see her. "Take a seat. Tell me what's going on in your lives. How's your mother? I hope you've got some good news."

"Well, no, Jewel," Harry, the older boy said, his deep voice cracking. "We couldn't think of anyone else to come to. We know you're a big-time lawyer now. We need help."

"Is something wrong?" Jewel looked from one to the other. "I don't know if I can do anything myself—" She indicated with her arm the stack of files: franchis-ing, floats, syndicates, whatever. "But I can certainly point you in the right direction."

"No," said Josh, staring at her with his bright blue eyes. "We want *you*. You know about our life, Jewel.

You know the people in it. You're one of us. From our town. We trust you.''

"Well, that's sweet of you, Josh." Jewel was touched by his words. "Suppose you tell me what this is all about. I take it you're here independent of your mother and stepfather?'' George Everett, never an attractive man. Jewel had always felt uncomfortable with him.

Both nodded. "Mum has betrayed us, Jewel," Harry said, turning his face away. "Ever since she married Everett, our lives have changed.''

Jewel acknowledged that with a sympathetic grimace. "He hasn't been unkind to you, has he?'' she demanded with sharp concern. "Abusive in any way?'' It didn't seem possible with Sheila, their mother, around. Sheila adored her boys.

"He's never hit us or anything," Harry said, thrusting a hand through his short chestnut-colored hair. "He wouldn't dare. Not these days.'' Both boys topped six feet and had strapping country physiques.

"It's still abuse, the way he talks," Josh insisted. "He's still the same smart-mouthed, oily character, and he's getting colder and colder." He paused uncertainly. "It's financial, the reason we're here.''

"Tell me," Jewel invited, instinctively pulling a legal pad forward. "I know your maternal grandfather Fletcher left you both a great deal of land just outside town. River frontage. I know it was held in trust by your mother. I know it was very valuable land then, which means it's far more valuable now. I know that after your mother remarried, she and your stepfather bought several thousand hectares of adjoining land.''

"Nowhere near as valuable." Harry's voice was so tight it was distorted. "Ours has the river frontage.''

Josh picked up the story. "Some time after you left

town to come down to Brisbane, Mum gave herself and Everett a lease on our land.''

"And listen to this—'' Harry burst out loudly. "It was for fifty years. A dollar a year. Everett began working it, then they started borrowing big money using our property as security.''

"Finally they mortgaged our property when they got into debt,'' Josh said.

"I don't believe it!'' Jewel had seen a lot of fraud and deceit in her business, but she was shocked. "Your mother would never allow such a thing.''

Harry shrugged, his expression unhappy. "Mum's not the same person you knew, Jewel. She's changed.''

"She's like a puppet.'' Josh closed his eyes tight, then opened them. "Everett pulls the strings.''

"So, where are you two living?'' Jewel asked, beginning to feel protective. She had known the Hungerford boys since they were toddlers.

"Not in the house. We've left. We've fixed up the workers' cottage. We live there now.''

"And you came all this way to see me?''

Josh folded his arms, suggesting he wasn't leaving until she helped them. "Yeah.''

"But there are good solicitors in Cairns and Townsville.'' Jewel named two of the major cities in the far north of the state.

"Sorry, we trust you, Jewel,'' Harry said. "Not them. We talked it over. We rang your mum. You'd never betray us. Everett knows all the legal guys up north. He can get around anyone, he's so smarmy, the asshole. He got the bank to lend him nearly a million dollars, remember? The thing is, Jewel, we don't have a future anymore,'' Harry said, his eyes holding hers. "Grandpa left us that land to work. The Hungerfords have always been on the land. It's our life. His legacy was our future.''

"That's always the way I saw it,'' Jewel said. "You realize your mother has committed a breach of trust? She held that land in trust for you, her two sons. She had no legal right to mortgage the property. In doing so, she and your stepfather could be said to have squandered your inheritance, which must be worth several million. You're in a position to start legal proceedings. When do you gain direct control, or is that some way off?'' She addressed Harry, but Josh spoke.

"Just over a year. When I turn eighteen and Harry turns twenty. Our birthdays are only a month apart.'' Josh sounded as if they could barely survive until then.

"For that matter, the bank has acted improperly. They knew perfectly well the land was held in trust for you boys. We *all* knew. The whole district. Your grandfather was a highly respected and influential man.''

"One of Copeland Connellan's top mining engineers in the north,'' Josh said proudly, his eyes wandering to Jewel's wall of plaques, tributes, degrees. "I saw on the board outside that this firm handles Copeland Connellan's legal affairs.''

"That's right, Josh.'' Jewel nodded.

Josh leaned toward her. "Mum always said you were really going to make something of yourself. You're a corporate lawyer, right?''

Jewel nodded again. "Corporate and commercial. I had to work hard to earn it. What about you? I take it you finished your schooling Josh?'' Both boys were very bright.

"End of last year,'' Josh confirmed.

"And you, Harry? What are you doing?''

"Nothing,'' Harry said glumly.

"But surely your mother wants you to go on to university or agricultural college?"

Both boys sat silent for a moment, looking exceedingly upset. "We're not talking to Mum," Josh said eventually. "We *can't* talk to Mum. It's impossible to see her without Everett. He doesn't let her out of his sight. That's his tactic."

"That's hard!" Jewel frowned. "You were all so close. How are you supporting yourselves? Where's the money coming from?" she asked.

"Grandpa left us some money, as well," Harry said. "I got mine when I turned eighteen. I'm taking care of Josh. We're in this together."

"It sounds like you've been worrying yourselves sick." Both boys looked as if they'd been carrying a weight of grief on their shoulders.

"It's terrible to know we've lost Mum." Harry swallowed. "It's...it's like she's joined some sect. And it's terrible to know what she's done to us. Are you going to help us, Jewel?"

Jewel settled back in her chair, pondering the fact that she was already loaded down with work. "I should speak to your mother," she said.

"You'll never get to her." Josh punched one hand into the other. "It's always the two of them. Everett's always alongside. I suppose a legal battle would cost a lot of money?"

"I'm afraid so, Josh. And from what you tell me, it would be very bitter. Are you absolutely certain you'd want to work the land if you won the case? Your stepfather and mother own and work the adjoining land."

"It's not as though we could even sell." Harry let loose with his anger and frustration. "It's not ours. We're in limbo. Going nowhere. Everett thinks he has it all over us. A couple of hick kids. You *have* to help us, Jewel. We can't deal with all these problems. You don't know how it feels.''

"Oh, I think I do, Harry, and my heart aches for you. Let me talk to my boss about it.'' Jewel started to drum her fingers on the desk.

"What does that mean?'' Josh clenched his jaw, obviously anticipating obstacles.

"I'm free to take on cases, Josh, but my boss is the senior partner in the firm. I'd have to discuss it with him.''

"But you can help us?''

"You can be helped. Understand that. I'd like to be the one. Where are you staying?''

"With a friend,'' Josh replied. "You wouldn't know him. We boarded with him at school. He's a good bloke. His parents are graziers on the Darling Downs. They have an apartment for when they come to town. Dex lives there—it's close to the university. Dex is a real bright guy. He's studying medicine.''

"Listen, why don't I take you both out tonight?'' Jewel suggested. "I'll have spoken to my boss by then. We can really catch up. You like Italian? Thai? Indian? Chinese? Don't for the love of God say McDonald's.''

"Italian is great.'' Harry grinned, looking as though he wanted to embrace her. "That's very nice of you, Jewel.''

"Hey, aren't you guys forgetting how nice your mother always was to me?'' Jewel answered quickly, shaking her head as she considered what the boys had told her.

"You wouldn't know her now, Jewel,'' Josh said again, bitterness in his tanned face. "Everett has taken her over. She's his now, the stinkin' fraud.''

AFTER THE BOYS HAD GONE, Jewel got feverishly down to work, refreshing her memory of the Omega deal by speed-reading through the file. At the end, she still came to the conclusion, as had Skinner, that the deal was airtight. Omega ex-executives would be ill-advised to go to litigation, but it seemed that was their intent. Bad advice from their lawyers, who would nevertheless line their pockets. It wasn't until after lunch that she had the opportunity to speak to Skinner about the Hungerford boys' situation. She expected—and received—an irritated-sounding response.

"I would've thought you had one hell of a job on your hands already," he said when she was finished.

"I can't walk away from this, Blair. I feel indebted to these boys. To their mother. She was very kind to me when I was a girl. She was directly responsible for a number of fund-raisers to send me off to university. Mr. Hungerford was alive at the time, and the boys were just kids. Really nice kids."

"Then, she's well and truly let them down, hasn't she. If what you tell me is true," Skinner said, his eyes narrowed. "Have you taken the time to check?"

"Of course. I'm thorough, Blair. You know that. Besides, there's money in it for the firm." Which, of course, was Skinner's bottom line. "The land I've been told would fetch around six million in today's market. The boys have a solid case. Their mother, apparently under the influence of her second husband, George Everett, was in breach of trust. She acted wrongly, and so did the bank."

"How could she be so stupid as to get in so deep?" Skinner asked. "It was just a time bomb waiting to go off."

"I intend to speak to her, with your permission, Blair."

"Ah, no." He shook his head. "You're not haring off to North Queensland."

"I can do it on my own time. This weekend. Maybe you'd be good enough to grant me Monday, as well. I'll be on the job. And it'll be wonderful to see my mother."

Skinner eyes sharpened. "Of course. She's still up there with your aunt?"

Jewel nodded, keeping her expression cool and calm. "I wanted her to live with me, but she doesn't like change."

"Oh, all right, then," Skinner lifted his shoulders in a nonchalant shrug. "It's a helluva distraction, but it has the smell of easy bucks."

"Thank you, Blair." Jewel stood up, preparing to leave.

"I noticed a small error in your preparation of the Mayne Goddard brief." Skinner fixed her with such a steely glance that she sat down again.

"Really? A misplaced comma, perhaps?"

"Don't be too clever, my dear. No, it's…" Skinner slipped his gold-rimmed glasses onto his nose. "Ah, here it is. Good thing I picked it up. It might have cost us. You said Shipton Technologies funded the initial deal."

Jewel breathed an inner sigh of relief. "They did."

"But surely it was Goddard on their own?" Skinner gave her a steady frown.

"Let me refresh your memory." Jewel spoke pleasantly. "It was supposed to be, but things changed. A man called Elliot stepped in to handle the negotiation, remember?"

Light dawned in Skinner's eyes. "Ah yes, now I do. You're off the hook, Eugenie, when I was so looking forward to catching you out. Shipton Technologies, of course." He gazed across at her, considered a minute. "By the way, if you were to pop in with some papers at around three-twenty this afternoon, I could introduce you to Lady Copeland and Keefe Connellan. They'll be here."

"My goodness. I assure you I'm appreciative of the honor."

"It's a gesture of my confidence in you, dear girl. So for God's sake, be on your best behavior. That sardonic tone might go over well enough with me, but these people are used to a lot of respect."

"I'll be so respectful they'll never know what hit them," she promised with a straight face.

"You might keep in mind that Keefe is a past master at gobbling up small fry," Skinner said acidly.

Like you hung heavily in the air.

CHAPTER TWO

BLAIR SKINNER WAS ALL SMILES, as he shook hands with his favorite clients, then waited until they'd seated themselves—he had special chairs brought in for such occasions—before he returned to his revolving leather armchair behind the desk. Lady Copeland had asked for this meeting, bringing along not her son, Travis, as might under normal circumstances have been expected, but Keefe Connellan. Keefe would provide company, support and advice. And few better, Skinner thought, scanning Connellan's handsome familiar face. Keefe had hair that was almost jet-black, and his eyes were equally dark. They were remarkable eyes, ablaze with intelligence and a shrewd intensity that a lot of people, including Skinner, found daunting, but they also had a marvelous capacity to light up with humor and an ir-resistible charm. Men as well as women felt it. Skinner, the clotheshorse, approved of Connellan's unmistakable sense of style—the dark-gray suit, beautifully tailored to fit his tall, athletic body, the very pale lilac shirt worn with an olive silk tie patterned with lilac, silver and midnight blue. Keefe Connellan looked what he was: a rich, highly successful young man from a powerful and influential family.

Lady Copeland, as usual, was lovely, but getting very fragile. Skinner knew she was seventy-five but she didn't look anywhere near that age. She always dressed beautifully, today in one of her exclusive little suits, in a shade of indigo that was particularly effective with her wonderful eyes. She wore glorious triple-stranded South Sea Island pearls around her neck, chin-length pearl-white hair classically framing a face whose bone structure would probably look good forever. Her skin was extraordinarily unlined. Granted, she had the money for the most expensive skin treatments in the world, but so did other clients of the same age and none of them looked as good. Davina Copeland was and remained a genuine beauty.

She was smiling at Keefe now. Skinner could see the ease and depth of affection that lay between them. They seemed to be seasoned confidants—even co-conspirators. Certainly this kind of bond didn't appear to exist between mother and son, which was possibly one of the reasons Lady Davina Copeland still held the reins of power in Copeland Connellan.

"So?" Keefe asked with his slow smile, deliberately breaking into Skinner's thoughts. "Perhaps we could get started, Blair. I have an appointment in just over an hour. Lady Copeland has filled me in thus far, but perhaps you can tell me more. On the face of it, I don't think we can rule out industrial espionage."

Skinner inclined his head in acknowledgment. "But we want proof."

"Of course." Keefe leaned forward, assuming like lightning a different guise—official, authoritative, keeping his brilliant black gaze on the lawyer. "And I'm quite sure we can obtain it. Inside the law. Just one question."

Skinner hoped he was prepared for it....

WHEN THE KNOCK CAME some twenty-five minutes later, Skinner was so intent on the discussion, he wondered for a moment who would have the temerity to interrupt him when he was with such important clients. Anger flared in his eyes, and he swung around in his revolving chair, remembering at the last moment that he'd instructed Eugenie Bishop to make a calculated appearance around that time.

"Enter," he called curtly, his expression fixed. All exchanges with Keefe Connellan raised him to this level of intensity. Keefe was more than his equal when it came to strategy and points of law. It didn't make him dislike Connellan; rather, Skinner strove constantly to be well regarded by the younger man.

As they all glanced toward the door, Jewel opened it and walked gracefully into the room, her demeanor poised and confident. Before Skinner could open his mouth to introduce her, Lady Copeland, suddenly looking years older, simply slid from her chair onto the carpeted floor.

"My God!" Skinner leapt up in agitation, wondering if he'd imagined the icy hostility that swept Keefe Connellan's face. Clearly they were both shocked. Connellan was already down on his knees, demanding a glass of water. Lady Copeland was already stirring, her face white as a sheet.

"Keefe," she said almost desperately, clutching at his jacketed arm. "Keefe."

"It's all right," he assured her in a strangely harsh tone. "We can handle this, whatever it is. Let me get you up." He put his strong arms beneath her and lifted her into the chair, keeping a steadying hand on her shoulder.

"Is there anything else I can do for you, Lady Copeland?'' Jewel was back within seconds, carrying a glass of cold water, which she offered to the woman.

"Who are you?" Lady Copeland asked in a quavering voice. She clearly wanted some sort of answer, but Jewel felt it was beyond her.

"I should've explained," Skinner said hastily. "This is one of our associates. Eugenie Bishop, Lady Copeland."

"Bishop?" Connellan turned to stare at Jewel.

"I don't understand." It was impossible to ignore the hostility that emanated from him, the half-horrified, half-fascinated expression on Lady Copeland's face.

"Here, let me help you." Jewel moved quickly, seeing Lady Copeland's hand shake badly. She didn't even pause to consider that Lady Copeland might reject her help. As it happened she didn't, allowing Jewel to assist her in bringing the glass to her mouth.

"I'm so sorry. Are you feeling better?" Jewel asked, bending to peer into the older woman's face.

"I'm fine." Lady Copeland gave a faint little smile that struck Jewel oddly as very brave after that sudden, shocking collapse.

"And why is Ms. Bishop here, precisely?" Keefe Connellan looked at Skinner with unconcealed contempt.

"Mr. Skinner was after a particular file," Jewel fired back levelly. She'd never met a man like Connellan. Who the devil did he think he was? She felt a wave of answering aggression. More to the point, what had she missed? She'd surely missed *something*. He was looking at her as though she was playing some high-stakes game. Or as if she had secrets to hide. What on earth was going on? Whatever reaction she'd been expecting, it wasn't this.

Connellan now held out his hand like a man used to a great deal of authority. "Show me."

"I'm sorry, Mr. Connellan, it's confidential." She kept her expression neutral.

"I thought it might be," he said. "I'd like to see it, all the same."

Skinner interrupted uneasily. "Look here, Keefe, Ms. Bishop is one of our finest young lawyers and my protégée. She did a lot of research for the Quinn Corp.-Omega takeover. I thought it was time you met her."

"So you arranged it." Connellan's tone was hard.

Skinner shrugged helplessly. "I don't know what you're getting at, Keefe. Or why you're upset."

Connellan took a step closer to Lady Copeland, his manner both protective and daunting. "Are you feeling better, Davina?"

"Perhaps a cup of sweetened tea?" Jewel suggested, already turning to go.

"Thank you, my dear, but no." Lady Copeland spoke quietly and gently. "I'm sorry if Mr. Connellan and I seem distracted."

"We can scarcely fail to be," Connellan said, his voice clipped. "I'm curious, Ms. Bishop. How long have you been with the firm?"

"Three years." Jewel returned his challenging gaze with one of her own.

"Ms. Bishop came to us with wonderful references," Skinner submitted, sounding quite confused.

"And where did you work before that?" Connellan asked.

Such unfettered arrogance, Jewel thought. She named the highly respected law firm in the north.

"But you wanted to come to Brisbane?"

She nodded a shade too curtly. "It's not too terrible

to be ambitious, is it, Mr. Connellan? I needed more demanding work.''

"Eugenia graduated top of her class," Skinner pointed out. "Indeed, she won the University Medal. Across all disciplines on all campuses, as I believe you did yourself, Keefe."

Connellan ignored him. "Go ahead, Ms. Bishop. As you might imagine, we're particularly interested."

"Really?" Jewel couldn't mask her surprise. "You only met me a minute ago."

Lady Copeland, who had listened without interrupting, now spoke. "What is your background, my dear?"

Jewel felt astonished by her interest. "I could show you my file, Lady Copeland, but shouldn't I be getting you a cup of tea?" She sought to keep her tone respectful.

"I'll ring for it." Skinner moved quickly to the phone, betraying an uncharacteristic agitation, not without a hint of excitement.

"I find it hard to believe you're a country girl," Keefe Connellan said, his black eyes moving so disturbingly over Jewel that she felt herself flush. She was developing a profound dislike of this too-handsome, too-arrogant, too-rich and powerful man.

"But I am, Mr. Connellan. Take it or leave it. In fact, I was born on an Outback cattle station."

Incredibly he laughed. "I hope you know what you're doing," he said strangely. Facing her, he was disconcertingly close.

"Doing?" Her vivid blue eyes sparkled with anger. Jewel was confident in herself and her own abilities. She refused to let this man belittle or insult her, no matter who he was.

But he smiled at her. A curiously unnerving smile,

for all that it lit his lean, darkly tanned face. "You'd better be good."

Lady Copeland spoke in a voice so strained it seemed almost theatrical. "It's all falling into place. Your father was a Steven Bishop? Overseer on one of our properties, Mingaree Station, some twenty years ago."

Skinner looked over at Jewel quizzically. He had always sensed this girl had some mystery to her. Was that what it was all about? Her father? What had Bishop done?

Jewel inclined her gleaming blond head, one side sweeping forward to shield her face. "He was. Perhaps you could tell me, Lady Copeland, why you and Mr. Connellan are so interested. My father died tragically, as you must know—or perhaps you don't. He wasn't important in your scheme of things."

"I didn't know him, my dear," Lady Copeland confirmed gently. "I saw him only once in my life, at my late husband's funeral."

"I was six at the time," Jewel answered, just as quietly. "I don't really remember Dad going, but my mother told me he attended the funeral with a party of cattlemen."

"What else do you remember?" Keefe Connellan asked.

Jewel turned on him with magnificent disdain. "He never came home."

In the midst of the bitterness, he suddenly sounded sincere. "I'm sorry."

"Blair, I wonder if you'd mind leaving us for a few minutes?" Lady Copeland unexpectedly took the initiative. "I would appreciate it."

Keefe Connellan intervened. "Davina, I don't think

this is the right time. You just fainted and you're still very pale. I should take you home."

"Ten minutes, no more." Lady Copeland threw him a trusting smile.

"Take as long as you want, Lady Copeland," Blair Skinner said, not meeting Jewel's eyes. "I have things I can attend to."

He went to the door, practically colliding with a secretary carrying a silver tea tray. The secretary smiled at Jewel, who went to her and said thank you, then put the tray down on a side table. As Skinner shut the door, Jewel poured Lady Copeland a cup of tea, asking over her shoulder if she took milk.

"No, my dear. No sugar, either, but perhaps today…"

Jewel ladled in two teaspoons and passed the elegant cup and saucer to Lady Copeland, who took it with a steadier hand. "Tell me about yourself," Lady Copeland invited, gesturing to the armchair Keefe Connellan had vacated. He stood, arms folded, and leaned against Skinner's desk.

"You're dying to tell someone, aren't you," he said.

"Pardon me, but are you insane?" Jewel let her own hostility spill over.

He stared at her for a few moments, his handsome face drawn into somber lines. "I'm so very sorry, Ms. Bishop, if I'm Goddamn offending you."

"Keefe!" Lady Copeland endeavored to soothe him. "Maybe she doesn't—"

"Doesn't what?" Jewel asked, finding the whole situation bizarre. Yet was it? Now that she was really looking at Lady Copeland, she was swept by a strange sense of familiarity.

"Does your mother live with you?" Lady Copeland asked, sipping her tea, then putting it down.

"My mother lives in Hungerford, North Queensland, where I was raised. Perhaps you can give me a clue, Lady Copeland. I have no idea what you're getting at."

"You haven't looked in the mirror for a while?" Keefe Connellan asked in a dark voice.

Jewel sat back wearily. "Could this possibly be the nature of your enquiry, Mr. Connellan? My appearance?"

Though she spoke sardonically, inside her was growing panic, confusion, even fear.

"So it's come to you at last. My, my, my!" he drawled, eyes snapping.

In desperation, Jewel turned to Lady Copeland, who was now excessively pale. "Please tell me! I swear I don't know what this is all about." Lady Copeland was gazing at her with such a strange expression but for the moment seemed quite unable to reply.

"We didn't get much notice, either," Keefe Connellan said, his handsome features drawn tight. "Tell me, are there many golden-haired, black-browed, sapphire-eyed women in your family?" he asked. "Don't look so stunned. You're a beautiful woman with very distinctive features."

"So?" Jewel spread her hands. "Please continue."

"But, Ms. Bishop, you've even got your hair cut the same way. Tell me, are you and Skinner enjoying this? I assure you your enjoyment won't last long."

Jewel stood up, her mind racing. This meeting had implications that were deeply disturbing. They could also cost her her job. "There's no way I can continue to sit here and listen to this," she said. "Either you come out with the information you appear to have, or

I'll break all the rules by walking out on you.'' Arrogant son of a bitch. He could get her fired, but she no longer cared.

Behind her Lady Copeland sighed heavily. ''My dear, I may be almost three times your age and I, too, am breaking all the rules by saying this, but you're the living image of me when I was in my twenties.''

''The question is, why haven't *you* noticed?'' Keefe Connellan demanded before Jewel could hope to speak.

He moved suddenly, taking her by the arm and guiding her toward a gilded mirror that hung between two ceiling-high Georgian bookcases.

''Please let go of me,'' Jewel said from between clenched teeth. Her confusion was growing.

He removed his hand immediately but continued to watch her with careful eyes, their two heads reflected in the mirror. ''Are you going to tell us what's going on, Ms. Bishop?'' he asked.

She felt as though she was hardly breathing. ''Fine, there's a resemblance,'' she conceded. ''I see it now, but I was never looking for it. Hardly! All I can say is that it's a coincidence. And for the record, Blair Skinner has never remarked on any such resemblance.''

''He must have known,'' Connellan said.

''Known what?'' She swung on him. Tall herself, she had to look up at him. ''What sense is there in keeping me in the dark? I'm not a fool. You seem to be implying that Blair Skinner and I have devised some strategy to bring me to Lady Copeland's attention.''

''Haven't you?'' he challenged.

''Please, Keefe.'' Lady Copeland spoke quietly.

Jewel ignored him and walked back to where Lady Copeland was sitting. She noticed that a fraction of color had come back into the woman's face. Jewel sat down so her own face would be level with the older woman's, staring into eyes she now saw with shocking clarity were indeed like her own. "I wouldn't for the world be party to any plan to upset you, Lady Copeland. Neither would Blair Skinner. He respects you greatly. It was exactly as he said. I've done quite a bit of work on the Quinn Corp.–Omega takeover. I'm well thought of in this firm. He felt it was time I met some of our more important clients."

"Surely you could up with something better than that?" Connellan stood tall, his expression cool and cutting. An imposing figure who clearly didn't believe her.

"I don't think I could come up with anything better than the truth. In any case, this isn't a courtroom, Mr. Connellan," she reminded him.

"But you're playing a dangerous game."

"Nonsense!" she said emphatically.

"Perhaps, my dear, we've all been taken by surprise?" Lady Copeland suggested, still looking as if she'd seen a ghost.

"Or you and Mr. Connellan have leapt to a conclusion," Jewel countered. "I don't allow myself to be used by anybody. That includes my boss."

"Maybe you could visit me so I could find out more about you." Lady Copeland for all her power and influence seemed to be pleading.

Jewel stared back at her, perturbed. "There *can't* be any connection between us, Lady Copeland, no matter how strong the resemblance. Isn't it said we all have a double somewhere?"

"Perhaps not so close to hand. I have to admit you play the game well," Keefe Connellan said dryly.

Jewel faced him, terribly unnerved but determined not to be thrown off balance. "Game, what game?" she asked. "Why do you seem to think it's your place to confront me, Mr. Connellan? Why this hostility? My God, it fills the room! I don't feel the same antagonism coming from Lady Copeland." It was perfectly true. Lady Copeland's demeanor was curiously nonthreatening.

Connellan merely shrugged. "To answer your question, I've known Lady Copeland all my life. I care about her. We're part of a tight circle. Whoever disturbs her, disturbs me. I wonder if you fully appreciate that."

"I'm not afraid of you, Mr. Connellan." Jewel met his gaze unflinchingly.

"Perhaps you should be." A faint smile curved his mouth. "What was the plan? First the meeting, then the blackmail?"

It was an insult too great to be borne. Before she knew it, Jewel's hand flew up spontaneously and she struck Keefe Connellan across his arrogant face.

The silence in the room was profound. Jewel felt her heart flutter.

"Oh God, I didn't mean that," she said.

"Yes, you did." Connellan rubbed his cheek thoughtfully. "It's a first, anyway. I'm sure you'll tell me next that you're the proud possessor of a black belt."

"I apologize," Jewel said, feeling his whole aura intensely. "But you have to admit you deserved it."

"What else have you got up your sleeve?" he enquired with mock politeness.

Jewel was utterly exasperated. "I want to hold onto my job. I deeply regret this upset, but I feel I'm the innocent victim here." She turned to Lady Copeland, who appeared to be hanging on her every word. "This is the first time I've ever laid eyes on you, Lady Copeland. I'm sorry if—for whatever reason—that makes you sad.'' And sorrow was the expression printed on Davina Copeland's face.

"Oh, it does, my dear.'' Lady Copeland flung a narrow hand to her heart. "Forgive me, but…you're not hiding anything from us?''

This would be ridiculous if it weren't so disturbing. "I'm sorry, Lady Copeland. I've already told you no. If we've finished our conversation, I should get back to work.''

Again Keefe Connellan intervened. "So how did you get this job? Who offered it?'' He glanced at his watch.

"I'm not sure this is any of your business, Mr. Connellan.''

"Oh, it is,'' he muttered grimly.

"I was recommended to Mr. Skinner by Professor Goldner from the university,'' she said, knowing he would check.

"So Skinner is definitely mixed up in it?''

Jewel sighed in disbelief. "I haven't the vaguest idea what you mean. I came with very good references and recommendations. Let's get that straight.''

"By all means,'' he said tersely.

"I hope you're discreet, Ms. Bishop?'' Lady Copeland suddenly appealed to her.

Jewel frowned. "Lady Copeland, what do I have to be discreet about? Do you think people will gossip if they notice our strong resemblance?''

Keefe Connellan exhaled loudly. "You bet your life they will. It's impossible to miss.''

"Do you think so? They'd have to be looking for a hidden mystery then,'' Jewel said. "However, it hardly matters, since I don't move in Lady Copeland's circles.''

"No doubt Skinner hoped to change that?" He spoke so sharply his words gave Jewel a twinge of fear.

They stared at each other like combatants, neither yielding, both tense. "No need to investigate Blair Skinner," Jewel said firmly. "He never puts a foot wrong."

"You mean *so far,*" Connellan returned curtly. "Playing us for fools would guarantee disaster." He moved then, touching Lady Copeland's delicate shoulder. "I think we should go, Davina. Jacob will take you home and drop me on the way. I have an appointment with Drew Westaway uptown. I'd break it, but it's critical." He glanced at Jewel, brilliant black eyes narrowed. "You can inform your boss we're leaving," he said, his face taut.

"If that's what you want. Let me say again that I deeply regret any upset I may unwittingly have caused you, Lady Copeland. I'll speak of it to no one."

Connellan laughed—an attractive if discordant sound. "That's a bit rich. Skinner can't wait to discuss this."

"What do you expect, given your attack on me? Naturally I have to say *something.*"

"Of course. Is your mother in on this, too?"

Nothing so far had prepared Jewel for that. She went white. "My mother is a very sick woman, so watch it, Mr. Connellan. I'd just love to slap you again."

"Only this time, I'll deal with it," he promised, gently propelling Lady Copeland to the door.

Nearing it, Lady Copeland paused. "If I asked you to come and visit me, would you consider it, Eugenie?" Her still-beautiful face revealed a strange longing.

Jewel found herself nodding, lured somehow by the use of her Christian name. "I think I want that, too,

Lady Copeland, just so long as Mr. Connellan is nowhere nearby."

"Are you sure about that, Davina?" Connellan shot a questioning look at her.

"Quite sure, my dear." She smiled at him and patted his arm. "I need to learn more about Eugenie. You see that, don't you?"

He turned, studying Jewel's resolute stance. "I do, in a strange sort of way," he admitted. "Just bear in mind that Ms. Bishop, for all her beauty and avowed brightness, could pry us all apart."

Shaking inside but using her characteristic self-confidence as camouflage, Jewel went in search of Blair Skinner, finding him in the boardroom frowning over a coffee.

"Well?" He looked distressed, and was without his usual bold quip. "Can I go back into my office?"

"They're gone, Blair." Jewel resisted a groan. "Connellan had an appointment."

"*Mr.* Connellan to you," Skinner reminded her stonily and stood up. "I don't understand this. They left without speaking to me?"

"I'm sure Mr. Connellan will be remedying that," Jewel answered abruptly, bringing a chill to Skinner's eyes.

"What exactly is that supposed to mean?"

"Beats the hell out of me, Blair." She gave a brittle laugh. "It'll be mentioned, so I'm not betraying a confidence. It seems that both of them—Lady Copeland and Mr. Connellan—figure we're playing some kind of game with them. I'm quoting Mr. Connellan himself."

Skinner actually blanched. "My God, Eugenia, you can't be serious."

"I'm deadly serious," she said.

He looked at her with a grim expression. "You're hiding something from me, aren't you," he accused. "I suspected it right from the beginning."

"Nevertheless you hired me. Why?" The *why* was starting to worry her.

"Because I thought there was something special about you," he answered testily. "Don't act like a dolt. It doesn't suit you. What caused Lady Copeland to faint? Keefe looked at me quite murderously. It was all about you, wasn't it. And your father. What on earth did he do? If you tell me he made off with Copeland money, I promise I won't scream. God knows, old Sir Julius broke a few laws. But then, he had us legal eagles to get him out of trouble. What does hurt is the fact that you've never seen fit to confide in me, Eugenie."

"I never thought I had much to confide."

"Sit down," Skinner advised briskly. "I know you well enough to realize beneath that brazen exterior you're falling to pieces."

Jewel took a seat. "I think you're right. What about getting me a cup of coffee—to show you care?"

This was received with a scowl. "You're really something. You know that?" He disappeared, then returned a moment later with two steaming china mugs. "Give it to me straight. Any lies, and I promise you'll be out of here just like that!" He snapped his fingers.

"You and me both." Jewel took a tentative sip. Too hot. At least the coffee was good. "Blair, I'm going to ask you something." She switched her eyes from the mug to him. "And I'd appreciate the truth. Have you been aware of the resemblance between Lady Copeland and me?"

Skinner's jaw dropped in amazement. Either he was

a wonderful actor or he had just suffered a severe shock. "What are you saying, Eugenie?"

"Have—you—ever—noticed?" She leaned closer to him, deliberately spacing her words.

"Sweet, sweet Lord! What a fool I am."

"Welcome to the club. I take it you haven't. However, the cat is out of the bag. Whatever cat it might happen to be." Jewel had just enough left in her to speak flippantly. It was her way of overcoming her own tremendous shock. "Lady Copeland told me she thought I was the image of herself when young."

Skinner put his knuckles in his mouth. He rose to his feet shouting, "That's right!" then fell back, lowering his head and holding it in his hands. "And they think the two of us set up a meeting!" he muttered despairingly.

"I think they saw themselves as two blackmail victims."

"If I've made enemies of those two, I'll have to move abroad. Oh, my God!" he cried. "I could weep."

"Ordinarily I'd enjoy that, but bear with me," Jewel said, taking another gulp of the strong coffee. "I told them you'd never, ever remarked on even a passing resemblance. You are a man of great integrity. I kept assuring them of that. I told them you respected Lady Copeland far too much to ever want to upset her. I explained that I'd never laid eyes on her in my entire life. The whole thing was one monumental coincidence."

"My dear, my mother taught me to be very suspicious of monumental coincidences," Skinner said. "This is not the end," he predicted. "So, how can we make sense of this? Now that the scales have fallen from my eyes, I can see you're a dead ringer for Davina.

I knew there was something familiar about you, right from the beginning. I even ran through a few film stars. The young Lana Turner with blue, blue eyes. That kind of look. Soft, sexy yet challenging.''

Jewel gazed at him in astonishment. ''You thought all this, Blair? Shame on you. I've always seen you as a good, solid father figure.'' A dreadful lie.

He shook his head. ''Just an objective judgment. I have eyes. Or so I believed.'' He stared at her directly. ''What would you advise?''

''You mean, you're going to listen?'' This all felt like a strange dream, except that she was actually hurting.

''What I'm saying is you were there the whole time. How did it all end?''

''In Lady Copeland inviting me to visit her.''

Skinner made a whistling sound through his mouth. It could have been admiration. ''And Keefe?''

''What a gorgon!'' Jewel said with a shudder.

''A gorgon, my dear, was one of three snake-haired sisters in Greek mythology. Of course, you didn't have a classical education.''

''All right, make that a bastard.''

Skinner snorted. ''Don't get on the wrong side of Keefe Connellan,'' he warned her. ''He loves Davina. They love each other. I could almost feel sorry for Travis. At one time, his father was threatening to dis-inherit him. Damn, I'm talking too much. Should I ring him?''

''Who, Connellan? I wouldn't give him that satisfaction,'' Jewel said disgustedly. ''But expect a phone call...''

IT WAS IMPOSSIBLE to concentrate on anything for the rest of the afternoon. There seemed no rational explanation for what had happened in Blair Skinner's office, but it all had to do with the striking resemblance between her and Lady Copeland and the fact that her father had once worked for the family. Jewel was outraged by the way Keefe Connellan had treated her. Outraged by everything about the man. Being with him was like being in an emotional and intellectual combat zone. He acted as though she was cruelly impersonating someone closely linked to Lady Copeland's life. Someone Lady Copeland really needed or cared about. A daughter, a granddaughter who'd died? Jewel couldn't figure it out.

More than anything, she wanted to call her mother to see if Thea could offer an explanation. A couple of times she'd even picked up the phone but knew there was little point in it. Her mother, even if she came to the phone, would be made highly anxious by any kind of questioning. Thea experienced bouts of severe anxiety, and talking to her would do no good at all. In fact, it might make a difficult situation worse. Her mother lived in a permanent state of depression, a kind of helplessness, even worthlessness, that Jewel often found overwhelming.

"Thank God you never took after your mother. I'd go crazy."

That was what Aunt Judith always said. A single woman with a crackling persona, sometimes cyclonic, far from unattractive—she'd once had a fiancé who had simply "vanished," a calamity at the time. It had been two weeks before the wedding and the theory was that he'd been taken by a crocodile on one of his nighttime fishing trips. Judith was thin, terribly thin, but always on the go, impatient, trying to do her best but totally unequipped by nature to deal with a sister who had "emotional problems." In all fairness Aunt Judith had tried to cope with Thea's physical and mental inertia, but her initial sympathy had passed quickly, mainly because she, like Jewel, was a person who was anything but stationary.

Her aunt Judith. Jewel owed her a great deal.

They'd gone to live with Judith after her father's death. Her mother had little money, but she still retained a half-share in the family home, a marvelous spooky old colonial Queenslander some miles out of town. Jewel would never forget her first sight of it. She was an imaginative child, and it had seemed to her the house of a witch. Set in a great blossoming forest with gem-colored birds and enormous blue butterflies circling the riotous overgrown gardens, it was filled with towering palms and soaring ferns and great mango trees whose fruit littered the ground. And there was Aunt Judith confirming her childish suspicions, standing on the deep shadowy front veranda overhung by a scarlet bougainvillea that had woven itself through the length of the white wrought-iron banisters and threatened to bring down the huge pillars that supported the luminous green roof. She stood there, thin arms outstretched, a wild mane of curly dark hair cascading down her back, her clothes like clothes Jewel had never seen before. Long and loose and floating with big stars all over them, like a magician's. She soon learned that outfit was called a caftan and Aunt Judith had painted the stars herself. After the harshness and the terra-cotta colors of her Outback home, it was like being invited into the Garden of Eden—where there were plenty of snakes. It was and remained a magical house, the place her mother and Aunt Judith had been born and where her mother now hid.

Aunt Judith had welcomed them, glad of their company. The day they arrived, the ceiling of the huge living room dripped colored streamers and bunches of balloons hanging from the lovely Chinese lanterns with painted wooden panels that shielded the lightbulbs. But Aunt Judith had quickly come to the realization that Thea wasn't going to be any company, let alone help. To herself, her little daughter or indeed anyone else. And Judith came to realize, not without shock, that her pretty sister, who'd run off to get married when she was barely nineteen, no longer cared if she lived or died. There was only the child to be salvaged.

Me, Jewel thought.

So they'd all settled into their strange new life— Jewel confronting lots of hair-raising experiences in what was virtually a wilderness. Aunt Judith ran a small, successful business in the town. It was a sort of treasure shop selling the handiwork of the artists of the district—a dizzying array of wonderfully dressed dolls and stuffed toys to patchwork quilts, imaginative clothing, exotic cushions, watercolors, oils, pottery, handmade jewelry, clocks, so-called sacred objects, you name it. As a child Jewel had always enjoyed helping Aunt Judith in the shop. Her mother had tried, frowning with concentration over the least little thing, but she couldn't manage it. Thea Bishop's slump into depression had not been gradual. It had been dramatic, dating from the very day her father was killed. Before that, her mother had seemed a different person. Sweet, loving, fun to be with. Then the terrible descent into a kind of quiet madness when only glimpses of her former self showed through. Jewel had lived all her childhood with the knowledge that her mother wasn't like other mothers, but a heartbreakingly sad person, a woman who could never be relied on to help Aunt Judith, to turn up at speech days or concerts or fetes or to fetch her from school in the afternoons. This she had accepted as testament to her mother's grief. A thinking child who had adored her father, Jewel could remember her own terrible pain and sadness when she was told her daddy had gone to heaven. How much worse for her mother to lose her beloved husband, her life's companion, at such a young age. The trauma held her mother in thrall. It refused to let go.

"For God's sake, Thea, other people suffer terrible losses and go on!" Aunt Judith, voice imploring, would urge her sister to try to keep her physical and mental integrity intact. "The child needs you!"

Her mother would stare back at them, lost in some subterranean labyrinth. She had started crying the day she learned of her loss and she had never stopped, falling deeper and deeper into an inertia that was agonizing to watch. Jewel, who loved her mother and was fiercely protective of her, never put her own confused and frightened thoughts into words, even during her mother's worst periods. Aunt Judith did that for her, coming home every night to a sister "off on another planet," under the influence of all the pills that were prescribed by her doctors. At the age of ten, Jewel had taken charge of her mother, reversing their roles, while Aunt Judith strove to keep all three afloat. This arrangement had endured until Jewel won a full scholarship to a leading girls' school, which she'd entered as a boarder with her aunt's full approval and support.

"One of us has got to spring the trap," was the way Aunt Judith had put it. Outwardly sharp and increasingly without sympathy for her sister's "self-inflicted" condition, Aunt Judith nonetheless refused to cast Thea aside. The two of them would "survive, but it won't be much fun!"

So many of the things Aunt Judith had said over the years stuck in Jewel's mind. Her aunt had not been a witch, thank goodness; she was a courageous and unusual woman, with a sharp tongue. The last time Jewel had visited her mother and aunt, just over a month before, they seemed to have eased into an arrangement that worked. Aunt Judith ran the shop, ordered in all the provisions and she'd hired a handyman to halfway tame the spectacular abandoned jungle they lived in, while her mother tried to keep the house in order and have a meal ready for Judith when she arrived home from work. For some years now, Jewel had been able to help out financially, easing the burden on her aunt who, to her great credit, had never complained about all the "extras." As well, Jewel bought her mother's clothes and enjoyed finding unconventional outfits for her aunt. Her aunt Judith had become something of a local celebrity, just as her mother had become the local misfit, the outcast, even if word was she still looked fetching.

Jewel tried hard to organize her chaotic thoughts. The best she could do was speak to her aunt over the weekend. In the early days, Aunt Judith had spent countless hours listening to her sister's mournful outpourings. Maybe Judith knew something that would shed some light on the bewildering situation that had confronted her. Briskly Jewel picked up the phone to book an early-morning flight to the "far north." North of Capricorn. Another world. After that, she would ring her aunt at the shop. It was the usual routine designed by both of them to shield Thea.

CHAPTER THREE

IT WAS AFTER SIX before she left the office, intending to take the bus the couple of blocks to her club, the Caxton. Named after an early female activist, it had been formed a few years back for young, professional women, mostly from legal circles. She enjoyed being part of it and meeting other young women whose interests matched her own. At the club she could relax and freshen up before going on to meet the Hungerford boys at the restaurant. They had assured her they could find it.

It was much too late to go home, home being a small townhouse in a trendy suburb near the river. She was paying it off, but not as quickly as she would've liked. There were too many other considerations, not the least of them keeping up the appearance her job required, especially since Blair Skinner had taken her under his wing. After such a strange and frustrating afternoon, the boys' unhappy home and financial situation had somehow paled into insignificance beside her own affairs. She would have to get herself back on track. Going up north to visit her mother would address two issues at once. Her own family mystery and how Sheila Hungerford, now Sheila Everett, had come to betray her adored sons.

Lost in thought, Jewel didn't immediately notice the big silver-gray limousine that was purring alongside her as she strolled along. Finally it caught her attention, and she swung her head. Shock was like a live wire sparking inside her. The face that looked out at her belonged to Keefe Connellan. She couldn't believe it. Was he following her? He was seated in the rear of the chauffeur-driven vehicle, the window wound down. He called to her, his tone of voice quietly authoritative.

"Ms. Bishop." The limousine slid into a loading zone a short distance ahead, and he emerged from the back seat, leaving the door open and looking toward her. "Could you spare a moment?"

Her pulse picked up and the blood tingled through her veins. She hated the way he was looking at her. "I don't think so, Mr. Connellan. I have an evening appointment." She spoke doubtfully, as if it were a regretful statement of fact. She was careful not to reveal her unease.

"Are you going home?" He, too, kept his tone polite—but managed to sound somehow derisive.

"As it happens, I'm off to my club."

"The Caxton?"

It seemed he approved. Not that she cared. She dropped her pretense, realizing she was under careful scrutiny. "Now, how did you discover that?"

He smiled, a white flash that attracted her in spite of herself.

"Would you believe I have a marvelous networking system?" he said. "Please get in. You're not five minutes away, if we drive you."

Jewel took a decisive step to one side, head up, shoulders straight. "That's quite all right. I like to walk."

"Obviously, since you're in the best of shape." His glance licked over her. "But indulge me."

"What, after today?" Those black eyes made her think of the Medicis and hidden daggers.

"I'm interested in talking to you further," he said mildly, his expression giving nothing away.

"Really? There's nothing to learn."

"We both know there is." He stared down into her face, then he put out a hand and gently grasped her arm.

Jewel's knees turned to mush.

"You're forcing me into your car?" She lifted her brows, feeling an unwelcome thrill she sought to banish.

"I never forget my manners."

"You forgot them this afternoon." Knowing she had little chance of getting away, short of screaming, Jewel slid into the back seat of the Rolls. A smartly uniformed chauffeur sat behind the wheel awaiting instructions. He didn't turn his head.

"The Caxton, Jacob," Keefe Connellan said. He got in beside Jewel, shutting the door.

"Yes, sir. I know it."

Keefe Connellan focused his attention on Jewel, while the chauffeur activated a device to bring up a glass partition between front and back seats.

"This is a lot like getting kidnapped."

He looked at her in mock amazement. "Please don't feel threatened. There's nothing wrong with privacy."

"So you're a private investigator now." Jewel leaned back slightly, her nostrils beguiled by the scent of the plush leather.

"Lady Copeland is someone I care about," he said curtly, revealing the anger beneath the smooth surface.

"She has a *son,*" Jewel said pointedly.

"Obviously." He watched her in a way she couldn't fathom. "She has a granddaughter, too."

"Amelia. Yes, I know." Jewel glanced out the window at the homebound crowds. "I've often seen her photograph in the social pages. She's very beautiful. Do you care about her, too?" She tossed her head defiantly, pleased that she'd rattled him.

"Why? Is it any of your business?"

"In my view, yes. If you think it's within your rights to investigate me, why should you object to my right to investigate you? Unless you think being very wealthy gives you some authority over the rest of us."

He turned his lean body so he was confronting her. "What is it, Ms. Bishop, that you hope to achieve? To get close to Lady Copeland? To make yourself a member of the family? You don't know Travis." He shook his head. "He won't be very pleased to welcome you. Neither will Amelia. You're already the cause of intense emotional anguish."

"How?" Jewel demanded, holding his eyes. "No speaking in tongues this time. How exactly?"

His answer, when it came, took her completely by surprise. "You're pretty damn amazing, you know that?"

"I don't care for you, either." She was barely able to remain seated beside him. Large as the interior of the Rolls was, she had never felt so claustrophobic. "In fact, I've never met a man I find so hateful."

"Words. Mere words, Ms. Bishop. What you are is somewhat wary of me. As you should be."

"Particularly as you appear to be stalking me."

His laugh was unexpected and profoundly attractive. "I prefer to say 'running a few checks.'"

"Well, I hope you've dropped Blair Skinner from your investigation," Jewel said. "He's as straightforward as anyone you could meet."

He pondered that a while. "I wouldn't have thought him the sort of man to pull something like this."

"Something like what?" Her eyes opened wide in indignation. "This colossal *con?* Is that what it's supposed to be?"

He smiled slightly, no humor in it. "Perhaps if I keep you off balance, you'll crack."

"To hell with that!" Jewel muttered, one arm extended toward the door. "There is where I get off."

"Of course." He nodded his coal-black head. "Perhaps you'll invite me inside for a drink. I haven't seen the place since they renovated. One of our subsidiary companies did the job. Leave the door," he advised. "You can depend on Jacob to open it."

Jewel took a deep breath, glancing at him slowly. "Oh, what it is to be rich!" she said in a bitter voice. "Attendants on every side—and the power to inspire fear."

"When did you decide you wanted that, too?" he asked tautly.

"I have enough money to live on." She shot him a disgusted look.

"You've got *no* money," he corrected, rather indolently.

"I beg your pardon." She thought she'd been holding her own but that got to her. He had taken the time to find out everything, it seemed. A massive invasion of her privacy.

"A very nice town house," he continued in a deceptively pleasant tone. "You're paying it off. And look at your beautiful clothes!" He shifted slightly to gaze at her, making her very conscious of her body. "Buying clothes must take a lot of your pay."

Jewel stared back for a few moments, her cheeks burning. "God, you're offensive."

"I just keep thinking about what *you're* trying to do," he countered quietly.

"What? Join the Copeland family?" She spoke crisply. "Come on, give me a clue. Instead of looking down your arrogant nose at me. Why don't you share your suspicions? That would be a good start. Obviously, your thoughts differ appreciably from mine."

He wondered how much longer she'd be able to keep up the act, drawn and repelled at the same time. Then he said what he had never intended. Judgment clouded by a beautiful woman? "I'm prepared to talk over a quick drink."

She blinked hard and looked away. "Otherwise, say goodbye to my career, my reputation?"

"That's a take-it-or-leave-it offer," he answered.

EVERYONE LOOKED AT THEM when they walked into the quiet elegance of the Caxton's lounge. There were a few male guests mixed in with the women. All were seated in comfortable leather armchairs ranged around circular tables, nursing drinks and talking in a relaxed fashion. Most of them Jewel knew. She smiled, waved and nodded her way across the room with its attractive contemporary carpet, while most of the eyes widened and the smiles grew.

"It's Jewel—and just see who she's with!"

What they couldn't know was that she wasn't enjoying it. She felt like a fictional character, aware of the little eddies of excitement that ran through the room. Keefe Connellan knew quite a few people, too, because he lifted his hand, that beautiful white smile flashing.

No sooner were they seated at a quiet table for two

overlooking the small rear garden than a waiter appeared, bending over deferentially. "Good evening, Mr. Connellan. Miss Bishop."

Jewel nodded, doing her best to smile. "Good evening, Archie."

"That's it—*Archie*." Connellan took a long look at the waiter. "You worked at the Polo Club for a while?"

"Yes, sir."

"And the Queensland. You get around, Archie."

Archie nodded, grinning delightedly. "I like a change. Could I take your order, sir?"

Keefe Connellan looked at the quietly seething Jewel, with her golden hair. "No one drinks much anymore. Not when they're going on to an evening appointment," he said, a little sarcastically.

"A martini," she said. "A very, very dry martini. One olive."

"Fabulous!" Connellan said. "I'll join you."

"When can we stop all this?" Jewel asked, after Archie had gone, his expression conveying his absolute fascination at seeing them together. "I think we've moved beyond the conspiracy theory."

"All right." He leaned forward, stared into her deeply blue, black-lashed eyes, aware that every man in the room was staring at her. Why not? Physically she was an inspiration. It was her character that worried him. "One doesn't have to be a super-sleuth to realize you're somehow related to Lady Copeland. Either that or you've had plastic surgery."

She forcibly shut down her mounting panic. "What do *you* think?"

"I can't even see the tiniest wrinkle. You have beautiful skin. This, of course, we already know."

Despite the mocking banter, Jewel felt chilled. "I

swear I have no idea what you're talking about. I know of no connection. I've lived my life a thousand miles from her. I've already told you that. It would save a lot of time if you answered my questions honestly instead of shrouding everything in mystery.''

''You didn't happen to discuss all this with your mother?'' he asked, eyes piercing. ''I'm prepared to believe she didn't tell you until very recently.''

''Tell me what? That I was snatched from the cradle? There was a mix-up at the hospital?'' She looked highly skeptical. ''That I'm someone's *love child?*''

''Hadn't you already suspected it?'' he asked quietly.

Jewel felt the pain attack her temples. ''I'm going to get up and go now. What you're saying is impossible. Unforgivable, really.''

''Please don't.'' He reached out, putting his hand over hers, an action she knew would be totally misinterpreted by everyone watching them. ''God only knows what people here would make of it,'' he murmured.

Her cheeks were flushed, and not only with anger. ''I don't understand any of this. I only met Lady Copeland today.''

''And it was a wonderful performance,'' he informed her, releasing her hand. ''She took to you immediately. It must give you hope.''

Jewel turned her head to gaze out the window. Outside in the small Italianate courtyard, a fountain was playing peacefully. No peace inside. ''You've allowed yourself to see some kind of conspiracy where there is none. My appearance and the fact that I met Lady Copeland are nothing more than coincidences.''

Little brackets appeared at the sides of his mouth. At another time she would have found them sexy. Not now.

"I don't think you're going to get many people to accept that," he said. "Feature by feature, the similarity is extraordinary. Skinner had to be blind not to notice it right from the start."

"Why should he?" Jewel met his eyes. "He wasn't expecting any such thing. Lady Copeland must be well into her seventies. I know she still looks wonderful, but one would have to know us both very well for the resemblance to register."

"Exactly," he said, his voice dry. "Hasn't it ever worried you that you resembled no one in your family?"

Jewel attempted to speak; for a moment she couldn't. Why should she tell him her most private confusions? "I could be the very image of my father, for all you know," she said angrily although she still had enough control to keep her voice down. "And this has something to do with my father, doesn't it?"

"It has everything to do with your father," he answered, grim-faced.

"And who is my father?" She was beginning to feel dizzy. "Come on, say it. There has to be some justification for this torture."

"I can't believe you don't know. You're a very clever woman. Fact-finding is part of your daily life. You've seen many photographs of Lady Copeland—who hasn't? She's always inhabited the world of glamour and power. Not only that, she's always been a beauty with a needle-sharp brain."

"No ornament like her granddaughter?" Jewel was stung into asking. Everyone knew that Amelia Copeland, the heiress, had claimed immunity from daily toil.

"I'm sure you made it your business to check out Amelia, as well." His eyes were black as jet.

"Are you sure she *is* Lady Copeland's granddaughter?" Jewel asked facetiously, raising her brows. "She doesn't resemble her in the least. Not in coloring or bone structure. Perhaps I'm the real granddaughter and your girlfriend's an impostor?" It was a deliberate thrust, and he didn't like it.

"Even if you *were* Lady Copeland's granddaughter, Eugenie, it wouldn't get you far."

"Really? I thought it would transport me overnight to the family home," she retorted.

"Perhaps that's what I mean," he said. "The Copeland
household is a dysfunctional one, to say the least."

"Perhaps you yourself create some of that tension," she accused him, herself on the attack.

"The fact that Travis Copeland and I are often at loggerheads has nothing to do with you. As you seem destined to find out. It's no secret. For almost fifty years, Lady Copeland has carried with her a photograph of her little daughter. Her name was Angela. Her golden child."

Jewel stared down at her hand. It trembled. "I had no idea Lady Copeland had a daughter."

His eyes contested that. "I'm amazed. A fact you missed? It's a matter of public record. The little girl died of bacterial meningitis when she was six."

"How sad!" Even her voice trembled slightly.

"Indeed it was. Although Lady Copeland has led a very full and active life, I suspect she's been weeping inside ever since. Angela was, from all accounts, a lovely little girl. A Botticelli angel. Sparkling with life. She looked pretty much the way you would have as a child."

Jewel fought hard to master her emotions. "My God!" she breathed. "You're very cruel."

He gripped the arm of the chair, his knuckles showing white. "And you're very—" He broke off immediately at Archie's approach with their drinks.

"Could I get you anything else?" Archie put down the drinks on the club coasters, then glanced from one to the other, obviously picking up on their tension.

"No, no, thank you." With a flick of his wrist Keefe Connellan produced a wallet, selecting a note that more than covered the price of the martinis. "Thanks, Archie."

"A pleasure, Mr. Connellan. Good evening, Ms. Bishop." Archie accepted the money and all but skipped off.

"I don't want this drink," Jewel said, feeling as nerve-ridden as if there were ghosts at the table.

"Just sip it," he replied. "I'd like to continue this…unique conversation."

"Why? I'm beginning to wonder if you're slightly unhinged," she suggested shortly.

The comment caused him to smile. "I don't think so. Whoever you are, Eugenie Bishop, you're not presenting your case—if you have one—in the right way."

"I have no case," she said angrily. "It's all in your mind. In any event, I'm flying home this weekend. I'll speak to my mother then."

"So she can come up with an explanation? Or perhaps tell you what you should do next?"

She returned his stare coolly. "My mother isn't a well woman."

"I'm sorry. What's wrong with her?"

Her blue eyes flashed. "She suffers from chronic depression. She's done so for many years."

"But surely she can be treated?" he asked, unexpectedly showing concern.

"There doesn't seem to be anything the doctors can do—and they've tried."

"Who's looking after her?"

She stiffened, although this time his tone was anything but confrontational. "I wanted her to come and live with me. But she dislikes change. She lives with my aunt Judith, her sister, in the family home."

"So there are only the three of you? No one else?"

"Unless *you've* come up with someone," she said with more than a touch of bitterness. "My father's death brought about great changes in our lives. My mother has been in deep mourning all these years."

"I'm sorry. That's tragic." He drank a little of his martini, set it down. "It must have affected your whole world."

"Of course." Jewel didn't touch her drink.

"So you sought to correct the past?"

Jewel suddenly reached flash point. She rose from her seat like the jet from the sparkling fountain. "My father was killed. It was a tragedy. Forgive me if I can't speak about it."

She left him sitting at the table, indifferent to the fascinated eyes that watched her progress across the room and into the lobby.

CHAPTER FOUR

IT WAS A LONG TRIP HOME. Two hours in the plane, another hour before she reached Hungerford by minibus, then the town taxi out to the house. The heat did not help her mood. She had almost forgotten how hot it was North of Capricorn, how humid. The driver left her at the gate. She picked up her overnight bag and began the trek through the garden, and its extraordinary lush beauty began the ritual soothing.

The place was drowned in golden-green light, heavy scents and birdsong. Dozens of brilliant rainbow lorikeets were dive-bombing the fruit trees, chattering and screeching. Everything grew in the utmost profusion here. Mangoes, bananas, custard apples, papaws, loquats and guavas; all manner of citrus trees—lemon, grapefruit, mandarin, lime; a whole grove of avocados and, lining the side fence, a row of long-established Queensland nut trees spreading their branches so they interlocked. These wonderful nut trees, native to the state, were *bauples* to the aborigines who had dined on them probably since the dawn of time, macadamias to the rest of the world. Some enterprising Hawaiian businessman had had the foresight to take them back home to found a profitable industry. But the *bauples* belonged to Queensland. Every child in the state knew the frustration of trying to crack the hard shells with a brick before exposing the most delicious of nuts.

Jewel walked on. Perspiration beaded her neck and her temples, trickling down her back. She approached two tall tank stands near the house; Aunt Judith always washed her hair in tank water, encouraging Jewel to do the same. Passionfruit vines climbed all over the stands. At this time of the year they were covered in the bronze-purple fruit. She had never tasted passionfruit as good as the ones that grew at home. Aunt Judith usually made up a beautiful tropical fruit salad fresh from the garden whenever she came to visit.

Someone had recently cut the grass, she noticed. Not a professional job, by any means, but a brave attempt to keep sections of the acreage clear and discourage the snakes. Such a fragrance rose from the earth. Intoxicating, really. Like incense. Jewel paused a few moments beneath a magnificent poinciana just past its flowering; she set down her overnight bag so she could breathe in all the exotic scents. Waxy gardenias massed themselves in the shaded areas; the frangipanis and ole-anders flaunted their beauty out in the brilliant sunshine, where the honeysuckle and ginger blossoms gave up their nostalgic perfume. When she'd first come to live here, Aunt Judith had warned her never to touch the oleanders, never to break off the pretty sweet-smelling flowers. Every part of the shrub was toxic. And Judith, being Judith, had gone on to tell her that a woman in the district had tried—mercifully without success—to murder her husband by adding some brewed oleander leaves to his coffee. Jewel had never forgotten that story.

She continued on her way, eyes focusing on the house as it finally emerged out of the semi-jungle. The intervening years had done nothing to lessen her belief that this place was magical. Haunted. Lost in time. The vivid red bougainvillea scrambled over the walls, giving every appearance that it was holding up the house now. She began to whistle the way she used to as a child copying the birdcalls, only this time it was an old song her mother had always loved. "Danny Boy." Her mother was easily startled by strange noises but she would recognize the tune and the whistler.

Before she'd even climbed the steps, her mother was there, rushing toward her with outstretched arms, a tiny creature, slight as a waif despite the oversize muslin dress, with big luminous green eyes and a wild cascade of dark hair.

"Darling, darling, girl."

Incredible, the love and pain that passed between them.

"Mama." Jewel gathered her mother to her, hugging her as if she were a child. Taller by several inches, Jewel felt infinitely stronger, infinitely older. How fragile her mother was. How delicate her bones! Her hair smelled lovely. She must have washed it. "Here, let me look at you." Jewel drew back, holding her mother's shoulders. "You never age."

It was almost true. Her mother, unlike other people, never seemed to grow older. In her late forties, Thea Bishop could have passed for a woman ten years her junior. At a distance, a teenager. She wore no makeup and really didn't need it. Her expression was open, yet her fragile mental state showed itself in every line of her body. "How are you, Mama?" Jewel asked, wondering how her mother could ever face up to the unpleasant questions she needed to ask.

"Terrific. I feel terrific. Never better, darling." The mildness of her voice was at odds with her words.

"What a wonderful surprise! I heard the whistling but I thought I was dreaming."

"But Aunt Judith told you I was coming?"

Her mother frowned in concentration. "Did she?"

"I'm sure she did, Mama, but no worries. I'm here now."

"And it's marvelous!" Her mother laughed aloud, then instantly sobered. "I pray and pray every day that the good Lord will protect you."

"And He does, too, Mama," Jewel said quickly. "Oh, it's good to be home. Let's go in, shall we?"

Aunt Judith came home not long after, thin to the bone, wearing a tiered cotton voile skirt in shades of orange, green and violet, with colored flowers sewn all over it and a rakish little V-neck sleeveless green top that echoed her clear eyes.

"You look great, Jewel!" They both moved to kiss.

"You look wonderful!" "I love the outfit!" They spoke together, stopped, laughed.

"Part of my summer collection!" Judith twirled. "I shut the shop," she told Jewel cheerfully. "I don't want to miss a minute of you while you're home."

"And you're going to love what I've brought you. Both of you." Jewel reached out to put her arm around her mother's waist.

"You spoil us," Thea said, resting against her daughter.

"Sure I do. Because I love you."

"I've been no use to you most of your life," her mother said in a completely different voice. Dull and self-flagellating. "I never took proper care of you. I never did the right thing."

"How about lunch?" Aunt Judith intervened briskly,

turning the conversation. "I haven't had a bite since six o'clock."

"No wonder you never put on a pound." Jewel joined ranks with her aunt, continuing to stroke her mother's trembling back. "I'll help. Give Mama a rest. What's it to be?"

"Ham salad?" Judith suggested blithely, obviously determined to be happy. "There's a beautiful ham in the fridge. Saves Thea worrying about cooking."

"I'm going to do the cooking while I'm here," Jewel announced, striving, as was Judith, to keep the mood light. "I'm a whiz with salads. All sorts of salads. You should try my Indonesian bird's nest salad with peanut sauce. Takes a bit of time, so we'll have to settle for avocado and grapefruit. All those lovely fresh ingredients. It'll go well with the ham."

"Or we've got some smoked salmon, if you prefer," Judith tossed over her shoulder on the way to her bedroom. "Over lunch you can tell us what else has been happening to the Hungerford boys. It wasn't right for Sheila to marry that Everett. I can't ever understand how it happened. He must have laid a spell on her."

Thea turned to her daughter, fear and despair in her look. She whispered, "It does happen. One mistake can change lives."

"Hush, Mama." Jewel spoke gently, very gently, unwilling to stir up the demons. "I can help the boys. I may even be able to help Sheila."

"And *me,* Jewel. God help me," her mother said.

THEY ATE ON THE VERANDA. Judith polished off her lunch, which included a fresh baguette from town, disproving a lot of people's theories that she never ate; Thea merely pushed the ham and greens around her plate but forked a few segments of the ruby grapefruit into her mouth.

Jewel filled them in on her discussion with the Hungerford boys, not sure if her mother was listening; she described their visit to the office and the pleasant catch-up meal they'd shared the night before. She didn't have it in her heart to raise the subject of Lady Copeland, much less her meeting with Keefe Connellan and his veiled accusations. Strangely enough, it was Judith who brought up the fact that the boys' grandfather had been a longtime employee of Copeland Connellan Carpentaria at their copper mine, Mount Esmeralda, some thirty miles inland.

"Frank Fletcher was their top engineer for many years, don't you remember, Thea? Sheila's father?" Judith spoke as though her sister were deaf.

"Why would we want to hear that name here?" Thea shuddered, her eyes filling with tears.

"*What* name?" Judith asked in astonishment. "Fletcher was a grand old man. He'd turn in his grave to know what was going on now."

"Who are you talking about, Mama?" Jewel risked asking, finding her mother's reaction ominous. "Copeland Connellan?" If so, Aunt Judith had really started something.

Thea's green eyes were burning, burning, blazing with intensity. "That name ruined our lives. I never want to hear it in this house."

"Well, it hasn't been used for the past twenty years," Judith said dismissively.

"Why does it make you so unhappy, Mama?" Jewel persisted, trying to keep the urgency out of her voice.

"The way they dealt with me and your father." Thea spoke tightly.

"Thea, does it do any good to go over this?" Judith implored. "Steve's accident could hardly be laid at their door."

"They destroyed him." Thea lifted a bread-and-butter plate and threw it. Then she bent right over, rocking her body.

"*How,* Mama?" Jewel ignored the shattered plate, placing her hand on her mother's neck. She desperately wanted to keep her mother talking, knowing that otherwise all information would be lost to her. "You've never mentioned one word of this all these years."

Her mother straightened, giving a great cry of anguish. "My only wish was to protect you."

"From what?" Jewel caught her mother's wrist and held it.

Thea's eyes filled again. "You've been happy, baby, haven't you?" she whimpered.

Judith exploded. "How the hell could she be happy? You've given up on life, Thea. You let go of the reins. Jewel had to turn into a woman by the time she was ten. You could've saved her from that."

"Judith, please," Jewel begged of her aunt. "Let Mama talk. Something's eating her away inside."

"Well, it sure as hell isn't hormones. Thea went into a decline twenty years ago. Don't tell me the Hungerford kids have stirred up some big mystery."

Mystery? Jewel felt her world begin to crash around her. "All along," she whispered, "I've been aware that so much has been kept from me."

Judith shook her head strenuously. "Not by me, love. I've kept nothing from you because I *know* nothin'. I've lived the good life and followed the commandments. Whatever is eating away at your mother, she's kept it all to her tiny self, the poor poop. In the early days, when you first came to live here, I did everything in my power to get her to open up. It was obvious she was in one hell of a mess. Not even losing Steve could account for it all. Hell, I lost Andy. The bloody crocs took him. But there was no one around to hold my hand or wipe my tears.'' She shook her head. ''We've had more than our fair share of misfortune. Losing Mum and Dad the way we did. They *would* drive into town in a bloody cyclone—'' Judith broke off sounding anguished and angry. She must have been remembering how a tree had come crashing down in their parents' path, crushing car and occupants.

''We're cursed, Judi,'' Thea said, holding her frail body taut. ''I've accepted my punishment.''

''Gawd, here we go again!'' Judith snapped. ''Tell me, whose life is perfect? Personally I find it incredible that you've kept this up so long. Accusing yourself of every kind of weakness. Anyone would think you'd *murdered* poor old Steve.''

Thea sprang from her chair, wheeling so sharply that her dress floated out. ''I did worse, far worse! Better he'd married any other girl.''

''Only he was hooked on you.'' Judith gave a broken laugh. ''You'll never figure your mother out, Jewel,'' she said, watching her niece with pity. ''I've known her longer than you have and I haven't got a clue.''

But Jewel had decided to try. ''So what does this have to do with the Copelands, Mama?'' she continued, although Thea shook her dark head quickly. ''You say *they* destroyed Dad? *How?*''

Her mother's eyes were a deep shining green. ''It was a tragedy. An unbearable tragedy. I can't speak of it. Love killed him.''

"Love?" Jewel's voice rose. "He loved you. He loved me."

"He *adored* you," Thea emphasized. "You were his golden child."

As little Angela had been Davina Copeland's? Jewel was struck by the same description.

"Then, why wasn't *my* love worth living for, Mama?" she asked, reliving for a moment the endless hurts and disappointments.

"That's right, kiddo." Judith applauded her, staring across at her sister in challenge. "Give it to her. Your daughter loves you, Thea. And you let her down."

"I didn't mean to!" Thea started to weep, falling back against the vine covered pillar, oblivious of the thorns.

"Yes, you did!" Judith began to shout, the usual ritual. "And quit the hysterics. Why, in God's name? I never thought Mum and Dad raised a couple of wimps. What happened to you? Anyone would think you carried the sins of the world on your shoulders. What bloody sin did you commit that you can't speak of it?" By now Judith's voice revealed a great weary anger mixed up with pity.

"What do the Copelands have to do with it, Mama?" Jewel, too, hammered away. "Do you realize my law firm represents Copeland Connellan?"

Thea's olive skin blanched and her head shot up. "You've never said." She sounded truly frightened. She even raised her hands to her eyes as though a ghost stood before her.

"Probably realized it was going to be a big problem." Judith flung her mane of dark curly hair, witchlike, over her shoulders.

"Mama, I'll take a plane out of here by nightfall if

you don't speak," Jewel threatened, feeling close to tears herself.

"She'll never set foot in this house again," Judith added for good measure. "What have you got against the Copelands, Thea? We all know Steve worked for them Outback. Hell, I thought you were happy there. You always said so in your letters. I've still got all the photographs you sent me. Do you want me to get them?" Judith half-rose, causing her sister to break out in moans.

"Nooo, nooo. For God's sake, have some mercy, Judi."

"Ah, cool it, Thea," Judith said disgustedly. "You're giving me the creeps. All this time, Jewel and I have been showing you mercy at the cost of *ourselves.* I think now we've been doing the wrong thing. What happened at Mingaree Station? What went on? Was there some...unpleasantness? Did Steve get himself into some disgrace? I've often wondered. What did Steve *really* look like? You only brought him home once and there's no good photo of him. I remember he was dark-haired, a nice guy. But who does Jewel look like? Look at her. *Look* at her like you've never bothered to look before. She's a beauty. Okay, so we were pretty when we were young, but neither of us could hold a candle to Jewel. She could be on the cover of some Goddamn magazine. Who the hell does she look like? It sure isn't you and I'm fairly certain it wasn't Steve. Where did she get the golden hair? The black brows and lashes? The violet eyes?"

"From Steve's mother, of course," Thea said, wiping her mouth with the back of her hand.

"That's bunkum!" Judith answered with a hiss. "Blondes like that can marry millionaires. You've said yourself, Steve's family didn't have a cracker. Might as well pack your bags, Jewel.'' She addressed her niece, pointing dramatically to the door. "Your mother is never going to come clean.''

Jewel felt her heart begin a long painful tattoo. "Yesterday for the first time, I met Lady Copeland,'' she announced, afraid, so afraid of what was coming. "She visited the office with Keefe Connellan. That's—''

"I know who he is.'' The words shot out of Thea as wildly as a bolting brumby.

"Keep going, Jewel,'' Judith all but shrieked her encouragement.

"Lady Copeland took one look at me and fainted,'' Jewel told them, stunned she was saying this. "She simply slid from the chair to the floor.''

It was as though no one breathed.

"Do you know what caused it, Jewel?'' Judith finally asked, the attack draining out of her.

"Do *you* know, Mama?'' As much as she loved her mother, Jewel was determined to back her into a corner.

"Know? How should I know?'' Thea, although she looked heartbreakingly frightened, had a furtive air.

"Then, I'll tell you.'' Jewel pulled her mother into a chair, a little roughly. "She said, and I could *see* it clearly, Mama, that I was the image of her at the same age. Keefe Connellan also told me he saw a striking resemblance. Even my boss admitted he must've been blind. It could be sheer coincidence, of course, but I don't think so. What does it mean? You're the only one who can tell us.''

Thea stared back at her, pale. "Darling, darling, take my hand.''

Jewel did so, tightening her two hands around her

mother's. "Whatever it is, Mama, remember I love you. Nothing will change that."

"But it *is* nothing, my darling," Thea wailed. She looked honestly shocked. "You're my daughter. Steven was your father. I know nothing about Lady Copeland. She never ever came to the station. Sir Julius himself came infrequently."

"God, Thea. I kinda hoped you'd make an effort," Judith burst out. "So who *did* come, Thea? Came a lot. Was it that bloody son of hers—what's his name, that nasty Trevor?"

"Travis. Travis Copeland." Jewel gave her aunt a stricken look. She felt ill. Somehow soiled.

"Did *he* visit the station, Mama?" Jewel shook her mother's frail shoulders.

"He did come at times," Thea breathed. "I never liked him. He was the most arrogant man. He thought there was nothing in this world he couldn't have."

"The question is, did he have *you?*" Judith leapt up. "The filthy, cowardly blaggard. Is that what this is all about? This long nightmare. Some bloody pathetic affair? When Steve was away on muster, did you let Copeland into your bed?"

"Judi!" Thea said in a small protesting voice. Her eyes rolled back and she slumped to the floor. Jewel jumped up to grab her. She settled her mother in the chair, supporting her with one hand.

"Mama. Mama," she moaned in dismay before turning on her aunt. "Lord, Judith, did we have to do this to her? She's so pitiful."

"She's strong as a bloody horse!" Judith raged, suddenly bursting into tears. "These weak ones, these weak ones, how they pull the rest of us down! We've pandered to Thea forever. Holding her hand. Drying her tears. Coping with her faints. They've always struck me as a bit convenient—like faints on demand. She has the doctors feeling sorry for her. Pretty little thing. She wouldn't have gotten half the pills or the sympathy if she'd looked like a horse. Maybe someone should've given her a good kick in the backside.''

Deceptively violent words, when her aunt was so obviously upset.

"I know, Judith, I know." Jewel shook her head. "Maybe everything's been a big mistake. But it's so painful to look at her.'' She sighed in relief as her mother came around or, as Judith suggested, simply stopped her fake faint. Jewel went down on her knees, staring into her mother's face. "It's all right, Mama,'' she said soothingly, unable to break long years of habit. "Everything's okay. Would you like to lie down for a while?''

"Why not? More avoidance.'' Judith laughed ironically, coming to assist Jewel as they helped Thea out of the chair and into the house.

"Your mother's mind isn't as scrambled as you think, my darlin',' Judith said after they'd deposited Thea on the bed and closed the door. "My advice to you is to keep hammering away at her. She's been hiding from her ghosts all these years. Now they're beginning to catch up with her.''

JEWEL DROVE JUDITH'S SMALL CAR over to the old Hungerford farm, traveling through the great sweep of river valley that lay beneath the cloudless peacock-blue sky. The beauty of this tropical landscape had always affected her—the marvelous lushness, the clarity and brilliance of the air. Farther west, beyond the ragged larkspur ranges, lay sun-bleached cattle country, the vast stations that carried the nation's great herds. But here on the verdant coastal strip, luminous green sugar lands ran for hundreds of square miles, as far as the eye could see, the deep red soil of the ploughed paddocks contrasting vividly with the green cane, the rich ochres of the earth touching early memories of her childhood desert home. Where the eternal cane stopped, the mango plantations took over, the tropical fruit farms growing all the exotic new fruits, many of which not even she could name. Beyond them the prosperous tea and coffee plantations on the tablelands were expanding now that the tobacco industry had foundered.

Thirty miles west, almost in dense scrub, lay the rich Copeland Connellan copper mine, Esmeralda, where the boys' grandfather, Fletcher, had been employed for most of his working life. Employed and grown wealthy. The Hungerford farm she remembered used to grow sorghum, maize, safflower and winter feed for cattle, but apparently with the unlawful acquisition of the boys' inheritance, the farm had become a much bigger operation. Her visit today was in the nature of a private visit to an old friend. Once any proceedings started—and she hoped that could be averted—she'd have to restrict all contact to Sheila and George Everett's solicitor. The boys had already told her Everett had removed the family's affairs from one of the biggest law firms in the north, putting them in the hands of some new guy who'd managed to rack up a fairly significant clientele.

All along her route, the bougainvillea broke out in open country, crimson, white, mauve, climbing in spectacular fashion over everything in sight—fences, trees, spindly old rotted shacks and abandoned rainwater tanks that must once have served tenants long gone. The impressive white timber gates that marked the entry to the farm were closed. Jewel got out, opened them, then drove through and closed them behind her. The long drive up to the house was lined by the ubiquitous coconut palms. It took her past the stoneworker's cottage; she could see it through the great shade trees, some of them still carrying small bouquets of scarlet flowers. A wide area around the cottage had been cleared, the grass neatly mown. Two wooden planter's chairs, a freshly painted yellow, had been placed in the shade of the front veranda.

How had it come to this? The boys in the cottage. Sheila and Everett up at the house. Obviously it only took one person to wreck a happy home. She didn't know much about George Everett. As yet, she hadn't had time to run her own checks, but what she recalled of him she hadn't liked. It was more an intuitive reaction than anything else. Before the marriage, he'd tried very hard to ingratiate himself with the people of the district, who collectively had thought him a very poor successor to the much-respected Stewart Hungerford, Sheila's late husband and the boys' father. Jewel's own trauma of the morning, the seriousness of this present situation and what she herself intended to do about it, put her in a sober frame of mind.

The house came into view, allowing her to see the changes that had been wrought over the intervening years. Not all of them for the better, she thought with a stab of dismay. The huge homestead was a Queenslander par excellence, entirely surrounded by wide verandas. It had a steeply sloping iron roof and a small hip that had been repainted. No longer the pristine white it had always been, with a green roof and dark green glossy shutters offsetting the pairs of French doors, it had been refurbished in Federation colors inappropriate

to the building. The once-luxuriant flower beds along
the house frontage had been dug up and replaced by
turf, the central fountain taken away. A clean sweep of
green lawn remained with nary a flower or shrub. In the
hectically blossoming tropics it was a relatively leafless
environment.

Not Sheila's work, she thought. The old Sheila had
taken great pride in her garden. This had to be Everett's
decision. If so, it was a wonder he hadn't had the great
fig trees cut down, as well. Perhaps too much work or
Sheila had rebelled. As Jewel parked at the base of the
curved flight of steps, she saw one of the filmy curtains
in the old drawing room stir. A woman's outline was
visible. *Sheila.* Thank God she was home. A further
blessing might be in store; George Everett might be out
in the fields.

Jewel took the steps lightly, trying to convey by her
demeanor that this was just a pleasant visit from a
friend. The front door with its lovely leaded side lights
had always stood open in the early days, so the cooling
breeze could waft down the wide central hallway; today
it was firmly closed. Jewel rang the bell, listening to its
familiar peal through the quiet, rather dim interior.

No one came. Nerves badly frayed by the events of
the morning, Jewel stood back, biting her lip. Surely
Sheila wasn't going to ignore her. It made her wonder
seriously what this marriage had done to the woman.
My God, these weren't Victorian times! George Everett
would have to be very, very stupid to ill-treat this particular woman. Jewel put her finger on the bell yet
again. More moments passed. She had no intention of
returning to the car. She was starting to feel so worried
about Sheila, she was even prepared to walk around the
veranda to the rear of the house. She started to do so,

glancing discreetly inside. The decor of the living room appeared to be changed. Where was the magnificent landscape painting that had always hung over the white marble mantel?

"Yoo-hoo, Sheila!" she called. "It's me, Jewel, home for a visit!"

The front door opened forcibly. Jewel whirled around to see George Everett staring at her, a deep furrow between his eyes, his stance aggressive.

"Why, Mr. Everett!" She turned on the charm. Usually it worked wonders, but George Everett, a powerfully built man with slicked-back graying hair and stony, searching, almost colorless eyes, wasn't responding. Undeterred, Jewel advanced, smiling and holding out her hand. "It's so good to see you!" She should choke on that lie. "Do you remember me? Jewel Bishop?"

The grim aspect lifted to a patronizing near sneer. "Of course I remember you, Miss Bishop." He took her outstretched hand, crushed it. "What are you doing back in these parts?"

Jewel would've loved to say "I'm after you." Instead, she kept up the smile. "Why, visiting Mama and my aunt. Just for the weekend. I couldn't let today go past without popping in to see Sheila. She was always so kind to me."

For a minute, Jewel thought he was about to slam the door shut. "Not today, Miss Bishop. Sheila suffers from bad headaches."

They locked stares. "I might cheer her up. I get to see so little of her. Why don't you just ask her if she could spare me ten minutes to say hello?" Jewel half turned and waved a hand in pretended admiration. "I see you've made a great many improvements since I was here last.''

He glared at her, obviously trying to see if she was having him on. He must have decided she was sincere. ''Got rid of all those damn flower beds, at least,'' he finally muttered. ''I had to, just so Sheila wouldn't work herself to death. Come in if you like, Miss Bishop.''

''Oh, please, it's *Jewel!*'' she cooed, knowing George Everett was the sort of man who detested clever women.

''And that's no exaggeration,'' he amazed her by saying. ''You're even more beautiful than you used to be.''

''Why, how nice of you to say so.'' Jewel grasped the opportunity to make a full sweep of the entrance hall, with glimpses of the main reception rooms that led off it. The Hungerfords had always been wealthy. But it appeared that quite a few of the treasures she remembered had either departed or been put in storage.

''If you'll take a seat for a moment, I'll go see if Sheila's fit to talk.''

''That's really sweet of you.''

''I'd appreciate it, however, if you could keep your visit short. I like to protect my wife as much as possible.''

Really? From *what?* Having a few friends in? Jewel positioned herself sweetly, hands on lap, legs crossed at the ankle, on an elaborately carved mahogany bench with rampant lions for arms—at least *it* was still there— and waited. She could've sworn there used to be a small side table right inside the door, genuine Thomas Chippendale. A Tang dynasty horse, hundreds of years old, used to sit atop it. She recalled the exquisite painting that had hung above the table, a watercolor by a classical Chinese master. Two white herons with lotus leaves and pink lilies and a Chinese poem written in calligraphy down the right-hand side. Nothing had been put in the place of those three objects, which wasn't a smart move. One could see where they'd been. The color scheme had been changed here, as well. Too dull and too heavy with all the dark timberwork. George would never make a successful interior decorator. He didn't have the taste to carry it off. Sheila was a warm, outgoing woman who'd always lived the gracious life, and Jewel couldn't imagine how she'd allowed this man to walk over her, let alone render her fraudulent. So perplexed did she feel on every front, Jewel felt like smacking her forehead with the palm of her hand. The only thing that stopped her was catching sight of herself in the hall mirror.

She was the skeleton in the closet! Generally speaking, every family had one. That didn't make her feel any better. The very idea of having a double sent a cold shiver down her spine. Of course, there were twins, mirror images, even stand-ins for film stars. According to popular wisdom, everyone had a double somewhere in the world. The thing was, she didn't believe it. Nor, despite what she'd insisted to Keefe Connellan, did she believe in coincidence. So what did that make her? Travis Copeland's illegitimate love child? She frowned for a minute, considering rape. That would be too dreadful. At this point, she didn't think she could even cope with the idea of her mother having had an affair. Yet the person looking back at her with those blue, blue eyes might not be Jewel Bishop at all. Literally overnight, she could be demoted to the status of a Copeland bastard. There were still a few people around who called the innocent that.

Her mother was hurting, had been hurting all these years. Now *she* was hurting, too. She had to face the fact that her mother might've been living a lie all these years. She could have lied to her husband, the man Jewel had called "Daddy" as a child. She couldn't visualize his face anymore but the memory of him was warm. She knew he'd loved her. Kept her safe. He had loved her mother, too. His "girls."

For a moment Jewel almost hated her mother for what she might have done to Steve Bishop.

Damn Everett! Where did he have Sheila stashed away? One of the outbuildings? They were taking a devil of a time. She stood up, suddenly tired of waiting, and then she heard footsteps.

Oh God!

George Everett had finally untied Sheila. He was leading her into the room the way a beefy, overbearing caregiver might lead in a psychiatric patient. Here was a shadow of the woman Sheila had been. The lovely chestnut hair Jewel remembered as long and flowing was cut in a thick wedge as short as a boy's, the slightly plump curvaceous figure whittled down to almost nothing, the widely spaced hazel eyes reflecting an inner misery Jewel could feel like a blast from the Antarctic. But those eyes when they fell on Jewel showed a hopeful ray of light.

"Jewel, my dear!" It came out as a soft wail. "How kind of you to come and visit me."

George Everett had done this to her.

Jewel took no heed of his possessive stance. Well might he look at her as if she was some sort of threat. She *was!* She swooped toward Sheila, using the advantage of surprise to prise her away from George.

"Do you think I could possibly forget your kindnesses to me?" she exclaimed. "It's so good to see you, Sheila. It's been far too long." The two women embraced, Jewel keeping an affectionate arm around Sheila's waist, even though the scowling expression on George Everett's face would have persuaded a lesser woman to let go. Who was this boorish man? How had Sheila been drawn to him? Some sort of sexual compulsion? Sheer loneliness? A need for a physically strong man to run the farm for her? Sometimes women made terrible mistakes without meaning to. She'd made a few herself. But nothing as bad as George.

"Jewel, you're a sight for sore eyes," Sheila was saying as she studied Jewel's chic informal getup. "So much polish!"

Not bad for a kid with a weird mother who forgot to buy her child shoes.

"We have lots to catch up on." Jewel turned to confront the silent, glowering George. "You won't want to be part of this, Mr. Everett. Girl talk."

"I've already told you Sheila isn't well," said George, obviously refusing to cooperate. "We can give you ten minutes."

"You don't trust me with fifteen?" Jewel joked, subduing the brief violent desire to tell him to get lost.

"Can I offer you something, Jewel? A cold drink?" Sheila asked quickly, an unbecoming flush mottling her throat.

"You wouldn't have a Coke, would you?" Jewel smiled at her. With any luck they might make it to the privacy of the kitchen.

"No, dear. I do have some homemade lemonade, though." Sheila made a little jerky movement backward, looking more and more distraught.

"That'll be fine. Why don't we go to the kitchen to get it? Would you care for some too, Mr. Everett?"

"I couldn't think of anything worse," he said.

How gracious. For one unbelievable moment, Jewel thought he was about to follow them, but he turned back, walking into the drawing room, instead.

Sheila wore a floral cotton dress that was dreadful to behold—she'd always been the trendsetter in the district with money to splurge. Once in the kitchen, she went quickly to the refrigerator, withdrawing a glass jug covered with cling wrap. "I made it this morning. I like it, if George doesn't," she added with the vaguest hint of defiance.

"I don't know that I like it when they're so *completely* honest," Jewel said flippantly. "What *does* George like—besides beer, I mean?"

"Beats the hell out of me." A glimpse of the old Sheila. "If I ever find out, you'll be the first to know."

Jewel paused, deciding she had to speak. "You don't look well, Sheila. You must have lost twenty pounds or more."

"More," Sheila told her in a wry voice. "There was a time I couldn't lose a pound, no matter which diet, but George soon cured me of that. I'm not a happy woman, Jewel."

"Can you talk about it?" Jewel said in her soothing lawyer's voice. "I'm your friend, Sheila. You have lots of friends, remember?"

"I used to have friends. Not anymore. George has cut me off, but the really sick thing, the shameful thing, is I've allowed him to do it."

"He is a very intimidating man," Jewel pointed out. "I've seen the boys," she told Sheila, quickly looking over her shoulder in case George was lurking in the doorway. "They're worried about you."

Sheila almost dropped two crystal glasses. "Saw them. Where?"

Jewel took the glasses out of Sheila's nerveless hands and set them down. "They're in Brisbane, Sheila, staying with an old school friend. They're fine. We had a very nice meal at a restaurant last night. It was great to catch up."

"They came to see you, didn't they." Sheila's hazel eyes filled with tears.

"I *am* a friend of the family," Jewel said gently. A lawyer, too.

"You always did have the knack of getting on with everybody," Sheila said, blinking hard. "If the boys are worried about me, I'm frantic about them. Without my ever wanting it, we've become estranged. They hated George right from the start."

"Maybe they didn't give George enough of a chance?" An absurd notion.

"George doesn't have your sympathetic personality, Jewel," Sheila said, quite unnecessarily. "He's a very stiff, stern man, though he wasn't too bad at the beginning. The problem is I never listened to anyone before I married him. So many people, including my own father, warned me it wouldn't work. But it was unbearable without Stewart. I had to fill the terrible void."

"You could have waited a while."

"I know." Sheila squirmed. "It seems obvious to me now. But I couldn't handle the sudden pressure in my life. Having a big farm to run. To continue to keep it successful for the boys. If nothing else, George is a good farmer."

Yet the boys had indicated the farm was on the edge of economic disaster.

"That doesn't give him the right to talk you into taking over the boys' property, Sheila." Jewel went to the heart of it. "That's illegal."

"I'm not clever like you, Jewel. I've done some really bad things."

"And the bank let you," Jewel added.

"Oh, they've always been on side. We had a name in this part of the world, Jewel."

"Absolutely correct." Jewel nodded. "Are you aware the boys aren't going to stand for it anymore?"

"You're not representing them, are you, Jewel?" Sheila burst out.

"Not today. I came to you as a friend only, Sheila. Not the boys' representative. I'm not supposed to talk legalities. But you must know you and the boys could settle all this privately. You and George don't have a leg to stand on."

"We stole their inheritance from them," Sheila said dolefully.

Jewel's voice was wry. "It's certainly the view of the town."

"Why do you think I don't go there anymore?" Sheila's eyes filled again. "I'm so ashamed. It was mostly stupidity, you know. George convinced me we'd be doing the best possible thing for the boys. We'd be trebling the income."

"And have you?" Jewel asked.

"No. But I don't know the details. George keeps such a lot from me."

"You still own this house, don't you, Sheila?" Jewel looked directly at the older woman.

"Yes."

"Then, you can tell George to get lost any time."

"Can I?" Sheila leaned closer, appearing amazed.

"You'd better believe it. You can do it if you want to. This is your house, Sheila—and your life."

"It's no life at all," Sheila said wretchedly. "I got

myself into this terrible situation and I don't know how to get out.''

"Find the strength for your boys," Jewel urged. "Surely seeing them robbed would put steel in your backbone?"

"That's the problem, Jewel." Sheila gave a broken laugh. "I've lost all my confidence. It went with Stewart. I adored him. Marrying George… For whatever reasons, I've become a gutless woman. The marriage would never have worked with George even if he'd taken a fatherly interest in the boys, which of course he didn't. I got a sinking feeling the minute I said, 'I do!' but I'd already made my bed.''

"Crises can be resolved, Sheila." Jewel sought to reassure her. "You have people who love you. Ask for help and you'll get it. You have to reach out, not struggle alone.''

A furious voice from the door shocked them. "How could she possibly be *alone?* She has me." George Everett strode into the room, his square-jawed face contorted with rage. "How dare you come into this house under false pretenses, young lady. What's your game?''

"Tennis." Jewel said after a moment's hesitation, trying to control her anger. "I used to be a good swimmer but I gave up on the training.''

Sheila reached out tentatively and touched Jewel's hand. "Don't, dear," she warned.

"Don't what? Don't provoke George? You may live in fear of him, Sheila. I certainly don't. You can take that threatening expression right off your face, Mr. Everett. Lay one finger on me and you'll be slapped with an assault charge. I should add that Judge Donovan in town considers me one of his grandchildren.''

"Don't play the fool with me," Everett shouted. "You young people know nothing about respect."

"Personally, I consider bellowing extremely disrespectful. I'm not getting into any argument with you, Mr. Everett. I came to see Sheila. I came on my own behalf and for the boys. They're very worried about her. As they need to be, from the look of her."

"She looks fine," Everett maintained furiously. "As for those boys, they're afraid to work for a living."

"They need an education first." Jewel stared back at him. "Their father would have wanted them to go to university or agricultural college. As it is, they've got nothing. And it's because of *you*, Mr. Everett."

At once his glowering expression changed, became wary. "Ah, so they got themselves down to Brisbane to cry on your shoulder?"

"It's obvious they couldn't look to *you* for support," Jewel shot back.

"Or me, either," Sheila said brokenly. "We've acted very wrong, George. We have to put things right."

It clearly wasn't a plan of action George intended to take. "Get out of my house, Miss Bishop," he said tautly, advancing not on Jewel but his wife.

"I'll go when Sheila tells me." Jewel stood her ground, afraid for Sheila. How did she know the man wasn't physically abusive? "It's *her* house, lest you forget."

"That's right, George." Sheila looked down pointedly at the strong fingers clamped around her arm. "Would you mind letting go?"

He stared at her balefully. "Have you lost your senses, Sheila? This girl comes in here stirring things up and—"

"Things that *need* to be stirred up, George. I have to

sleep at night. I have to be able to look at myself in the mirror. Poppa would turn in his grave if he knew what I'd done.''

"Don't be ridiculous!" Everett cried in his brow-beating voice. "It had nothing to do with stealing. I've slaved to make this place work. It's a far bigger operation and eventually it'll all go to the boys.''

"It's theirs *now*, Mr. Everett," Jewel pointed out quietly. "Or it will be, as soon as Sheila puts things right.''

"Ah, the lawyer!" He looked at her with contempt. "You're a troublemaker.''

"Go, Jewel," Sheila implored. "Please go. I thank you for trying to help me.''

"I haven't finished yet, Sheila," Jewel said in a determined voice. "Why don't you leave with me?''

Everett was livid. "How dare you come between man and wife?" he demanded. "What is it you fancy yourself now, a marriage counsellor?''

"If I were, I'd tell you your wife is frightened of you, Mr. Everett," Jewel retorted. "That's no way to live. No way for any woman, let alone the Sheila Fletcher Hungerford I knew. You've got control of her. I perceive that as being very bad, very dangerous. She needs help.''

"Not from you." He appeared genuinely menacing.

"Then, maybe the local police sergeant. No woman should be intimidated, especially not in her own home. Sheila has a perfect right to ask you to pack your belongings and go.''

By now George Everett's colorless eyes were almost bulging from his head. "My God, you have a hide!" he cried, in a filthy temper. "But then, you had a very odd upbringing. You and your crazy mother and that eccentric aunt.''

"You make them look like pillars of society," Jewel said sharply. "My mother does no one harm. My aunt runs a successful legitimate business, which is more than I can say for you."

"Get out!" He ground his teeth, the blood mounting alarmingly to his face.

Jewel walked past him, reaching out for Sheila. "Are you coming, Sheila? My crazy mother and eccentric aunt would love to have you." She prayed Sheila would have the strength to make a bid for release, but Sheila looked as though she was remembering slaps in the face. Or perhaps beatings. Could anything be worse?

"I want you to leave, Jewel," she begged. "I'll see you to the door."

"Very well, Sheila." Jewel didn't give Everett so much as a sideways glance. "If that's what you want."

"I said *I'll* go, George." Sheila spoke with dignity. "I've got a little too used to being chained to your side."

Yet he came after them, though keeping a small distance.

"I'm so frightened," Sheila whispered as they stood in the open doorway, her voice so low Jewel had to bend her head to hear. "So ashamed."

"Don't give up, Sheila," Jewel said, hugging the older woman to her as if providing a protective shield. "I'll be back."

CHAPTER FIVE

SKINNER GAVE HER the extra time she needed, which turned out to be a week, without the slightest dispute. A huge relief! As long as there was money in it for Barton Skinner Beaumont and she kept up with her other legal work, it appeared schedules could be adjusted. Much had happened since she'd called on Sheila Hungerford that fateful afternoon. The most significant event was that George Everett had been turned out of the Hungerford family home. Sheila had sounded terrified when Jewel had left the farm, and Jewel, totally averse to abandoning a friend in trouble, drove straight back into town to the local police station manned by burly Gordon Matheson and his well-muscled constable. A responsible lawyer, known to them forever, she didn't have a lot of difficulty convincing them Sheila needed police protection.

As a consequence, they'd all returned to the farm, where George greeted them so warmly that the police might have been guests and Jewel a good friend. It was a charm card that Jewel, for one, had never suspected he had in the pack. Handsome in a big, dark, glowering fashion, George played the solid, highly respected citizen quite at a loss as to why this visit could actually be official and not something to do with a police fund-raiser. Despite George's concern for his wife—he claimed her migraine was much worse—Sheila was

eventually summoned, displaying to their horror the be-
ginnings of a black eye, the swollen lid closing. Even
then, she was loath to say George had caused it, though
they all knew he had. Jewel was well aware that physical abuse is a demeaning experience, the victims often
feeling too humiliated or ashamed to confide in anyone.
It was an irrational response but easily understood.

In the end, Jewel persuaded Sheila to speak of
George's treatment, dreading what shocks might lie in
store…and there were quite a few. Once started, Sheila
couldn't seem to stop, so after a while they all had to
sit down. They heard of the psychological abuse, which
had caused Sheila's alienation from her sons and her
friends, the occasional physical abuse when George
felt provoked into giving his complaining wife a back-
hander.

Jewel's visit had precipitated a whole chain of events.
George, protesting violently, was allowed time to pack
a bag before being escorted into town. Sheila spent the
night with Jewel. The boys reconciled with their mother
over the phone and lost no time in catching the first
available plane home. Sheila's former family solicitors
were reinstated, arranging a restraining order to keep
George Everett away from Sheila and her boys, and
divorce proceedings were placed on the agenda. First
thing Monday morning, Jewel started her own lengthy
search, uncovering the fact that George Everett had si-
phoned off a considerable amount of the loan he and
Sheila had received to upgrade the property, using the
boys' inheritance from their grandfather as security to
the bank. With mother and sons reconciled, Jewel was
now in a position to act for all three. Litigation against

George Everett would proceed to win back the boys' property. The whole scenario had worked out well for everyone. Except George.

AUNT JUDITH DROVE HER to the airport early Monday morning, ten days later, leaving the shop in the care of her assistant, Dolly, who practiced white magic and read tarot cards at the Sunday markets.

"I just can't believe what's going on around here anymore," Judith said, still in the grip of multiple shocks. "You were pretty good taking on George Everett." Judith glanced at her niece with admiration. "The whole thought of it worries me. He's one scary guy. I'm still trying to figure out what Sheila ever saw in him. Maybe he was more affectionate toward her when they first met...."

"Come on, George Everett never had a tender moment in his whole life. Anyway, he doesn't scare me." Jewel moved her hand to touch her aunt's. "Besides, as soon as he saw Gordon, he backed right off. George is the kind who only treats *women* badly."

Judith smiled wanly. "Poor old Sheila. I'd just love a man to take a swipe at me. I'd clobber him with whatever I could lay my hands on. But for the marriage to finish just like that!" Judith gave an amazed hoot.

"According to Sheila, it was finished almost as soon as it began. She made a very bad decision at a critical point in her life. But the boys are safely back home."

"Two fine strapping lads," Judith said with satisfaction, "who at last know the truth. What happens now?"

"I'll get cracking with the action against George. Sheila's solicitor will act for her on the divorce. Basically, I'm around to protect the boys. We'll win.

The boys will get their property back. As for Sheila, she's probably had enough of men.''

"I honestly can't see her remaining a single woman." Judith frowned for a moment. "Sheila's one of those women who always has to have a man around. She was blessed with Stewart.''

"Let's just hope she doesn't take on another George.''

"Everett must hate you." Judith turned her head briefly, an expression of worry on her face.

"Doesn't he hate everybody? Who cares about the Everetts of this world?'' Jewel looked out the window at the lush tropical landscape. A beautiful black horse, coat gleaming, was pounding around a paddock on delicate thoroughbred legs.

"You don't think he could be nasty?" Judith persisted.

"It's possible. Very possible. But he's already in a very bad position and Sergeant Matheson made that very plain— None of which solves my own *huge* dilemma.''

"No." Judith jutted out her chin. "We have to face it, kiddo, your mother had an affair and she's been blaming herself ever since. You are the result of that affair. The depth of her grief can now be revealed to us two suffering souls. She always felt extremely guilty, as one tends to do when one breaks the commandments.''

"But she wasn't responsible for Dad's death," Jewel argued emotionally. "He had a car accident, didn't he— or is that a lie, as well?''

"No lie. He did.''

"You're certain of that, Judith?" Jewel asked. "Because I'm going to look it all up in the archives, going back to Sir Julius Copeland's funeral. The man I called Daddy died that day.''

Judith struggled to keep the distress out of her voice. ''He slammed his car into a power pole.''

''God!'' It had never been explained. ''Was it raining or something? Did he lose control? Dad could drive anything. Anywhere.''

Judith shook her head, her voice grim. ''I don't know, love. I only know your mother's been punishing us all ever since. Maybe your dad—Steve—was suspicious. Maybe he found out something. Maybe he met Lady Copeland? He certainly would've seen her at the funeral. That was twenty years ago. She would've been in her fifties. You say she's a beauty now.''

''She'll always be a beauty,'' Jewel said. ''He may have been taken unaware by the resemblance. He may have jumped to conclusions.''

''He may have discovered the truth, girl. It all adds up. Travis Copeland used to visit the station on behalf of his father. Your mother was a very pretty girl. A dark-haired Mia Farrow. Strange how this all has happened,'' Judith mused. ''The Hungerford issue fueled it.''

''Deception runs through everything,'' Jewel said, her face bleak. ''I don't think I can bear this, Judith. I had an identity. Who am I now? I don't even think I want to continue with the firm. They represent Copeland Connellan. From the way Keefe Connellan spoke, he wants me out.''

''Does he now! How could he blame *you* for anything?'' Judith demanded hotly. ''You had no control over your own birth.''

''Hard to argue with that, but he seems to think I'm manipulating the present situation.''

"I'd like to have a few minutes with him." Judith set her teeth.

Jewel managed a discordant laugh. "You think George Everett is scary? This man is the real thing. He can tear you up with his eyes. He doesn't have to say a word. Besides, even *I* think it looks suspicious. I could have worked my way into the firm. Put myself into the best possible place for drawing attention."

"Your boss didn't notice anything," Judith pointed out.

"He noticed *something*. He just needed a little nudge to put two and two together." She sighed. "The Copelands won't want to know me. I'd be nothing more than a terrible embarrassment. A huge problem they'd probably pay to go away. Blackmail is obviously on Keefe Connellan's mind. They're the elite, the Establishment, among the most powerful and influential people in the state."

"To hell with that!" Judith burst out in disgust. "They're no better than the rest of us. Probably a damn sight worse. To most people it would be a seven-day wonder. Anyway, I thought you told me Lady Copeland wanted you to visit her?"

"She does." Jewel gave her aunt a tight smile. "I think I've touched some chord. She wasn't at all angry. She wasn't fearful or judgmental."

"Especially when her adulterous son comes into it. Why should she judge you?" Judith challenged. "You've done nothing wrong. You're a splendid young woman—you could take your place anywhere."

"Travis Copeland has a daughter," Jewel said quietly, after a short silence. Emotions were running high inside the car.

"Amelia, isn't it?" Judith asked, adjusting the sun shield against the mirage.

"Amelia wouldn't want to know me," Jewel said, shaking her head.

"Her loss." Judith, obviously feeling tender and protective, looked ferocious. "But you don't know she feels that way, do you? She might love to have a sister. Surely to God there's enough money to go around."

Jewel nearly choked. "I don't want their money," she said violently, her words resounding in the small car's interior.

"Bless you, your mother could do with some." Judith paid no attention. "I figure your bloody father had something to do with it all. Your birth father, I mean—not Steve."

"He mightn't have known a thing about it." Jewel didn't want to consider the specter of a father's lifelong abandonment. "Mama might have kept it from everyone. She kept it from you, her own sister."

"Thea always did have a great talent for keeping secrets," Judith said wryly. "We didn't even know she had a boyfriend until she and Steve turned up at the door. Next thing, they're married. A week after that, they were a thousand miles away, working some damn cattle station. Of course at the time we thought Thea was pregnant. The big rush to the altar and all. But she didn't have you until two years later. Always knew something wasn't right, but I could never flush Thea out."

"We're still not having much success," Jewel observed, not without underlying humor.

"Makes you wonder what'll happen on Judgment Day." Judith glanced at her niece, green eyes ironic. "The good Lord asking and Thea refusing to talk."

Despite the anguish Jewel was battling, she chuckled at that, heartened by the powerful attachment between them. "You know I love you, don't you?"

"I know exactly," Judith said and smiled.

THE DOMESTIC AIR TERMINAL was full of people coming and going. This was one of the jumping-off points for the crowds of tourists going to the beautiful resorts of the Great Barrier Reef. Jewel checked her luggage and made her way to the departure lounge. The torrent of conversation had apparently affected the pressure of Judith's foot on the accelerator, so she'd made record time, which gave Jewel a full thirty minutes before boarding time. She debated having a cup of coffee, then decided against it, walking over to the small shop that sold souvenirs, paperbacks and a range of magazines.

She was almost there, when a physically large, hard-eyed man loomed in front of her. Too late for her to react, George Everett clamped her arm so tightly she couldn't shake it off, though she wrenched hard. He then proceeded to maneuver her swiftly out of the mainstream and back against a large pillar, which effectively concealed her.

"Don't think I'm finished with you," he snarled.

"What do you want, Mr. Everett?" Jewel didn't have to work up to anger. It exploded out of her. "And take your hand off my arm. You're already in big trouble."

"Unfortunately, yes." He grimaced. "Because of *you*. How quickly you messed up my life. I still can't believe it."

"Your life was messed up long before I came on the scene," Jewel said with contempt.

"You think I count for nothing, don't you." He fixed her with his gaze, as a big cat might fix its quarry.

"I try not to think about you at all." Jewel made no attempt to conceal her scorn. "Any involvement with you is over, so I'll ask you to please leave me alone."

His colorless eyes were like poisoned wells. "I love my wife, whatever you choose to think." He pressed closer, probably in case she tried to make a break.

"It's got nothing to do with me. I do remember Sheila telling us all of your physical abuse, if that's your idea of *loving.*"

He raised one large hand, made a fist. "You shut up."

Jewel was stunned by the fact that this was actually happening to her. Associates of Barton Skinner Beaumont didn't get into ugly public fistfights, but this brutish man was infuriating her. "Don't threaten me, Mr. Everett," she said coldly. "You'll regret it. Fair warning. I'm a lawyer, remember? What are you doing here, anyway?"

"What do you think?" He regarded her with such enmity; if they weren't in a public place, Jewel might have panicked. It might take very little to turn this man dangerous, more dangerous even than Sheila had led them to believe.

"I'm here for my say," he exclaimed violently, thrusting his face forward. "I'm entitled to one, aren't I? You ruined my life, putting ideas into Sheila's head. Going to the police. How dare you! By the time Sheila finishes with me, I'll have nothing left."

"You started with nothing, as I recall." Jewel began her move, inwardly agitated, outwardly composed. "You could've had a good life had you shown any decency. Instead, you started on a criminal course of action. Please get out of my way now, before this all gets out of hand. I'm not impressed by your scare tactics."

Everett's stolid frame remained rooted to the ground, blocking her path. His skin was slicked with sweat and his breath reeked of whiskey. "Then, you're not reading me right, lady," he rasped. "Don't think you're going to crucify me and get off scot-free. You're talking to a desperate man...."

"Then, make it easier on yourself by walking away," Jewel retorted with vigor, though warm dread was spreading through her body. It might help if she screamed. People were so busy with their own affairs, they weren't really looking in this direction. It didn't help that Everett's bulk was hiding her, either.

GEORGE EVERETT SPAT the word "bitch!" over and over. Something in this woman's face, her contempt for him, her inherent spirit, was tipping him over the edge. For most of his life he'd intimidated others. Women were a pushover; Sheila was the proof. Now here was this one, this blonde, the way she held her shoulders, the way she held her head, figuring she was a man's match. He'd show her, for shaming him. He wasn't just anyone. He'd led a comfortable life since marrying Sheila, the life of the local squire. Now this girl had ruined everything.

Everett recoiled, pulling back his powerful arm....

ABOUT THE SAME TIME Jewel arrived at the airport, Keefe Connellan was seeing off a small party of Japanese clients en route to Hayman Island, one of the great island luxury resorts of the world. Connellan had flown them up on the company Learjet, all talking business until the last moment, but now it was time for a little R&R. Afterward, when the Japanese businessmen had boarded the Sikorsky helicopter that would ferry

them to the Great Barrier Reef island, he walked back
into the terminal to find his pilot, Dan Halliwell. Dan
had gone in search of a coffee, so Connellan moved in
that direction, thinking he'd have one himself.

He was walking through the terminal, oblivious to all
the attention directed his way—a kind of celebrity he
had long since put into perspective—when he was
stunned to see the young woman who had so cleverly
insinuated herself into Davina's life. Eugenie Bishop.
The young woman he himself was so dangerously
drawn to, even as he realized she could plunge them all
into turmoil.

In any company she would stand out, he thought. Her
spun-gold hair seemed to draw all the light, although
she'd pulled the full sweep of it back off her face and
arranged it in a coil on her nape. She wore a casual
white outfit with the easy glamour that seemed to be a
part of her, as it was very much a part of Davina—a
sleeveless tunic top over a side-split straight skirt that
showed a tantalizing glimpse of one long golden-brown
leg, strappy sandals on her narrow feet. In the tropical
heat she put him in mind of a lily. Cool and immaculate.
Her companion was a tall, broad-shouldered, heavyset
man who was standing, in Connellan's opinion, far too
close. Crowding her. The man had his back turned but
he was obviously staring down into her beautiful face.
Why not? Most men wouldn't be able to take their eyes
off her. Whatever they were talking about, it wasn't
relaxed or friendly. As he watched, the discussion grew
more intense. She was already effectively hemmed in
by the man's bulk, although she appeared to be trying
to leave. Connellan immediately increased his stride in
response to a gut feeling that she could be in danger.
Intimidation of women was deplorable at any time; in

this instance, he was ready to take physical action if he discovered that Eugenie Bishop was being threatened.

She was staring up at the man, her face smooth and composed. It was her "legal" face, but he was still set on finding out what was going on. She might look in control—he'd already found she had an authority of her own—but he had concerns about the big man's body language. It spelled anger and aggression. Emotions he was all too familiar with in the cutthroat world of big business. Yet he sensed *this* confrontation was personal.

He had almost reached them, fully intending to break in on the conversation whether she welcomed it or not, when the man's face was fully exposed to him. Anger bordering on the psychotic was imprinted there, an expression that propelled him into a dazzling burst of action.

At a run he roared, "That's enough!" Instantly all the noise and chatter stopped and everybody turned to gape at him. One woman screamed.

He saw the heavyset man fling a glance over his shoulder. Then, too far gone to stop, the man swung at Jewel. Mercifully she ducked reflexively, so the blow missed her face and landed on her shoulder. Keefe reached Everett, spun him around, pinning one arm to his side and wrenching the other up between his shoulder blades.

"What the hell is going on here?" he demanded. He was fully prepared to deliver a disabling blow to this howling bully, who was blubbering incoherently that he was being hurt.

Jewel realized she was shaking badly. "I'll tell you when I've regained my balance." All around her was relief, excitement, incredulity. What was Keefe Connellan, of all people, doing here, bringing the weight of his physical strength and impressive presence to bear? She had difficulty taking it all in.

"You bitch!" Everett's face was scarlet with impotent rage, his big body writhing.

"Be quiet," Connellan warned him, his voice revealing disgust and revulsion. "Or I might just knock your head off."

"No, please, no." Jewel placed a staying hand on Keefe Connellan's arm. "He's not worth it. Security is on the way." She turned her head to see two uniformed men come running, alerted by the commotion.

"Let me go. You're breaking my arm," George Everett, the wife beater, was yelling.

Connellan clamped his arm tighter. The first security man reached them, producing a pair of handcuffs that he swiftly clamped around Everett's wrists.

"What's happening here, Mr. Connellan?" The security man, who knew Keefe Connellan by sight, now asked, trying to absorb the situation.

Connellan nodded toward Jewel, who'd pulled herself together sufficiently to explain. "I'm a lawyer. My name is Jewel Bishop. This man here is George Everett, the husband of a client, Mrs. Sheila Hungerford Everett."

"Of course, Mrs. Hungerford...Everett!" The security man corrected himself. "A well-respected lady."

Jewel continued her explanation. "Mrs. Everett has taken out a restraining order against her husband. Divorce proceedings instigated by my client will follow. Mr. Everett, appears to blame me for his current situation."

"It appears you'll need a restraining order, too," Keefe Connellan advised sharply. "I remember you now, Everett, from talk around the district. How many times have you done this, throwing punches at women?''

George Everett groaned and shuddered, apparently without the strength to fire up again. ''She drove me to it. I only did what any other man would do.''

''You're a bully with a twisted mind.'' Connellan returned his gaze to the security men. ''The police will have to deal with this. We'll have to make formal statements.''

''I've already given them a call,'' the older guard told him. ''They should arrive in a few minutes.''

Connellan looked across at Jewel, filled with a huge rage at what had been done to her. ''Are you all right?''

''I'm okay,'' she said, nodding. ''I don't know if I could've gone another round if you hadn't shown up. Thanks… I'm supposed to be on the next flight to Brisbane. It'll be boarding shortly.''

He shook his head. ''I think you'd be much more comfortable if you flew back with me.'' Connellan turned to acknowledge his pilot, who, on hearing of the ruckus, had come running. ''The company jet is out on the tarmac. We've just dropped off a party of Japanese clients en route to Hayman.''

''I don't think…'' Shaken by the incident, Jewel found herself weakening.

''Make it easy on yourself,'' he suggested, overcoming all her resistance. ''First, though, I want to see this guy Everett led away.'' He reached out and took her arm with such gentleness, it made her rethink her initial hostility. ''Why don't we go and sit down while we're waiting for the police? You've had a shock.''

''Much better than a broken nose,'' she said in a wry voice, wincing as she moved her shoulder. There would be a bruise where Everett had struck her.

IT WAS MORE THAN AN HOUR LATER that the Copeland Connellan Learjet was given clearance to take off. Once airborne, Jewel unsnapped her seat belt, embossed with the company logo in red, blue and silver, the same logo that was imprinted on the jet's tail. It was hard for her to believe she was traveling with a man who—only ten days before—had questioned her integrity, her motivations, her very identity. Now he'd established himself as her rescuer. A sobering thought. She wondered if she'd be tough enough to deal with him. He was seated in an armchair just across from her, dark head lowered as he read what looked like a balance sheet—familiar territory for Jewel. His name and position had made things easy for her with the police. He'd outlined what had happened, allowing her a necessary calming period before she had to relate her part of the story. George Everett had been led away, protesting he'd merely been having a conversation. He was to be held in the police detention center until he'd sobered up. Jewel readily informed him that she would be bringing an assault charge, which she hoped might stop him from bothering her again. But for now, she had to put the incident, upsetting as it was, behind her. It was far from the only upset of her professional life.

Jewel shifted her gaze from Keefe Connellan's glossy black head to look around the jet's interior. It was carpeted and furnished like a study, with plush armchairs in a deep champagne color and fixed timber tables polished to a mirror finish. Very attractive. This man had been born to privilege, while her life, until recent times, had been a struggle.

Jewel turned to look out the porthole, watching the shimmering sunlight glance off the silver wing. Having a company jet was certainly the way to travel.

"Feeling better?" Keefe Connellan asked with concern, shutting a file and putting it aside.

She turned her head, not forgetting to smile. "I don't need any medical treatment, but I was still thinking about George. Lucky you were there. It seems quite incredible."

"How the hand of fate guides us," he replied in a gently sardonic voice.

"Yes, indeed. I've been traveling back and forth for years now and I've never seen you at the airport."

"Not surprising," he said. "I don't usually check in our overseas clients. Travis likes to do that."

"Ah, Travis," she said. "How strange you should even bring him up."

His faint smile acknowledged the mockery. "You've had a shock. I was making small talk—giving you time to recover. Speaking of less confrontational things, I recall meeting Sheila Hungerford, as she was then, years ago when both her husband and her father were still alive. It was at an amateur race meeting she'd organized. Quite a lot of fun. I wasn't long out of university, although it wasn't my first visit to Esmeralda. Her father, Frank Fletcher, was our senior mining engineer there for many years. She was a very happy woman then. Very pretty, too."

Jewel sighed deeply. "She made a bad mistake when she married George."

"So it seems." He held her eyes. "A little patience and she might have met someone far better. I can't imagine how a woman like that, who seemed to tolerate no nonsense from anybody, could tolerate physical abuse. She had a whole town to turn to."

Jewel shrugged—a little movement that reminded her

of her sore shoulder. "In the beginning she chose George. She thought she wanted him. Pure and simple."

"And you're going to handle the litigation?" he asked.

"Yes. I'm not finished with George Everett yet."

"Then, I'm sure it will all work out. Tell me, how did the trip go with your family?"

She looked at him and saw that he was dangerous to her. In so many ways. "Plenty of talk. Plenty of food. What with Sheila—she stayed with us that first night—plenty of action. How's that for an answer?"

"Sort of evasive. I'd say it would help a lot if you could lay your cards on the table."

"If I had cards. Is it blackmail you're implying?"

"Routine question. I'm acting for Lady Copeland. You're acting for yourself. Surely we can get together on this. If you are who I think you are."

"And who am I supposed to be?"

"I thought we'd established that." He met her eyes. "Travis Copeland's daughter. It would put you in a very strong bargaining position. You're a lawyer. I have a law degree. We both know how to work the system."

"Well, I'll certainly try," she said with mock bravado. "If I am Travis Copeland's daughter, don't you think he should pay?"

His gaze didn't shift. "He could certainly afford to. Is that it—revenge?"

She shook her head. "Revenge I can do without. Besides, do I look like a vengeful person?"

His smile wasn't without humor. "If you are, I can't see it. You look like a very sexy angel, if there's such a thing. But you don't know Travis Copeland. I'm not trying to upset your little applecart when I say he won't want anything to do with you. He'll refuse to recognize you even if your identity's staring him in the face.''

''Really?'' Jewel began tapping the side of the armchair. ''There's such a thing as DNA.''

''You surely don't think you'd get him to take a test?'' He looked at her with acute skepticism.

''He could be *made* to,'' Jewel said. ''If I put myself in the position of one of my own clients, I'd feel very confident.''

He shook his head. His own voice hardened. ''A man like that wouldn't stand for public humiliation.''

''What do *you* stand for?'' Jewel challenged him outright.

''The truth, Ms. Bishop. And you're not telling it.'' She let a few seconds pass. ''Before I met you, I never had a problem with people believing me.''

He leaned forward in his chair, his shoulders hunched. ''How do you know I don't yearn to believe you? But we're dealing with very serious matters here. Matters that might be beyond you. When did you first hear the whole story?''

She fixed him with her gaze. ''What whole story do you mean, Mr. Connellan? That I'm Travis Copeland's love child?''

He gave a slight yet daunting smile. ''Look, I don't blame you if you're profoundly angry. I just don't want this to become a nightmare. I'm very fond of Lady Copeland. She's getting on in years and her health isn't as robust as it used to be. A tremendous amount of pressure was put on her as chairman of the Copeland Connellan board.''

''She must be a very clever woman.''

''Indeed she is. One of the reasons I admire and respect her so much.''

"But you have a problem with Travis?"

"Nothing like the problems you might cause for yourself. Travis's brutality in emotional matters is legendary."

"You don't trust me."

"Were you expecting me to?"

Jewel looked down at her linked hands. "I was expecting absolutely nothing."

He made a small disbelieving sound. "How many millions do you think the Copelands are worth?

"Oh, brilliant!" she scoffed. "I read *Business Review*. 'The Rich 200 List.' I know how much they're worth. I know how much the Connellan family is worth."

"Expecting too much might be your downfall," he warned.

Jewel glanced out the porthole, her tone deliberately flippant. "What's money?"

"Quite a lot when you haven't got it," he retorted.

"Well, *you've* got it and you seem to want more. And power, as well?"

"Why not?" he said, clearly not uncomfortable with the charge. "I won't stop until I'm the chair. In the meantime, I'd settle for CEO."

"Over Travis Copeland?" She uttered a mock gasp.

"We're both in the running. I believe I'll succeed."

"So you have considerable ambitions of your own." It was said with more than a flash of sarcasm, which he acknowledged with a brief nod.

"The press never fails to point that out. I'm also obsessed by the thought that Julius Copeland did some terrible things to my grandfather in business. Julius Copeland could be very cruel."

"Lovely relations I've apparently got." Jewel's smile

was self-deprecating. "What I don't understand is how your knightly affection for Lady Copeland came about."

His brown muscular throat tensed. "On her husband's death, Lady Copeland quickly reversed his underhanded dealings. My family had reason to be grateful to her. My grandfather was a far cleverer man than Julius Copeland, but he was no match for him when it came to ruthlessness."

"So there it is." Jewel threw out her hands. "You and Travis are still around to fight the war. It would seem we've both suffered at Copeland's hands. For your information, though, I have no intention of claiming Travis Copeland for a daddy. I think he's a complete bastard. By the way, just to frustrate you, Mother swears I'm Steven Bishop's child."

He studied her for a moment, then drawled, "She must love games, too."

"Even when I beseeched her," Jewel continued, leaning back and putting both hands behind her head.

"Jewel, I don't believe you." His eyes moved lightly over her, yet they made her extravagantly conscious of her own body.

"Of course you don't." She slowly straightened, pulling the gold clasp from her hair. "And who said you could call me Jewel?"

"I couldn't call you anything else." He smiled. "It goes with your starry eyes. What does your aunt have to say?"

"You'd better take care," Jewel warned. "My aunt has a very hot temper. She can't stand to see me criticized in any way. She actually said she'd like to spend an hour with you."

"Maybe then we'd be able to work out the puzzle,"

he reasoned, his voice unperturbed. "Your aunt must know the story."

"What she knows is very sad." Jewel showed him her profile. "All these years later I've only just learned that Dad slammed his car into a power pole. I loved him. I still remember his love for me. If he thought I wasn't his daughter, it would have destroyed him."

Keefe Connellan looked at her with a mixture of sympathy and suspicion. "I think he knew that, don't you, Jewel?"

"Why do you say that?" Jewel was suddenly afraid.

"Oh, for God's sake!" His handsome face showed his impatience. "You must know Travis Copeland and Steve Bishop had a scuffle right outside the cathedral the day of Sir Julius's funeral. Travis was punched to the ground and suffered a broken nose. It was something I'll never forget."

Jewel felt unnerved. "You saw it?"

He gave an emphatic nod. "I attended the funeral with my parents. The incident was hushed up as much as possible, but many people witnessed it. You're asking me to believe that a clever professional woman like yourself, a lawyer, hasn't checked all this out—even if your mother frustrated your every attempt to learn the full story?"

"As I told you before, my mother suffers from depression," Jewel said. "She has a terror of being asked questions, so I no longer ask them. I've spent all my life believing Steven Bishop was my father. I understood and never questioned that he was killed in a car crash. I didn't deliberately position myself at Barton Skinner Beaumont, as you seem to think. However, like you, I'm ambitious. An old professor of mine recommended me to the firm. I'd never laid eyes on Lady

Copeland or you until that day in Skinner's office. At the time I thought Lady Copeland looked strangely familiar, but the fact that she recognized *me* took my breath away. Until that moment, I had an identity. You've successfully taken it away from me."

He stared at her, frowning, carefully weighing her words. "How could I? You couldn't possibly hope to keep the resemblance secret. Davina has had her portrait painted three times. All of them hang at the house. You could have posed for the one in the early days of her marriage." He paused. "Once you took a step into Davina's world, everyone would find out—and the flurry of rumors would begin."

"Yet she wants to see me." Jewel raised her eyebrows.

"Of course she wants to see you. She's had precious little love in her life. You touched her heart."

"Quite a feat for a gold digger," she taunted. "Lady Copeland has a son, a granddaughter. Surely she receives love from them."

"My view of Travis is that he has no true feelings," he said, his tone more dismayed than judgmental. "Amelia is very…well…self-absorbed. She's her father's heiress. The daughter he wants. She's good-looking. Excellent at playing hostess. She has no job, no profession, but she excels at sports. She plays golf with her father and friends. Tennis, squash. She goes out on the boat with him. She does everything he requires and wants of a daughter."

"I hope that's what *she* wants, too?"

"It's all about money, Jewel. Lots of it. Amelia has lived like a princess. She's not about to give that up."

She stared at him, trying to suppress a very strong,

if edgy, sexual attraction. "Then, I'll make sure I keep my distance from her."

"Too late to go back, Jewel," he said quietly. "Things were set in motion as soon as you came in contact with Davina. What's going to be the outcome? That's the question."

CHAPTER SIX

A FEW DAYS AFTER she returned to work, Jewel received an invitation from Lady Copeland asking her to lunch at the Copeland riverside mansion on Friday at noon—an honor Blair Skinner received with delight.

"Doesn't that prove something, Eugenie?" He looked up from his jotting to chortle. "When I hired you I just knew you'd turn out to be Somebody." He smacked his lips over the "Somebody."

She held up a cautioning palm. "Don't tell Keefe Connellan that. I'm Jewel Bishop at the moment. Don't let either of us forget it."

"Not me, my dear." Skinner shuddered and slightly loosened his silk tie. "The last thing I'm about to do is fall out with such powerful people. Take as much time as you want. You're a worker, I'll say that for you. You'll catch up. Please give Lady Copeland my warmest regards. You're going to love the house. It's just splendid."

"When were you last there?" Jewel asked, raising her eyes to his smooth, polished face.

"Not for a few years now," he admitted freely. "Not since Travis and his darling daughter took over the reins. Honestly, I've never met two people so completely vain."

That amused her, coming from Blair. "Why didn't you ever see Lady Copeland's portraits?" Jewel asked, with a worried frown. "I understand they're all over the house."

Skinner looked surprised. "My dear girl, I assure you I've never seen a one. They must've moved them. Who told you this, anyway?"

"Keefe Connellan."

Skinner swallowed visibly. "He can't possibly still suspect me of anything, can he?" he asked, seeming startled.

"What if *I* decide to suspect you?" Jewel waited a few seconds, then leaned forward in her chair to whisper, "Only fooling. I would've thought they'd hang at least one in the living room."

He shook his head, at the same time tossing down his expensive Mont Blanc pen. "Maybe they're upstairs. I never did get upstairs."

"Not a peek into the bedroom?"

"I never got into the library, either."

"See what you've missed?" Jewel rose from her chair. "If I get the chance, I'll ask to see the portraits."

"Will you? I'd love to know what they're like." Skinner kissed his fingertips. "*Bellissima,* I'll bet. Such a beautiful woman. And she'll love you. It's all plain sailing there. I don't know if I can say anything so positive about Travis. Or Amelia, for that matter. That's a very pampered girl. And she's been named as heiress."

"So she's a big step ahead of me," Jewel said with dark humor. "Anyway, let's take this one thing at a time. I'm simply having lunch."

"You go out and have a wonderful day," Skinner urged. "It's not everyone who gets invited to lunch with Lady Copeland. I, for instance, have never received a call. You're honored, my dear."

"I don't feel honored, Blair," Jewel paused, speaking seriously. "I feel under a lot of pressure. It could degenerate into a big storm. Suddenly I've found I want to be sure of who I am—the way I was just a few weeks ago."

"That's easy," he said, eyes shrewd. "You're Lady Copeland's granddaughter. Travis Copeland's daughter. The most we can say for Travis is maybe he was lonely. In need of comfort. I knew his wife—thin, thin, thin, with a blade of a tongue. I think the old man, Sir Julius, pushed Travis into marrying her. She was a Watson Smythe."

"Really? I'm not familiar with the name."

He looked at her in astonishment. "My dear, they're the landed gentry. You really will have to bone up. Especially now you're moving into the big time."

"Bye, Blair," Jewel said.

"All the best," he called, laughing lightly. "Never forget I gave you your big chance."

As THE TIME FOR HER MEETING with Lady Copeland approached, Jewel tried hard to get a grip on herself and the major issue that now confronted her—the business of her real identity. It wasn't easy contending with such a bombardment of mixed emotions, an overload that seemed too chaotic for her mind to contain. On the one hand, she felt a sense of excitement, as though she was being handed some wonderful present, swiftly followed by moments of extreme inner turmoil, a sense of rootlessness, as though she'd suddenly become a foreigner in her own country. Was she really who they all thought her to be, or was it some incredible coincidence, after all? The fact that Steven Bishop, an enduring memory in her life, wasn't her father at all seemed the saddest thing, so much so that she couldn't let it register yet. She needed time to absorb the shock and pain, the question mark over his sudden, violent end.

She thought she would never adapt to thinking of Travis Copeland as her father. She felt absolutely no sense of relatedness to him, although she'd experienced an immediate rapport with Lady Copeland. And if all that wasn't enough to confound her, there were her encounters with Keefe Connellan, who seemed to be playing a pivotal role in this whole tremendously unsettling business. The hours she'd spent with him remained shockingly vivid in her mind. She put it down to the swiftness of their involvement—that and his extraordinary aura. It distinguished him from any other man she had ever known. She'd even discovered, with some trepidation, a powerful sexual attraction to him. At twenty-six she'd come to take it for granted that she was the ''controlling'' one in her relationships with men. All her boyfriends had claimed she could wrap them around her little finger, and it had seemed, even to her, to be the truth. She knew that would never be the case with Keefe Connellan. This was a man who threw out challenges, and so far she was the one very much on the defensive.

She found herself puzzling long and hard over his relationship with Amelia. Both families appeared to have had expectations of a match. Amelia had lived a life of privilege, which probably meant she was used to getting everything she wanted. So where had the courtship gone wrong? Actually, if she was being honest, Jewel had to admit that the idea of a serious relationship between Keefe Connellan and Amelia dismayed her. And how would Amelia react to the sudden discovery of a half sister? The result, moreover, of an illicit relationship in her father's past. Being the Copeland heiress no doubt gave great meaning to Amelia's life. Now for something like this to surface! A scandal. Let alone Amelia's grandmother inviting a total stranger to their home, even if only to delve into the stranger's past. Travis Copeland could be counted on to continue disowning her.

Small wonder Jewel felt both excitement and fear. What happened next ultimately depended on how well she and Lady Copeland related to each other. If Davina Copeland believed she was her granddaughter, surely it had to be so. Then, Travis Copeland was the one who had abandoned her and her mother. A terrible and cowardly thing to do.

After Keefe Connellan's revelations, she'd read everything she could find on Sir Julius Copeland, going way back to the early days when he and Stafford Connellan had started out on their mineral exploration, a scant year after they'd both graduated from university. She read about the Copeland pastoral interests, which were huge. She read about Travis Copeland's wedding to Sonia Watson Smythe. The wedding of the year! The old newspapers showed a handsome, smiling young man with a surprisingly prune-faced bride on his arm. Jewel saw the birth notice of their first and only child, Amelia, and the many society page articles once Amelia was launched on the social scene. Countless photographs had been taken of her with a certain drop-dead gorgeous man.

Keefe Connellan.

Jewel studied the photographs with a curious lurch of the heart. Who had dropped whom? Or had their romance degenerated into a love-hate? She read every line of reportage on Sir Julius's funeral. She read how Travis

Copeland had been accosted outside the cathedral by a young man believed to be a disgruntled employee. An employee so unimportant they hadn't even printed his name.

She knew that name. Steven Bishop. Not her birth dad, it now seemed, but the best dad in the world. She couldn't bear to think his accident might not have been an accident at all. What had been in his mind when he slammed that car into a tree? His young wife's infidelity? Travis Copeland's adultery with a young woman he would never have given the time of day, on his home ground? She'd found the tiny article reporting his death tucked away along the side of page four. It was written up like another fatal case of drunk driving. She couldn't find any reported link between Travis Copeland's assailant at the funeral and the young man whose life had ended hours later.

How the rich and powerful could arrange their cover-ups!

She and her mother had never seen Steven Bishop again. They hadn't even brought his body back. Aunt Judith alone had flown to Brisbane for the cremation that followed. Her mother had been engulfed by what she and Aunt Judith believed to be a wife's inconsolable grief at the loss of her mate, her spouse.

But Jewel had come to realize that other unresolved feelings had presided there. Guilt too acute to be grappled with. Quite simply, guilt had rendered her mother powerless. On one occasion she had become depressed enough to want to die, but the overdose of pills she had taken only made her violently ill.

In a sense she'd been orphaned at six, Jewel thought. Emotionally orphaned, anyway. Her mother was there physically but rarely in spirit. God knows what would have happened to her without Aunt Judith. Judith had kept her sufficiently on track, encouraging her "cleverness," telling her if she worked she could break out of the "terrible rut" that had claimed the sisters' lives.

And how she'd worked—with great energy and spirit, a compulsive student throughout her academic life. She knew she wanted a future, a life in complete contrast to the depressed and negative one of her mother. Maybe her fighting spirit, her commitment, her daring was inherited from her grandmother, Davina Copeland.

Her stomach tight with nerves, Jewel turned into the broad leafy avenue—the Millionaire Row—lined with the imposing mansions of the rich. A mixed bag of architectural styles, she thought. There were the carefully preserved or meticulously restored grand colonials, large and elegant with enveloping lacework balustrades and valances on the wide verandas so suited to the city's subtropical climate. There were Gothic-style "lodges," built of stone, more suited as English country residences. The fairly recent Italianate villas were all set in large beautiful tropical gardens with fountains playing in the heat. Long wrought-iron fences with massive wrought-iron gates kept out the world; the gates hung on huge pillars, while the fences were adorned with flowering bougainvilleas color-matched to the houses.

The Copeland mansion was as big as a village. Lined on either side by jacarandas, it presented itself to the street as one of those palatial villas the senators of ancient Rome used to retire to when things got hot either politically or on nature's front. This was the only residence that saw the need for solid walls. To keep the family in or keep the neighbors out? To add to the cloistered look, few windows punctuated the bold facade, at least on the first floor, yet in the third-floor tower, she saw three. Obviously no one was about to creep up on them. The tower might even be manned by security guards.

Jewel pulled into the flagstone driveway, lowering her window so she could press the button on a brass box mounted on a pedestal. There was a glass-covered hole she took to be the seeing "eye."

Hello, there!

It was all a far cry from the sprawling Queenslander she'd grown up in, with its wild but incredibly pictur-esque acres. This might have been a six-star hotel de-signed by the late Versace.

A disembodied voice said, "Yes?"

"Jewel Bishop for Lady Copeland."

The massive gates immediately opened, allowing Jewel to cruise up the drive. Moments later she was standing in front of the huge classical facade. With the river to the back, she presumed the mansion would open up along the rear, perhaps with lots of large windows to take advantage of the beautiful view of the wide, deep river. A breeze that usually came in from the bay about noon was already springing up, fanning the sun-ray pleats of her delicate silk shirtdress. It was a shim-mering shade of beige that suited her coloring. Expensive it might have been, but she loved the beauty of movement of the skirt. She'd slung a wide leather belt around her hips; it matched her handbag and her tan sandals. Looking good gave her some of the confi-dence she needed.

Bracing herself, Jewel walked up the short flight of steps, too nervous to smile. A pleasant-faced, middle-aged woman, breathing a little heavily, dressed in what appeared to be modern-day livery, met her at the door, telling her Lady Copeland was looking forward to seeing her. The woman was trying unsuccessfully not to stare—not that Jewel blamed her. She showed Jewel through a vaulted entrance hall exhibiting busts of hawk-nosed Roman emperors, its austere effect softened by two massive bronze planters filled with white orchids. Then they moved on to an enormous living room, with another barrel-vaulted ceiling, painted this time by someone with pretensions to the Da Vinci style. Loads of antiques and paintings, very unusual glass chandeliers and baroque mirrors, a marble fireplace. Dazzled in spite of herself, Jewel followed the woman into another large room at the rear of the house with French doors leading onto a flower-filled terrace. Beyond that was a great sweep of emerald lawn set with towering palms, running down to the sun-splashed sequined river.

Lady Copeland was seated within hailing distance in a large-scale armchair that all but swallowed her. As soon as Jewel entered the room, the woman rose, a lovely smile of welcome on her face, right hand extended.

"Eugenie, I'm so glad you could come."

Jewel didn't know whether to laugh or break out in sobs. Instead, she moved forward gracefully to clasp the delicate hand, her own smile in place. "I really appreciate your asking me, Lady Copeland." *Grandma?* God, this was overwhelming.

"Well...well...." Lady Copeland continued to hold her hand, turning her head slightly to speak to the woman who'd brought Jewel through. "Thank you, Holly. We'll talk for a little while, then you can serve lunch. Say in half an hour."

"Very well, Lady Copeland." Holly, who'd been staring at Jewel in apparent fascination, dismissed herself slowly, as though backing away from a sovereign.

Her expression was three parts respectful to one part avid speculation.

Lady Copeland ignored her. "Please, Eugenie, sit down." She indicated one of the oversize armchairs that could easily have served as a bed.

"Thank you." Jewel wondered for a frivolous moment if Lady Copeland was about to tell her of some complex genealogy, according to which the two of them were descended from the royal House of Savoy. What else could account for this sumptuous fortress furnished in such princely fashion?

As if she could read Jewel's mind, Lady Copeland threw her hands in the air. "To understand all of this, my dear, you'd have had to know my late husband, Sir Julius. Stafford Connellan built a very beautiful house—you may know it. Stafford and Margaret had exquisite taste and Julius thought he had to go one better. The result was this. A house fit for Julius Caesar. Sometimes I think my late husband convinced himself he might've been descended from that line."

Jewel smiled at the little irony. "It's very impressive, Lady Copeland. So...you don't see yourself as the woman who married Julius Caesar?"

Davina burst out laughing. "I've made a few attempts to tone it down, but the house will pass to Travis when I'm gone. He loves it. He never got on with his father but he's passionately loyal to his memory. Astonishing, really. Later I'll show you some of the antiques Julius acquired. If you put them end to end they'd probably stretch around Australia. There's even a Renaissance portrait of a Venetian noble, fine haughty face framed by a ruff. Julius bought it because the dealer said it looked like him."

"And does it?" Jewel asked.

"Extraordinarily enough, it does. Julius could look very distinguished when he had to. All those years in public life. You know the saying, street angel, home devil—he was a bit of a home devil, I'm afraid."

"But you loved him?"

Davina Copeland's still-vivid blue eyes gazed off into the past. "He was a man of great energy, marvelously handsome. A true buccaneer. How I actually came to marry him remains a mystery to this day. I don't ever recall saying *yes*. He must have swept me off my feet."

"It happens," Jewel said wryly, recalling for a moment Keefe Connellan's impact on her. Too full of nervous tension to ease into the reason for this visit, she said rather emotionally, "I believe my own father, the man I *called* my father, was there on the day of Sir Julius's funeral? Steven Bishop."

"He was, Eugenie." Davina Copeland's voice held a world of regrets.

"I treasure his memory," Jewel murmured. "I remember the love he had for me and for my mother."

"How is your mother?" Davina asked. "Have you spoken to her?"

Jewel inclined her head. "This...situation has transformed my life," she answered evasively.

"Of course it has. What do you think our meeting has done to me? I've lived all these years believing I had only one grandchild."

"Are you really *that* sure?"

"Come with me." Davina Copeland stood up purposefully, leading the way through more grand spaces to a small feminine study that offered sanctuary from the rest of the house. No splendid embellishments here. Restraint, refinement and, above an English gilt side table adorned with pink roses, a wonderful portrait of a beautiful young woman in evening dress. "Proof?" Lady Copeland asked, her eyes on Jewel as she stared up at it.

"It's an incredible likeness," Jewel said, her throat tight.

"Julius loved this one." Davina touched her abundant upswept hair. "It used to hang in our bedroom but I had it moved here. Too many reminders of growing old. It's not easy resembling oneself less and less." She laughed. "There are other portraits. Julius reveled in commissioning them, supposedly as a record of his love. This is the one I really wanted you to see."

"You've taken a huge step inviting me here." Jewel turned to face this elderly woman who was looking at her with such—God, was it love? If it was, Jewel wanted to capture it, hold on to it. "Do you *really* mean to acknowledge me?"

"Of course I do," Davina maintained, her tone firm. "You're my own flesh and blood. Surely you didn't expect me to turn my back on you?"

"A great many would. I couldn't blame you if you did. We could still see each other without any formal acknowledgment." Jewel wanted to make perfectly clear that she was after nothing.

"I think you *would* blame me, Eugenie," Davina said quietly. "It wouldn't work, in any case. You saw Holly's face. Why have people gossiping behind our backs? It doesn't suit me at all."

"Even if it creates a scandal?"

"At my age I'd jump at a scandal."

"You sound a bit like me." Jewel smiled. "Your sense of humor. But other members of the family mightn't be so welcoming."

Davina exhaled, sank onto a nearby sofa and gestured

for Jewel to join her. "That's their problem. I would, of course, speak to them. I wanted us to talk first."

Jewel could actually hear the loud pulse of her heart. "I have to tell you, my mother denies any relationship with...your son," she said hesitantly. "In fact, she became hysterical at the very mention."

Davina nodded. "One can understand the path your mother took. Her terrible sense of grief and guilt when life caught up with her. She's lived all these years under a great burden. I'm hoping if we can straighten things out, the burden will be lifted. A simple test would prove Travis's paternity—as if we need proof. It all adds up. The protagonists were in place. Your mother was young, vulnerable, no doubt lonely with her husband away. Travis can be very charming and persuasive when it suits him. At any rate, he's had a great deal of success with women. Your mother could have been in awe of his position, too. These things happen in life. We can all make bad choices." She paused for a moment. "I have no wish to upset your mother. On the other hand, I'm not going to be denied my granddaughter. I could have loved you, helped you all these years. Both of you. You can't know what this means to me." Her lovely mellow voice was trembling with emotion.

Jewel leaned closer. "I could understand better if I knew what's missing from your life. You have your son. Your granddaughter, Amelia. Most people would see that as a blessing."

Davina lifted a slow hand. "My dear, I'm moving through a period of my life in which I feel very much alone. I know people think I've always had everything, but I haven't and I don't. My health isn't as good as it was. I've had to curtail most of my activities. I used to keep very busy with my charity work and support groups. I've given up hope of reaching my son. Strange thing to say, but it's true. His father was always much more important to him than I was. Travis sees himself as the head of the family, and the fact that his father left the reins to me has only alienated us further. I'm sorry," she said with a shrug, "but that's the way it is. As for Amelia? Her father's attention is what she's always craved. I love her and I know she loves me in a charming childlike fashion. But her father is the dominant force in her life—as Julius was in Travis's."

"And Keefe Connellan?" Jewel found herself needing to know. "I can't see him as a substitute son."

"Good Lord, no. All that vigor and masculine intensity. Travis has high hopes for a match with Amelia, although their romance appears to have gone off the boil. Keefe is very high achiever. I know he'd be looking for a woman who could expand his horizons—intellectually, emotionally, in every other way. An equal. Amelia has allowed her father to clip her wings, to diminish her. It saddens me. Women are only ornaments to Travis. Their job is to keep *him* happy. That even applies to his own daughter. I've tried to interest Amelia in other things beyond pleasurable pursuits, but her father runs her life."

"What about her mother?" Sonia Watson Smythe Copeland, member of the ruling elite.

"Her mother had the same experience with her as I have," Davina said. "Amelia idolizes her father. She's spent her life striving for his approval. Both of them maneuvered Sonia out." There followed a long, rather difficult silence. "Sonia isn't an easy person," Davina continued. "A certain…stuffiness, but I've always had a lot of sympathy for her. Ultimately Travis broke her heart."

"How awful. You're being very frank with me, Lady Copeland."

"Just so," Davina smiled. "I'm not normally. But I feel very different with you, Eugenie. I feel I already know you. It's wonderful, wonderful…."

Lady Copeland sounded so poignant Jewel thought she would suddenly find herself in tears. Instead she took the woman's frail hand. "Isn't that what love's all about? You know, my dad always called me Jewel— because of my blue eyes. *Our* blue eyes. It ceased to be a nickname and became my given name. I've been Jewel all my life. I'd like you to call me that."

"I would be honored to do so," Davina said, tightening her hand.

Davina had her back to the door, so it was Jewel who saw Amelia first. Saw the horror in her dark almond eyes.

Davina caught Jewel's dismayed expression, turning her head in response. "Amelia! What are you doing at home, my dear?" she asked in some bewilderment. "I thought you were going waterskiing with your friends?"

Amelia Copeland remained frozen, her face, more handsome than beautiful, distorted by a mixture of emotions. None of them pleasant.

"I was *warned*, Davina," she said, her white teeth tightly clenched.

"Warned?" Davina Copeland stood up, all of a sudden the very figure of authority. "What on earth do you mean?"

"About this girl here." Amelia took several steps toward Jewel. "Who *are* you?"

"She's my guest." Davina Copeland stood between

them, anger spilling out of her eyes. "How dare you, Amelia."

But Amelia's emotions had erupted out of control. "What's she *doing* here? Who is she? Why does she look like you?"

Davina moved toward her granddaughter, but Amelia shrank back. "I'm afraid there's no other way to say it, Amelia dear. I believe this young woman—her name is Jewel Bishop—is my granddaughter, just as you are."

Amelia's cry was almost a howl of rage. "She can't be! Where did she come from? I've never seen her before in life. Why can't she speak for herself?"

Jewel stood up resolutely, although her stomach had somersaulted twice. "I know this must be a terrible shock to you, Ms. Copeland, but the shock was no less for me. I've only very recently come into your grandmother's life."

"And what are you after?" Amelia reached out to grasp a small porcelain statue as though she was about to hurl it. "It has to be *money!*"

What had she expected from her new life but horror and suspicion? "I'd prefer to know who supposedly warned you," Jewel said, keeping her voice even. "Could it have been Keefe Connellan?"

For an instant Amelia's fine features were wiped clean. "Keefe?" she asked, almost blankly.

"He knew I was coming here. If he didn't know the exact date, he would've had a fair idea."

Amelia tossed her dark hair over a golden-brown shoulder. "Who else would it be? Keefe will do anything to protect me."

"From what?" Davina asked crisply. "Keefe didn't tell you at all. Did he? Please don't lie to me, dear."

"He did." Amelia didn't waver. "Why would he

trust someone like *that?*'' She threw an accusing hand in Jewel's direction. ''Someone plucked out of nowhere to betray me. Someone who could've had cosmetic surgery, dyed her hair. You can't really know a thing about her except that she *claims* to be your granddaughter.''

''Please sit down, Amelia,'' Davina begged. ''I realize this is a big shock to you, but I'm confident you'll come around to seeing things my way. Jewel has never made any claims.''

''I don't believe that,'' Amelia shot back with undisguised bitterness.

''Nevertheless, it's true. I had every intention of speaking to you and your father, but your unexpected return has changed all that. I'd like you to sit down and listen to what I have to say.''

Amelia, tall and whipcord slim, remained standing. ''I've never, *ever* thought you were a fool, Gran.''

''Indeed, I'm very happy to hear that,'' Davina said, studying her granddaughter. ''I would remind you that this is my home. You live here because of my love for you—and my generosity.''

A high flush of pink appeared on Amelia's cheeks. ''I'm sorry. I apologize.''

''And I accept your apology, Amelia. It's not often you forget yourself. Please, won't you sit down?''

Amelia, dressed in a bright red camisole with hip-hugging jeans and a silver-studded belt, slid into a chair like a model fresh from the catwalk. ''If I must,'' she said with no attempt at grace. She bore little resemblance to her grandmother, either in appearance or manner. Still, Jewel felt genuine sympathy for her. This was the heiress. The legitimate child. A member of one of the richest families in the country, with everything that entailed. Amelia was probably so pampered and protected, a thing like this could actually destroy her. She, Jewel, had been cast in the role of fortune hunter. Even her name marked her. Jewel! The long-lost claimant. As for Keefe Connellan, she'd handed him the information he needed when he was the last living person she should have trusted with anything—particularly considering his relationship with Amelia. Clearly he and Amelia were still close.

While both young women sat tensely, Davina Copeland outlined the sequence of events for Amelia. She spoke of the Copeland Outback station Mingaree, part of the Copeland pastoral empire to this day. She fixed people in place and time. Travis Copeland, Thea Bishop, her young husband, Steven Bishop, who had since died. She didn't mention how or when. Jewel could see that Amelia, like her, had never known.

"I just don't believe this, Davina," Amelia said, when her grandmother finished. "Why is this person here? Is that hair even natural? Why would she turn up now? God, is she some substitute for the daughter you lost? I mean, I don't feel I've ever belonged to you, really." She took a deep breath. "What do you think Father is going to say to all of this? He'll be furious."

"Life has a way of unlocking the secrets of the past," Davina said, her fragile shoulders a little hunched. "We have to handle this like a family. I believe your father may have suspected he fathered Thea Bishop's child, Amelia. I recall now that he was very keen on taking over the job of overseeing the station. Then it abruptly stopped. He didn't want to go there at all."

"But that doesn't mean a thing." Amelia looked as though she was about to burst into tears. "What are you trying to do to us, Davina? We have a proud name. A position. People expect—"

"We have what started with my husband. Your grandfather," Davina cut in. "Some journalist recently dubbed him a robber baron. I believe that journalist intends to write a biography, needless to say without my help. Anyway, your grandfather certainly didn't do it all by the rules. Since he died, I've tried to change that. I've chaired Copeland Connellan and I don't believe there's anybody who'll tell you I didn't do a good job. We're rich, Amelia, but the foundation of the wealth is, in some respects, questionable. Nonetheless, you've benefited from it. You grew up wanting for nothing, with the assumption that you are the heir. Jewel didn't have it anywhere near so easy. Not that it appears to have done her much harm."

"So *what* is she?" Amelia repeated forcefully, pointing across the room. "A rocket scientist?" Despite the sarcasm, it was obvious she was reeling from shock, although the full impact probably hadn't reached her yet.

"I think I can establish my credentials," Jewel said, trying to get Amelia to look at her. "I'm a lawyer. I specialize in company law. I'm with your grandmother's firm, Barton Skinner Beaumont."

"Lawyer?" Amelia repeated the word almost stupidly, then crowed in derision. "Of course you are! I suppose it was only a matter of time before you and Gran met up. Which must've been your intention all along."

"No." Jewel shook her head. "Being with her firm had nothing to do with it. Pure coincidence. I was fortunate enough to win a University Gold Medal, which helped me along the fast track, and landed up at Barton Skinner Beaumont. As your grandmother has told you, that's where we met for the first time."

"And where's your documentation?" Amelia challenged. "I assume you have some. Birth certificate, that sort of thing."

"I was reared as Steven Bishop's child," Jewel said, distressed by Amelia's violent reaction to her but trying not to show it. What had she expected, anyway—sisterly love? "I've always believed he was my father."

"Well, he *is*. *My* father isn't." Amelia's dark eyes burned.

"You're welcome to him." Jewel stared back unflinchingly. "If he was aware of my existence, he made no attempt to see me, let alone send along a birthday card. He made no attempt to make my life or my mother's any easier. And it *was* hard. Meeting your father all those years ago had a devastating effect on my mother. She's a very vulnerable person. Easily hurt." She paused, then added coolly, "Paternity is easy to prove these days—as I'm sure you know."

Amelia got to her feet, thrusting her hands into the pockets of her jeans. "You surely don't think Father would undergo any humiliating tests for *you?*"

"I'm not asking him to." Jewel shrugged. "I'm not asking for anything, except to know who my family really is."

"And that's all you want?" Amelia flashed her a contemptuous look.

"Be quiet for a minute, Amelia," Davina intervened sharply. "I haven't the slightest doubt Jewel is my granddaughter, just as you are. I can see by your face that you're finding the resemblance between us unnerving. If you turn your head and look at that portrait of me, you can see Jewel might have posed for it. The resemblance is that close."

"It's incredible." Amelia glanced briefly at the portrait. "It's incredible, this whole business. I won't let you bring shame to this family, whoever you are." She sat down again, staring at Jewel.

"What happened in the past isn't my fault, Amelia." Jewel tried hard to relax her own tension. "I'm the innocent party here."

"By your own admission, you're a smart lawyer," Amelia retorted. Jewel sensed that she resisted believing any of this, but much as she might want to, Amelia couldn't explain away the extraordinary resemblance. "You're just playing an old woman along."

To Jewel's ears it sounded dreadful. Where was Amelia's love and respect for her grandmother now?

"Is that how you see it, Amelia?" Davina Copeland's voice was low and dangerous in that serene and beautiful room.

Amelia recovered rapidly. "S-sorry, Gran," she stammered. "I'm just describing it the way this person here is seeing it. Apart from the bizarre resemblance, there's no *real* evidence."

"There's a mountain of it, Amelia," Davina said. "You're just hiding your head in the sand. Like it or not, Jewel is a blood relative. Your half sister, in fact. It would make everything so much easier for us all if you could give her some understanding and compassion. Don't see Jewel as a usurper. She's your own flesh and blood."

Amelia banged her long legs together in sheer frustration. "How do you intend to go about telling Father? Or are you going to issue a press statement?"

"That will do, Amelia," Davina ordered quietly, although anger glittered from her violet-blue eyes. "The whole situation has to be thoroughly discussed, then we'll come to an agreement as a family. It might help you to know that I need no further proof. Jewel is my granddaughter, just as you are."

"You keep saying that! Oh my God!" The words died on Amelia's lips, then she rallied, her glossy head shooting up. "Have you really thought this over, Gran? All it's going to bring is a horrible scandal. God alone knows what Mother will make of it. She'll be nastier than ever. She hates Father as it is."

"Perhaps he's given her good reason, Amelia," Davina said stiffly. "And she doesn't hate him at all. Your father likes to put that mischief about. Your father, as we both know, has had many affairs. We've both come face to face with them."

"But he hasn't married anyone, has he?" Amelia said, almost gratefully. "He's a very handsome, powerful man. He can have his affairs if he wants. And he's not just going to pack up to suit you."

Davina clearly had had enough. "He might have to behave a little better if he thinks he's going to inherit this place!" she said tartly, her slim hands stirring in her lap. "You are your father's rightful heiress, Amelia. Please don't be frightened. You'll never be cheated of that."

"Then, find out what her price is, Gran," Amelia said. "Pay her off, if that's what it takes."

Jewel stood up, unable to listen a minute more. "I don't think you understand either of us, Ms. Copeland. I'm not interested in making any claims on your family's money."

"Put it in writing," Amelia responded, glaring up at Jewel as if she blamed her for everything. "Everyone has a price. Father's always telling me that."

"Perhaps you shouldn't be so willing to listen." Jewel snatched up her handbag. "I don't give a damn about this house, luxury yachts, luxury cars, the whole social scene. I earn a good living. I like what I do. Helping people makes me feel good. I have a nice town house. Good friends. I find, however, I do want my grandmother. Forgive me for that. I'll drop any interest to being your half sister, if you'd prefer.''

Amelia curled her lip. ''Oh, you're clever!''

''I believe I am. Moreover, I have integrity.''

''Don't go. Please don't go yet,'' Davina Copeland implored rather breathlessly, as Jewel showed her determination to leave.

''I must.'' Jewel's expression softened as she looked into Davina's eyes, glittering with unshed tears.

''And don't come back,'' Amelia cried. ''Leave now. Get the hell out of here.''

Adrenaline spurted into Jewel's veins. She didn't have to take this from anyone. She stood poised and calm. ''Please be quiet,'' she said in a voice that carried the confidence of achievement and the expectation that she would be obeyed. ''I'm here on the invitation of Lady Copeland. I'll leave when she tells me. I'm very sorry you've found all this such a shock. Nevertheless, I'm not impressed by your behavior. Where is your pity? Your sense of blood? Your reactions begin and end with yourself. I didn't start any of this, Amelia. It's just as you've been told.''

''In that case, God help us.'' Amelia buried her face in her hands.

CHAPTER SEVEN

JEWEL RETURNED to the office depressed, fighting mad, and minus her lunch.

"How did it go?" Blair Skinner stood framed in the doorway, his eyes bright with interest.

"Terrible. Absolutely terrible," Jewel said, the tips of her fingers on an aching temple.

"Tell me all about it." Skinner advanced into the small room, taking the chair opposite Jewel's desk. "Hmm," he murmured, looking around, "we'll have to get you a better office. So, what happened? I told my secretary I wouldn't be accepting any calls."

"You're becoming very nosy, Blair." Jewel stared at him for a minute or two.

"Dear girl, I've been nosy all my life," Skinner answered promptly. "It's the only way I ever get to know anything. But you surprise me. I thought the whole thing would go off extremely well."

"Except, Amelia showed up," Jewel said stonily. "She was supposed to be out on the river waterskiing and having a jolly time with her layabout gang, only someone tipped her off."

"That you were there?" Skinner's expression was incredulous.

"Exactly. She claims it was Keefe Connellan."

That clearly disturbed him. "But how could he possibly know?"

"I told him," Jewel confessed, her tone filled with self-disgust. "I even told him I was looking forward to the meeting. I didn't say exactly when it was, but he could've found out easily enough."

"Dear God!"

"Don't act so surprised, Blair. Wouldn't you expect her to be the *first* to know? Weren't they an item? Neither of them has found anyone else."

Skinner still looked doubtful. "I don't think Keefe would be in a hurry to upset Lady Copeland. It doesn't sound like him."

"He's...he's wicked," Jewel said wildly.

"So it wasn't the nice reunion Lady Copeland had in mind...."

She shook her head. "Amelia was shocked—and pretty damn rude. I don't know what I expected from her. I thought a well-brought-up young woman could have handled it better. I'm reasonably certain I would have."

"It didn't degenerate into a screaming match, did it?" Skinner asked, hunching forward.

"Not really. She just carried on like a maniac. I'd have had a hard time swallowing lunch, so I left."

Skinner stared at her. "You've had a bad day. I don't imagine Lady Copeland was pleased, either."

"She was very upset." Jewel's voice conveyed her concern. "If I'd been her, I would've thrown Amelia out. She showed no consideration whatsoever for her grandmother. It was all for herself. And, just between the two of us, for dear *Father*."

"What else is new? Did she threaten you with anything?"

"Not really. If she could've called down a thunderbolt from heaven, she would have. I think it's the money that's getting to her." Jewel pondered. "I'm sure she'd be agreeable to paying me off. I might work on it."

"You're joking!"

"Yes, I am, but I might want to leave her guessing. I can understand her feelings—I'm still in a state of shock myself—but I could never speak to anyone the way she spoke to me. I'm charged and convicted. A gold digger. Guilty as hell."

"Those Copelands trust nobody," Skinner confided. "Cross Travis, and he turns absolutely feral."

"Well," Jewel said, "I'm certain he already knows about me. Maybe Connellan keeps him posted, just like Amelia."

"Oh, no." Skinner, loyal to his favorite client, ran a finger down his chin. "I've known Keefe Connellan a lot of years. I've seen and heard nothing but integrity. A lot of people say so. Travis, now, is a vile, vile man. If I were you, I'd have nothing to do with him."

"I don't think I can cope with this," Jewel said, vigorously pulling a paper clip apart. "He's supposed to be my *father*."

"You don't have to respect him," Skinner said, concentrating on his own paper clip. "It's Lady Copeland we're interested in. She's a woman who has a lot of power but she doesn't hit you over the head with it every other minute. If Lady Copeland accepts you, my dear, you're in."

"In *where,* Blair?" Jewel threw her paper clip away.

"Into riches, my dear. Do you want me to get you the latest *Business Review Weekly?* You can catch up on 'The Rich 200 List.'"

Jewel leaned across the desk, fixing her gaze directly on his. "Blair, up until recently, I'd been enjoying every minute of my life. I never got bored and I was never confused. I knew who I was and what I was doing. I wish I hadn't even laid eyes on Lady Copeland and that backstabber Keefe Connellan.''

"Well, it's natural to feel like that right now," Skinner replied, "but what you're saying about Keefe just isn't true."

"Even if it isn't, this whole thing is shaping up to be a disaster of monumental proportions." She sighed. "You can't blame Amelia for seeing it that way. Her father will want to run me out of town."

"Or hire someone to push you under a bus," Skinner suggested with a delicate shudder.

"Thanks, Blair." Jewel gave a hollow laugh. "I'll make sure I always have plenty of people around."

Skinner laughed. "You must realize, dear girl, they need time to let the unthinkable sink in. I just knew that Amelia was a bitch. I *knew* it."

"And you still want me to become part of the bunch?" Jewel frowned at him.

"My dear, you'd be like a breath of fresh air," Skinner pronounced. "You could be the salvation of that whole family. Bring them back to reality." He lowered his voice. "Do you want me to help you?"

"How?" Jewel asked, her voice cracking confusedly.

"I'm not without influence in both quarters. Like Connellan, I come from an old Establishment family. My quiet promotion of you should mean something. Everything had gone a bit stale the past year or so, then you whooshed into my life—and now, look! I mean, it's so *rare* to come across a missing claimant to a huge fortune."

"Would you like me to offer you a finder's fee?" she asked sarcastically.

"Not at all, but I *would* like you to be grateful. Remember that when they appoint you to the board of Copeland Connellan."

"Sure. No problem." Jewel groaned. She opened a file. "I might as well get back to work. It never goes away. See you later, Blair."

Skinner went out of the room chortling. "And to think I've taught you so much!"

Twenty minutes later, Jewel picked up the phone to hear a man's voice say, "Ms. Bishop?"

Jewel scowled. The caller's identity was unmistakable. "Mr. Connellan," she snapped. "You must have the hide of a rhinoceros."

"That's right. It's been said before." He laughed, a low-pitched mocking sound. "Are you having a bad day?"

"I'm sure Amelia told you exactly what you wanted to hear. It all went very badly."

"What did?"

"Why, the meeting of course," she said brightly. "You know, the *meeting.*"

"Lunch with Davina?" he asked, sounding fully alert.

"Oh, you're so *smooth,*" she said disparagingly. "You mean to say you didn't know about it?"

"Bite my tongue if I tell a lie. I don't know any more than you told me."

"Really? I didn't realize you were such a good actor. The first thing you did was pass the information on to your girlfriend."

"All right," he said. "I give up. This is making me insane. Can you unscramble, please?"

"It goes something like this. You're a twister, a very devious person. I'm angry about that. Goodbye, Mr.

Connellan. One. Two. Three. I'm hanging up." Jewel slammed down the phone.

It rang a moment later. Jewel waited only long enough for him to say, "I hope I can get a word in edge—" before she slammed it down again.

The man was a rotter. And he could win an Oscar for his performance. She had to forget all about him. The excitement, the humiliation and the anger. A shocking assortment of emotions.

When the phone didn't ring again, she felt almost miserable and couldn't understand it. She would *love* to tell him off! "Face it," she muttered to herself, "George Everett was an angel compared to my so-called family and their best friend." She returned to her preparation of the Hungerford brief.

AROUND SIX, with the summer sun still bouncing off the pavement, she left the building, intending to do some shopping. There was a little party going on at the Heritage. One of the legal secretaries had just become engaged. Jewel thought she might pop in for a while. She felt she needed a little fun. Not to mention support and understanding.

There were lots of people about. In fact, the "River City" was crowded. She stood beneath the green heart of an umbrella tree and slipped on her sunglasses.

The Rolls materialized from nowhere, gliding up alongside her. "Where are we going, Ms. Bishop?" a dark, familiar voice called out.

Jewel considered stalking on, like women did in movies, but at the last moment veered off to the curb, showing her anger. "Haven't you got anything better to do?" she asked.

"As it happens, I want nothing more than to have a

conversation with you,'' he replied suavely. ''Our best yet. Would you like to get in?''

Jewel stared at him, long and hard. ''You've got a nerve.''

''Agreed. That's the kind of man I am. Don't let's hold up the traffic.'' He got out of the car and handed her in.

''What is this? Another setup?'' she demanded, before her anger drained away. ''Same chauffeur, I see. And once again the window is up.''

''We're in need of privacy, aren't we? Actually, I called you earlier on the off chance you might like to come out to dinner tonight.''

''Good grief!'' She moved her back against the plush, seductive-smelling leather. ''That's the last thing I expected.''

''Of course, if you'd rather not…'' His eyes slid over her, giving Jewel a series of violent little shocks down her spine.

''I wish I knew what's going through your mind.'' The disgust in her voice was genuine.

''Nothing that should alarm you. Dinner, then?''

She turned on him, almost calm with despair. ''What do you *want?*''

''To tell the truth, you fascinate me. And you're a beautiful woman.''

''You've met beautiful women before.''

''Not one who claims to be Davina Copeland's granddaughter.''

''I don't *claim* anything.'' Her mouth parted in outrage. ''What exactly does this have to do with you? You surely don't want *more* money?''

''What do you mean?'' He met those blazing blue

eyes, wondering why he was doing this, complicating his life endlessly.

"Your romance with Amelia isn't working out," she said tartly. "It helps to have a backup, doesn't it?"

"Are *you* offering?" He wondered what might happen if he just seized her and kissed her. That luscious mouth! Her silken legs were so close to his, demurely crossed at the ankles.

"No, I'm asking *you* the questions," she said. "You are not a person I want to get involved with."

He nodded. "Sound reasoning on your part. Now, are you going to tell me why you hung up on me?"

"Perhaps I don't like interruptions," she said. "Also, I was furious that you told Amelia about my luncheon date with Lady Copeland. It was very upsetting, especially for Lady Copeland. She told me herself her health isn't good."

He frowned, looking quite daunting. "You're jumping to conclusions."

"Conclusions?" Her voice was rising and she deliberately lowered it. "You've been a step ahead of me all the while. Amelia told us you tipped her off."

"Really? I can't think of anyone who lies more easily than Amelia."

"You deny telling her?"

He gave a near-Gallic shrug. "You're asking me to deny too much these days. I would never do anything to hurt Davina."

"You don't mind hurting me." She spoke sharply.

"Aren't you a woman who can look after herself?" He gave her a brilliant black-eyed look.

"You bet." She nodded in emphatic agreement. "How did Amelia *know*, then?"

He didn't consider for more than a few seconds.

"Well...if I had to guess, I think I'd settle on Holly. I imagine she got a big surprise seeing you close up."

"Her mouth stayed open so long, it was a little vulgar. But why would Holly tell Amelia?"

"It comes with the territory. Holly adores her."

"Really? Having met Amelia, I must say I'm surprised. I'd have expected Holly to be more loyal to Lady Copeland."

He glanced out the window as they stopped at the lights. "I think Holly sees herself as a long-term employee."

"What does that mean?" Jewel asked, her heart suddenly thumping with fright. "Lady Copeland isn't ill, is she? I mean, seriously ill?"

"She has a heart condition but medication keeps it under control. She has to look after herself, though."

"Then, I'm even less impressed with Amelia for upsetting her," Jewel said in dismay.

He took her hand. "I like you when you're being kind," he said, stroking her skin. "Don't forget I warned you. Travis and Amelia aren't the sort of people one threatens in any way."

She tried to get her hand back. Couldn't. Tried to control her racing pulse. "Are we talking about accidents? Accidents to me?"

"Don't worry. I'm keeping a close watch on you." His expression turned grim.

"Why, exactly? Your attitude was quite deplorable when we first met."

"And it could be again. I didn't say I absolutely trust you, even now." He linked her fingers with his. "But you're funny. You're sexy. You're beautiful. You're resourceful. You're clever. Do you want me to go on?"

"What I want you to do is give me back my hand."

"If I can." Slowly he released it. "What time would you like me to pick you up?—although I have to admit I lose all sense of time around you."

"Would eight o'clock suit?" She glanced at him. "That gives me a chance to get home, shower and change."

"What can I say except I can't wait!"

THE RESTAURANT was a luxuriant, softly lit room with perfectly laid tables, silver service, sparkling glasses; small garlands of flowers surrounded the lanterns that held lighted candles. The walls were covered in a deep green shimmering fabric that matched the green leather, brass-studded chairs; the green was also picked up in the striking floral fabric on the banquettes. At various points, gilt-framed mirrors were set into the wall, reflecting the beauty of the room and the female guests, who always wore their most expensive clothing when dining here. On the river side, great windows reached from floor to ceiling, granting a spectacular view of the city by night, all humming lights and glitter, with the City Cats, the ferries, plying up and down, landing their passengers at the base of a broad terrace with leafy trees in large pots. It was the ideal place to be at ease—if one was affluent and well-connected. Keefe Connellan, of course, was perfectly at home.

"So?" He looked across a riverside table at her with that faint smile she found too darn sexy. "What did you see in your last male friend? I've heard you were both madly in love."

"He was nowhere near the catch you are," she retorted, openly taunting him.

"What kind of work did he do?"

"I'm sure you already know that. He was a lawyer,

like me. And great in bed. I thought I'd mention it in case you planned to ask.''

''Well, that's good.'' Those attractive little grooves appeared at the side of his mouth. ''You certainly can't say it about everybody.''

''I'm not tasteless enough to ask about Amelia.''

''Very wise. I wouldn't tell you. Anyway, let's not talk about our exes. I can't think why, but a sudden flare of jealousy just hit me.''

Of course, he was teasing her. ''Why don't you go into movies?'' she suggested with a trace of hostility. ''You've got the looks—and the talent.''

''The problem is, I'm fully occupied in my own world.''

''And you're extremely ambitious.''

''Famous for it,'' he admitted. ''I also intend to put certain wrongs to right.''

Jewel toyed with her champagne glass, but her gaze remained intent on him. ''Does this include smacking Amelia's and Travis Copeland's heads together?''

He laughed, looked off across the gently opulent room. ''You've got quite a repertoire of little jokes.'' He paused, then told her grimly, ''I hold onto my memories, Jewel.''

''I pray I'll forget mine,'' she responded, then immediately regretted the admission.

''Was it that bad?'' His black eyes, heavily lashed, lit with interest and—was it sympathy?

''Yes,'' she said curtly.

''Yet despite this disadvantaged childhood, you managed to establish yourself in a competitive world.''

''And deserved to,'' she returned with some spirit. ''I worked very hard. At one point in my university days, I was even unpacking crates in a warehouse.''

"Do you think that hurt you?" His interest appeared flatteringly intense.

"No, not really." She shook her head, which set her hair dancing. "I had plenty of energy."

"And you still have." He smiled, letting his appreciative gaze travel over her. She was wearing a simple one-shouldered dress in a color that reminded him of African violets. The material, soft and supple, lightly skimmed her body yet it seemed to mold every womanly curve. Candlelight enhanced the deep violet of her dress, throwing a shimmering haze around her. It accented up her beautiful coloring and the perfection of her skin. This was a woman who could steal a man's heart…but she wasn't about to steal his. He had too many other pressing concerns. The mess Copeland was making of things. The way he was raising the hackles of important Asian clients with his arrogant manner. This was something relatively new, but when Travis felt threatened, he resorted to these airs of superiority. God knows how Travis Copeland would react to this challenging young woman. She wasn't the type to be easily cowed, unlike Amelia, who, for all her pampered background, was. A few sharp words from her father were enough to send Amelia into an emotional decline. He knew that wouldn't happen with Jewel. She was too much of a fighter.

"What are you thinking about?" Jewel asked, as he continued to regard her in thoughtful silence.

"I was thinking you wouldn't be a woman to cross," he answered lightly. "Tell me, what caused the split between you and your last boyfriend?"

"Why don't you phone him and ask? Anyway, 'boyfriend' is a silly term."

"I don't think anyone's come up with anything better,'' he reasoned mildly. ''The guy you were in love with, then.''

Jewel quickly looked away. ''Maybe my own ambitions overshadowed my romance. He was and is a fine, decent man, but for some reason I couldn't deal with the thought of marrying him. No doubt a result of my dysfunctional early life. Abandoned by my so-called father, losing my true father—all that. Who was the last woman to share *your* bed?'' she goaded, unwilling to let him ask all the unsettling questions. ''I can see you're having difficulty remembering.''

He held up an elegantly shaped, darkly tanned hand. ''No, I can tell you exactly. She's an old friend and very charming.''

''Married?'' She raised her winged brows.

''I don't make a habit of desiring married women,'' he murmured.

''Do you desire *me?*'' It was said in no way seductively but as a straightforward question.

''I'm attempting not to.'' He couldn't help it; he laughed.

The smile alone would make most women fall into his arms. *But not me,* Jewel vowed. She hadn't the slightest wish to get burned. ''Part of you will never forget who you are,'' she said, slowly tipping her head to one side. ''A Connellan, with all the responsibility— and all the privilege—that implies. You won't mess up your meticulously planned life.''

''How well you know me,'' he jeered, eyes unreadable.

''Your life hasn't all been glamour and power, has it?''

''Not at all.'' His handsome face sobered. ''Losing my father was a tremendous blow. I could've searched the whole world over and never found a better role model. My mother and my grandmother went through a long, deep period of mourning. Both of them would tell you they found strength because they had me to raise. They had to put up a fight to retain what we had until I was ready to take over. And then we had Davina on our side. Davina is a woman of honor.''

''It's obvious she's very fond of you.''

''The caring is mutual,'' he said. ''I'll do anything to protect her, especially now that she's growing older and frailer. It's been very exhausting, even for a woman like Davina, to cope with Travis. For many long years, that house was a battlefield. A complete contrast to the peace and harmony of my own. If Amelia reacted badly when she walked in on you and Davina, you have to remember the Copeland fortune is *everything* to them.''

''If that's the case, I should pity her,'' Jewel said, experiencing anger all over again.

''Maybe you should. Most people think Amelia has it all, but I've seen her go through real misery.''

''Because of her father?'' Jewel stared at him.

''Travis plays far too important a role in her life,'' he said. ''She's always tried desperately to please him but never really succeeded. Not that anyone could. Travis had a tough time with his own father, so the pattern of oppression and disapproval continues.''

''How awful! Why doesn't she simply leave? Why's she living there? She's a few years older than I am. I'd expect a woman of thirty to have some initiative and a few skills. Why doesn't she learn to support herself?''

''You're not listening, Jewel.'' There was a hard edge in his tone. ''Amelia is the heiress waiting to ascend the throne. She lives for that day. It's the one reason she puts up with so much.''

"Doesn't he love her?" Jewel felt increasingly disgusted with Travis Copeland. "What's wrong with the man? Doesn't he have any sense of remorse, any tender feelings?"

"He *does* love her in his own peculiar way. He wouldn't, for instance, countenance your claim to her throne. Still, he's a bully as opposed to an out-and-out tyrant like Sir Julius. And if you want to know about Travis's tender feelings and his capacity for remorse, you should ask his ex-wife, Amelia's mother. She's a tough lady, but he cut her to pieces."

"Charming. I don't think I'd like to meet him."

"You wouldn't, except for one thing. Davina wants her granddaughter," Keefe Connellan told her. "Her other granddaughter. *You.* Much as Travis strains under the yoke, his mother is head of the family. What she says goes."

"There's still no positive proof." Jewel allowed the bubbling champagne to fill her dry mouth.

"Instinct and a wealth of circumstantial evidence."

"Why the shift in *your* attitude?" she asked bluntly.

"Initially, I saw you as engineering the whole thing. With Skinner's full support."

"And now?"

"What I think doesn't matter at all. Davina has taken you to her heart." He gave her that seductive, practiced smile and another faint shrug. "Shall we order? The lobster looks good."

Jewel hadn't realized she was so unashamedly hungry. She even felt reckless, which didn't augur well. No doubt due to the champagne, combined with Keefe Connellan's exhilarating presence. It immersed her in an intoxication the likes of which she'd never known.

She had to keep reminding herself that beneath his striking exterior lurked a human calculating machine.

The food was delicious. One incredible dish after the other. A salad of lobster, quickly fried with roasted pine nuts and watercress, dressed sparingly and arranged on slices of warm baby potato. This was followed by steamed Red Emperor served in a banana leaf with papaw chilli and coconut salsa. Afterward, Jewel surrendered to a small ginger soufflé with Calvados cream, while he settled for a slice of almond tart with burnt-honey ice cream.

"That was wonderful!" she said sincerely, finally laying her spoon down. "Just splendid. I've been here a few times before, but it's so very expensive and hard to get in without reserving well in advance."

He smiled without commenting.

"How did you manage it?" she asked.

"It helps to own this block."

"Of course." She rolled her eyes. "I should've known."

"Are we going to have coffee? Or did you plan to invite me to your town house?"

"I don't know." Her brain was reeling at the thought of him inside her home. It wasn't like her to feel so vulnerable. She preferred being contained. "You're a dangerous man." She made the admission. Indeed, his sexual allure was a powerful weapon.

He nodded, his lean face creasing into a smile as though she'd said something totally inoffensive. "Definitely, but not to you. I make it my business never to hurt women."

"As though it were that simple."

"I meant *deliberately*. My mother brought me up to be a gentleman. Having said that, shall we go?"

"Why not?" she agreed briskly. "You know, I'm just the teeniest bit intoxicated. It's…an interesting sensation." And not one she was used to.

"I promise you I won't take advantage of it." He gestured to a hovering waiter, requested the bill, pulled out a card.

"I never said it was affecting me *that* badly," Jewel responded a shade edgily. "I'm absolutely certain you'll have no difficulty whatsoever keeping your hands off me."

His dark eyes swept her briefly. "Let's see if you're right."

WHAT FATE HAD IN STORE for Jewel, she was totally unprepared for: her first view of her father.

Keefe Connellan had maneuvered her effortlessly through the dining room, acknowledging friends and acquaintances along the way. Jewel was very aware that, unlike her, he knew everyone there. Once they'd left the restaurant proper, their exit via the elegant foyer was blocked by a large party of late diners, some four or five couples. The men were all in dinner suits; the women, none of them young, visions of glamour in surprisingly fashionable evening dress. They looked as if they'd come from somewhere else, as indeed they had. A little "do" at Parliament House. Jewel registered their affluent, civilized air but little else. She had never been one to stare, even at people who liked to be stared at. Consequently she was caught off guard when a tall, dark impressive-looking man with the silver temples of a forties movie star strode toward Keefe, holding out his hand.

"Keefe!" he cried indulgently, stopping before them

as though he'd sprung a huge surprise. "I *thought* I'd see you tonight."

For a moment, Jewel wondered if she'd simply dissolve. Death by tremendous shock. *Travis Copeland.*

Here was the man she now believed was her father, yet there was no trace of recognition in her. No piercing grief of the abandoned child. Rather, something about him repelled her. She didn't gauge her reaction as extreme, either. Even Keefe Connellan with his habitual air of command seemed about to spin on his heel but must have decided to shake the older man's hand. Whatever Connellan had been thinking a moment before was now masked by a smooth social smile.

"What's happened to Orlando's, Travis?" he said. "I thought it was your favorite dining spot?"

"Some of the ladies figured they'd like a change. Last-minute decision." Travis Copeland's ice-blue eyes, so light against the dark hair and tanned skin, moved on to Jewel, but his gaze was totally devoid of appreciation. "And this, of course, must be your friend, Ms. Bishop." He said it as though it were a joke.

I'm an adult, Jewel thought. *I don't get crushed by some megalomaniac bully.* Yet instinctively she moved closer to Keefe Connellan, who did far more than she'd expected. He put his arm around her in a gesture that was protective without being patronizing.

What grace, what style! There was sadness in knowing they were, in fact, opponents.

Travis Copeland didn't relish Connellan's grace. If eyes could wound, his did.

"My God, she's so much like my mother it's eerie." Obviously warned by Amelia, he yielded to a faint gasp. "Amazing! They do say we all have a double in this world."

"So they do." Keefe's voice was polite. "*This* time, however, the resemblance is of a more personal nature."

Another glimpse of venom. Only in the eyes. The dark, handsome face continued to smile benignly. "You surely don't trust her." He lowered his voice.

"Trust has nothing to do with it, Travis. I have complete confidence in Jewel's story. So does Davina, which is more important."

Travis laughed and glanced at Jewel quickly. "My mother's an old woman. A lonely old woman. At this stage of her life, she'd accept anyone as her granddaughter. Your friend here, Keefe, although she looks like Davina, is probably a real pro."

In other words, a cheap tart. *I should stamp down hard on his foot,* Jewel thought. Aunt Judith would have, and cursed him, as well.

"Some people will do anything to get noticed," Copeland continued in that mock-humorous upper-crust voice. "But eventually we'll get to the truth."

"There are ways of doing that quickly," Keefe suggested in a mild voice.

Copeland shook his big, arrogant head. "I've got no idea what you're talking about, Keefe. No idea at all. Yet I have the feeling you're accusing me of something." He gave the younger man a half droll, half censorious look.

"I'm attempting damage control," Keefe answered, his expression grave. "For all of us. For the business. I notice that some of your friends are mighty interested in this conversation. I think Natalie Carlyle's about to beckon Jewel over."

"Don't be ridiculous." Travis threw a nervous glance over his shoulder. "Jewel! What an outlandish name," he said. "A made-up name just like your story, Ms. Bishop."

Jewel found she couldn't bear to look into those frozen eyes. She turned her head, pretending to study a nearby flower arrangement.

"I'll get back at you one of these days, Keefe," Copeland murmured in a quick aside, as he prepared to rejoin his party. "Do remind me."

"Hell, Travis. I'm shaking in fear."

They had to run the gauntlet of Copeland's dinner guests, all of them known to Keefe as he was to them. He flashed that charming smile, tossed in a few cordial "good evenings," and then they were out in the star-spangled night, a cooling breeze blowing off the river to cool the turmoil in Jewel's blood.

"That man is *scary*," she said in a heartfelt tone. "It's not often I run into someone who frightens me as much. I thought you were tough, but you're like Sir Galahad compared to him."

"I told you I was raised to be a gentleman. Anyway, he can't hurt you. I promise."

Jewel was having difficulty keeping up the breathless pace. "I'll remember that when I get my first threatening letter. He looked at me like I was a despicable nobody."

"You're infinitely more respectable than that," he said with casual amusement. He recognized another half-dozen patrons, also leaving the restaurant. Smiles and waves. Plenty of curious glances.

"Well, thank you. But didn't you think he might turn up here?"

He pressed his hand to her back as they forged across the busy street. "Actually, Travis and his friends have always preferred the Paxton."

"You mean they don't patronize anywhere else, even occasionally?"

"Don't blame me for this." The uptown traffic stopped at the lights across from where his BMW was parked.

"I *am* blaming you," Jewel said. "That was what my aunt Judith would rather crudely call a 'balls-up.'"

"So it is. So it is." He suddenly burst out laughing. "I'm half in love with Aunt Judith already, but I swear to God, Travis was the last person I expected to see tonight."

"Is nowhere safe?" Jewel's breath was fluttering. "He hates me. More than that, he loathes me. He kept smiling that cold, nasty smile when the steam was nearly coming out of his ears."

"You're a puzzlement to him, that's why." He used his remote to unlock the car. "Why didn't you say anything?" He turned to look down into her face.

Jewel shook her head violently. "I'm never going to say anything to him. Ever. Not a word. He's not the only one who doesn't want him to be my father."

He opened the passenger door for her. "He knows in his heart that you're his child. I've had years and years to measure his reactions. I could tell you shocked the living daylights out of him."

Jewel was incredulous. "You can't be serious."

"Get in," he ordered, using his CEO voice.

"Please," she murmured.

"Get in, *please.* Either that or I'll have to sweep you off your feet."

"I rather think I'd like to be swept off my feet," she told him audaciously, but obeyed, slipping into the passenger seat while he closed the door.

The next moment he was behind the wheel, pulling

into the traffic. "So where's it to be? Your place or mine?"

She knew he was joking but her whole body felt saturated in heat. "I can offer you coffee," she said with feigned composure.

"I'll accept it gladly."

"Just coffee. Maybe a little conversation."

"My dear Ms. Bishop, that's understood."

She thought he might have the most attractive laugh she'd ever heard.

It had been a night of very real shock and pure pleasure. Her life was becoming increasingly complicated. Until recently, it had been one long lie. She'd been reared to believe Steven Bishop was her father, and in the ways that counted, she still believed that. Having met Travis Copeland, she felt pity for her mother—young and inexperienced, lonely, confronted by the devil in human form. Travis Copeland was handsome now; Jewel could picture him as a swaggering young man with his intoxicating background of power and riches. She could see her mother made to feel so pretty, so desirable, his hands on her....

"What's the matter?" Keefe Connellan turned his face to her, as she sharply drew in her breath.

"I was thinking how easy it would've been for a man like Travis Copeland to seduce my mother," she said, recognizing both sympathy and anger. "Even easier for him to disappear. I've read everything I could about the day of the funeral. The news reports indicated that he was attacked by an unnamed assailant. A disgruntled employee, they said." She swallowed with difficulty. "Poor Steven Bishop! He didn't rate a name. The rich know how to cover up their mistakes," she added bitterly.

"Travis isn't going to be able to cover *you*," he pointed out.

"I don't think he's about to let me into the family, either."

"He was waiting for some response from you."

"Why do you think I spent so much time staring at the flowers? His broken nose never did heal properly, did it?" she added with satisfaction. "One up for Dad. It must have been frightful for him to realize he'd been so betrayed."

"Add to which he'd learned the truth about the daughter he adored. Still, he should've given himself time—a chance to adjust."

"That is, if he *did* commit suicide. It might have been an accident."

"Only, it wasn't. The police were as good as certain."

"I was so small. I didn't grasp anything that happened back then. I still miss him, you know."

He glanced at her in the intimate darkness. "I can understand that." After a pause he asked, "Have you ever been head over heels in love?" he finally asked, surprising her. "I mean the passionate, romantic love you read about in books?"

"Have you?"

He shook his head. "I haven't been married, either."

"Weren't you almost engaged to Amelia?" She found herself desperate to get to the heart of the matter.

"I've known Amelia all my life," he said, "but in the end, I don't think I know her at all."

"She's that deep?" She affected an astonished voice.

"In a word, no."

"But things were very cozy between you. Still are?"

"And you never really loved your lawyer. Did you live with him?"

"Good Lord, no! I couldn't bear to have a man messing up my house. And I'm not in favor of live-ins without commitment."

"Indeed," he drawled.

"Have your fun."

"On the contrary. I like a woman who demands respect."

ON THE WAY into her stylish little town house, her high heel caught in a crack in the pavement. "Oh!" Damn it, these were her best evening shoes.

"All right?" He caught her to him as she tripped, one arm locking around her waist. "You know, I think you're right. You're borderline tipsy."

"I am not." She denied it indignantly. "It's my shoes. Anyway, even if I were, running into my so-called father would've sobered me instantly."

"Now *that* I believe." He looked about him with interest. "I know the architect who designed this building. A dynamic guy. I'm interested to see how it turned out."

"Well, it's exactly what I wanted," Jewel said, inserting the front door key in the lock. "Fresh, clean, with the illusion of spaciousness and light. Lots of maple, which I like. Come in."

"After you."

Jewel reached for the panel of light switches that completely illuminated the downstairs area. She was glad now that she'd spent so much money on several beautiful white Phalaenopsis orchids she'd placed in strategic spots. They floated like exquisite butterflies in the low golden glow, adding their own magic to the furniture, the objects and the various attractive but relatively inexpensive paintings she'd bought over the years.

"I'm impressed with what I see," he said. "Did you do your own decorating?"

"I certainly did," she said.

"Then, I admire your taste." His dark eyes moved appreciatively around the open-plan area.

"For that, you may get invited again."

"I'd enjoy that very much." He turned to look at her. The lighting gleamed on his thick hair, black as a crow's wing.

"Why? What are you up to, Keefe Connellan?" She was half smiling, half serious.

"Surely you realize you'll be joining one big happy family."

"So you've decided to like me?"

"Maybe." He smiled, too.

"I think you have quite a capacity for strategic responses."

"I mean what I say."

Jewel dropped her evening purse on an armchair. She walked through the living-dining area, defined by free-floating timber panels, on which she'd hung paintings, to the small functional kitchen with its high-gloss steel fixtures and dark green granite countertops, "How about a cheeseburger?" she asked flippantly. "Or I can make you a steak. Or a—"

"I don't think I can fit it in. Just coffee. Unless you want me to stay the night."

Jewel let a few seconds go by, hoping her face didn't betray how she felt. Her dress might had been peeled away, exposing her naked trembling body. This man was taking her places she'd never been, introducing her to sensations she'd never experienced. Nevertheless, she managed to say lightly, "Nice try, but I don't. I trust your ego's not suffering because of it."

"Actually, it's a rule of mine never to sleep with a woman on the first date." He bent to read the signature on one of the paintings. "I like this."

"I'll have it delivered to you in the morning," she joked.

"No, it's very good. Where did you get it?"

"The Young Contemporary Studio." She spooned the freshly ground coffee into the plunger. "That's where I got them all. I love paintings but I can only afford the up-and-coming."

He straightened. "All of these show talent. Is there a terrace?"

She gazed at him thoughtfully. "You're genuinely interested in my house?"

"Of course I am. One doesn't have to pay a fortune to achieve good design. You obviously have a sense of style."

"It couldn't have been inherited from Sir Julius. Nero would have felt at home at the Copeland villa." Jewel paused in her coffee-making to turn on the terrace lights. Paved in slate, it was set with a single recliner and four large Asian pots filled to overflowing with pink flowering hydrangeas and a single contrasting blue agapanthus.

She watched him move out into the starlight, as she struggled with feelings she could only describe as intense. The last thing in the world she wanted was to make a fool of herself with this man. She closed her eyes for a moment, shutting out his deeply exciting presence, deliberately trying to control the heavy beating of her heart.

When she opened them again, he was standing right in front of her.

"You startled me," she gasped.

"Only because you were lost in thought." Watching her, he lifted a hand to grasp a handful of her hair. "You're a very beautiful woman," he said, those brilliant eyes like smoldering lamps.

"And you're a very disturbing man."

"How's that?"

Despite herself, she felt her back arch. "Power has its own high voltage." Wasn't she already scorched?

"You can't be saying I have power over *you?*"

"I wouldn't be fool enough to let you use it." She had the oddest sensation that the whole room was receding, leaving them both enveloped in a heat-induced mirage.

"How would you go about stopping me?"

"By pushing you away." She brought up her hands to place them against the lapels of his suit jacket, acutely aware that they were trembling.

"Desire's a funny thing, isn't it?" he mused, his voice low and absorbed. "Like a moth to a flame. You know you're going to get burned, yet you can't resist it."

With his hand still caressing her cheek, he bent his head until his mouth covered hers.

Peaches. She could taste peaches.

From then on, she had difficulty thinking as the full rush of sexual desire hit her body.

The kiss seemed to go on and on, almost as though she was dreaming, except that the reactions of her body were too real, too convulsive. She was feeling it all too deeply, allowing the entry of his tongue, her own entwined eagerly with his. Her nipples, budded to the point of pain, thrust against the supple fabric of her dress, and the silken place between her thighs began to throb.

God, she had been wanting this for years but had never reached it. And all with a kiss! Her own mouth was nectar, open and molded to his, her body yielding as his hand sought and found the curve of her breast.

How easy it would be to surrender. How easy to let him pick her up and carry her to bed. A fantasy lover taking her from the wildest elation...to possible despair. If you gave someone that power over you, it became almost impossible to protect yourself. She wasn't the first and she wouldn't be the last to experience manic surges of emotion, of passion, that affected the rest of her life. Her mother, for instance. Becoming like her mother had once been her greatest fear.

"You're a siren, aren't you," he accused, as though he, too, was questioning their actions. "The Lorelei, luring a poor sailor onto the rocks."

It was a new view of herself for Jewel. "Isn't it gratifying we've both got good heads on our shoulders." With a supreme effort she drew back, one of the hardest things she'd ever done. "Sexual attraction. That's all it amounts to. There's no protection against the body's chemicals, hormones, neurotransmitters, whatever."

"Depend on you to come up with an explanation." His voice was infused with dark laughter. "All the same, I don't think I knew what a kiss was until tonight. You have the most seductive, provocative mouth."

"Perhaps it's because of you." She was amazed she sounded so normal. "Usually I'm so controlled."

"So am I. But what a difference tonight." He kissed the arc of her throat.

She almost wished he'd do that forever. "We'll know

better the next time. It must be a terrible thing to really be in love.'' She swept her hair aside so he could nibble her ear. ''The power one hands over to another human being is too complete.''

''Agreed, but it's either take a risk or miss out on *this*.''

More gossamer, burning kisses. They were fracturing her determination to end this extraordinary episode. ''The coffee's ready.'' She spoke as decisively as she could.

''Great. I need it.'' He thrust a hand through his hair, missing a dark lock that fell forward onto his temple. It softened the rather severe look of his face in repose.

They each backed off, staring into one another's faces until Jewel belatedly turned away, lifting the coffeepot.

''My mother stopped living when Dad was killed.'' She made the confession spontaneously. ''He'll always be 'Dad' to me. After his death I had a lot of responsibilities.'' These were the experiences and feelings that defined her, and she wanted him to understand.

''That made you a woman of substance.'' He found the coffee cups and saucers without being told where they were.

''It's made me very, very cautious,'' Jewel said. ''I suppose I was about ten when I swore I'd never allow myself to be put in the same position as my mother. Grieving terribly for a dead husband. Love meant loss. Pretty much the end of life, even when you were young. Now I know that not only was Mama grieving for Dad, she couldn't rid herself of her guilt and her degrading memories.''

He had no wish to defend Travis Copeland. Still, he caught her arm, trying to comfort her. ''It may not have been as you think. Only two people know. Your mother and Travis. They could have formed a genuine emotional attachment.''

Jewel shook her head. "It was pretty short term. He made sure he stayed away. Davina told me that. Travis Copeland is a cruel person, and I know I could never love him, even if I'd been raised as his daughter.''

"Amelia idolizes him despite all her unhappy experience," he said, rather discordantly.

"It must have something to do with her personality. Maybe she's a masochist. Some women are. They love men even when they're brutal and abusive. Not me. I'm not in the market for that kind of humiliation. After tonight, I want nothing to do with Travis Copeland.''

CHAPTER EIGHT

HE ARRIVED HOME in a fury, not caring if he disturbed the household. He knocked at Amelia's door first. She'd returned from a private dinner party only ten minutes before, so she was still in her short chiffon slip dress.

"Father, what is it?" she asked in hushed tones, glancing past him down the hallway. He swept past her without a word, so Amelia immediately closed the door behind her.

"I saw that girl tonight. Thea's girl," Travis told her savagely.

"Jewel Bishop?" Amelia's strained half-smile was wiped from her face.

"And you'll never guess who she was with," Travis exploded, pitching Amelia's beautiful expensive evening purse off an armchair so he could sit down.

"Don't tell me. *Keefe*." Amelia's golden-skinned, oval face went pale as she sank into the chair opposite him.

"Yes, Keefe Bloody Connellan," Travis confirmed, looking steadily and harshly at his daughter. "How old are you now, Amelia?"

Inside Amelia withered. "You know perfectly well, Father. I'm twenty-eight."

"And how long have you been trying to get Keefe Connellan to marry you?"

Icy fingers clutched her heart. It seemed now that

she'd spent her life on a knife edge, always evading her father's disdain. "It feels like a hundred years," she said with a sigh that might have been a sob.

"Well, that girl had him in tow." Travis Copeland's heavily handsome head shook as though he had palsy. "What does that say for *you?*" He answered himself. "Not much."

"She's very beautiful, Father," Amelia told him. "Any man might fall in love with her."

"Love, love. What's love got to do with anything?" Travis looked back, incredulous at her simplistic thinking. "Keefe's a born manipulator. He's most likely using the girl. Mother's fallen for her story like a ton of bricks. God knows, she's her mirror image. I tell you, I got an appalling shock. I—"

"Who is she, Father?" Amelia interrupted him.

"She's a bloody impostor, that's what she is." Travis, used to deference, shot his daughter a furious look.

"Gran doesn't think so." It took courage for Amelia to say it.

"Your grandmother is in her dotage," he said scornfully. A little more courage trickled into Amelia's veins.

"I've never met anyone less unhinged. Gran gives us all strength. So…you're saying she's *not* your daughter?"

Travis stared at her, his expression malignant. "I have *one* daughter. Everyone knows that."

"You *had* one daughter until Jewel showed up." Amelia heard the nervousness in her voice.

"Don't use that ridiculous name," her father thundered.

"It suits her," Amelia said. She hadn't been able to

stop thinking of Jewel. *Those beautiful violet eyes.* "She has Gran's eyes."

"Why don't you accuse me of betraying your mother and be done with it?" Travis snapped. "I couldn't care less."

"I suppose not." When her father wasn't setting out to charm, she realized he didn't really love her. Any affection he showed was for the benefit of an audience. "None of us can keep up with your affairs, Father. Gran said you flew into Mingaree Station often in the old days. Then you stopped."

"So?" Travis Copeland's heavy, muscled body went rigid and intense. "I did many things for my father. I was his right hand."

Even Amelia knew that wasn't true. "The question is, what are we going to do about her? Pay her off?"

"Frighten her off is more like it." Travis Copeland swore beneath his breath, his face twisted with emotion. "She never said one word, but you should've seen her eyes. How dare she look at me as though I were beneath her contempt! Who does she think she is, the little nobody? Who's she plotting with? Keefe? He'd do anything to ruin me."

Amelia pressed her hands together so tightly they looked bloodless. "That's not true, Father. I hate to hear you talking about Keefe like that. He's a good man."

"He's a top-notch wheeler-dealer, you mean. Mark my words, he's got some plan going. You obviously don't interest him, for all the time and money that's been spent on you. My God, you've got the looks but you're just like your mother. Frigid. Not a trace of sex appeal, let alone fascination. That girl has it. Even I could see that. I tell you, Amelia, I couldn't be more disappointed in you. I had great hopes for our two families to be united. Keefe would owe me his loyalty then. But you couldn't get him to propose. Great God, it doesn't have to be a love match! Surely you understand that. Families like ours have to think in bigger terms. We have to think of the Fortune. You enjoy being rich, don't you?''

"Of course I do, Father," Amelia said. "But being rich is *all* I am," she whispered with unusual honesty. "You've never encouraged me to use my brain. But I know we have real trouble this time."

"You know that, do you?" He mocked her cruelly. "Why do you think I'm here? I don't usually start up a conversation this time of night."

"Gran is going to recognize her," Amelia told him carefully.

"Over my dead body." His anger was so intense he kicked Amelia's evening purse out of the way. "Or *hers.*"

Amelia felt ill. Her father was such a violent person he sometimes terrified her. "Gran is still a powerful, mentally strong woman. She's head of the family. Not only that, she has an ally in Keefe. Keefe and his family. They won't be swept aside, Father. Keefe is going to get back every last penny the Connellan family lost."

The icy eyes, cold and hard, flashed. "Whose side are you on, my dear?"

"*Yours,* Father. I'm always on your side." And that had been her whole life up to date.

"As I expect you to be," he told her. Indeed, Amelia's blind loyalty was important to him. "I can't have this girl destroying our world. Making a spectacle of me."

"Even if she *is* your daughter?" Amelia's heart was hammering so hard she was short of breath.

"I will *never* recognize her." Travis looked squarely into her eyes.

"So she *is* your daughter," Amelia blurted, feeling her own identity had been wrenched from her. "I wanted to have her thrown out of the house today, but I knew in my bones she had a right to be here. The look on Gran's face wounded me terribly. The love that was in it. For *her*." She shook her head. "There's no trace of Gran in me. You've had such a hold over me, Father. I used to hate Mother for saying I spent my entire life trying to please you and no one else. But it's true. And…and Jewel is my half sister."

"Whose mother is feebleminded," Travis shouted back, startling her. "An emotional wreck. So even *you* have betrayed me behind my back? Now, at this time of my life."

"I told you tonight that Jewel was here at Gran's invitation," Amelia reminded him desperately. "But you were on your way out, and there wasn't time to talk about it further."

Travis Copeland came to his feet, glaring. "I'll get rid of this girl," he cried. "Have no doubt about that. *You* are my heir. The child of my marriage. Your inheritance is safe. You had a chance to please me by marrying Connellan. In one swoop, a marriage would've put everything to rights. United families can't fight each other. Keefe would've seen sense. An alliance was crucial, still is, but on *my* terms, which means you. After tonight I've come away with the feeling that you're not up to it."

The disappointment in his voice was so bitter, Amelia felt like collapsing at his feet, begging forgiveness. "There might be a chance, Father. I know Keefe cares for me."

"Then, why doesn't he marry you?" Her father let out a growl of frustration, then started walking to the door. "Dear God, that it should come to this...."

"You're not going to disturb Gran, are you, Father?" Amelia was plunged into the depths of anxiety. Anything was possible with her father in this mood.

"Oh, go to bed." He spoke as though he disliked her intensely. "The meeting with my mother can wait until morning."

"OKAY, TRAVIS, what is it?" Davina, who was standing in front of an exquisite French *secretaire* looked critically at her son. She had known perfectly well that Amelia would inform her father of Jewel's visit. Consequently, she was prepared for this confrontation. Travis had inherited all Julius's worst qualities, including the rages, but few of his strengths. It was an arrow in her heart, for she continued to love him despite the conflicts that had filled their lives.

"I wanted to speak to you about the girl, Mother." Travis Copeland instinctively began carefully. His awe of his mother had been well-hidden for many years, yet he felt compelled to swallow his anger and bitterness. It was now nine o'clock and his mother had kept him waiting for an hour while she dressed.

"Your *daughter,* Travis?" Davina, being Davina, stripped away all pretense. "She is your daughter, isn't she, Travis? Thea Bishop's child."

Travis licked his dry lips, his expression changing to one of self-loathing. "She isn't the only woman who's tricked me."

Davina laughed grimly. "You mean there might be more grandchildren tucked away somewhere?"

Travis snapped his fingers. "Of course not, Mother.

She was just a silly little girl. I was kind to her, and how did she respond? She was all over me every time I turned up.''

"You mean she was ready and waiting for an affair?"

"Aren't they all!" Not sweet little Thea, no. Both of them had surrendered to a powerful impulse. Travis shook his head to clear the memory that survived.

Davina sighed heavily, hardly guessing her son's thoughts. "You have a callous hand with women, Travis. Even your father didn't have that. Riches can spoil. They spoiled you. Had this Thea been the sort of young woman to have easy affairs, she wouldn't have let you get away with fathering her child. She'd have slapped a paternity suit on you and fast. She wouldn't have spent the past twenty years bitterly regretting an act or acts that tore her family apart. I should've known to go further when I saw that tragic young man, Steven Bishop, strike you at your father's funeral. I guessed you'd taken advantage of his wife, of course. Sonia thought the same thing. Neither of us knew about the child. But *you* did.''

"I didn't know there was a child." Not at the beginning, anyway. That part was true. He swallowed on a hard knot in his throat. Didn't anyone realize he had his own capacity for pain? "I didn't believe for one moment she was mine.''

"That won't hold up as an excuse, Travis." Davina was shaking her head, every pearl-white hair in place. "Jewel is the living image of me when I was young. You don't often see resemblances like that. You don't see natural blondes with black lashes and brows.''

"I never saw any resemblance," Travis said, moving his eyes away. This was becoming unbearable.

"You're lying. You're not a fool, Travis, whatever else you are. You abandoned her and her mother."

"What else was I supposed to do?" he cried, not concealing his feelings of impotence. "Tell me, Mother. Go to Father? Tell you? Tell that cold bitch of a Sonia who offered me her body exactly like a sacrifice? All three of you would've torn me to shreds. The scandal would have been shattering. God Almighty, Father thought he was Caesar." He shrugged helplessly. "Do you really think I'm the only man who's had to turn his back on his child?"

"No, I don't. I'm a woman of the world. But you were bound to help them financially, Travis. Your father's been dead twenty years. You and Sonia are divorced. And why would you ever think *I'd* turn my back on my own granddaughter? I'd be damned forever if I did."

Travis gazed at his mother with wondering eyes. "So you're going to ruin all our lives?" he challenged, his strong jaw thrust out. "Yours, mine, Amelia's? You've never really loved her, have you."

Davina's hand went to the dull ache in her breast. "You've twisted Amelia's character, Travis. You deliberately took her away from her mother and me. You wouldn't let our relationship flower. You're wrong when you say I don't love her. I love her very much. That's why I don't want to see everything that's good in her disappear."

"Why is it, Mother, that you blame me?" Travis asked in a hoarse voice, going far back into his childhood and adolescence, remembering his virtually arranged marriage to a woman who'd turned out to be frigid in bed. She *hated* it. Nothing like the desire that had flowed between him and…and…the sort of woman he'd really wanted—sweet, soft, sensitive to his needs. A woman who actually used to hang on his every word…. Unlike his father and mother, who were too brilliant, too motivated and too self-disciplined, too tremendously sure of themselves and their place in the scheme of things. Both of them had turned him into the man he was, full of frustration and fury. Sometimes he thought he couldn't bear what he had become.

Now he tried to explain his strong dependence on his daughter, Amelia, who sprang to his defense, no matter what. "Anyone would tell you I've been the most indulgent father on earth to Amelia, Mother," he said, truly believing it. "She's wanted for nothing."

"Except your *unconditional* love, Travis," Davina pointed out. "There are always strings attached. If she doesn't please you, you're sarcastic to her, even hostile. You've given her hell over Keefe. Don't you know you can't make people fall in love on demand?"

"Why would you be telling *me* that?" Travis showed his profound resentment. "Father as good as forced me into marrying Sonia."

"She really loved you, Travis." Sonia had never been Davina's choice, but she tried to be fair.

"She *screamed* the first time I tried to make love to her on our honeymoon. How do you think that sits with a man, Mother? I've had plenty of affairs since then, not a one of any consequence, but at least no one's let out a scream."

This was news indeed to Davina. She sat down as though she'd suddenly lost the power of her legs. "I'm very sorry, Travis. You never told me that before. I know you had a difficult marriage, but you must remember you ignored my advice. I told you not to get mixed up with the Watson Smythes. They're such an odd family.''

''My God, and ours isn't?'' Travis said. ''By the time I was married, Father had me convinced I was an idiot. 'Boofhead'—isn't that what he called me? Sonia carried on in the same vein. No wonder I fell in love with Thea. She was a different human being altogether. Gentle and loving. Full of mercy.''

''Oh, my dear boy.'' Whatever Davina had been expecting, it wasn't this. She'd even faced the worst possible scenario—rape. ''Why didn't you come to me?'' She stared into her son's wretched eyes.

''I couldn't.'' Travis recalled how he had tried. ''Father would've heard about it eventually. He'd have cut me off without a moment's hesitation. That's the way he was.''

Davina drew a short, shallow breath. ''He wouldn't have done it, Travis. I wouldn't have let him. He used his power over you like a whip. I think he thought it would make you stronger. Extraordinary, isn't it? You've always been insecure and your way of confronting it has been to put terrible pressure on others. Amelia's particular terror is that you'll cease loving her altogether. You've made her feel she *has* to get Keefe to marry her as part of that deal. But Keefe and Amelia don't suit each other at all.''

''Really?'' Travis was livid. On his own and Amelia's account. ''So what's *your* dream, Mother? Bring this girl into our lives and let her marry Keefe?''

''This girl, Travis, is your daughter,'' Davina said once again. ''As much your daughter as Amelia. I want you to meet her.''

Travis laughed in his mother's face, his own expression ghastly with pain.

"For once, Mother, I've beaten you to it. I met her last night. Well, not exactly *met.* We weren't properly introduced. She was out dining with your beloved Keefe."

"Was she?" For a moment Davina felt faint. "Now the whole thing's out in the open. You were at the same restaurant?"

"Yes." Travis nodded uncontrollably like a puppet. "We were arriving. They were leaving."

"I suppose all of your party saw her?" The scene flashed before Davina's eyes.

"They saw her, all right, but no one passed any remark. Not to me. They left that for later. She's the very image of you, Mother. She has nothing of me or Thea."

"You sound disappointed." Davina's tone was ironic. She had tried so hard to win her son's love, but he'd never really responded. Too much like his father, believing men ruled the world.

Now he confirmed it, if only to his mother. "I've never liked women who feel they're equal to men," he confided, in the genuine belief that male superiority had been carried unanimously. "You should've seen the way she looked at me."

"You've had your share of approving nods, Travis," Davina said. "Don't be so mean-spirited. Perhaps you should consider Jewel's point of view. She hasn't had an easy life. Far from it. Thea apparently still suffers from severe depression. We'll have to make things easier there, Travis, if they'll let us."

"So you're determined to bring her into the family?" Travis stared at his mother as if she'd gone mad.

"For God's sake, Travis, can't we put things right?" she begged, her eyes bright with unshed tears.

"You're not seeing the implications, Mother," Travis

said. "This is the child of one of my mistresses. It was over long ago. Now you want to subject us all to long-term punishment. Where's your pride, your sense of family?"

"It's my sense of family that's speaking, Travis." Davina had recovered her composure. "Blood ties. This family has done bad things. I want to make amends. Compensation, if you like. I want this with all my heart. But let's look at this in a way that might suit you better. Many people will admire you for recognizing your child. Even after all these years. No one needs to know you haven't provided for them."

"What do you mean by that?" he asked sharply.

"I mean we should offer Thea Bishop compensation for raising your child. The burden fell totally on her and her sister. Given her state of mind, she couldn't have done it by herself. These women need some sort of settlement. It's only justice, and we must persuade them of that."

Travis was seized by a mad desire to laugh. "Why don't I just visit Thea in her jungle home?" he said. "Maybe we could even get together again. I could marry her in one of her lucid moments. That would solve the problem, wouldn't it, Mother? Why didn't I think of it before? Thea and I could marry and legiti-mize our daughter."

"Travis, please stop," Davina implored, holding her head. "It doesn't help to talk crazily."

"What's so crazy about it?" He'd had his arms crossed over his chest, and now he threw them wide. He was a big, powerful, angry man. "It's no crazier than introducing my bastard to society."

"Nobody talks about bastards anymore, Travis,"

Davina pointed out coldly. "If a child feels unloved and unwanted, the damage can never be repaired."

"Then, you'll have to accept some blame there, Mother," Travis said. "I barely saw you and Father when I was a child. My God, most of the time I was left with Rosie Lennox, a servant in the house."

"Rosie was a tower of strength." Davina looked down at her hands, beautiful once, now knotted with arthritis. "A lovely, kind, woman. I didn't leave you with just anyone. I had to accompany your father everywhere, Travis, whether I liked it or not. It may not have been right or for the best, but your father became my universe."

"You wouldn't attempt this if he were still alive," Travis challenged her.

"I suggest you didn't know your father as well as you think. Julius went ahead with whatever he believed in and to hell with everyone else. He acted according to his own judgment and he acted swiftly. I'm certain he would have made the decision to bring Jewel, his granddaughter, into the family. I think that, unlike me, he would've gotten to the bottom of what went on at Mingaree Station all those years ago, and you wouldn't have escaped. You must have found your father's death a great relief."

Travis's face lost color. "I never expected you to be vindictive, Mother. I idolized Father, as you very well know. I revere his memory. I'm only saying this new development might destroy us. Certainly our high standing in society."

Davina rose and walked to the open doors that led to her private balcony. "Travis, we'd lose our supposedly high standing in society tomorrow if Copeland Connellan crashed. We're powerful because we're rich.

The Connellans are powerful because they're universally admired and respected. That's why you've been trying to get Amelia and Keefe married off.''

Travis recoiled. "I know my duty. I wish to see my daughter married well.''

"Far better she be happy,'' Davina said wearily. "I married well. So did you. Where did it get us?''

"Are you saying you didn't love Father?'' Travis looked his shock.

"Travis, dear, your father was magnificent but he wasn't lovable. In my next life, I'm going to choose someone quite different.''

"There is no next life, Mother.'' Travis shook his head. "This is all we've got. Meeting that girl gave me an enormous shake-up. I'm not the ruthless, heartless bastard you seem to think. I want to love, but I don't seem able to. It's like you say—I see myself with Amelia, giving her the same awful time Father gave me. It's almost as though I was programmed in childhood.'' He fell silent for a moment, then started up again in quite a different tone. "Keefe put his arm around that girl last night. I know a protective gesture when I see it. He put his arm right around her when I reached them. Just like a shield.''

"Keefe is a born gentleman.'' Davina sighed and returned to her armchair.

"Oh, and I'm not?'' Travis lifted his head.

"Maybe as your father's son, it's been beyond you. Without your father there, both of us would've been completely different people.''

There was great truth in that.

"But everyone loves you, Mother,'' Travis assured her, suddenly struck by her frailness. "They all look up to you.''

"I don't deserve it," Davina answered quickly. "And I certainly won't deserve it if I turn my back on my own granddaughter. I haven't got all that much longer, Travis. I feel a strong need to put our house in order. I want you to phone your daughter Jewel and persuade her to come to us this weekend. It's a long weekend, so that gives us three days to get to know each other. You and Amelia will remain at home all that time, so you can both cancel your engagements. I want you to invite Keefe, as well, and that nice young man who works for us, Greg McCall. I know for a fact that Amelia enjoys his company, and he's a very pleasant young man to have around the house. Better yet, he's loyal and discreet. The young people can swim and play tennis. There's plenty to do."

Shock and horror clouded Travis's eyes. "You can't be serious, Mother. Even if I wanted to, which I don't— My God, she'd never speak to me."

"Then, you'll have to use your charm, Travis." Davina refused to back away. "You *do* have it when required. Aside from everything else, I want us to sort out our strategies before the press get hold of this thing. From what you tell me, you and Jewel were seen in conversation last night."

"She never said a word to me." Travis knew he sounded fierce and full of indignation.

"That's beside the point. Jewel's resemblance to me, even if I am an old woman, is striking. People aren't fools. Some of them remember me from my prime. Most of them love scandals. You can guarantee the phones have been ringing off the hook. What I'm suggesting to you now is that we beat them all to it with an announcement. That we act as *one* family," she urged.

"Dear God!" Travis buried his head in his hands. "You're ruthless, Mother, once you get started."

Davina shook her head. "Travis, don't you think I feel for you? I know you hide behind that mask. I know all your insecurities. But I love you. Nothing will change that. You are my son. We can't let our wounds fester—we have to bring them into the light of day. The world is a changed place, far more tolerant. Less hypocritical. I promise you, this will be no more than a nine-day wonder. Jewel isn't someone to be ashamed of. On the contrary—she's a daughter to be proud of. It is my dearest wish that you'll come to see that. Do this for me, Travis. It may be the making of us all."

JEWEL WAS STILL IN HER NIGHTGOWN, drinking her morning coffee and reading the newspapers, when Travis Copeland's call came through.

"Hello?"

His voice was so clear, so immediately identifiable, Jewel almost dropped the phone. "It's Travis Copeland here," he said. "And there's a good chance I might be your father."

She didn't know whether to be shocked or infuriated by his offhand announcement. "Thank you for ringing, Mr. Copeland, but I simply don't care." Jewel put down the receiver as if it burned, her whole body trembling. What right did he have to call her? In her own home, yet. She picked up her coffee cup and drained it, going to the kitchen to get more. What did he expect? That she'd forgive him for his paternal shortcomings? For the hard life she and her mother had led?

The phone rang again ten minutes later. Jewel swept up the receiver and spoke in a rush. "I'd appreciate it if you didn't ring my home."

"With no hint of the caller?" Another voice. A different kind of jolt. This one she liked. "How are you, Jewel?" Keefe asked. "Since it's Saturday, there's no chance of getting you at the office."

"I'm fine. Really," she said automatically, trying to disguise a certain breathlessness. "I've just had a phone call from someone you'd never guess if you lived to be a million."

"Travis Copeland, right?"

"I'm impressed. Yes, it was Travis Copeland."

"Actually, it's not a guess. He called me."

Jewel propped herself up against the wall. "Not about me?"

"I was too astounded to make it all out" was the response. "Apparently, he and Davina want you to come and stay with them for the long weekend. Travis was about to issue the invitation, when you hung up on him."

"I admit it. I did. Has he gone mad? Last night he looked like he wanted to hit me over the head with a blunt instrument."

"He's a different man this morning." The low attractive laugh was hard to resist. "I'd say he's had a session with Davina."

"So his mama snaps her fingers and he jumps? I haven't the slightest intention of going back to that house."

"Not even to see your grandmother?" he asked.

Jewel considered. "I'm sorry about that, but no. The whole idea of it dismays me. For one thing, Amelia couldn't have been any part of that decision."

"Amelia hardly knows what it is to make a decision. If you decide you *can* do it when Travis rings again, give me a call. I've been invited, as well."

Jewel straightened her arm to reach a chair. "If you're trying to confuse me you're doing a darn good job," she said, sinking down.

"Think about it, a foursome. You. Me. Amelia. And a very nice guy named Greg McCall."

"And how's he involved in all this?"

"It's a house party," he explained. "Greg and I get on well together. I have the impression he's keen on Amelia. She certainly likes him. He's in our legal department, so you two should get along, too. He's well-bred, well-educated and he knows where all the bodies are kept."

"Quite. Such is life in big business," she said crisply. "I'm not going, so you can cease your blandishments, Keefe Connellan."

"It really isn't my kind of event, either, but if you're there… Are you sure you don't want the opportunity to beat me in a game of tennis? They have a grass court. Amelia is very, very good. And Travis might be past his prime but he still plays a mean game."

"Absolutely not. I've won my share of games but I haven't played for ages."

"We can still have fun," he cajoled. "We could have lunch together. Lose ourselves, if we wished. It's an enormous place."

"Why do you want me to go?" she asked point-blank.

"I'm not entirely sure." Suddenly he sounded serious. "I'm not close to Travis, but he's a complex character. I never really knew Sir Julius. I do know there were a lot of people pleased to say farewell to him. Though he'd never admit it even before a firing squad, I'd say Travis was one of them. I'm very fond of

Davina, as you know. I've known Amelia all her life. She could be my cousin.''

She sat there, rejecting that. "It didn't seem that way to me. Lovers might be more accurate. I can't decide whether or not you're on the level. I know I've kissed you, but I don't know you very well.''

The laugh sounded in his voice. "That's why I'm eager for us to spend the weekend together. So we can remedy that.''

"I really don't believe you.'' Jewel sighed.

"Shall I come over? Try to convince you?''

She shook her head although he couldn't see her. "I'm still trying to get over what happened last night. You're not the man I want to get involved with, Keefe.''

"I'm afraid you already are involved,'' he said. "I'll get off the line. Travis is going to ring back. When he does, for all our sakes, give him a chance.''

CHAPTER NINE

KEEFE FOUND HIS MOTHER in the lush tranquillity of the garden, discussing new design ideas with Arnold, their head gardener. Arnold, "a happily transported Pom," as he described himself, had once worked as a landscape designer for rich clients around the world. He'd been with the Connellans for ten years or so, and under his direction the extensive grounds surrounding the family home had turned into one of the country's great gardens. Year after year, his mother and Arnold opened the garden to the public during the full glory of spring; now they were planning for the year ahead. Serious business. Neither of them seemed to run out of creative ideas, which they discussed endlessly and enjoyed passionately. They were standing in the scented shade, looking toward the river. The brilliant morning sunlight was shining on the deep broad stretch of water, lending the dark green surface a remarkable quality, with bright flashes of color like the heart of a fire opal.

"Hi, there," he called, his shoes sinking a little into the plush emerald-green carpet of lawn.

"Darling!" His mother turned, throwing out her arms in welcome. "Where did you spring from?" Keefe maintained his own inner-city penthouse apartment but called in on his mother and grandmother almost every other day.

"Hi, Keefe, how's it going?" Arnold asked, preparing to move off so mother and son could talk.

"Fine, Arnold." Keefe smiled, putting his arm around his mother's waist, while she stood on tiptoe so she could kiss his cheek. "More plans in the making?"

Arnold, a big, well-set man in his early sixties, nodded. "We have rather a splendid statue coming in. Came out of a Sussex garden. A lady Sphinx. Your mother and I are trying to hit on the best site. It will be enormously heavy, so when it goes down, it stays down."

Keefe, who felt privileged to have this man working for them, said, "Why not place her exactly at the center of the break in those trees across the river? It could be an impressive backdrop."

His mother's dark eyes smiled into his. "We'd more or less decided on that, darling," she said happily.

"Great. I like to get it right. I can't tell you how pleased we are, Arnold, with what you've helped us achieve."

Arnold couldn't control a pleased blush. "There's nothing I've enjoyed more. I mean that. This is a fine place to work and your mother's the best boss in the world."

"Not boss, *colleague*," Rebecca Connellan corrected affectionately.

"Well, I'll be off." Arnold smiled and doffed the cap he always wore. "I have a couple of helpers coming in this morning. We're going to dig a narrow canal running the full length of the west wing, with a fountain at the end. The sight and sound of playing water is wonderful in a hot climate."

"I'll look forward to seeing it," Keefe called. He

knew to the cent the considerable amount of money it had taken to establish such a garden and maintain it, but the pleasure provided by these lawns, these trees and formal arrangements and flower beds was worth the expense.

"So, where are you going this weekend?" his mother asked. "Sailing?" She knew Keefe loved his boat, which he kept at a bayside marina.

"That was the intention, but something else came up. Come and sit down for a moment." He took his mother's arm, guiding her to a stone bench set beneath a huge jacaranda. "Travis rang me earlier on, inviting me over to the house for the weekend."

"How absolutely extraordinary!" Rebecca stared at her son, fascinated. "Why did he do that?"

"Davina." He shrugged. "She's put pressure on Travis to meet his long-denied daughter."

"Oh!" Rebecca reeled slightly. "That's going to cause problems."

"It is."

"How did dinner go?" Rebecca patted her son's hand. She and his grandmother, Lady Connellan, had been kept informed of the whole business from day one. "I'd love to hear."

Keefe told her. He left out only that one unplanned, heart-stopping kiss. He might be able to talk about it in a day or two. Not now. Not even to the mother he adored.

"Good grief! It'll be all over town, I suppose." Rebecca sounded somewhat aghast. "Natalie Carlyle is never happier than when she's spreading gossip. This is going to create quite a scandal, Keefe. Are you sure this girl had no real idea of who she is?"

Keefe looked at his mother and half smiled. "Jewel's story is that her mother kept her secret well locked away."

"Do you believe her?"

"Yes and no. A man could believe anything looking into those dazzling blue eyes. She's very beautiful. Very sexy. And a whole lot more. Make no mistake."

"A multilayered woman," Rebecca murmured, pleased in one way but a little fearful, too.

"A clever, stylish, ambitious woman," Keefe said. "Who knows what secrets lie behind that beautiful face?"

Rebecca stared at her son thoughtfully, seeing the intrigue in his eyes. "It sounds very much as though she's going to overshadow Amelia."

"Could be," he agreed wryly. "She won't do it on purpose, though. She's very likable." He caught her eye and gave her his beguiling smile.

"Then, I have to meet her," Rebecca responded. "She seems to have made quite an impression on you."

"And here I was trying to conceal it. Don't get any ideas, Mother. Neither of us is taking the other seriously."

"That's a relief. The implications could be quite staggering. Amelia's been madly in love with you for years."

"Oh God, when I was hoping it had all worn off. We grew up together. Copeland Connellan—it's almost incestuous. My relationship with Amelia was finished a good two years ago, in spite of her father's pressure. She should turn her attention to someone else. There are plenty out there."

"Amelia doesn't want to be loved for her money," Rebecca said with sympathy.

"Then, she should develop her talents in more fruitful directions," Keefe suggested with a shrug.

"The first step would be to get away from her father. Travis is a throwback to the Dark Ages. Amelia's bored, unhappy, unfulfilled. She's finding it extremely difficult to get over you." Rebecca, who cared for Amelia, was worried about her.

"And I'm sorry for her. But I don't love her. I tried. Mostly I pity her. Travis has built this whole thing up, encouraging Amelia to think the two of us would be gloriously happy. Pure fantasy."

"That's sad. I feel sad," Rebecca said. "And somewhat concerned. Amelia would be devastated if you ever found yourself in love with her half sister. Travis wouldn't like it much better. He loves Amelia, as much as it's possible for him to love anyone."

Keefe compressed his mouth. "I think I'll wait a while, Mother, before I fall in love with anyone."

"Not too long, darling," Rebecca said. "Nan and I are so looking forward to a wonderful romantic wedding. Followed by two or three christenings."

"Let's get the wedding over first," he suggested dryly. "Sure you both haven't picked out baby names?"

"All we want is for you to be happy." Rebecca rested her head onto her son's shoulder. Keefe was the source of her greatest happiness in life. He'd been so special since he was a little boy. "When you meet the right woman, I'll be able to tell just by looking at her," she said with genuine conviction. "The past has left a mark on all of us. The future is all that matters now.''

Gracefully Keefe picked up his mother's hand and kissed it. ''As long as you and Nan need me,'' he said.

TEN O'CLOCK SHARP, he picked up Eugenie Bishop, aka Jewel of the golden hair and glorious blue eyes. With very little effort this woman could bewitch him, he thought, but he wasn't going to allow it to happen. Threats surrounded them. His mother knew it. Nan knew it. So did he. Davina was so desperate to find the grandchild of her heart that she was turning a blind eye to the world she lived in.

Jewel was waiting for him outside her town house. He was acutely aware of her—physical beauty, plus all those other assets that, in the end, a man needed for a lifetime if he was going to find any happiness.

''You're right on time,'' he said, slamming the door of the BMW and moving to the pavement to collect her single medium-size suitcase. Quite a departure from Amelia, who needed half a dozen pieces just for a weekend.

''I'm always on time,'' she said. ''The business world does not embrace people who are late.''

''You look gorgeous.''

''If so, I'm not the only one.'' She cast an approving eye over him.

''How are you feeling?'' he asked, stowing her luggage in the trunk.

''Confused.'' Her whole existence had been turned upside down. And not the least of her confusion was due to this man. There was something so compelling about him, so complex and potentially dangerous, she instinctively found herself trying to repress her natural feeling. Which was to gravitate to him as if he were a magnet.

"Don't worry. So is everyone else." He smiled at her, sending a ripple of excitement, like a warning, the length of her spine.

A moment more, and they were both inside his car, silent as he circled the cul-de-sac and purred off in the direction of Coronation Drive, which ran parallel to the magnificent river on which the city was built.

"It appears Lady Copeland is shaping all our lives," Jewel remarked eventually, looking out at the picturesque paddle steamer plying weekenders and tourists up and down the river.

"She's certainly trying to," he agreed wryly, giving the impression that he shared her concern about where these various relationships were going.

"I hope she's aware that the best laid plans go awry," Jewel said. "Disaster might be staring us all in the face."

He shrugged, as though to minimize her worries.

"Just so long as we don't start killing each other," she said.

"God forbid!" He didn't even smile.

"Tell me, is this Greg McCall my real or fake partner for the weekend?"

He glanced at her briefly. "Greg is more susceptible to beautiful women than I could ever be."

"Being in your position, the heir to a considerable fortune, would keep you from doing anything too extreme," she reminded him.

"I kissed you, didn't I?"

"Ah, yes, but you're well able to deal with that." Her warm, clear voice was almost sardonic.

"Well, I'm giving myself a couple of days for the effect to wear off."

THEY DREW INTO the Copeland driveway some twenty minutes later.

"Nice place!" he said.

"Do I detect an element of friendly contempt?"

"I'm sure most people would consider this a palatial home."

"Would anyone have the money to buy it even if it was offered?" she asked, and brushed back the fall of her hair.

"Not unless it was a Hollywood movie star, but perhaps they wouldn't be interested in the address." He stopped speaking to lower his side window and press the brass button on the stand. "Jewel Bishop and Keefe Connellan," he said.

Immediately the towering gates swung open, and Jewel's jaw clenched.

"*What* am I doing here?" she asked.

"It'll be fine, don't worry," he assured her.

"Fine for *you.* You're Keefe Connellan. Most people think you're Amelia's boyfriend. You're also a business partner of theirs, someone they need. While I'm sort of…a threat."

He turned his head. "Jewel, you can be sure Davina has made it very clear that she intends to bring you into the family, regardless of their views on the matter. And Davina's the one who counts."

"What about me?" Her eyes flashed. "With all due respect to my grandmother, regardless of her power over the rest of the family, she has no power over me. If I'm nothing else, I've learned how to be my own woman.''

He let out a soft laugh. ''Now, that's something I find very attractive. Relax, Jewel. All the evidence points to your true identity. You're a Copeland, whether you like it or not. You've accepted your father's invitation—''

''Only because you came along,'' she cut in.

''All right. I've agreed to be your white knight, but unless you plan on moving overseas, this issue has to be confronted. The *family* has to be confronted.''

''Don't I know it.'' She gave a heavy sigh. ''But I don't have to be a Copeland to have a life. The life I want.''

He stopped the car at the base of the low, broad flight of steps, switched off the ignition and turned to her, one arm lying along the back of the seat. ''You want to know who you are, don't you?'' He stared into her eyes.

''Yes!'' God, if she wasn't careful she'd fall crazily for this man. And where would that get her. ''I want to discover the truth,'' she said, trying humor to cover her nerves. ''If I can't get it from Travis Copeland, I'll have to drag it out of my mother.''

THE DOUBLE-DEALING HOLLY was at the door to greet them. She addressed Keefe with a face full of admiration, telling him the family was gathered in the atrium. It turned out to be yet another grand space, this one enhanced by a stained-glass domed ceiling, four very large Palladian glass doors that led out onto the terrace and the most spectacular Venetian chandelier Jewel ever expected to see. Davina, beautifully dressed and coiffed, sat regally in a sumptuous armchair that more than encompassed her fragile frame. She was flanked by her son Travis and Amelia—for all the world like two griffins holding up a shield. What made it so extraordinary for Jewel was the fact that they all smiled.

"Jewel, Keefe, how lovely you've arrived." Davina remained seated, while Travis rose slowly and Amelia made a graceful swoop across the marble floor to embrace Keefe Connellan warmly. The main thing accomplished, she then turned to Jewel, holding out her hand.

"Hello there, Jewel. We're all so glad you could come. Father?" She inclined her head as her father approached, a near identical smile to his daughter's painted on his lips.

"Jewel, my dear. Welcome to our home." To her shock he kissed her, bending to brush her cheek. "Forgive me for the last time we met. Shall we start over?" He looked very persuasively into her eyes.

"I'd appreciate that, Mr. Copeland," Jewel said.

He grimaced. "Why don't you call me, Travis?"

"As you wish."

Travis turned next to Keefe, extending his hand for the ritual shaking. "Many thanks for coming, Keefe. Greg won't be here until lunchtime, since we have things to discuss on our own."

Jewel moved on to where Lady Copeland was sitting so expectantly, her eyes full of a blue radiance. "How are you, Lady Copeland?" Jewel asked gently.

"I feel wonderful now that you're here," Davina said. "You can't keep calling me Lady Copeland, my dearest girl. For the time being, you may prefer to call me Davina. Amelia alternates between Davina and Gran. Now, won't you both sit down. We were waiting until you arrived before I rang for morning coffee."

It entered a few minutes later, on a large trolley wheeled in by the multipurpose Holly. The trolley was covered by a starched white damask tablecloth overlaid by another of very pretty palest pink lace. A small posy of pink roses rested on top, as well as a silver service, tea, coffee, delicate bone china cups and saucers and little wafer-thin sandwiches. Nothing so homely as scones, but a range of delicious, bite-size sweet confections to indulge in.

"Would you like to be mother?" Amelia exclaimed. Her heavyhanded attempt to be witty suggested that she was desperate to be friends. Jewel and Keefe had been supplied with little side tables, while the family faced a banquet-size coffee table. "Gran's hands are a little shaky these days."

"Sometimes they're shaky," Davina said. "But yes, Jewel, if you would?"

"My pleasure," Jewel answered easily, not given to pretensions or excessively formal rules of social etiquette. Besides, she was well aware of the challenge behind Amelia's sisterly smiles.

All the photographs she'd seen of her half sister didn't do her justice, Jewel decided. Amelia was very good-looking with her clear golden skin, her large dark eyes and long flowing ribbon of dark hair. She was also naturally very stylish, as tall as Jewel but thinner, pared down to the bone. She was wearing a jade-green silk shirt tucked into boldly printed silk trousers that picked up the color of her shirt. Her flowing hair was slicked back behind her shell-like ears. *Daddy's girl*, even if Daddy was an ogre from time to time. It was perfectly obvious, too, that Amelia was still hell-bent on pursuing Keefe Connellan. Amelia openly adored him with her eyes, she seemed almost to be paying homage, and Jewel found she didn't like it at all.

For several minutes she was kept busy playing "mother," showing her own brand of confidence. Surely one didn't have to study pouring tea? She had learned all about it watching her aunt Judith, who actually did most things right. The little lemon-cream cheese tartlets were so delicious, had she been at home Jewel would've licked her fingers. As it was, she was hungry enough to eat a second when Davina pressed it on her, but Amelia extravagantly shook her head to all offers. She drank her coffee strong and black. Unsugared. But then, she was a young woman conscious of her figure to the point of obsession. The pressures on the heiresses of this world to stay very thin had to be huge, Jewel thought.

"This is so extraordinary for me," Amelia said, reaching out to touch Keefe's arm. "I've never had a sister."

"I wasn't aware I had one, either," Jewel remarked mildly. "We all seem to be agreeing that I'm part of this family, but there's been no proof."

"You surely don't expect me to present you with some?" Travis Copeland gave a wolfish laugh. "You are the image of Mother. I knew you were my daughter the moment I laid eyes on you. I can't believe your mother's never spoken of the past, but then, I understand she suffered a nervous breakdown."

That set Jewel's teeth on edge. "I wouldn't express it exactly that way. My mother has suffered her private hell."

"I'm deeply sorry," Travis managed to say thickly, avoiding her eyes.

"A normal reaction," Jewel said, continuing to look straight at him. "You never thought my mother might have borne you a child?"

"Of course he didn't!" Amelia's dark eyes flashed outrage.

Jewel ignored her. "Then, why do I keep thinking of myself as abandoned?"

"My dear, it would have created so much misery," Travis explained. "My father would have ensured that. But the fact is, I had only Steve's suspicion to go on."

"Which should have been more than enough. You never thought of checking? Confirming his suspicion? Providing a bit of money for my education?" Jewel was aware of Keefe's eyes on her.

"My dear, I really couldn't do that." Travis threw up his hands, as though self-interest was entirely reasonable.

"Forgive me, but I can't help thinking of that as wicked," Jewel said. "You had a responsibility to find out, and if—"

"Aren't you being overemotional?" Amelia broke in, suddenly fanning her hair out wildly.

"Not at all." Jewel shrugged. "It's a professional judgment. I think a jury would conclude the same."

"A jury?" Travis Copeland's handsome face turned cucumber-green. "What on earth are you talking about, girl?"

"Jewel is talking hypothetically." Keefe intervened, giving Jewel a keen glance. "You must appreciate, Travis, that she spends her life as a lawyer. A very good one."

"It sounds like blackmail to me." Amelia flew to the

defense of her father, her eyes betraying jealousy at Keefe's intervention on Jewel's behalf.

"We'll ignore that," Davina said, sitting very straight.

"No, it *could* sound like blackmail," Jewel responded, looking at her grandmother, "but that's not what I'm here for. Please, all of you be assured of that. My integrity is very important to me. And, needless to say, I'm not such a fool that I'd go around threatening blackmail. What I want is simple. I know hardly anything about you and I want to know more. I want to be able to come to terms with the injustices of the past. My mother's been the real victim in all of this. She stopped living twenty years ago. That short affair and her husband's tragic death all but destroyed her. Now, twenty years on, I think my biological father should be made to admit to a lot of the blame." Jewel turned her eyes to Travis. "When did you first realize I might have been your daughter?" she asked quietly.

"Until you turned up in this house, we didn't know about you at all," Amelia said furiously and got to her feet, only to be told to sit down by her grandmother.

Jewel smiled and shook her head. "That might be true for you, but not your father." She turned to Travis, gazing directly into his eyes. "I think you must have wondered from the very beginning."

Travis jerked his head away. "I couldn't afford to know. It would have ruined me, my dear."

Sadness touched Jewel's expression. "If you'd searched all your life, you'd never have found a more vulnerable woman than my mother. She would never have made trouble for you. She wants no part of you now."

"I'll make it up to her," Travis promised in a surprisingly remorseful tone.

"How?" Jewel's voice remained quiet.

"I'll acknowledge you. Is that what you want? I'll pay compensation."

"You'll never get my mother to take money from you." Jewel shook her head again. "I don't think she'd accept your heartfelt regrets, either. After all, she denies to this day that she even had an affair."

"She loved me," Travis suddenly said, something about his expression intimating that floodgates inside him had opened up.

Amelia stared at him in horror. "What are you saying, Father?" she demanded, flashing an aghast look at her grandmother, who seemed unmoved.

"I loved her," Travis repeated. "I still carry an image of her in my heart. She was the sweetest, gentlest little thing. I could have found happiness with Thea. God knows, I found it nowhere else."

Amelia wasn't the only one who was shocked. Jewel suddenly reached over and seized one of her father's hands. "You loved her and you deserted her? How could you do that?"

Travis gave Jewel's hand a stiff little shake. "My dear, we were both married at the time. My first concern, I admit, was to keep it all from my father. To keep it out of the papers. Things are a lot easier today than they were twenty-odd years ago. A whiff of scandal would have ruined us." He sighed heavily. "You have no idea what my wife was like. The Antarctic should've been her home. She didn't want me, but God help anyone else who did. I admit to numerous affairs over the years, but not a one of them she didn't unearth. At least my women friends knew the score. All of them women of the world," he added wryly. "Except Thea."

"So, are there any more sisters I should know about?" Amelia asked bitterly.

"No—and I don't think you were listening, Amelia. Thea Bishop was the only woman to ever touch my heart. I'm not a brutal man. I didn't rape her. It was love. Love on both sides. It wasn't premeditated, either."

"You're just saying that," Amelia accused him, her dark eyes full of tears.

"It's true." Travis's voice was low and urgent. "I want you to believe that, Eugenie." He turned to Jewel. "I know that's what your mother called you. You were conceived in love. Illicit love but love all the same. Thea may have agonized, thinking I was glad to be rid of her, but that was far from the truth. If I'd been even half a man, I would've taken steps to protect her. Instead, to my everlasting self-contempt, I cut you both out of my life—Thea and the child I suspected was mine…. I told myself you'd be all right. That our affair didn't happen. After a while, I really believed it. I had my rightful heir. My only child. And that's not the worst of it. I heard along the way, maybe eight years ago, that Thea was virtually a recluse in her family home."

"Any more confessions?" Amelia's tone was glacial. For once she was staring at her father with open criticism.

"Maybe you and I should talk in private, Eugenie," Travis suggested, looking so woebegone that Jewel started to feel sorry for him.

"Well then, you won't need me!" Amelia jumped up from her chair, ready to bolt.

"Don't run away, Amelia," Davina begged. "Please, dear..."

"I'll go after her," Keefe offered. "It'll work out but there might be a bit of drama first."

"Tell me about it!" Travis said wearily. "I'm already having nightmares."

After Keefe had gone looking for Amelia, Davina turned to her son. "You want to talk? Then *talk*."

"It's all too bloody late." Travis swallowed. "Eugenie probably despises me."

Which just happened to be true until moments ago.

"I did." Jewel shot him a pitying glance. "But I hadn't known you'd once loved my mother. Is it true? Don't lie to me, please. I won't forgive this lie." She gazed at him fixedly but he didn't back away.

"You could put me in front of a firing squad but now that I've proclaimed my true feelings for Thea, I'd never recant. I was very much in love with her. She made me feel good about myself. If she'd been unmarried, a young woman of my own circle, I would've married her in an instant. And you know why? Thea would have shown me how to be a man. How to be a husband and father. Instead, I did something that destroyed us all. But consider how it was all those years ago. I was a married man with a child already. Amelia. A girl, incidentally, I've helped ruin. I know that—I admit it. I should've divorced Sonia years ago and been honest about my relationship with Thea. None of it would've been easy and I was a coward. I took the easy way out."

"That's true, but at some point you could've put things right. Or made them better at least. Maybe it's better if I don't stay," Jewel said abruptly, seeking her grandmother's eyes. "Amelia is very upset."

"We *all* are, dearest girl." Davina nodded. "But we have to move on. Your father and I have agreed that we want the world to know you as a Copeland. You are my son's daughter. My grandchild. Regardless of the distress and confusion, I'm excited about it. We need to be a family. *Right away.* We need to make up for all the wasted years."

"It can't be done overnight, Grandma." Jewel spoke spontaneously, almost demolishing Davina. Tears jumped to the older woman's eyes.

"We need to *celebrate,*" Davina cried, wiping her eyes with a linen napkin. "You should try to approach Thea, my boy," she said eagerly to her son. "Beg her forgiveness. Tell her that what existed between you was good. You should talk to her."

Travis studied his mother, as if she'd imparted the greatest truth.

"She's *exactly* the one I want to talk to," he said, almost rapturously. "If anyone will forgive me, it's Thea."

CHAPTER TEN

JEWEL WAS UNPACKING in the vastness of the guest suite allotted to her, adorned and patterned in every shade of blue, when a knock came at her door. She went to it, straightening her already-straight shoulders. This could be her half sister, Amelia, in a fighting mood.

Keefe stood on the threshold, a wry expression on his face. A face she found so attractive it made her head spin.

"I hate you, Keefe Connellan," she said.

He sauntered past her into the room, tall, lean, superbly athletic. "Did I say I labored for your love?"

She gave an amused little laugh and returned to her unpacking. "We've already agreed the last thing you intend to do is abandon yourself to love. Did I ask you to come in, by the way?"

"Now, now, you weren't going to keep me outside." He walked through the open Palladian doors onto the balcony, which looked out over the garden. "Did you ever start something!" he said in a low, mocking voice.

"There is nothing but nothing like the feeling of power," she said, equally mocking. "But what did you expect me to do? Sit there like a good little schoolgirl?"

"I didn't expect you to suggest putting a noose around poor old Travis's neck. When you mentioned juries, I thought he was going to be ill."

"Poor old Travis!" Jewel scoffed in an unsympathetic voice, feeling she could disappear completely in the room's towering armoire. "It might've taken a while to reach this point, but—wait for it—he's planning on taking a trip to see my mother. He'd better go armed," she muttered. "Aunt Judith might shoot him just for being on the premises."

"Is this something Aunt Judith does regularly?" And then, in a more serious tone, he asked, "Do you mean that about Travis?"

Jewel clutched a pair of tennis shoes to her heart. "Every word of it. Did you manage to comfort Amelia?"

"I'm famous for my comforting powers," he said smoothly, sinking into an antique armchair.

"Really? Then, you're going to wind up as her husband one day."

"Would that matter to you?"

"How do *I* come into it?" she retorted, snapping the lock on a suitcase.

"It can't have slipped your mind that we shared a brief passionate interlude," he said. "Kiss after kiss. And never for a moment did you pull away."

"I'll make sure it doesn't happen again," she said, lowering her eyes but unable to restrain a slight laugh.

"So, are you jealous of Amelia?"

"I avoid jealousy at all costs. But I will admit to a slight flutter when I saw you both in the garden."

"I was merely being kind," he informed her, watching her every movement. "Were you by any chance spying on us?"

"You learn a lot that way." She paused to shrug. "But, no, I was just taking in my surroundings. Both of you were too absorbed to notice."

"Amelia is in a state of shock," he told her. "Emotions all over the place. She doesn't know her exact position in the world anymore.''

"You mean she's horrified by the thought of a scandal," Jewel corrected.

"That, too." He stretched out his legs, crossing them at the ankles. "I found it very touching that Travis has been holding onto tender memories of your mother all these years."

"I could've passed out when he said it. Actually, now it's all about my mother. Nothing to do with me. Mama, apparently had a talent for getting the best out of him. To be honest, I would never have guessed. I don't think he fancies me as a daughter at all. I'm probably too much like Grandma."

One black eyebrow shot up. "*Grandma,* is it now?"

"Yes, it is." Jewel turned to look at him. "She's so frail. I want to care for her. I want to save her more pain. It'll be easy to love Davina. My hopes aren't so high for my dear father. Or your girlfriend, for that matter."

"Tut, tut." He stood up and came to her. "I think I should kiss you again. You need sweetening up."

He brought his hand up beneath the thick golden fall of hair.

"Are you intending to transfer your affections to the prodigal daughter?" she challenged him, her mind filled with images of him and Amelia in the garden, only ten minutes earlier.

He swooped and kissed her. A hard kiss. So weighted with emotion it sent shock waves to every pressure point in her body.

"It won't help if you're suspicious of my every move," he said with an edge.

"How are you asking me to interpret the things you do?"

"I would never want a woman who didn't trust me."

"Where does that leave me? Or can't you distinguish between kissing and sparring? I looked over the balcony in all innocence a few minutes ago and I saw you sharing a very tender moment with Amelia. That's okay. I understand there's a lot of feeling between you. You've told me you don't love her, but I'm finding it a little difficult to believe."

"And why exactly is that?"

"You have the most frightfully arrogant expression on your face," she said, without answering him.

"And your eyes are as blue as a blowtorch," he returned caustically. "Please don't misinterpret my motives. I do care about Amelia, but I was never destined to fall in love with her. Does that clear up your confusion?"

"Just so long as you don't tell me you're prepared to take a chance on the second daughter?"

"The nerve of you!" he murmured very quietly. "The fact is, Jewel, you're turning into a Copeland right before my eyes."

That hurt her, as was intended. "All right, I'm sorry." She sank her teeth into her lower lip. "Confusion seems to be the order of the day."

"Hell, yes," he agreed. "If we want to fight, maybe we should take to the tennis court. I saw you with a pair of tennis shoes. Do you want a game?"

"Like I told you, I haven't played in ages," she answered casually.

"I have a feeling you're bluffing."

"You're not a poor loser, are you?"

"I don't ever see myself as a loser, Ms. Copeland."

"That's good. Neither do I. And it's Bishop."

"All right, Ms. Bishop. Tennis court in about twenty minutes." He walked to the door, paused. "See you later," he said with a breezy wave.

JEWEL WAS ALMOST READY to go downstairs, when she had another visitor. This time it was Amelia, whose brown eyes widened when she saw her. Jewel was dressed in snappy white shorts that showed off her small shapely bottom, matched to a snug navy-blue T-shirt with a white designer logo emblazoned across an equally pert bosom. Jewel's golden blond hair was caught back in a businesslike ponytail. She wore white socks and white navy-trimmed tennis shoes.

It took Amelia a few moments to speak. She seemed quite thrown off, whatever it was she'd come to say. Finally she looked up from her examination. *"Tennis?"* she burst out, as though it were a blizzard outside and not a piercingly bright day.

"Yes, would you care for a game? I am told you're very good."

"I excel at most games," Amelia replied with no attempt at modesty. "Who are you playing *with?"* She appeared flustered.

"Actually Keefe has challenged me to a game."

"Keefe! Good Lord," Amelia said sharply. "Keefe could go five sets with Pat Rafter."

"That's okay." Jewel turned back to collect her tennis racket, resisting the urge to rap Amelia on the head with it. "I'm hoping not to make a complete fool of myself. Can I help you with anything, Amelia?"

Amelia moved to stand directly in front of her. "Don't take Keefe from me, will you, Jewel?" she pleaded in an unexpectedly girlish voice. "Don't, okay. I couldn't bear it."

Jewel could understand that. "I've only known him a very short time," she said gently, feeling a wave of pity combined with frustration.

"It only takes one glance." Amelia nodded sorrowfully several times. "Keefe is *mine*. He's always belonged with me. I just wanted to ask you not to take him from me. You're very beautiful and sexy. I don't have that, the sexy bit. I think you have to be born with sex appeal. Just look at you in that gear," she complained. "I can't look like that."

"Why would you want to?" Jewel said. "You're very attractive, very stylish."

"I don't have your flair." Amelia shook her head. "I have people to help me put my wardrobe together. I bet you don't bother."

"I couldn't afford it, Amelia. Besides, I think I know by now what suits me. It just takes a little time and experimentation getting things together."

Amelia was obviously finished with the small talk. "This is a momentous time for our family," she said darkly. "You know the news is all over town. It spread like wildfire."

"What news?" Jewel demanded. "Tell me *exactly*."

"That you're the result of one of Father's affairs." Amelia seemed happy to oblige. "Well, the only one to surface so far. Father has betrayed me—" Her voice cracked.

"Try not to see it like that, Amelia. Things happen in life. People do lots of things they regret."

Amelia scarcely heard her. "I'm going to find it very hard explaining this to my friends."

"Then, don't explain," Jewel suggested. "It's none of their business, anyway."

"And Father telling us he was in love with your mother! Did you ever hear anything to equal *that?*" She said it as though her father should be delivered to the nearest asylum.

"Strange to say, I think it must have been true. You can't see into your father's heart, Amelia."

"He told me once that I was the only person he loved."

"Amelia, you can believe that he loves you, but— forgive me—you're too fixated on him. You need a life of your own. A family of your own. There must be a dozen eligible guys wanting to rush you to the altar."

"I—only—want—Keefe." Amelia spaced the words very carefully. "That's why I'm begging you not to take him away from me."

Jewel held up a hand. "If he loves you, Amelia, I couldn't. *Wouldn't.*"

Suddenly Amelia relaxed, rushing to hug Jewel. "Oh, thank you," she said. "I really am sorry for the way I spoke to you that first day. I thought you probably were after money. Most people are."

"I'm not most people, Amelia. I'm your half sister."

"I know!" Amelia gave her a brilliant smile. "I just need a little time to get used to the idea. It's been such a *shock.*"

"For me, too," Jewel reminded her. "But it makes our grandmother happy. You're pleased about that, aren't you, Amelia?"

"Yes, yes, of course I am," Amelia cried, but it wasn't reflected in her eyes. "If you wait a few minutes, I'll go and get changed into my tennis outfit. I could give you a few tips to polish your game."

"That would be great," Jewel answered promptly, playing humble. "But I'll go ahead, if you don't mind. Keefe doesn't strike me as a man to be kept waiting."

"How *does* he strike you?" Amelia returned swiftly.

"Very masterful," Jewel said honestly. "Charming, clever, high-voltage, very polished, given to arrogant moments. But one can't help being impressed."

To Amelia, all of that must have added up to infatuation because she frowned. "He's practically a genius. Father says he's going to end up running the whole company. I might as well tell you, Keefe's extremely wary of you." This was said with a very solemn expression.

"Wary? In what way?" Jewel asked, thinking her half sister had all the attributes of a troublemaker.

"I don't know, actually." Amelia looked a little bewildered at Jewel's challenging expression. "I think he had you investigated. Gran would agree to that if you were to come into the family."

"How very commendable," Jewel said, tilting her chin. "I suppose you were all afraid I might sell the story of how I grew up to the *Women's Weekly,*" she muttered furiously, receiving a troubled look from Amelia. "Then there's the question of my inheritance. What do you think? A lump sum? A generous yearly allowance? Something in line with yours. I'm fairly reasonable."

With a horrified expression, Amelia retreated, moving backward. She fell over the same antique armchair Keefe had sat in, flushed with embarrassment, then sprang up again. "I must ask you to speak to Gran about these matters, Jewel," she said in a rush. "I can't help you with anything. It has nothing whatever to do with me."

"Of course it has," Jewel answered decisively. "We're half sisters, aren't we? We share the same blood. But to put your mind to rest, I promise you, Amelia, I'm only fooling." She laughed. "If the family went to such lengths as employing snoops, I'll have my bit of fun, too. See you on the court. I just might have a few tips of my own."

KEEFE WAS WAITING FOR HER by the time she arrived at the beautiful grass court. Palm trees, golden canes and tree ferns flourished in this section of the garden, with two sides of the wired enclosure completely covered by a climbing vine with beautiful white flowers.

"Hi!" Keefe greeted her casually, but his eyes sparkled with appreciation. "It took you a while, but the result was worth it."

"I should hope so!" Jewel unzipped her racket a little more forcibly than necessary. "I can't *believe* these people are my relatives," she said.

He came to sit on the bench, relaxed and vibrant in a red T-shirt he wore loose over white tennis shorts. "This is only a guess, but I think old Julius had something to do with it. What's the problem?"

She shook her head as though to clear it. "I don't think either of us was predicting a great weekend, but Amelia deserves good marks for a spot of troublemaking. I've just been listening to her tell me how I've been investigated."

"Darling, wouldn't you investigate me if I were in your position?" he asked, drawing her down onto the bench beside him.

"Who said you could call me 'darling'?" she chided.

"There's just something about you, I guess. Darling comes easy. Why worry about it?"

"I don't think *you'd* be very happy about being investigated." She studied him severely.

"I think I'd recognize that there's a fortune involved."

"I've told you—I don't want their money," Jewel protested. "Or if I got some, I'd start giving huge donations to my favorite charities."

"Which are?"

"Oh, the Children's Hospital, Leukemia Foundation, breast cancer research, the Salvation Army, RSPCA. I could go on."

"My dear girl, the company is quite involved when it comes to philanthropy," he pointed out, contemplating her long satiny legs. "Surely you know the tremendous charity work Davina has done over the years?"

"What about the others?" she retorted.

"The others are a lot tighter with their money," he admitted. "However, my own family has done a lot of work in that area."

"Well, good for you." She couldn't resist slapping his tanned knee. "I must apologize for my lapse in manners."

"That's okay," he said.

"However, that doesn't give you permission to go on spying on me."

"Not anymore." He threw back his head and gazed heavenward. "I have all the proof I need."

"Good thing *you're* not a fortune hunter," she said, her eyes on the clean cut of his jaw. "You'd be way too good at it."

"Oh, nothing like that. Are you going to give me a game?" He stood up and grasped her hand, pulling her to her feet.

"Sure I am. But we'll have to be sharp. Amelia's changing into her tennis gear as we speak."

"What?" He didn't sound pleased.

"She's also going to help me polish my game."

"How exhilarating! Let's go!"

They were enjoying a prolonged warm-up, each evaluating the other's game, when not one but three people arrived at the court, all smartly outfitted in immaculate tennis whites. Amelia, flanked by her father and an attractive young man who flashed them an engaging smile. Greg McCall.

"How's it going?" Travis called, looking so good for his age Jewel couldn't help but be impressed.

"Fine," Keefe answered for both of them. They left the court so he could introduce Greg to Jewel. Greg had brown hair and hazel eyes, with pleasantly rugged features. He proved charming but in no way ingratiating to his bosses and the super rich, and Jewel would have liked him for that alone. His steady handshake warmed her, she also liked the way he was able to keep any trace of curiosity out of his eyes as he spoke to her.

"What about you girls having a quick game?" Travis suggested, giving Amelia's shoulders an encouraging squeeze. "You can learn from her, Jewel. Amelia is an excellent all-around athlete. No need to feel badly if you're outmatched."

"What about a little bet?" asked Keefe somewhat dryly, caught between warning Amelia and letting Jewel's racket talk for her.

"Keep your money in your pocket, dear boy," Travis murmured. "Ask anyone how good my daughter is."

"I know," Keefe agreed lazily, "but you have *two* daughters."

"Don't worry about me, Keefe," Jewel said. "I'll try my best."

"Let's get down to business." Amelia spoke in a brisk tone. "I'm a very good coach, Jewel. For all you know, I might be able to uncover some ability in you."

Ah, the optimism of ignorance, Keefe thought, watching the women walk out onto the court. They looked beautiful, both of them, in different ways. Both thoroughbreds, natural athletes, although Travis and Amelia had a nasty habit of seeing the tennis court as a battlefield. He was sorry he hadn't been able to get a bet on with Travis. He'd been prepared to wager Amelia would crack first. Once deprived of her overriding confidence, Amelia had a tendency to collapse.

But Amelia was on her mettle. Her father's highly critical eyes were watching her. So were Keefe's and although she wasn't worried about him—Greg's. Having won the toss, Amelia elected to begin the game without benefit of a warm-up. She knew what she could do. She knew the number of good players who'd lost to her, so she wasn't prepared to waste time. This was destined to be one very short, very educational game for the half sister she would've been happy never to meet. Whose very existence was threatening.

Jewel wasn't quite ready, but that didn't stop Amelia. She sent down a center line ace Venus Williams would have died for. A shot even she had never produced before. "Fifteen love," she called, trying not to smile. After all the recent trauma she and her father had suffered, Amelia was looking forward to this. This was something she could do. This was something that made her father proud. Being a winner was everything to him. Her next serve she belted so hard it slammed into the net. The follow-up she put at Jewel's feet, scarcely able to credit the way Jewel picked it up, converting it into a sharply angled crosscourt winner.

"Fifteen all," Jewel called, giving Amelia a warm smile.

"That was lucky."

Jewel didn't reply.

In a way, it was the worst possible scenario, Keefe thought, his back pressed against the bench. Neither Travis nor Amelia had learned not to jump to conclusions. Since Jewel had lived her childhood and adolescence without material advantages, they automatically assumed she'd missed out on all the extras provided by top schools. In point of fact, Jewel had won a full scholarship to just such a school, which took into account both her academic and sporting prowess. Amelia wasn't the only natural athlete in the family. Jewel was a very good tennis player; had she made it her career, she might have reached the international circuit.

It was a three-set match none of them was destined to forget. Jewel took the first set 6–3, with Amelia so accustomed to winning, it rattled her badly. Instead of receiving encouragement from her father, she was forced to endure a barrage of criticism that was like a whip on raw wounds. Travis had grown into a professional bully, Keefe thought as he glimpsed Jewel's expression. It suggested clearly that Travis had better not try harassing her.

The young women returned to the court. It was obvious to everyone that Amelia had to improve her game. Which, thanks to her fighting spirit or fear of her father, she did. She hung in there to take the second set at 7–5. The third set, the decider, saw Amelia overextended, just as Keefe had predicted. Jewel brought her brains to the game. Also, she had so much energy, so much commitment, so much natural focus, that she stuck to her game plan and polished off the set at 6-2.

"That's one darn good player!" Greg jumped to his feet, clapping vigorously. "They're both great," he added hastily, catching Travis's ferocious frown, "but Jewel has incredible speed around the court."

"Amelia simply threw in the towel," Travis fumed. "I can't for the life of me think why Jewel was holding out on us." He looked affronted. "She's obviously an experienced player."

"She'd have told you if you'd asked her," Keefe said, hoping poor Amelia wasn't in for another tirade. She really didn't deserve such a father. And he'd prefer not to watch Travis humiliate his daughter.

"Amelia has a lot of work to do." Travis was still muttering. "She's getting downright sloppy. Of course, she's not used to Jewel's serve-and-volley game."

"Jewel would beat me," Greg admitted freely, looking at Keefe with loaded eyes.

"We can believe *that!*" Travis threw him a glance full of contempt. "I believe Amelia's beaten you every time you've played, dear boy."

"And you, too, sir," Greg said with a grin.

Those were the occasions when Amelia, carried away by the killer instinct she'd inherited, forgot herself to the point that she didn't allow her father to win.

Jewel put a friendly arm around Amelia's shoulders as they left the court. "That was wonderful!" She smiled. "I really enjoyed our match, Amelia."

Amelia eased away. "I'd call it an out-and-out attack," she said almost accusingly.

"Oh, come on!" Jewel realized she didn't fully understand the pressures put on Amelia by her father. "I wanted to win. Didn't you?"

Amelia stopped, gazing into Jewel's eyes. They were of a height. "Why don't you be straight with me, Jewel? You were showing off."

Jewel stared back at her in astonishment. "That's insane! I was having a good time. You're taking this too seriously, Amelia. There's no need to get so upset. I thought what we had was a healthy competition. Next time around, you'll probably beat me."

"I expect I will," said Amelia, who looked as if she might fall over any minute. "You took me off guard. I'm not used to your type of game."

"Oh, you can study it easily enough," Jewel said, all pleasure in the game draining away.

When they joined the men, Travis gave Jewel a smile that was almost savage. "Well, well, well," he jeered, breathing rather hard, "you are a dark horse, Eugenie."

"Ignorance is bliss," Keefe remarked suavely, standing up to offer the women a drink. "That was a great match. We enjoyed it."

Travis stared at Keefe as though he'd betrayed the family. "*You* may have enjoyed it, Keefe. I certainly didn't. Amelia didn't play intelligently at all."

"Why don't you give her a break," Jewel said, patting a cushion so Amelia could sit down. "That wasn't the Wimbledon Final, you know."

"Allow me to advise my own daughter. Amelia was raised to be a winner." Travis glared at Jewel with outraged eyes.

"But surely there has to be more to life?" Jewel picked up a hand towel and pressed it to her heated face. "Like discovering one's identity."

Keefe gave her a quick glance that said, *Don't press too hard,* but Jewel had had enough of this domineering man.

Travis's throat worked convulsively. It was clear that he took offense at Jewel's remark. "You have a great deal to say for someone so young." He gave Jewel an icy glance that was meant to be intimidating.

"Surely you recall I'm twenty-six, Travis," she said. "Not so young."

Do be careful, Jewel, Keefe thought. Travis Copeland could be dangerous. "Why don't you and I have a game, Travis?" he suggested before all goodwill disappeared.

Travis responded with his wolfish smile. "I'm not ready for you, Keefe," he was forced to concede. The last time he had attempted to play Keefe, he'd suffered a distressing bout of tachycardia. "What about you, Greg?" He turned to the younger man with confidence. Greg McCall was an employee. He wouldn't be fool enough to beat Travis. Even if he could.

"It'll be a real pleasure, sir." Greg had long been recognized as a diplomat.

After the two had taken the court, Amelia quietly burst into tears.

Jewel, who'd been enjoying her cold drink, scrambled up. "Amelia, what is it?" She put a comforting hand on Amelia's bare arm, but Amelia shook it off.

"Can't you learn some respect when you talk to my father?" she said, gulping down sobs.

"Not when he's so cold and cheerless, Amelia," Jewel replied. "So cruel to you."

Amelia wasn't going to accept that. "My father *adores* me! He's only trying to be supportive."

"God, is that how you describe it?" Jewel turned away, disgusted.

"You *do* have to take charge of yourself, Amelia," Keefe remarked gently, stroking Amelia's cheek. "I've never understood why you allow your father to bully you.''

''It's discipline.'' Amelia raised drowned eyes to his. ''I stop thinking about myself and concentrate on what I should be doing. If anyone was cruel today, it was Jewel. She tried to make a fool of me in front of everyone.'' Amelia's voice was raw with emotion.

Jewel's own temper came up like a gale. She watched Amelia pitch forward into Keefe's arms, burying her shiny dark head against his chest, begging for the comfort apparently only he could provide.

''Is she for real?'' Jewel demanded angrily, looking over Amelia's shaking figure into his eyes. She pulled the clasp from her ponytail, shaking her head so hard her hair flew about like a golden cloud. ''Why doesn't she just tell Travis to get stuffed?''

Keefe tried but failed to bite back a laugh. ''I think she'd be a little fearful of using that word.''

''Well, I don't need her picking on me.'' Jewel grabbed her racket decisively. ''I thought *I* had a rough childhood, but Amelia's must have been hell.''

She was outside the court walking at a swift pace to the house, when Keefe caught up with her.

''Jewel.'' His voice was deep and cajoling. ''This sort of thing goes on all the time. Amelia's been the victim of emotional domination since she was a child. By her father and to an extent by Davina. Don't pull away.'' He closed his fingers around her wrist. ''Davina's a very forceful, dynamic woman.'' He tried to explain. ''Amelia had to live in her grandmother's shadow. Which isn't to say Davina hasn't always loved her and tried to influence her in the right decisions. It's her money. Never forget that. Their whole lives are defined by it. The Money. Amelia and the money can't be parted. I honestly think she'll put up with anything so long as she's not cut off from the source. Her clothes alone must cost a fortune. I've never seen her in the same outfit twice.''

''Am I supposed to *envy* her? I don't. Go back to her,'' she said, her whole being alive with nerves. ''She obviously arouses protective emotions in you.''

''Oh, don't be stupid.'' He gave her arm a shake, a muscle twitching along his jaw.

''I'm *not* stupid!'' Waves of anger and frustration emanated from her. ''Why did I let you talk me into coming here? These people are crazy. You're talking *stupid?* Amelia acts like a silly schoolgirl. It's pitiful. I'm ashamed of her. I'm ashamed of myself for coming here.''

''It's a dilemma, all right.'' He moved her along, his tone somber. ''The only trouble is, you can't back out. You're one of them.''

''It's too bloody dreary. I don't *want* to be one of them. It'll never work. There's no dignity—they're all unbalanced.''

''Darling, you're preaching to the converted.'' His voice was as ash. ''So what are you going to do?''

''I'm not going to sneak away, if that's what you think,'' she said quickly. ''I'm all for doing the right thing. I'll speak to my grandmother. Tell her I've seen enough of the Copeland brand of family love. Travis Copeland is cruel and Amelia's like a greedy helpless child.''

''That's the way he raised her.''

''Well, it didn't work out too well, did it? I'll have to warn my mother. I think she'd lose her mind completely if he ever turned up at the farm.''

He let out a laugh. "Don't worry. Aunt Judith will fend him off."

"Aunt Judith works most of the time—I have to get away," she said abruptly. She felt too flushed and hot, dazed and defenseless against his sexual aura. "I have to clear my head."

"Why don't I take you out on the bay?" His vibrant voice turned seductive, effortlessly charming her.

"And *you* really disturb me, as well." She brushed her hair from her face. "What is it you want from me?"

They stood in the brilliant sunlight, staring at each other, Jewel with bitter pleasure. Half in love with him, half resentful of his power.

"God, you're a fire-eater, aren't you." He gave a soft grunt of amusement.

"And what about you? What's all this about? Why do you look at me like that? I'm a working girl. There's an heiress back there waiting for you. Why are you wasting your time on me?"

"We're in this business together," he said, resorting to mild humor. "You could almost say our...partnership was inevitable."

He had a talent for sending her into a frenzy. "*What* business?"

"You may be a working girl today, Jewel, and a very successful one, but you're entitled to a good slice of the Copeland fortune for *who* you are and what you've suffered. Your mother and aunt are entitled to compensation, as well. You may talk disdainfully now about how you don't want their money, but it's *your* money as well. Make no mistake. Sir Julius was all kinds of a bastard who did unimaginable things—but he would never have turned his back on you. How could he? Not only are you his granddaughter, you're the living image

of the only woman he ever loved. For his pains, he died
knowing she never loved *him*."

"How horrible!" Jewel had difficulty taking all of
this in. "I can't believe she married without love."

"One could almost pity him," Keefe remarked rather
bleakly. "Maybe Davina was waiting for it to hit her,
and it never did. Their marriage was virtually arranged.
She was already in love with someone else."

"This is unbearable." Jewel threw back her head. "I
don't know a damn thing about these people."

"What you need to know I can tell you," he offered
quietly.

"There are times you make me feel I'm talking to a
real Cesarea Borgia," she said with narrowed eyes.

"Never!" He shook his head, and his beautifully cut
black hair settled instantly back in place. "All his plans
failed and he died in battle. You, however, are beautiful
enough to have been the legendary Lucrezia who managed to turn pious. And could even have been pious all
along."

"Cesarea, on the other hand, lived and died evil,"
she pointed out, her bones melting when he suddenly
took her hand and carried it to his mouth.

"I'm not evil, Jewel," he said. "I'm a man determined to right the things that are wrong."

AMELIA, stalking them through the garden, was blasted
with shock when she saw them on the path ahead of
her. She squeezed her hands together in dismay, her
dark eyes glittering like glass. They were standing absolutely still beneath the shade of the overhanging
golden canes. Not talking, just staring at each other.
Caught up in each other's eyes. The atmosphere between them was so highly charged it singed the air. That

any other woman had the erotic power to do that to Keefe! It was more than she could bear. Here was the destruction of all her plans.

In that moment she hated Jewel. Hated her with all the pent-up rage and bitter resentments that were in her. Tears ran down her cheeks to her chin. She had tried so hard, as hard as anyone could imagine, to get Keefe to love her. She knew she always looked wonderful, poised and charming. They were bonded in so many ways. Friends from childhood. Heirs to the very rich. Now she found she couldn't escape her lack of self-esteem. Most people thought of her as the girl who had everything, but she lived with terrible feelings of dependency on her family, as though without them she was nothing. To please her father she had sacrificed her personal freedom. She'd failed to continue her education, just frittering away her life, without the qualifications to carve out some sort of career that might have made Keefe respect her.

Instead of accepting any blame, she now turned it on Jewel, the usurper. The viper in the nest. In almost one stroke, Jewel had taken her grandmother from her, and even her father had relented his entrenched position. Jewel would soon lay claim to a share of the family fortune at least equal to Amelia's own. But far beyond those grievous considerations, she was turning her large beautiful dazzling blue eyes on Keefe. She had a way with men. Greg had difficulty keeping his eyes off her, in those skimpy shorts and the figure-hugging T-shirt. She was so ostentatious! *Jewel.* Preposterous, like her name. If she could've had Jewel annihilated at that moment she would have done so. This was someone who didn't belong.

Amelia shrank back, giving full rein to the demons

that had grown up with her. She couldn't get over it. Keefe didn't love her. He had never loved her. Her tragedy, her great ocean of pain, was that she'd never cease loving him. Even now, she knew she absolutely had to have him. Only one woman could win, and it was going to be her. She had to talk to her father. Really talk this time. If they gave Jewel enough money, she might go away. Perhaps forever. The one thing she could never be allowed to have was Keefe.

Amelia wiped away her tears with the back of her hand. She had to act on her heart's desire, and to hell with the consequences.

CHAPTER ELEVEN

JEWEL FOUND HER GRANDMOTHER in the plant-filled solarium, quietly reading a book. She glanced at the title. Margaret Atwood's *The Blind Assassin.*

"Enjoying it?"

"Loving it." Davina looked up, her face radiating welcome. She marked the page, then closed the book, setting it down on the small table near her. "I've read everything she's written."

"That makes two of us." Jewel smiled, regarding her grandmother with equal pleasure.

"We share the same taste," Davina remarked. "Amelia has no time for reading, alas!"

"That's sad." Jewel sank into a chair. "I think people who miss out on reading must be somehow deprived."

Davina sighed. "Of course, Amelia's very sports-minded. She excels at tennis and golf, and she's very handy on the yacht. Which reminds me, why aren't you with the others? I thought they'd all gone off to the tennis court."

"Most of them are still there. Keefe and I sort of left them to it." Jewel exhaled, finding it hard to free her mind of all the rebuffs. "I'm afraid I committed a cardinal offense. I beat Amelia. She didn't take it too well. Neither did her father."

"Oh!" Davina pursed her lips, obviously getting the

full picture. "Can't you think of Travis as *your* father?" she asked quietly.

"No more than he can think of me as his daughter." Jewel shook her head. "I accept you completely as my grandmother. I think I connected with you almost immediately, but I don't think Travis and I are ever going to be close. I have too much to say for myself and he's not a man who approves of freedom of speech in women."

Davina laughed aloud. "My dear, he's famous for it. Even his father didn't portray such grandiosity, if there's such a word. Pomposity. It's Amelia I'm concerned about. Travis gives her hell when she loses."

Bullies do indeed know how to choose their victims, Jewel thought. "Why does Amelia let him?" she asked, frowning. "She's a woman, not a child who has to stand there and take it."

"It's all too much for me, my dear," Davina lamented. "As I've told you, Travis has always ruled Amelia's life. I tried for years and years to do something about it, but now I've learned not to interfere. There's sorrow in it, but Amelia has to break her own bonds."

"I certainly hope she succeeds," Jewel said with feeling. "If she doesn't, he'll never see her as an adult. He absolutely trashed her every time we came off the court, yet she took it as the most constructive form of criticism."

"I know. I know." Davina closed her eyes. "I also know how odd it is, but that's Amelia's usual reaction. Sonia opted out of the marriage. She opted out of trying to steer Amelia in the direction of escape. Whatever either of us said, Amelia only resented it. She worships her father."

"How awful!" Jewel burst out honestly, but her grandmother didn't seem to mind. "The thing is, Grandma, I don't think I can stay here the whole weekend. Travis doesn't want me. Neither does Amelia. I feel I'm here under false pretenses, since Travis will never see me as his daughter. I'll always be someone foisted on him. I don't think Amelia will ever care about me, either. We'll never be on equal ground. I can understand what an embarrassment both of them find me."

"But Keefe? What about Keefe?" Davina studied her granddaughter closely.

"Keefe is an enigma." Jewel glanced away so Davina couldn't see into her eyes. "Being involved with him would have far-reaching consequences. I've been in control of my life up to date, and that's how I plan to continue. Nevertheless he wants to take me out on the bay."

Davina inspected her with love and sympathy. "Then, why are you sitting here? Go!"

"You don't object?" Jewel met her grandmother's blue eyes. "We're not asking the others, which could seem very rude except that they've been uncivil to me. Greg McCall excluded. He's very pleasant."

"Yes, he is." Davina inclined her head with approval. "You go, my dear. But please come back for dinner. Will you do that?"

"For you, yes." Jewel rose to kiss her grandmother's cheek. "I have to tell you, Grandma, I'm very attracted to Keefe. And if I'm any judge, he's attracted to me. I'm proceeding as cautiously as if I were in the middle of a minefield. For one thing, I know Amelia might take any relationship between us as a derailment of her plans. Her plans and her father's ambitions."

Davina grasped Jewel's hand. "It's pretty much

about winning, Jewel. Marrying Keefe has always been Amelia's goal. It's not about being happy. It's getting Keefe to marry her. End of story. So unrealistic. Travis has convinced her she has to do it so things can continue the way they have. Keefe is working toward taking over as executive chairman of Copeland Connellan. He's got most of the board in the palm of his hand, especially since he was the one who pressed to buy Borodin Gold Mine. It's proved very profitable for us, relatively low-grade but a huge field. Keefe's full of ideas, but there's Travis as Julius's only son and heir.''

"Who do you want as chairman?'' Jewel was nothing if not direct. "Your opinion must count for a great deal.''

"That's true. There's no question in my mind about Keefe's capabilities. He's young, that's all. I don't want to burden him too soon. And there are other matters.... Matters from the past that have never been resolved. Keefe as a Connellan is determined to take back everything his family lost through my husband's maneuvers. This was after Stafford died. I did everything I could to make restitution but I couldn't force my son's hand.''

"So it's a power struggle,'' Jewel said. "If Amelia were to marry Keefe, that would put Travis in bed with them, as well.''

Davina laughed outright. "That's one way to describe it. Travis believes that cozy arrangement will ensure him the top spot. He'll keep the position until he allows Keefe to take over.''

"Mightn't Keefe do better marrying me?'' Jewel's eyes became watchful and shadowed.

"Is this a hypothetical question, my dear?''

"Yes, it is. I've just suggested to Keefe he's a modern day Cesarea Borgia.''

"Dearest, he's nothing like that." Davina shook the hand she was holding.

"All right, Machiavelli. After all, Machiavelli modeled *The Prince* on Borgia."

"You think Keefe, too, is making plans?" Davina held Jewel's eyes steadily.

"You just told me he was."

"He'd never marry a woman he didn't love. You can believe that, my dear. I know Keefe very well indeed. I've gotten to love him as if he were my own grandson. He's very much like another man I knew, his grandfather Stafford."

"You must talk to me about him someday," Jewel said. "Can't the two of us be family without involving anyone else?"

"Impossible!" Davina shook her head. "Once people see you, everyone will know. I couldn't call any of this off, Jewel, even if I wanted to, which I don't. I realize some things are going to hurt—there are complications already—but I must act according to my conscience. You are my granddaughter, just as Amelia is. As a family we must take responsibility for you and what has been done to you and your mother. I've been reflecting long and hard about your financial situation."

Jewel sat down again suddenly. "Grandma, don't think I'm ungrateful but I'm not here for money," she protested. "I'm here to open my heart to my family. Unfortunately my family, apart from you, seems hellbent on driving me away. Amelia has already begged me not to take Keefe from her."

"Really?" Davina looked dismayed. "Do you see Amelia wearing Keefe's engagement ring? No. For all that Travis and Amelia want it—as though everything they want has to happen—Keefe has never succumbed.

He doesn't love Amelia. I've told her that as gently as I can, but she insists he hasn't turned to anyone else. Which is true, and it's giving Amelia false hope. Keefe could have anyone he liked. I think one could safely regard him as one of the most eligible men in the country.''

''Amelia wouldn't love me for taking him from her,'' Jewel said soberly.

''Jewel, she never had him.''

''Try telling *her* that.'' Jewel's voice was wry. ''She'll never believe it. The idea's too deeply entrenched. Perhaps she's even a little emotionally unbalanced as far as Keefe is concerned. Not that anyone could blame her. He's that kind of man.''

NO WONDER THEY CARVED WOMEN into the prows of ships, he thought. While he sat in the flybridge nosing *Odysseus* into a sheltered inlet, she stood up front, a strumming breeze making a crackling pennant of her golden hair. A few moments before, drenched in brilliant sunlight, she had unselfconsciously stripped off her T-shirt, exposing the brief bra top of a bikini patterned in a swirl of turquoise, navy and white. She still wore her white shorts, but he hoped he was going to see the rest of her. She was a beautiful creature, yet *beautiful* wasn't enough to describe her. She had so much warmth, intelligence, life. She carried herself with the confidence and inherent poise that came with such a physical gift. Davina had it, too. So did his mother.

He knew Jewel was upset, although she was hiding it extremely well. He was upset, too. Mostly on her account. He was disgusted with Travis and Amelia. There—he had to say it. He'd spent years on Amelia, urging her to develop her own identity. She wasn't even trying or she *couldn't,* so powerful was her father's hold on her. Keefe had to recognize that part of the problem was Amelia's addiction to being an heiress. That was all she knew, but it didn't entirely explain her emotional attachment to her father, which his own family considered crippling and extreme.

Amelia, not generally given to bouts of anger, would be furious at being left behind. A natural enough reaction—had she and Travis not gone out of their way to make Jewel feel unwanted. An outsider. For his own part, he had to accept that it was pretty risky bringing Jewel out with him today. They were entirely alone in a world that was suffused in glorious blue—the dense cloudless blue of the sky and the sparkling sapphire of the fifty-mile spread of deep water, as precious to the inhabitants of the river city of Brisbane as their beloved Harbour was to Sydneysiders.

The bay was dazzling, famous for its mud crabs. Nothing to match them, except maybe the delicious delicate Moreton Bay ''bugs''—like a cross between crayfish and crab. The waters of the bay were teeming with fish. He should know. He'd made plenty of hauls. Red Emperor, pearl perch, snappers, black bream, whiting and the humble mullet; prawns of all kinds, huge jumbos, banana and tiger, king prawns and tiny school prawns just waiting to be caught. The oysters, too, were superb. The locals found them even more delectable than the famous Sydney rock oysters. Children learned crabbing and prawning at an early age. In their teens they went on to yachting. Almost everyone owned a boat of some kind, working through all the weekly chores so they could get out on the bay during the weekends and revel in all that it had to offer.

Even the trees and the vegetation on the small island

Odysseus was approaching were overgrown with lark-spur. On a summer weekend like this, with the weather perfect, the boaters were out in force. Every type of vessel was on the water: fishing dinghies powered with outboards, the more up-market family cruisers, most impressive power boats, one magnificent super-yacht belonging to a super-rich Southerner he knew, luxury motor launches like his own *Odysseus*. One day he'd take Jewel out on his fast little sailing yacht, *Sea Change*. It had been designed to run. And run it did. He took it out in all weather, thrilling in its performance. Off to their left, near one of the three large islands that almost enclosed the bay and kept it so safe, was a flotilla of graceful sailing ships from the local yacht squadron, rearing and plunging like racehorses. About the only thing missing was a submarine.

They dropped anchor less than ten minutes later, grateful for a lovely, secluded spot. He knew the bay like the back of his hand.

"Can I dive in to cool off?" Jewel called, looking into the crystal depths. "Or should I be worried about the sharks?"

He laughed. "Only the odd Great White."

"No jokes!"

"You're quite safe here. I go in all the time. So does everyone else."

"Great!" Like before, she unzipped her shorts and stepped out of them as unselfconsciously as if she'd been alone, folding them neatly before turning her attention to her windswept hair, which she pinned into a high knot. "Coming in?" She turned her head, a mesmerizing figure silhouetted against the lush tropical background of the island.

"When I'm finished admiring you," he told her

dryly, although the expression in his eyes was without reservation.

"Don't be long." Her pleasure in her surroundings was radiant. Her large beautiful eyes were extraordinarily luminous, close to the color of a gas flame. Today he could happily have drowned in the color blue. This was what he loved, what he had always been deeply involved in, like his father and grandfather before him. *The sea.* Jewel loved it, too.

In this horseshoe-shaped inlet, the water was dead calm, the dazzling blueness of the bay giving way to a deep bewitching green. He watched her go over the side in one graceful dive that didn't even create a splash. As an athlete it appeared she was very, very good. Something she and Amelia appeared to have inherited from their father, though Jewel mightn't like to hear about it.

After a moment or two he joined her, the two of them moving through the water as sleekly as seals.

"Heaven!" She turned on her back, treading water.

Yes, heaven. He could see *Odysseus* reflected sideways in the water. He could hear the faint creaking from the hull. They stayed in about fifteen minutes before returning to the boat. He'd called a restaurant near his city marina, asking them to make up a fairly simple picnic lunch, which they'd delivered right on time. Fresh caviar, chicken sandwiches, fruit and cheese, some little sweet things—he'd let them choose—a chilled bottle of Riesling. Very much his choice. Davina wanted them back for dinner, so best make it light. Amelia and Greg might be enjoying—well, hardly *enjoying* under the circumstances, which he realized he didn't give a damn about—a more elaborate lunch back at the house. He knew where he preferred to be.

Jewel went below to dry off and dress. She was back within minutes, wearing a different bra top. This one was fuchsia pink with the same white shorts. Her wet hair she'd scraped back from her face into a ponytail, revealing the perfection of her bone structure and small, close-set ears. He remembered the sweetness of those ears, their satiny texture. He remembered the curve of her breasts, though he'd never seen them so provocatively revealed. Not that it was intentional. He had the feeling Jewel shied away from being deliberately seductive. Which was just as well. Even spending a few hours together was complicating their lives. Endlessly... endlessly... The very thought tightened his nerves to an exquisite pitch. At that moment, he wanted her so badly the sheer pleasure of it was agony.

She, however, was deeply absorbed in setting out their picnic lunch, commenting as she did that *Odysseus* was easily the most luxurious high-performance motor yacht she'd ever been aboard. Brought up in tropical North Queensland alongside the eighth wonder of the world, the Great Barrier Reef with its immense Grand Canal, she'd spent a lot of time on all sorts of boats and found it great fun.

"You'll love *Sea Change*," he said, knowing she would.

"I expect you've taken Amelia out on it?" She bestowed a swift glance on him.

"Not on *Sea Change*, no."

"Good."

He went below, sliding a quick comb through his hair before changing. There was no other boat in their general vicinity. They had this whole place to themselves.

By the time Keefe returned to the saloon, Jewel had lunch all arranged. She'd even opened the wine, finding an ice bucket inside a cupboard in the streamlined galley.

"Okay, then, sit down." She kept her voice and expression calm. She was determined not to give much away. She'd always been in control of herself, of her male friends. Until now.

This was such a beautiful place. So lonely—no, not *lonely,* it was too bright, too sunlit for that, but alone. It might have been a lost world. She was in love with this man and she'd never felt less secure. Maybe that was what made things difficult about loving, she thought. The loss of self. The almost reluctant passing over of one's heart. Once given, she knew she'd never get hers back.

"What are you so serious about all of a sudden?" he asked, his brilliant eyes perceptive, almost reading her mind.

"I'm fighting something," she confessed.

"Could it be fear of me?"

"Something like that." She delicately licked at wine on her lips. "You're a remarkably unsettling person."

"I thought we were having a wonderful time."

"We are. Perhaps that's the trouble. These sandwiches are really good." She bit into one. "Here—" She passed him the plate.

"Thank you." He let his eyes roam over her. Her hair was so glittery it was casting a gilded veil over her skin. He felt if he touched her now, he wouldn't be able to stop himself from making love to her.

They ate slowly and quietly, in apparent harmony, both of them beset by a sun- and sea-drugged excitement. Both of them continually on edge.

Afterward they took the few dishes to the galley, where Jewel insisted on washing them up and putting them away. The galley, indeed the whole fifty-footer, seemed too small for both of them. Finally, she polished a couple of glossy red apples and took them to where he was sitting, looking out at the ever-changing colors of the water. From cobalt to the shallow lulls of emerald with a little amethyst mixed in.

"Want one?" She passed him an apple playfully, having taken a single crisp bite.

"Don't tempt me, Eve." His vibrant voice suddenly altered.

"It was an innocent gesture." Only half true.

"Was it? I can hear your heart pounding."

There was no way either of them could deny the tremendous sexual charge between them. Sensations curling over and over, like waves.

"If we make love, Keefe, our lives will change," she said, basking in his strong male beauty.

"They've already changed in a thousand ways," he pointed out.

"For the good? Can you say that? I never started this quest for a family. I thought I had my family. My mother, my aunt, my father who'd died at an early age. Now I have Travis and Amelia staring at me like I've smashed their world to pieces simply by appearing. Then, there's *you*." Momentarily she closed her eyes. "Whatever's happened between us, it's happened too fast."

A breeze ruffled his hair, pushed that lock onto his forehead.

"You want to fight it. Is that what you want?"

"I *want* to." It should have sounded final. It didn't.

"Is that a yes?" A crooked smile.

It shook her so much she thought she'd lost the ability to breathe. Her whole body felt weak, and she pressed back against the cream-colored leather uphol-stery. "Don't do this to me, Keefe," she begged.

"Me?" He paused for a moment, then moved to sup-port her. "I just need to kiss you." He turned her face to him. "I could abandon myself to you, to your whole body."

He opened her mouth with his own. "Let's go and make love and the rest be damned," he urged, aware of the faint shaking in his arms, his hammering pulse. He had never felt such an overwhelming need for sex. Not just blind sex. He wanted to merge himself with this woman with the thick golden hair and skin that tasted of honeyed nectar and sea salt.

She exposed him, his masculinity, to the point that he felt adrift and unprotected in an ocean of elemental power.

"You want this, Jewel?" he whispered, staring down at her, her every feature so revealing of the turbulence within her.

A hushed "yes," a whisper of breath against his cheek.

They rose together, he keeping his arms around her, bodies connected, both of them lost to the tyranny of passion.

EVERYTHING CHANGED for Thea Bishop in the days that followed.

Alone in the old colonial the next week, with Judith at her craft shop in town, and the kettle bubbling in the kitchen, Thea went hesitantly to the front door to an-swer the chimes. Afterward, when she'd had time to absorb all that had happened, she wondered why she hadn't fainted dead away.

Fully expecting to see their neighbor or perhaps their

handyman, Tom, she found herself looking into a face she'd never expected to see again. A face that even after all these years, she knew as well as her own.

"Thea, little Thea," the man said in deep cultured tones. "Don't be frightened. Don't run away. I know you haven't been well, or happy. It's all my fault. I can never forgive myself but I'm here to beg forgiveness of you."

Her voice when it came was dry and cracking, like an old woman's. "Travis."

"Such a job to track you down." The handsome face was working with emotion. "Eugenie wouldn't tell me."

"This is a dream, isn't it?" Thea asked. "I'm asleep."

"Not a dream. I wanted to come to you and I have. Will you let me in?"

"For what reason, Travis?" she asked faintly. He hardly looked twenty years older, if anything, he was more handsome, more substantial, his shoulders beneath his light jacket broad and well-set. The only real give-away was the silver wings in his hair, and even they seemed distinguished rather than a sign of age.

"Don't look at me like that, my dear," he begged. "I'm not an apparition. I want to say I'm sorry. So sorry. Why did you never tell me about your daughter?"

She felt so dizzy she had to clutch at the door. "But Travis, you didn't want to know. You had to return to your wife, your child, your marriage. Your father was a very important man."

"My God, I've regretted it all the days of my life," he groaned. "Please, Thea, can't I come in? I've had such a trek. Why, oh why, have you buried yourself in this godforsaken wilderness? It must be alive with snakes.''

''There are snakes, Travis. We see them from time to time but they don't bother us. This is my home. My refuge for the past twenty years. Come in.'' She moved away from the door, staggered a little, and just as he used to, he gathered her up in his arms, carrying her into the house.

''Oh, Travis!'' She directed her gaze upward to his handsome face. After the years of agony, nothing had changed at all.

''Shh! Be still, my little love,'' he cajoled. He didn't understand why she should forgive him, given the magnitude of his sin, but he knew in his heart that she already had. It made him doubly aware of the great wrong he had done her.

He set her down in a deep chintz-covered sofa that had seen far better days, coming to sit beside her, taking her soft hands. She was every bit as pretty as she used to be. That lovely innocence, the sweet vulnerability. Thea, his Sleeping Princess. Her body, though still tantalizing through the funny old-fashioned dress she wore, was almost childlike in its slenderness. Eugenie had nothing of her mother in her. Eugenie was the dominant female, like his own mother. He liked women who played the passive role, like Thea.

''Now tell me, dearest girl,'' he whispered, gazing down into her small face framed by the same glossy mane of curly dark hair, ''how I can possibly make amends. I'm ready to do anything, *anything*,'' he repeated, genuinely believing it, ''to return you to a full life. I know what's best for you. Listen to me. Trust me.'' He took her into his arms as she began to cry.

WHEN JUDITH RETURNED HOME that evening to find the man who'd been the cause of so much pain and unhappiness sitting like a lord in their living room, with Thea literally at his feet on a velvet stool, she did something she hadn't done in a long while. She erupted like a small volcano.

"I don't believe this!" she screamed, staring incredulously from her middle-aged-going-on-teenage sister to the wickedly impressive roué who was staring back at her as though at any moment she'd sail around the room on a broomstick. "We've had twenty years of hell! Sheer hell, with *you,* Thea, not giving a tinker's damn about your daughter, always holding your head in despair. And now you're sitting like a handmaiden at this man's feet. It defies *belief.* How could you possibly have the gall to come here, Copeland? And without permission. This is as much my home as Thea's. Good God, man, you've given me legitimate reason for murder!"

At that, Thea and Travis shot up, Copeland taking Thea's hand as though they were about to exchange marriage vows before execution. Though it killed him to apologize to this truly dreadful woman who reminded him of Sonia, he endeavored to do so.

"Please, Judith—may I call you Judith?" he appealed to her, using all the charm that had helped him out of many a bad situation in the past. "No one could be more ashamed of my actions years ago than I am. Ashamed because I took advantage of Thea's vulnerability. But I never regretted our short time together. I say this before God. Thea is the only woman I have ever loved."

"Oh, yeah?" Judith gave him a cold scathing glance. "It's a wonder the good Lord doesn't strike you dead.

I've had it on excellent authority that your life's been one affair after another.''

"None of which touched my heart," Travis continued, while Thea looked on in faint bewilderment, as though she'd never heard any of this before. "Only Thea managed to do that," Travis said in the grip of repentance. "This is the first time we've been together in twenty years and it's been a marvelously healing experience. I understand your shock at my coming here, Judith. It may seem incomprehensible, but I had to act. My mother is determined to bring Eugenie into the family.''

Instantly Judith's green eyes narrowed. "Ah, I figured there was an angle. You mean there's a conflict of interests. Right? You don't want Jewel?''

"Of course I want her," Travis stated with a heartfelt expression. "What must you think of me?''

"Why worry about my opinion?'' Judith said sternly. "It was Thea who was the victim. Thea and poor tragic Steven Bishop, whom you've failed to even mention. You're a weak, vain man, Travis Copeland, with no self-discipline whatsoever.''

Thea couldn't stand that; she stirred restlessly, tugging at her ankle-length muslin skirt. "Oh please, Judith, have some mercy,'' she pleaded, not wanting to see the man she'd once been so desperately in love with stripped of his pride. "Travis is not the same man who walked off and left me.''

"*Walked* off?'' Judith's voice soared. "I thought he took a fast ride home in his private plane. You're a fool, Thea! It worries me that you don't seem to have learned a thing.''

This was going badly. Thea and Travis turned to stare

at each other, as though one or both were waiting for a signal.

"Please, Judith, won't you sit down?" Travis suddenly said soothingly. He'd always been known how to charm women. Well…perhaps not Sonia. "Thea and I have some news for you."

"Yes, Jude," Thea chimed in promptly, looking so small and soft that most people would have hesitated to touch her in case they left a bruise. She smiled at her sister encouragingly.

"I don't think I could take your news right now," Judith said. "How long have you been acting crazy, Thea?" she asked, deeply troubled.

The extraordinarily youthful-looking Thea stared back, wide-eyed. "I've never been crazy, Jude. I really haven't. I was depressed."

Judith collapsed into a sagging armchair. If she stood a moment longer, she felt she'd lose the power of her limbs. "Has Jewel heard your news?" she demanded. "I really can't imagine what it might be, unless you plan to run away together."

"But that's it!" Thea cried joyfully. She let go of Travis's hand to dash over to her sister. "It's what we both want."

"God Almighty!" Judith warded off her sister, pressing her hands together.

"It will solve such a lot!" Travis came to add his pleas. "I know Thea can make me happy."

Judith's chin shot up. "I'll settle for you making *Thea* happy, thanks very much."

"I will, I will," he promised, as though that settled everything. "I'll take Thea to a friend of mine. She'll outfit her from head to toe and spare no expense. Thea is still a remarkably pretty woman. When she's dressed properly, with her hair cut and styled, it would be hard to find a prettier little thing.''

"God!" Judith moaned, hanging her head. "Is this what you want, Thea. To be cleaned up and made presentable, just like Eliza Doolittle?''

"Why do you always put things so crudely, Jude?'' Thea asked with resigned good humor. "Travis tells me he's always loved me, and I've never forgotten him.''

"Aw, hell!'' Judith was the picture of disgust. "I don't know what line he sold you, Thea, but he's really just thinking of himself. As usual. When Lady Copeland launches Jewel as a family member, her granddaughter, there'll be quite a scandal. I know people. They love to talk. If you and your one-time lover here decide to marry, that'll take the steam out of things. His PR people will dress it up as one of the great love stories of the century. So long as they remember to leave out Steve,'' she added bitterly.

"Steven loved me. I loved him. He would have wanted me to be happy.'' Thea lifted her small chin proudly.

"Okay! Fine. You deserve one another,'' Judith said, shaking her head. "Don't waste your time inviting me to the wedding. But you'd both better watch out if I discover that Jewel's suffered in any way,'' she muttered fiercely. "Jewel's the only one of us who matters.''

Judith went to her room to put through an urgent phone call to her niece—one of many to come.

She reflected ironically that Travis Copeland might very well end up paying for his sins in taking on Thea. After all, Thea had worked hard most of her life making *them* miserable.

CHAPTER TWELVE

"IT'S QUITE POSSIBLE your mother's gone mad," Judith concluded after she'd put Jewel in the picture.

"Obviously, she knows something we don't," Jewel said, her mind reeling at Judith's news. "You really think they were in love?" She asked the question with faint optimism. It would make everything so much better.

"Let's say they had the hots for one another at the time," Judith answered, then relented swiftly on Jewel's account. "They both say so, darl. We're dealing with something outside my comprehension. I've begged your mother to give it careful thought, but that didn't do much good. She and I suppose her fiancé have gone over to dinner with—wait for it—Sheila Hungerford."

"Wh-at?" Jewel was staggered.

"I expect Thea's going to ask her to be bridesmaid," Judith said with black humor. "Sheila's an old friend, at any rate. And she doesn't gossip. I suppose she'd be a good person to have on side. While I think of it, how are you doing with Sheila's affairs?"

"The brief will be ready in about three weeks. The case will be heard in the Supreme Court, but I don't anticipate it'll come before the court in under a year. Sheila knows all this. I keep in touch with her and the boys."

"Well, it all worked out there. Good old George has disappeared."

"They'll find him when they're ready," Jewel said. "So will I. I proceeded with the assault charge."

"So you should. He asked for it. Just one thing, love. People stupid enough to commit crimes, to risk going to jail, are dangerous people."

"He's been warned off, Judith. Don't worry. It's Mama we should worry about."

"I'm done with that, sweetheart," her aunt said. "I'll never allow myself to be caught up in Thea's affairs again. Including her wedding."

"But you *have* to come," Jewel protested. How would her mother even get to the altar unaided? She'd had to be supported in everything for twenty years. "Anyway, if you don't go, I don't go. I mightn't go even if you are there. Travis Copeland hasn't made a good impression on me. I'm not anxious to have him for a father, let alone see him as Mama's husband," she said disgustedly.

"He's only got one thing going for him," Judith added in a near-cheerful tone. "He has lots and lots of money."

"Money doesn't do much good if you're desperately unhappy," Jewel said. She loved her mother even if Thea was totally unreliable.

"Maybe he's been just that," Judith suggested, as though she was thinking it over. "At the risk of sounding like a lunatic myself, I couldn't help noticing that he appears to be genuinely fond of our little Thea. He's been holding on to her, and her to him, like they're both frightened the other will disappear. Like I say, when it comes to love, I haven't got a clue. By the way, your mother rang you, but she couldn't get hold of you."

"She could have left a message on the answering machine," Jewel said a little sharply. "I never in my wildest nightmares figured that Travis Copeland would want to marry my mother, take care of her."

"It might help shut the tabloids up," Judith offered cynically. "Their little affair will be dignified by marriage. I just know I'm going to read that they were childhood sweethearts. The way he agreed so readily to go over and meet Sheila makes me think they discussed it. Sheila and the Hungerford name is part of his plan—I'm sure of it. Then there's the fact that Sheila's father was a highly valued employee of Copeland Connellan and a rich man in his own right. I swear they're thinking along those lines."

"Maybe Mama *should* be locked up," Jewel said, rolling her eye expressively.

SHE HAD TO SPEAK to Keefe. Underneath, he was intensely passionate, as she'd found to her pounding excitement, while on the surface he maintained an elegantly cool, analytical and decisive mind. He just might be her means of staying sane. This was a serious quandary. Hadn't her mother been damaged enough? Perhaps that was the problem. It was her role in life to protect her mother. Like her aunt Judith, she'd come to regard it as a long-term responsibility, a personal obligation. And now her mother was planning to marry the man she'd been desperate to keep out of their lives.

It made no sense at all. Her mother, the victim, had turned to the source of her pain. For all Jewel knew, she could be going through some form of dementia. She agonized until she could get hold of Keefe. It was well after nine o'clock, but he'd already told her he'd be working late on a deal with a Southeast Asian mining syndicate. A tough deal, he'd added. In the days since they'd made such passionate, shattering love—the memory of which still gave her a rush—their relationship had deepened so dramatically, it was as though half a lifetime had passed. Indeed, the thought of him was interfering with her work. She actually wondered if Blair Skinner knew about this powerful shift in her emotions because he'd been surprisingly kind to her, not burdening her, as usual, with additional workload.

"I was just about to ring," Keefe said when he answered the phone. "Negotiations aren't proceeding as cordially as we'd hoped. I'd appreciate your input on this. Women often make better negotiators than men. More finesse, more diplomacy when dealing with difficult situations. Why don't I pick you up? We could have a late supper. Or we could arm ourselves with food and go back to my place. I badly need to see you. Touch you. Have you beside me. That's all."

"I need to talk to you, too," she said, fully aware of her own yearning. It must have sounded in her voice.

He laughed, his tone deepening. "Is it trouble?"

"*Trouble* is too soft a word."

Seconds ticked by. "I'll be there soon."

Thirty minutes later, the BMW was outside. When Jewel was seated in the car, inhaling a lungful of expensive leather and of sexy, dangerous *him,* he turned to stare at her.

"You're all right, aren't you?"

"Did you think I was pregnant?" She looked at him searchingly, and color flooded her cheeks.

"Well, if you were, I think my heart would melt."

She swallowed hard, startled by the tenderness in his voice. "Do you mean that?"

"Jewel, you're going to have the most beautiful baby

in the world," he assured her. "I'd be genuinely delighted to father it."

"Then, you'll have to be very patient," she warned him. "I'm not as wild and irresponsible as all that. My mother's the wild one. Turn off the engine so you can hear this," she urged, and waited for him to do it.

"Right, fire away." He traced her lovely features with a glance, feeling no longer an observer but her lover. This was the woman who had assuaged his every hunger, his every want, his every need. He was burning to make love to her again. She seemed to be trembling, so he reached out to stroke her hair. "It can't be that bad. Obviously you're upset."

"You will be, too," she said. "Aunt Judith called tonight. Mama and Travis Copeland intend to marry."

Complete lack of interest. "Are they eloping?" The way he said it, she could tell he took it for a joke.

"How do I know?"

"Are you serious?" he demanded.

"Yes." She nodded. "Travis is up in North Queensland as we speak. Mama carried him off to Sheila Hungerford's house for dinner. Sheila is a woman of taste and discernment. Most of all, she's highly regarded in the district, even when she was living with the notorious George. Her father was—"

"Darling. I know who her father was." He began to gently massage the nape of her neck, still staring at her with his brilliant black eyes. "I don't believe this."

"That makes two of us. Three, including Aunt Judith." Jewel shuddered. "I'd rather not know what Amelia will make of it. Now my mother's in on the scam—that's how she'll see it. Not only will Amelia have to take a big cut in her eventual inheritance, possibly even her trust fund, but Mama, as Mrs. Travis

Copeland, will be entitled to something, as well. Like two hundred million.''

''How come you're so accurate?'' he asked dryly. ''Anyway, Travis is doing it for a reason. He's always got a reason. He wants to put a respectable spin on the whole affair.''

''I remind you that I'm the result of 'the whole affair,''' she said emotionally.

Empathy flashed through him. Empathy and an overwhelming desire. ''Come back to my place,'' he urged, turning on the ignition. ''We can stop at a deli down the street. They stay open until ten. I'm hungry. I haven't eaten all day. And I'm starved for *you*. God!'' It was halfway between a groan and a sigh. ''When I think of the way you've changed my life...''

And I've let myself fall in love, Jewel thought.

TRAVIS COPELAND and Thea Bishop were married very quietly by a minister at the old colonial farmhouse where Thea had been born. Only family and close friends attended. Twenty people in all. Trusted people. Secrecy was understood under pain of being struck off the Copeland social list. The bride looked ravishing in a cream lace and chiffon gown reminiscent of the twenties. She wore it with panache. It suited to perfection her almost boyish figure. Her abundant dark curly hair had been expertly cut and styled, caught back at one side by a starburst of diamonds. Diamonds were at her ears, and around her throat she wore a necklace of very large, very lustrous South Sea island pearls. Her small ivory embroidered shoes were handmade. With twenty pairs of wondering eyes on her, she looked and acted as though this was the happiest day of her life. Even Travis stayed absolutely charming, every so often cuddling, kissing and touching his new bride, who smiled with newfound contentment as he tucked her into his tall, splendidly fit-for-his-age body. The happy couple were to honeymoon on a small exclusive Barrier Reef island, where the guests' privacy was so valued the staff eventually went cross-eyed from trying not to make eye contact. Or so Jewel had heard.

Jewel, as bridesmaid, wore a dress of palest pink chiffon over ivory silk, cut like a slip, the delicate fabric embroidered all over with bead-encrusted rose-pink flowers. There was no adornment in her golden mane, but an outsize pink silk rose trailing sequined ribbons was pinned to one shoulder. Judith, dramatic in her favorite emerald, had declined the position of bridesmaid, but Sheila Hungerford, who'd dropped the "Everett," stood in as matron of honor, looking very attractive in a silk dress and matching jacket the color of a good chardonnay.

Travis insisted the wedding guests be driven to the splendid Sheraton Mirage at Port Douglas for dinner and an overnight stay, to celebrate his wedding. But after joining their guests in a glass or two of champagne, husband and wife were anxious to fly out to their fabulous island so they could start their twenty-year-deferred honeymoon.

"Give me your blessing, darling," Thea whispered into Jewel's ear when it was time to leave.

"Do you really need it, Mama?" Jewel kissed her mother's sweet-smelling cheek.

"Of course I do, darling," Thea said. "I've lived for so long in so much pain."

"We *all* hurt, Mama." Jewel couldn't help pointing that out. "But all Aunt Judith and I want is for you to be happy."

"Thank you, darling." Thea's green eyes were a dazzle of tears. "I'm not so sure about Jude. I think she's cloaking a lot of anger behind the bright smile and brittle manner."

"You couldn't have managed without her." Jewel, loyal to Aunt Judith, kept on smiling. "Judith's straight as an arrow."

"Travis thinks she's one tough lady."

"What woman *isn't,* who can answer back?" Jewel quipped, trying to keep it festive. "I just can't believe he's stolen you away."

"I love him," Thea said, blinking the teardrops from her long lashes. "I always did, deep in my heart."

So much for twenty years of hell, Jewel thought. She wondered how her mother had the gall to say it. This wasn't the day to remind her mother of Steve Bishop, either.

"What will you do now, Judith?" Sheila Hungerford asked later when the happy couple had flown away.

Judith slapped a palm down on the dining room table, laughing shortly. "I may catch up with my own life," she said.

THE NEWS HAD SCARCELY BROKEN that Travis Copeland had secretly married a woman from his youth he'd never forgotten and who had borne him a child, when Davina decided to launch Jewel upon society as Travis's daughter and her grandchild. The great occasion—so what if Davina and Thea were the only ones to see it that way?—was to be in the form of a masquerade, the guests' costumes to depict legendary characters from literature. Chaucer to Capote and all stops in between. Three hundred invitations had been sent out. Not a single soul declined, including Travis Copeland's first wife, Sonia, who was currently expecting a marriage proposal from a distinguished career diplomat touted for an important overseas posting.

"Ever want to go back to where you were?" Blair Skinner, who was on the invitation list, asked Jewel one morning when she turned over the Hungerford brief and several others before they were sent to counsel.

"Just about every day," Jewel confessed. She was feeling depressed, plagued by myriad doubts and on the receiving end of Amelia's seething hostility.

"Sorry, dear, you're stuck with it. I suppose it's only a matter of time before you change your name to Copeland—or is that Connellan?" Skinner asked slyly.

"Forget it, Blair. I'm not telling." She waved him away.

"I'll bet your half sister, Amelia, is livid about your liaison with her ex-boyfriend."

"She sure isn't happy about it," Jewel said, "although he never cared for her in *that* way."

"I suppose I have to believe it, dear, if you tell me so," Skinner responded archly.

"All right, they went to the movies together. All I know is that nothing is ever as it seems. Anyway, I've got something that's really going to shock you."

"Really? What?" At the door, he turned back, an avid look on his face.

"My mother and f-father—" she could hear herself stammer "—are blissfully happy."

A bemused expression crossed his face. "How very strange."

"I knew you'd be interested."

"My goodness, yes. I never cease to be amazed at how little we humans know ourselves. Especially when we're talking about matters of the heart. I say," he said wistfully, "wouldn't it be nice if Travis turned into a nice guy under your mother's influence?"

"Do you actually think we could be so lucky?" Jewel was absolutely convinced it was never going to happen. Not to her, anyway. Her mother, who had acted irrationally for years, was the only one Travis Copeland wanted to care for.

His wife, not his daughters…

IF THERE WERE BIGGER PARTIES around the country, none got more media attention than the masquerade to be given by Lady Copeland at the family's riverside mansion. The city's social elite were expected to vie for the spotlight in an extravaganza of costumes. The women naturally would want to look their most beautiful. There was a lot of speculation about Natashas, Laras, Scarletts, Becky Sharpes, plus heroines from Jane Austin, Edith Wharton, perhaps Du Maurier's Rebecca, and the expected contingent of Shakespearean heroines and various Greek and Roman goddesses. A few women had apparently misunderstood; their costumes, already delivered, depicted historical figures like Cleopatra, Elizabeth I and Marie Antoinette.

Jewel had solved her problem with relatively little bother or expense. A couturier friend had run up a simple white toga that actually looked very good when she tried it on. The fabric was particularly soft and supple. With her hair swept off her face, her features rather than her golden mane demanded attention. She skillfully used makeup to accentuate her eyes, full mouth, skin and bone structure. A gleaming rhinestone-encrusted gold band encircled her head in classical Greek style— she'd had to let her hairdresser do it that morning— allowing her to call herself Helen of Troy.

Thirty minutes before the revellers were due to arrive, she was staring at herself in the mirror of her guest room, turning this way and that, when her grandmother called through the door.

"Open up, darling. It's only me."

Outside, Davina stood in her four-thousand-dollar gown of midnight-blue silk taffeta and lace, a dazzling diamond choker around her throat, diamond pendants at her ears, rows of pearls cascading down her front, her hair dressed in a high roll and supplemented with a double chignon at the nape—Oscar Wilde's Lady Bracken.

"You look fantastic," Jewel said, falling back to admire.

"I love playacting." Davina laughed. "'Is this the face that launched a thousand ships and burnt the topless towers of Ilium?'" she asked, studying Jewel with great pleasure.

"Either that, or I've just come from the bath. You don't think it's too simple? I didn't have the time for the Lady of the Camellias."

"You look wonderful!" Davina said. "So beautiful you're not quite human."

"My God, I am human!" Jewel protested, turning back to the mirror.

"Of course you are. That's what they used to say about me." Davina smiled. "Beauty can be a load to carry. It can be deeply resented, intimidating to some. But you have a lot of warmth in your face. You aren't the ice queen I used to be."

"Your life hasn't been happy, has it, Grandma?" Jewel said, looking into her grandmother's blue eyes.

"Not really, darling, but things have changed since you came into it." Davina made a visible effort to brighten. "Your father's the Great Gatsby, by the way. Needless to say, your mother's Daisy. She looks extremely appealing in her costume, and Travis has decked her out in very expensive jewelry."

"Oh, well, one of us had to get some," Jewel quipped, not really caring.

"Jewelry wouldn't suit the classical perfection of that gown," Davina said. "Otherwise, I'd go get you a few pieces. It's a superb cut."

"Of course it is. Daniel's very good." Jewel smoothed the toga over her hips. "And what's Amelia wearing? She wouldn't tell me."

Davina's expression was both sad and puzzled. "I'm not actually sure, dear. I only know she's got on a great deal of makeup and a magnificent ruby-red period costume with a big crinoline skirt and very little bodice. She doesn't look like herself at all."

"I wish she was happier about things," Jewel lamented. "The marriage has put a lot of pressure on her. She was her father's great favorite, the 'woman' in his life. Now Mama's completely taken over that role. Amelia must be feeling it."

"Well, she is." Davina could scarcely deny it. "But Travis is entitled to a life. I think your mother's going to demonstrate, not only now but in the future, that she can keep him happy."

"Such is the power of love," Jewel said, shrugging ironically. "My mother tortured herself for years. Travis stopped all that just by turning up at her door. It's going to take time for Aunt Judith and me to come to terms with that."

"But Judith's feeling better isn't she, dear?"

Davina and Judith had met at the wedding, taking an instant liking to each other. In fact, over the past week, with Judith in Brisbane for the masquerade, they'd become real friends. It had even been suggested that Judith sell the farmhouse—Thea had gone on record as saying she wouldn't take her share, something Judith didn't feel at all guilty about. Judith could then come and live in Brisbane to be near her sister and niece. Davina had promised Judith she'd find just the place.

Now Jewel agreed. "Yes, she is feeling better, and she deserves to. I would've had no life without Aunt Judith. Both of us are still worried about Mama. I know she seems radiant but I don't think she could face any more mental stress. It's crucial that Travis treat her well."

"Do you know, my dear, I think he will," Davina said not only to comfort her granddaughter but because she believed it. "In his own way, Travis has had a frustrating life. Anyway, I'm not concerned with Travis and Thea at the moment. It's you. This is *your* night. Travis and Thea have made their lives. You have a future, and I won't die happy unless I set things right. I've already told Travis and Amelia that I intend to change my will. It'll be taken care of this coming week. You will become one of the major beneficiaries, as you should be."

Jewel drew a deep, steadying breath. "Grandma, all I've wanted is to have you really care for me. Life is meaningless without family and love."

"Well, my darling—" Davina took Jewel into her arms and gently kissed her cheek "—I love you. I love you so much it makes me dizzy. Sometimes I think you're my own little girl come back to me, but of course you're a completely separate person. Your own person. My granddaughter." She sighed. "Very few of us can go through life without traumas. Some of them terrible. Money can't stop people from dying."

"Why are we talking about dying?" Jewel asked her grandmother in alarm.

"I'm not dying, darling." Davina shook her head. "I'm just speaking about the way life is. Whatever is ahead for you—and I wish you all the good things in life—you won't want for money. That's all I wanted to say. Your share will be equal to Amelia's. I have some jewelry, too, that I want you to have. You're entitled to a little extra. I'd also like to reward Judith, although I know she wouldn't hear of it. I'm good at getting around people, however. Both of you had a long struggle. It's not going to continue. Now, my darling, I must be off. Our guests will be arriving soon, and we all have to stand in the receiving line. What's Keefe coming as?" she asked as she moved in regal fashion to the door.

"There's another one who wouldn't tell me." Jewel smiled. "He'd be devastating as Rhett Butler."

"But of course! *That's* who Amelia is," Davina exclaimed. "Scarlett O'Hara. One usually sees the green-and-white costume that opened the film. It's the sensual red one she wears when Rhett makes her confront Melanie. I should've guessed."

"I hope things go well, Grandma," Jewel said. "People can be awful."

"Not in my house," Davina said, fine features tightening. "Not to me or mine. I'm honored to have you for a granddaughter, Jewel. I'm even happy about your mother. She's taken over the burden of Travis. Anyway, this is going to be a marvelous night. A night to remember."

Amen.

AMELIA WAS GLIDING DOWN to the hallway in her blood-red gown, when Jewel stepped out of her room.

It was impossible for either of the women to ignore the other, but Jewel was convinced Amelia was about to try.

"Hello there, Amelia. You look magnificent," she called. "I hope you've got your Southern accent down pat?" Jewel moved toward her half sister smilingly, hoping that tonight of all nights Amelia would relent her harsh stand.

"And what are *we?*" Amelia retorted, her dark eyes whipping over Jewel's white-clad figure and classic gold sandals. "A vestal virgin?"

"Just the opposite," Jewel said, determined to be pleasant. "I'm supposed to be Helen of Troy."

"Ah yes, the most beautiful woman in the world. How vain!" Amelia said darkly.

"Don't you ever let up?" Jewel sighed. "I'm not in the least vain. I just didn't have the time or money to go in for a more elaborate costume."

"Money." Amelia's brows furrowed slightly. "But that won't be a problem for long. I understand that by this time next week, you'll be an heiress."

"Being an heiress hasn't helped you." Jewel didn't delight in saying it.

"I'd advise you, Ms. Integrity, not to cross me," Amelia responded, her expression the spitting image of one of her father's.

"I'm not trying to cross you, Amelia. I wish you could understand that. The last thing I want to do is make you unhappy."

"Unhappy! Dear God!" Amelia muttered. "There's no way I'm ever going to accept you or your silly little mother. God, she's not even fully grown, just an itsy-bitsy flower child. I don't know how Father could be remotely attracted to her.''

''Actually he *was,* years ago. And just about everyone else likes having her around. I understand your feelings, Amelia. So does Mama. But you'll get married, too. You'll have your own life.''

''You enjoy mocking me,'' Amelia cried. ''You've done everything in your power to take Keefe from me. Stabbing me in the back. But then, Helen of Troy was a deceitful woman driven by passion into betraying her family.''

''Actually, most writers regard her as the innocent victim of her own beauty,'' Jewel said. ''And I haven't taken Keefe from you, Amelia. But I can't deny that our relationship has deepened.''

''You're sleeping with him,'' Amelia accused her. ''I *begged* you to leave him alone. Your behavior's been monstrous!''

''Amelia, you're shouting,'' Jewel warned her, fearing Amelia would be overheard. ''Grandma is so looking forward to tonight. Please don't upset her. You'd only enrage your father. He doesn't want any trouble in the house.''

''Father will never love you,'' Amelia pointed out vengefully, glaring at her half sister.

''I can live with that.'' Jewel shrugged. ''Anyway, I had a father. A great father. His name was Steven Bishop. But I might get to love *your* father a little if he makes my mother happy.''

''*Your* mother!'' Amelia almost spat the words. ''*My* mother is a lady. I despise yours.''

''I wouldn't make that obvious to your father,'' Jewel said. ''He just might take a different view of you. We have to go downstairs, Amelia. Please compose your-self. People will be arriving.''

"You go ahead," Amelia ordered, quaking in her outrage. ''I want no part of you.''

"Then, that's your loss." Jewel moved away, trying to leave bitterness behind. ''We could've been friends.''

But never with Keefe between them.

BY TEN O'CLOCK, the gala was in full swing. Round white-clothed tables had been arranged throughout the solarium and the rear terraces, the floodlit gardens and the aquamarine swimming pool. Glorious floral arrangements were placed strategically, and hundreds of potted cymbidium orchids had been brought in to grace the house. The huge billiard room had been cleared of its furnishings, transformed into a ballroom where dancers whirled in the brilliant glow of antique bronze-and-glass chandeliers.

Everyone appeared to be having a wonderful time, having taken in their stride Travis Copeland's new bride, so youthful and fetching in her exquisite pale-green chiffon gown—and did you see those emeralds? The near-unanimous verdict was that she was entirely socially acceptable, indeed, several society matrons planned on inviting her to their homes in the immediate future. And the daughter! After all the gossip and its implications, Jewel was considered a huge success, not to mention the very image of dear Davina. No wonder Amelia seemed to have her nose well and truly out of joint. She'd get over it, though. God knows, there was enough money to go around. The motto of the evening soon became *Enjoy every minute*. Especially the sump-tuous supper that was to come. Most of the guests had taken a peek at the delectable dishes being brought in.

Davina Copeland had always been famous for the high quality of her food and drink. Despite the excellence of domestic champagne-style wines, the guests were more than happy to drink Moët all night.

Keefe, who'd had a lot of work on his agenda, had decided to come as James Bond. He wore an excellent dinner suit, already in his closet, and easily acquired from his mother's garden the red carnation dictated by the early Sean Connery movies. He already had the height, the dark hair, the dark eyes and the tan. It was the easy way out, but he'd never been one for fancy dress. The only concession he made was to slick back his hair, Connery fashion.

It was to prove a decision that caused many a woman's heart to flutter. They found themselves continually watching him in the crowd. He had such enormous style. Not a man there to compare with him, and many were powerful and handsome.

Fully realizing how unpredictable Amelia might be in her present mood, Jewel decided the smart thing to do was adopt an easy attitude with Keefe, dancing with almost every man who beat a path to partner her. Keefe noticed. He could scarcely help it, but he divined without too much trouble that Amelia's attitude was the cause of Jewel's casual manner. Amelia, in fact, was bothering him to distraction, following him from room to room, leaning on his arm at every opportunity, playing to an audience of three hundred. *She* was the one Keefe Connellan was in love with, or so she meant to proclaim. Not the dazzling blonde with her grandmother's extraordinary aura. Amelia was the woman in his life. Or would be if only he'd come to his senses.

Finally Keefe had had enough. He took Amelia's elbow quietly and drew her out onto the terrace, walking some distance along so their voices wouldn't carry.

"Amelia, what's up?" he asked, not wanting to hurt her but not wanting her to follow him around, either. It was becoming impossible to capture a moment with Jewel, the object, the sum total of his passion. The moment he'd laid eyes on her in her white gown, her beautiful hair bound Grecian-style, he'd felt such an assault of sexual pleasure he thought it must've been apparent to everyone massed in the entrance hall. Judging by the knowing smile on his mother's face, his feelings were transparent.

Now Amelia raised her dark eyes to his look of feigned bewilderment. "I don't understand, Keefe. What do you mean?"

"Oh, cut the act. You do understand." He tried unsuccessfully to keep the hard impatience out of his voice. He'd known Amelia all her life; he did care for her. But not in the way she wanted. Now he had to explain. "You've been twining yourself around me all night. You should be off enjoying yourself. You're giving out entirely the wrong message. Surely you realize that?"

Here she grasped his hand, her voice impassioned. "Keefe, I love you."

His anger died. "And I love you, Amelia. But as a friend."

"You slept with me," she burst out.

His face turned intimidating. "Keep your voice down," he told her sternly. "When did I make love to you? Years ago. God knows, it was all a mistake."

"A *mistake.* How cruelly put."

"Amelia, I don't want to be cruel, but there's danger in your obsession. You can't cause a scene."

"You're in love with Jewel," she accused him flatly.

"Jewel has opened my eyes to so much." He could scarcely tell her Jewel was the image of his heart's desire.

"She'll bring you no happiness," Amelia warned, her dark eyes glittering.

"You know you're acting like a bad loser. That's what it amounts to. I've tried many times to let you down lightly, but it didn't work."

"If you don't love me, I'll *die*," she said through clenched teeth.

"Oh, rubbish." Keefe was disgusted. "Honest to God, Amelia, sometimes you sound insane."

"I'll destroy her," she threatened. "I'll destroy every chance the two of you have at happiness."

Keefe stiffened, reached out and held her arms. "Cause Jewel any harm and you'll answer to me. Understood?"

But Amelia, hysterical in her efforts to connect with him, threw herself forward and kissed his mouth. That beautiful cruel mouth. There was no one for her but Keefe. No one. No future. To lose him would be intolerable. To lose him to her half sister, a defeat she couldn't live with. There had been too many defeats already.

JEWEL WAS WEIGHTED DOWN by her own need to be with Keefe, despite her half sister's unreasonable demands, and she finally went in search of him. Her passage through the main reception rooms was marked by frequent stops as guests went out of their way to show their approval and acceptance. Her rise from nowhere to the top of the social tree was what fairy tales were made of, after all.

Keefe was nowhere to be seen. That left only the length of the rear terrace. Guests in all manner of costumes—including, for some reason, a plethora of the ghastly Hannibal Lector—were gathered outside the great ceiling-high doors, but just as she was about to go back inside she caught sight of Amelia's darkly glowing red gown.

As her eyes adjusted to the dimmer light, she realized Keefe was with her. They appeared to be caught up in a wild clamor of conversation. She couldn't hear a word but intuitively knew it was profoundly confrontational. Their public kiss came next. The classic ploy. Planned in advance. It could have come straight out of a romance novel. No expression of affection, but a greedy, gloating, defiant statement. On Amelia's part. Jewel wasn't such a fool she didn't know that. She'd read the books, seen the movies. The only hitch was that Keefe wasn't fighting it the way he should. *Was* he? It was a long kiss. Three thundering heartbeats. No hint of censure or revulsion there. Cooperation aplenty. Most men regarded kissing women as an extremely pleasant pastime. Few felt a sense of guilt; they believed it their right. However, Jewel spared that fact little thought. She focused on finding out exactly what was going on. Her own half sister! Shameless hussy!

Another idea struck her. Was it possible that Keefe, as a Connellan, wanted *both* Copeland sisters to belong to him? It might just be bizarre enough for him to find it exciting. Even as she thought it, she had to reject the idea.

In her cloud-white gown, Jewel sailed down the terrace toward them, prepared to confront them directly. She had no intention of creating a scene; she simply wanted to set the situation straight. Her mother had been the victim of an unscrupulous man—even if he'd married her twenty hellish years later. Jewel's life was going to be different. Let the rapture depart if it had to. Her progress, noticed by everyone on the terrace, provoked a near-ecstasy of anticipation. Most of the guests had seen that impassioned kiss. Most of them secretly thought Amelia Copeland a cold bitch. For all her polished good looks, she was perceived to be strangely lacking in sexuality. Now *this!*

Jewel's eyes when she directed them at Keefe were ablaze with blue light. She looked stunning, imperious....

"May I speak to you, Keefe?" Her voice was subdued, but it came out a little too much like a command. He could just walk away.

"Why don't you leave us alone," Amelia cried, flooded with jealousy. "Get out." The words spilled hoarsely from her throat. "I'm the only one who can make Keefe happy. The only one. All *you* can offer—"

"Be quiet, Amelia." Keefe's voice was filled with muted fury. "Why don't I take you upstairs?" he suggested, handsome face taut. "You're not feeling well. Jewel, take her other arm."

"I don't want to touch her." Jewel had had just about enough of Amelia.

Though Amelia gasped, enraged, she didn't fight being led away. Her big moment had been exciting and frightening at the same time.

"You can let me go now." Once upstairs she struggled to be free, wondering if it wouldn't have been wiser to keep her mouth shut.

"All your life you've known how to behave. And now *this,*" Keefe said, his voice so disgusted it hurt her.

"You're the whole world to me." Amelia turned to him and started to sob. "I know you better than she ever will. You've abused me, Keefe. Abused my trust. You told me you loved me." She leaned forward again to kiss him, but this time he fended her off.

"Cut it out."

"Is this true?" Jewel rounded to face him. Perhaps it was. Amelia when she was behaving herself was an extremely attractive package. Perhaps they'd shared a deep commitment.

"Of course it's true!" Amelia put a heavy hand on Jewel's shoulder. "I begged you not to come between us. Why did you do it?"

From nowhere, Aunt Judith appeared, a mesmerizing figure as Miss Havisham, her wealth of dark curly hair realistically frosted with silver and what appeared to be cobwebs, her green eyes heavily mascaraed, aglitter. "What's up, sweetie?" She looked quickly at her niece. "Everything okay up here?" Judith's antennae, honed to perfection over the Thea years, swiftly summed up the situation. A frozen tableau—the impossibly snobbish Amelia in a magnificent sexy gown that didn't suit her, Keefe Connellan who made even her poor old battered heart beat a little faster, and her beloved Jewel, whose lovely face had paled to the snow-white of her toga.

"Who asked you here?" Amelia responded with a rudeness Judith didn't regard well.

"Your grandmother, actually," Judith shot back, a power to be reckoned with. She gave Amelia a head-to-toe inspection. "You might tell me why, with a grandmother like that, you've got so few manners."

Amelia stared at her, momentarily speechless. Something about Judith instantly stripped all defiance away.

She was no longer the self-assured heiress. She was a young woman tottering on her feet. "What is it you want?" she asked more agreeably.

"I've spent a lifetime looking after my niece's interests," Judith informed her grandly. "As for you, young lady, it seems one of the guests has had a little chat with your father. Apparently you've been drinking quite a bit."

"Like a fish," said Keefe, who found Judith's presence bracing. "I've just suggested to Amelia she lie down for a while."

"Rather lie down than fall down," Judith commented, not unsympathetically. "Why don't you and Jewel return to the party, Keefe?" she said. "I'm sure Travis will be up here in a moment. I'll keep an eye on Amelia. That way I can get between her and her father."

"Has someone *really* spoken to him?" Amelia nervously bit her lip. "Or is every word you say a lie?"

"Well, you'd know about lying." Keefe turned away, looking utterly fed up.

"I rarely lie, my girl," Judith said, looking decidedly formidable. "Maybe your father will forgive you. Anyone can overindulge."

"I haven't had *that* much." Amelia shook her head, feeling suddenly exceedingly foolish and hugging her body fearfully.

"Why don't we pop along to your room," Judith murmured, sounding genuinely kind. She took Amelia's arm. "Don't worry—I'll stay close. I've never yet met the man to intimidate me."

"Isn't that the truth!" Jewel gave her aunt a grateful smile.

A moment more, then they heard footsteps along the corridor. From the heavy tread, a man's footsteps.

"Wonderful. That'll be Travis," Keefe said, hastily throwing open a door and drawing Jewel inside. "Such dreadful people, the Copelands," he groaned.

"Are you including me?" Jewel spoke into the darkness, intoxicated by his very touch. *Possessed.* She didn't want to be. Not yet. There were nagging doubts in her mind.

"Of course not." He leaned close to her, licked her earlobe with the tip of his tongue, igniting her flesh.

"What room are we in?" she asked, so close to him it was no more than a breath.

"I've no idea." He pulled her back against him, slowing caressing her breasts. "But I'm not going to risk turning on the light. God, I've missed you, missed you." This through clenched teeth. "You've been keeping yourself from me all night."

"Amelia is suffering." She said it as though it was his fault. And hers.

"Let her suffer," Keefe answered almost ferociously. He was still disgusted with Amelia's Academy Award–winning performance. "She needs to get her life sorted out." His hand fell to Jewel's hips, gripping them with the urgency of his hunger.

"Did you ever love her?" Jewel pivoted in his arms, putting her hands against his chest to fend him off.

His frustration was unrestrained. "For the last time— we had a brief, ill-advised affair. I don't want to sound like an utter cad, but it left me with the feeling that I'd been trapped."

"So you dumped her?"

"You wanted me to go ahead and marry her?" he

challenged, lowering his head to barely kiss her. A warning.

"Might you at some stage want to dump me?" she asked with a heavy heart.

"Only if you pushed me into it by constantly talking about Amelia," he answered crisply. "Amelia is my friend. Maybe she's not even that anymore. I told her many times it was over, but she refused to listen. It's all so Goddamn boring. Amelia's trying to sell you quite a story. I'm surprised she hasn't offered to show you an intimate video." Now his voice was caustic.

"The affair must have been fairly intense to cause so much misery," Jewel persisted, not knowing where this was leading. Maybe a first-class argument.

"Actually, Amelia moved through it like a somnambulist," he said. "You don't know what you're dealing with here. There's a kind of paradox to Amelia. She's passionate with words, but she might as well have been Joan of Arc in a full suit of armor in bed."

Her breath was unsteady in her throat, her nipples drawn to painful peaks by his ministrations.

"Not like you. Never like you." Now he kissed her. "What do you want me to do, go down on my knees?" He did so pressing his face against her body, his arms encircling her hips, drawing her to him.

"Keefe!" Flames crackled and burned.

"You're beautiful. So beautiful!" Slowly he stood up, still holding her, bringing his lips to the base of her throat. "You feel like silk." He moved his mouth over hers, causing a great surge of emotion. "I want you so badly. Feel me. I'm hard with it." There was a sharp catch in his breath.

She couldn't stop her hand from sliding down, her whole body trembling as she curved her hand over him.

"I want to fill you with my need." He withdrew his mouth from hers to look into her eyes. "I want to make love to you for a thousand years. You have to come home with me tonight, my Jewel."

Everything in her was rising to him like sap to a tree, when suddenly, without warning, the door opened and the light in the room flashed on, exposing paneled walls, a bar, deep armchairs and enough electronic equipment to blow half the fuses in the city. Travis Copeland was staring at them with such disapproval that he might have caught them rolling madly around a bed, stark naked, disgorging frenzied cries.

"When it pleases you," he said icily, as though he had a bishop's miter on his head, "you might come downstairs. I have to tell you, Keefe, you've upset Amelia terribly."

"You're one to talk," Keefe drawled, in no way impressed.

"I see you've transferred your affections to my other daughter." Travis looked at the wordless Jewel.

"I don't know how it's any of your business, Travis. Your attitude toward Jewel could hardly be called fatherly."

"She is nevertheless my daughter," Travis said. "What I'm not sure of is *your* strategy." With that he stalked off, pointedly leaving the door open.

"I have a feeling that, given the opportunity, both Travis and Amelia would have made terrific actors," Keefe said. "They seem to be able to take on any role at will. Glenn Close wasn't half as menacing as Amelia. Now Travis is *your father*. The man destined to give you away. What a thought!"

"No one is giving me away," Jewel snapped, one moment overwhelmed by passion, the next perversely hostile. "As far as I can see, it's difficult to believe a single thing any man says."

HE'D BEEN FOLLOWING HER for weeks, watching, waiting. He knew where she lived. He knew where she worked. He knew her daily schedule—what time she got up, what time she left for work, what time she left her office building in the evening. He knew about her affair with Keefe Connellan. He knew they slept together. Most of all, he knew that her grandmother, the high and mighty Lady Davina Copeland, had received her into the family. He knew all about the gala masquerade at the Copeland mansion, thrown in her honor. He'd seen the photograph of her with her grandmother in that morning's paper.

Today he'd tracked her to the Copeland mansion where he supposed she might stay for the night or, he fervently hoped, go home. Connellan would probably drive here in his bloody expensive BMW. Chances were, Connellan would stay. Then again, he might not. They tended to be a bit erratic. Connellan was a high-flier who probably had plenty of early-morning calls.

At the moment he was sitting very uncomfortably in his car outside the Copeland place, lost in the shadows, hoping she and Connellan would drive out. It was past two in the morning—he'd been parked down the road since seven. He'd been watching a lot of guests finally depart. They must have had a wonderful evening, damn the lot of them. There was much laughing, many happy calls of good-night. If he had to, he'd wait until those massive wrought-iron gates finally closed. He had plenty of time on his hands now that she'd ruined his life.

Bitch! She wasn't getting away with it. He didn't care

about anything anymore except getting even. He'd waited so long he was growing impatient. Ten minutes later, off guard for a moment while he lit another cigarette, he lifted his head to catch sight, first of her gleaming hair, then of her in the passenger seat of a big Mercedes. He didn't know the driver. Who the hell would? He had a damn deerstalker on his head, the fool. He couldn't see the face but it certainly wasn't Connellan. No one could miss *him,* arrogant bastard. They were a pair, those two. He gave them a few moments, then turned on the ignition and drew away from the curb.

At least she was going home.

AT ALMOST THE MOMENT Blair Skinner, with Jewel in tow, drove through the gates of the Copeland mansion, Keefe was asking Judith, who was having a very good time with a Mad Hatter aka Queen's Counsel, what had happened to Jewel. They couldn't finish the evening like this, more or less estranged and all because of bloody Amelia. He'd seen his mother off a good hour before, and Davina had long since retired.

"But she's gone, darling." Judith paused, champagne glass halfway to her mouth. "She left with that fellow she works for."

"Skinner," the Mad Hatter said. "You think there's something between them?"

"Isn't my niece gorgeous?" Judith smiled.

"I know someone else who's gorgeous." The Mad Hatter gathered Judith up for a dance. Judith was loving it.

Keefe, however, felt on edge, under a lot of strain. He hurried to his car, fully intending to pay Jewel a visit. He *had* to straighten out the situation. Amelia got her kicks stirring things up. But Amelia had problems—and so would he if he couldn't convince Jewel she was very important to him in every way. He'd waited a long time to fall in love. It was the most wonderful feeling in the world. At the same time, it was an agony. In his corporate life he'd been trained to conceal most of his feelings. A negotiator knew better than to show his hand, but he'd made no attempt to hide his desire from Jewel.

Maybe that was it. She knew, couldn't fail to know, how much he wanted her. He had to make it abundantly clear that he loved her, too. He loved her, although at the beginning he'd struggled *not* to love her. He had expressed in every possible way his physical hunger for her; now he had to communicate his love. He was a great communicator on the job, but he'd be a failure if he couldn't convince Jewel she was the best thing ever to happen to him. He wanted to marry her. His mother had suggested he do so quickly.

"She's a wonderful girl. Someone special. Don't let her get away," Rebecca had said.

Up ahead, he saw Blair Skinner's Mercedes stopped at a red light. A small beat-up car was behind it. For some reason he noted the number plate, filing it away in his mind. The car was heading in the same direction as Skinner. Nothing unusual about that. So was he. At this time—he glanced at the clock on the dashboard—nearly two-thirty, there was very little traffic. In many ways it had been a wonderful night. A triumph for Jewel. It wasn't just that she looked beautiful, though no one could fail to be moved by her beauty, but she was so warm, friendly and intelligent with a sense of humor that people found contagious.

What was that guy *doing?* Twenty minutes later, the

question resounded in him. Skinner had stopped in front of Jewel's town house, and she got out, waving to him as he drove away. Skinner could at least have pulled around to the right side, Keefe thought. Now Jewel had to cross the road, even if it was quiet and hushed.

Keefe knew the moment before she stepped onto the pavement what was going to happen. "God Almighty!"

The guy was trying to kill her. Keefe sensed it immediately. The small car accelerated, quickly picking up speed. Startled, Jewel looked toward it, half dazzled by the high beam, an easy target caught in the spotlight. Without the slightest thought for himself, Keefe trod on the accelerator, and the BMW responded with a real burst of power, smashing into the back of the small car ahead, sending it careering off the road and plunging into a tree. Within seconds, Keefe was out of his car, running toward Jewel who was standing there in shock.

"Are you all right?" He put his face right up to hers, as if she were deaf. "Jewel? Are you all right?"

"Fine." But she shook her head. "God, this is a nightmare."

The horn of the small car was blaring. The driver's body must be pressed against it.

"Get back," Keefe ordered. "I have to move him out of there. The car could catch fire."

"Oh, Keefe, oh no!" She clutched at him with desperate urgency, but he broke away, going straight to the crashed car. Already he could hear the sound of a police siren. Natural human curiosity was drawing people in night attire onto the street.

The man was alive but his breathing was labored. His head and torso had struck the wheel. At first, because the assailant was so disheveled, Keefe didn't realize who it was. Then it struck him.

George Everett.

A long second passed as Keefe considered leaving him there. The man was an attempted murderer. But leave him to God. Leave him to the police. Keefe pulled Everett clear, although it didn't seem likely that the car would catch fire. The police siren was closer now. Everett was coming round, groaning tortured obscenities.

Keefe glanced up as a police officer approached, shining a torch. "You'd better get an ambulance," Keefe said.

"On the way. Here, let me get a look at him. Mr. Connellan, isn't it?" The policeman was staring.

Keefe nodded. "And this is George Everett. I've had dealings with him before. Tonight he attempted to run down Ms. Jewel Copeland as she went to cross the street to her town house. She's standing in front of it now. I'm ready to make a statement. You might have to wait a little while for Ms. Copeland's. She's had a tremendous shock."

"We'll take care of it, sir," the officer responded, and Keefe walked back to the woman he loved.

IT WAS ALMOST DAYLIGHT before the street had settled. Everett's car was a write-off. Keefe's car had come off much better, but it was in no condition to drive. He'd already decided to sell it after repairs and buy another. Not that he intended to go anywhere. He felt he could never again leave Jewel's side. At least, not until George Everett had been safely locked away. Both of them had made statements to the police. It would be all over the newspapers; no way to avoid it. No way to avoid the necessary phone calls, either. They decided Davina and his mother should be allowed to sleep.

Travis took the call at the house, sounding absolutely shocked. He then asked to speak to Jewel, confounding her with a truly fatherly response.

"This is one weird night," Jewel said after she put down the phone. "Weirder and weirder. Travis sounded so...different. Like he really cared. He's going to call later to make quite sure I'm all right. He wants us both to come over to the house when we're ready."

"Just as I figured," Keefe said dryly. "You're starting to get to him."

"Did it really have to take almost getting run down? Anyway, I wouldn't be here except for you," Jewel said. "He was really going after me! Trying to kill me. Isn't that dreadful?"

"It is and he was," Keefe agreed grimly. "He'd been tailing you from the house. Probably watching you for weeks. Losing the good life has obviously turned his mind."

"It's a horrible feeling knowing someone hates you so much they want to kill you," Jewel said, deeply disturbed.

"Try to remember he's an ugly character, my darling." Keefe came to sit beside her on the sofa, drawing her into his arms. She'd taken off her white gown and freed her golden hair. Now she was wearing a pink satin robe. "We'll have to tell Sheila before she gets it from elsewhere," he murmured.

"Why didn't she see the menacing quality in him?" Jewel asked, settling her head on his shoulder with a deep sigh.

"I can guarantee he was on his best behavior until they were married." Keefe turned his mouth to kiss her hair. "Anyway, I don't want to talk. I want to hold you.

I want to love you. I want to keep you safe forever. Life can be very fragile.''

"It can indeed.'' A faint shudder ran through Jewel's body. "I love you, Keefe,'' she said, lifting her head to press a kiss on his jaw. "I love you with all my heart.''

"Then, you'll marry me?'' His dark eyes looked long and full into hers.

"No one in the world could stop me. You're my destiny. You're the one person my guardian angel hand-picked for me at birth.''

"And I've had you locked away inside me,'' Keefe responded. "I've had an image of you all my life.''

"A blue-eyed blonde?'' she teased, shifting in his arms so she could stare up into his face.

"Believe it or not, yes.'' He bent to kiss her. The kiss lingered and lingered. Finally he swept her up into his arms, carrying her through to the bedroom.

They made love for a long time. Until the terrors of the night subsided into the past. The future was what mattered. They were going to live it together.

EPILOGUE

Six months later
Mingaree Station, Southwest Queensland

SEEING THE DESERT IN FLOWER was a transcendent experience. Like a day trip to heaven. Jewel reveled in witnessing the rebirth of countless millions of wildflowers that spread for miles across the fiery red sand dunes and the dark golden spinifex plains. The vast area of the Channel country, the riverine desert, had been flooded for weeks courtesy of tropical cyclone Norman. The floodwaters from the far north of the state had poured their bounty into the great central Three River System, the Georgina, the Diamantina and Cooper's Creek, carrying liquid gold to the wild heart. It was this that ensured the survival of the magnificent desert flora.

Once the floodwaters had subsided, they'd decided to make their trip. This was the place where Jewel had been born. Where she'd lived until age six. This was a kind of rebirth for her. Rebirth and an end to all the closely guarded family secrets. She had wanted her mother to come, if only to pay homage at Steven Bishop's grave—for Thea *had* loved him, until Travis Copeland entered her life—but Thea had chosen not to resurrect the old painful memories. The past was the past. Just that. Besides, Travis—although happy for

Jewel and Keefe to make the trip—had been opposed to his wife's going. He had shunned Mingaree for many years now. An excellent manager was in place. Thea these days was a happily married woman—beautifully dressed, pampered and cosseted. She adored being Mrs. Travis Copeland. Thea had assumed the role like a great actress might assume the role of some fictional heroine. Thea had always been pretty. And she was still youthful looking; Judith said it was because her sister had left all the strains of living to *them* for the past twenty years. But they both loved Thea as they might love a fey child. They had lived to protect her, and now it was Travis Copeland's job. A man who needed to be needed more than most. As Judith remarked to her wondering niece, "The world is full of bizarre people, darl. Thea and Travis are a pair."

Secure in the love of her grandmother, Jewel found she was able to cope with the rest of her family. She and her father would never exactly hit it off, which might be a good thing, since—as everyone had noticed—Amelia tended to be insanely jealous. She simply couldn't abide not being the favored daughter. Jewel and Amelia were never going to be close, dashing Jewel's hopes, but the situation had improved considerably since Amelia had a new man in her life; Greg McCall had finally prevailed. These days, Jewel's relationship with Amelia was warily cordial.

What pleased Jewel most was the fact that Judith, who had withstood so much and put her own needs far down the list, had at long last found a soulmate. Her barrister friend, with a mind as sharp as her own. They were on the brink of tying the knot, and Jewel was thrilled for her aunt. If anyone deserved to be pampered and looked after, it was Judith, not her mother. Her aunt

Judith had been her tower of strength. Judith finally was to have her reward.

"I've always had a pure heart, love. That's the reason," Judith told her, grinning.

Absolutely!

As for her? Jewel was so happy in her marriage that her radiance spilled over on everyone around her. Keefe was her husband, her most perfect lover, her closest, most intimate friend. And her colleague. She had moved very comfortably into the Copeland Connellan legal department, bringing her skills with her. Keefe told her many times he was proud of her. Her husband, who held her heart in his two hands. As she held his.

It was Keefe who had arranged this trip out to Mingaree, using the company plane. The plane would return for them when they were ready to go back to Brisbane. But for now it was glorious to revisit her desert home. To lay the ghosts, to pray at the simple grave of the young man who had loved her and raised her to age six. To cover that grave with a carpet of "snow," an exquisite desert bush with pure white flowers like frangipani. Her mother had assured her she'd cared deeply for Steven. According to Thea, they'd been happy until Travis Copeland had entered her life—apparently like a cyclone. At any rate, Thea had been swept away. After twenty years of denying it she'd finally admitted to her and Judith that she'd always known Jewel wasn't Steven's child.

"Just like that!" Judith jumped up to exclaim, after Thea had contributed that monumental bit of information. "You're such a pain in the ass, Thea." Judith shook her head wonderingly, while her sister smiled back as though Judith had paid her a compliment.

Ah well, her mother and Travis had paid for their

sins—Jewel constantly had to remind herself that Travis was indeed her father—and they had nothing more to fear from judgmental society.

"It's time for forgiveness and reconciliation," Judith pointed out ironically.

Mingaree was the place to do it, Jewel felt. It was her territory. She'd remembered it in her dreams. Was there any sight so splendid as the great sweeping sand hills? They ran in continuous lines some quarter of a mile apart, calling to mind the great inland sea of pre-history. The highest dunes rose to one hundred feet and more, straightening out to half that height as they ran northward. Great masses of pure clean sand, blood-red in color, heaped and carved to perfection by the trade winds that blew incessantly all year round. Now at this wondrous time, the entire landscape—so savage in drought—was mantled with the exquisite beauty of the desert flora. Many of the plants were so delicate, one would've thought they couldn't possibly survive the blazing sun—yet they thrived in their trillions.

Heart uplifted, Jewel experienced a wave of euphoria. Life was so good! A little distance away, her husband was gathering a bouquet of yellow and white paper daisies from the fiery sand.

"What have you got there?" she called to him, starting to make a track through a fantastic yellow-and-white carpet, accented by fallen mulga branches that pointed skyward like wonderful abstract sculptures.

Keefe flashed her a loving smile. "I don't know yet. Maybe a garland for your head." Holding the pretty daisies in one hand, he put his other arm around his wife, drawing her to him and kissing her golden hair. "Isn't this a magic place?" He gave a sigh of great contentment, turning his face to the peacock-blue sky.

In the short time they'd been on Mingaree, he had watched the desert work its miracles. His beautiful Jewel's wounded heart had healed completely. The truth about her childhood, her true parentage, had finally been revealed; the ghosts of so many painful memories were laid to rest.

Jewel, his wife. He loved her above all else.

She raised her lovely face for his kiss. "A miracle, darling," she agreed.

A Wicked Lady

by

Anne Herries

Chapter One

'Belmont has the ear of the Regent,' Wellington said and grimaced as he looked at the younger man. 'If these rumours are true, I need to count on the Prince's support in the coming months.'

It was early November 1814 and they were in Vienna, where Wellington had recently taken up his post as plenipotentiary extraordinary at the great congress to discuss the future of Europe. Rumours abounded, but the ones that had just reached them were more serious than many and had worried the Iron Duke, better known to the soldiers who adored and followed him, often to their deaths, as Old Hookey.

'The message I got was vague.' Lord Giles Benedict, the Duke of Belmont's heir, grimaced. He was a handsome man, though he often looked stern and unapproachable to those who did not know him well. 'The story about Napoleon plotting an escape from Elba is probably true enough, for we have suspected that it would not hold him for ever—but these assassination rumours are rather more ambiguous. Belmont was mentioned, as was your own name, sir—and, indeed, the Regent himself.'

Wellington made a scoffing noise. 'It wouldn't be the first time they've tried to get rid of me and failed,' he muttered gruffly. 'You can forget me, sir. I am well protected—but I would not have the Regent murdered, nor indeed Belmont dispatched to an early grave.'

'Nor I, sir. I'm rather fond of the old boy, reprobate though many think him.'

'And that does you credit, especially if as I've heard he is about to take a young wife, who may well cut you out of the succession.'

'You know my mind on that, sir,' Giles said and frowned. 'Is it your wish that I continue to investigate these rumours?'

'As I mentioned, I need the Regent to stand firm,' Wellington said, scowling. 'You know those fools in London, Benedict. If Napoleon escapes and raises an army to fight for France, I want a free hand. This time we have to beat that tyrant for once and all and no favours granted. In my opinion he has been given too much freedom to date, and if this is not finished he will be a thorn in our sides for evermore.'

'Then I shall see Ellwood on his way and visit my informants in Paris to further my inquiries; after that, we shall see.' Giles's brow furrowed. 'I know you have no care for your own safety, sir, but I would beg you to take care. England needs you.'

'Be damned to them all,' Wellington growled. 'I have an appointment with destiny, Benedict. I feel it in my water and no wretched Froggie is going to stop me keeping it.'

Giles smiled, knowing his commander of old. They were firm friends and had been since their time together in India—a time that had been hard for Giles, a time that he had buried deep inside himself and had no wish to remember.

'Then I shall see what more can be discovered,' he promised. 'But first I must see Ellwood off. He will carry your message to the Prince, for he is a firm favourite in that direction and your voice will be heard.'

'Report to me when you are in Paris. I have special couriers, who will bring your message to me secretly,' Wellington said. 'And take care, Benedict—these are dangerous times.'

'Like you, I bear a charmed life, sir,' Giles said with a grin. 'I too believe I have a destiny to fulfil...'

'You cannot do it,' objected Sir Roderick Hazelmere. He looked at his sister in mild shock and some amusement. 'No, Maggie! Only think for a moment. It won't do. It really will not serve.'

He was a handsome young man, fair-haired with deep blue eyes and a sweet smile. Usually of an easy-going nature, he could be thoughtless at times, but the brother and sister were fond of each other despite having been seldom in each other's company these last years.

'What is so very terrible? I am merely proposing to set up as a Society hostess in London—and to introduce a very charming young lady as my protégée.' Margaret Hazelmere raised her fine dark brows at him. 'I cannot see that my desire to help a friend to find a respectable husband is such a horrendous crime.'

'She is Lord Monkford's bastard, that's what the fine ladies of London will not stomach if they discover what you're up to,' Sir Roderick replied. 'They would send her packing if even a whisper of this got out—and you with her. You ought not to consider it, Maggie. Think

of the scandal it would cause. We should never be able
to hold our heads up in Society again.'

'That is precisely why I intend to masquerade as the
Comtesse Magdalene de Grenelle,' Margaret answered
serenely. 'After all, who is to know me? It is years since
I was last in England. You said yourself that you hardly
knew me when you arrived a few days ago. If I set
myself up as a widow and call myself by a French
name, no one can deny me.'

It was nearing the end of November 1814 and they
were sitting in the sheltered garden of a pretty villa in
the south of France, taking advantage of an exception-
ally warm day. The villa was the home to which the
Contessa di Cabria had retired soon after her husband's
death some six years previously. A very wealthy
woman, she had taken her sister's child to live with her
when both Margaret's parents died within days of each
other from a virulent fever. Roderick, having inherited
his father's title and a small estate, had been sent to
university. However, it was soon discovered that he had
no bent for studying and his aunt had bought him a
commission in the army, placed the generous sum of
ten thousand pounds in trust for him and informed him
that he could expect no more of her.

'The remainder of my money, which is I confess considerable, will be your sister's when I die,' the Contessa
had told him. 'You have intelligence, looks and the
good fortune to have been born a man. It is up to you
to make your own way in the world. I shall do my best
for your sister. She will be provided for whether she
chooses to marry or not. If she takes my advice she will
think very carefully before choosing a husband. If I had
not been forced by necessity, I should certainly have
remained single.'

Margaret had been fifteen when she went to live with her aunt. She was then a shy, pretty girl with grey eyes and straight dark hair, which she had worn in plaits around her head. At five and twenty, she had become a very elegant, very assured young woman, her thick shining hair now coiled in a sleek twist at the back of her head—a style that showed off the white column of her neck to perfection.

Her beauty was remarkable, but she wore it with a cool serenity, which led others to mistake her for something other than she truly was. Beneath the mask she had been taught to show the world lurked a very passionate, slightly naughty nature. Had she been born a man, Margaret might have chosen to be a politician, a man of business or a judge, for her wits were sharper than many of the men she had met in her aunt's salon, but it was more likely that she would have been an adventurer. There was a reckless streak in her that she had tried to suppress, but which would not be quite controlled, no matter how often she scolded herself.

'Pose as a widow…' Roderick looked at her thoughtfully. To him she remained his younger sister, but there had been a change in her since his last visit, which had been some months before his aunt died. He had been with Wellington for some years, but his army career had now ended and he was at liberty to please himself.

Looking carefully at his sister, he had to acknowledge that she had the poise and authority of a woman of some stature. Her clothes were of the best quality and elegant, but it was not only that. She had an air of assurance that made her appear older than her years, and there was no doubting that her manner carried weight. Her frowns had thrown him into a quake before now. He loved her dearly as a sister, but would not care to be married to a woman of Margaret's character, for she was too determined. If she set herself up as the Comtesse de Grenelle, there was no true reason why she should not be accepted. For the past few years Margaret and her aunt had lived quietly, receiving only a few close friends—people who were unlikely to travel to England and even less likely to betray her.

Her brows arched at him, a challenge in her eyes. 'Yes—why should I not call myself a widow if I choose?'

Roderick could have given her a hundred reasons, but he doubted that she would be swayed by any of them. His sister was too independent, too set on having her way, and would not be deterred from her plans by his objections.

'But I do not see why you want to do this,' Roderick said. 'Caroline is pretty and quite charming. Surely you could find a suitable husband amongst your friends here, where there is less criticism of a background such as hers—why must you introduce her into the cream of English society? I am sure there are scores of men who would be willing to offer for her if you were to give her a small independence. Why subject her to the scrutiny of people who would simply look down their noses at her if they knew the truth of her birth?'

'Because it is a challenge,' Margaret replied, smiling at him. 'And because it amuses me. Aunt Kate told me so many stories—about the stuffy ladies who rule society, and the rogues who call themselves gentlemen. They are frauds and villains, Roddy—and deserve to be taught a lesson.'

'Steady on,' Roderick cried, a dark red colour creeping into his cheeks. 'You cannot condemn the whole of

English society simply because one or two of them stray
a little.'

'A little!' Margaret laughed scornfully. 'My aunt was
herself seduced by a member of her own family, who
shall remain nameless. She was barely sixteen, Roddy!
When it was suspected that she was with child, a marriage was hastily arranged with a man more than three
times her age—a man who made her life unhappy for
many years.'

'Good Lord!' Roderick looked at her in astonishment.
'I had no idea. Is that why she was packed off to marry
abroad? What happened to the child?'

'She miscarried after a fall and was never able to
have another child,' Margaret said. 'You can have no
idea of the things she suffered, Roddy—and as for poor
Caroline…'

'Yes, do tell me about Caro,' Roderick said, a gleam
of interest in his eyes. 'I have often wondered how our
aunt came to adopt her.'

'Caroline's mother was the daughter of a landless
gentleman, who was forced to support himself by being
of use to his wealthier friends. She was seduced by one
of those so-called friends when she was fifteen. When
her father discovered she was with child, she was sent
abroad with a duenna to have the child. She was too
delicate and fragile to bear children at such a young age
and she died. Her child was abandoned to the care of
strangers and the duenna disappeared, taking what
money and jewels still remained. If our aunt had not
rescued Caroline, she too might have died. She would
certainly have been cast out into the street to earn her
living as best she could as soon as she was old enough.'

'No—poor child!' Sir Roderick's blue eyes clouded
with anger. He was as fair as his sister was dark, he

taking after their mother and Margaret their father. 'Good thing Aunt Katherine was there.'

'She had become friends with Caroline's mother,' Margaret went on. 'She would have been with her at the birth if she could, but her husband forced her to accompany him on a journey to his villa at the Italian lakes. When she returned Caroline's mother was dead, but she was able to trace the child and she paid the people who had taken her in when the duenna fled. Her husband never knew that she placed the child of her friend with the nuns in one of their orphanages—or that she visited from time to time. Caroline came to us when she was sixteen. It was my aunt's intention to take her back to England. She believed it right that both Caroline and I should have at least one season in London society, even though she did not approve of marriage—but then she became ill and died.'

Margaret's voice caught with emotion and she got up from the small wooden bench, wandering over to gaze down at the beautiful scene below. The sea was a wonderful turquoise colour, lit with silver where the wintry sun touched it, and the surrounding hills were thick with lush greenery. It was a paradise on earth, and she had been so happy here with her aunt. There were times when she felt she could not bear to leave this place where she had been so content, and yet of late she had grown restless.

The sudden illness and death of the woman she loved had left Margaret feeling bereft and at a loss, all their bright plans at an end. It was because of her deep love for the woman who had been both mother and friend to her these past years that she had come up with her daring plan, because it would in some small measure pay back the debt Aunt Kate believed she was owed by

Society as a whole. And also because the sheer audacity of it appealed to her sense of humour, which her aunt had always maintained was rather outrageous.

'It is because of your wicked humour that I do not think you should marry, my love,' Kate had told her once. 'You are too independent, too proud, and too much of a free spirit to be a good wife, Maggie. Most men want a meek obliging girl as their wife—and those who can appreciate a woman like you are usually interested only in seduction.'

'Then I shall not marry,' Margaret had replied with a little shrug. 'Why should I, after all? You have made me independent. Why should I surrender my freedom for the sake of a man?'

'I have made you dislike men,' her aunt had said, touching her hand and looking sad. 'It is possible to find happiness with a man sometimes, dearest—and love, too, I dare say. I was unfortunate, but you may fare better.'

Her aunt's stories had given her a deep scorn for men of a certain type, but it was another who had made her feel that she did not wish to marry. Margaret had never spoken of the incident to her aunt and did not do so now.

'If I am offered love, I may take it,' Margaret had replied. 'But I do not need to take marriage, too.'

'Would you end as poor Caroline's mother did, dying in shame and alone?'

'It would not necessarily be like that,' Margaret replied, an audacious gleam in her eyes. 'If I took a lover I should know that it was not a permanent arrangement, and I should make my own plans. Throughout history there have been women who have dared to love and flout convention—why should I not do as I please?'

'And most of them have come to a sticky end, my love.' Her aunt had shaken her head over this, amused and yet worried for her dearest child. 'I have taught you too well,' she said on a sigh. 'I thought only to set you on your guard, but I have made you cynical. Be careful, dearest Margaret. You may discover that love is not so easy to control as you imagine.'

They had been so close, so loving, and now Aunt Kate had gone. Margaret had never once felt alone while her aunt lived, but now there were times when the sense of loneliness became almost unbearable.

Margaret was close to tears when she felt the touch of a hand on her shoulder and turned to see her brother standing just behind her. Handsome, gentle, what the English were pleased to call a dandy, she cared for him, but knew he had his own life and that he preferred to be in London. At one time she had hoped they might travel together, but Roddy had no taste for it. He was a year older than she was and they had remained good friends, writing regularly to keep in touch, though their lives had taken separate paths for the past ten years.

'I am not against you, Maggie,' he said softly. 'I think you should come back to England—but why not as yourself? We could find someone to introduce you into society, and Caroline could accompany you as a friend.'

'I have been used to being my own mistress,' Margaret replied, blinking back her emotion. It was foolish to cry for it could change nothing. 'I would drive any duenna to tears within a day, Roddy. No, no, I cannot put any poor woman to so much trouble.' She gave him a provocative smile that brought an answering humour to his own lips. 'All I need is for you to acknowledge me, dearest brother. You have many friends in society. You have only to say that I am known to you—that you met me while staying with our aunt.'

Roderick laughed, giving in to her, as she had known he would in the end. He shook his head at her, a gleam of mischief in his eyes.

'Well, I suppose it will be rather a good joke,' he said. 'And you are right, certain members of Society could do with being paid in their own coin. But if I agree to support you in this madness, Maggie, you must promise you won't let me down. If something happens, you must keep our secret—you must disappear rather than be exposed as yourself.'

'Yes, of course,' she promised, giving him a quick hug. 'Nothing will happen—but if it should the Comtesse de Grenelle will simply disappear.' Her eyes danced with wickedness as she gazed up at him. 'You must remember to call me Comtesse from now on or you will have people think I am your mistress.'

'Good Lord!' Roderick said. 'So they might if I am too familiar. I shall have to be careful, Maggie.'

'If you must use my name, call me Magda,' his sister told him. 'Better people should think we are lovers than brother and sister.'

'No, indeed it is not,' he replied, looking shocked. 'I never heard of such a thing. I shall call you ma'am, or Comtesse when in public.'

'Thank you, Sir Roderick,' his sister said and curtsied. Her head was bent, her manner demure, but when she looked up the recklessness was there in her eyes. 'Oh, my dearest, dearest Roddy—it is all going to be such fun!'

He looked doubtful for a moment. Maggie didn't know what she was taking on or what old cats some of the Society hostesses could be—but if it was what she wanted he would do it. Besides, he had reasons of his own for wanting her to bring the lovely Caroline Hammond to London.

The weather had been against him for the past two days, his ship held at Calais by the storms that had made even his captain cautious of putting to sea. Armed with news of Bonaparte's intention to return to France and raise an army once more, Lord Clarence Ellwood looked impatiently at his companion.

'I'll be damned if I'll wait much longer, Giles. If the wind doesn't abate by the time the tide is right, I'll go, whatever Jackson says.'

'Don't be a fool, Ellwood.' Giles Benedict raised his splendid dark brows. 'Your news is important rather than urgent. Wellington has suspected it for months, but we need you to tell the Prince that things have begun to move. What we need to know more urgently is what is likely to happen when Bonaparte lands—is he likely to be greeted by a popular uprising or will it be a limited response?'

'The Old Guard will rally to him and France will fall to his advance,' Ellwood said. 'There's not much love for the Bourbons, I can tell you, and many will welcome the emperor back. Depend upon it, Giles. I suppose your plan is to remain in France a few days longer to see what you can discover.' Ellwood was five and twenty, devoted to Wellington, with whom he had served as a young subaltern on the Peninsula, and Giles Benedict was his particular friend.

'I mean to discover what I can of this talk of a woman spying for Boney,' Giles replied with a frown. His information was not clear, but it seemed certain that a woman was deeply involved in the plot. 'I have heard whispers of an attempt to assassinate various members of the English aristocracy, including Wellington. If that could be achieved before Bonaparte's return, it would almost certainly result in a victory for the French.'

'You have little faith in our allies, it seems.' His friend's summing up of the situation amused Ellwood. 'Or our generals—though I am with you there. Not many of them can hold a candle to the Iron Duke.'

'Old Hookey is our talisman,' Giles replied with a wry smile about his mouth, a mouth that could be hard or generously soft, depending on his mood. He was an attractive man in his early thirties, though not as handsome as his companion. Ellwood was fair with blue eyes while Giles had hair the colour of a raven's plumage, and his eyes were very dark, almost black at times, but with a silver flame in their depths, especially when he was angry. 'The troops love and trust Wellington to a man. If he should be murdered, morale would be shattered. He has been warned and will be on his guard, but there are others who may be more vulnerable to the assassin's ball.'

'You mean Belmont and the Regent?'

Giles nodded. 'Neither of them are likely targets in my opinion. I dare say it is Wellington they will go for if they get a chance, but I have done what I can in that direction for we shall need him when the time comes, believe me. Besides, I happen to like the fellow, cursed awkward as he may be at times.'

Ellwood laughed, because this was very true. 'That's putting it mildly, Giles old fellow, but I agree. Your mission is more important than mine and you should stay on for a few days, see what you can learn.' His attention wandered as he saw the carriage stop a little distance from where they were standing. A man of

about Ellwood's age had got down and was assisting a
young woman to alight. 'My God! What a beauty. Look
at that hair—it's like spun gold, Giles.'

Giles Benedict smiled, his gaze taking the direction
his companion's had taken previously. The girl could
not have been above eighteen in his estimation and was
certainly lovely, but he found himself looking more intently at the woman who had followed her from the
carriage. At first sight not as stunning as the fair girl,
perhaps, but with a certain style. There was something
about her that seemed familiar, but he could not place
her in his mind. Had they met at some time—or had he
merely seen her from a distance? The memory was ob-
scured for the moment, but he would no doubt recall it
in time.

The younger woman was laughing at something the
man was saying, laughing up at him in a manner that
some might call flirtatious, though it could equally as
well be quite innocent. She had what he thought of as
English colouring, but her skin had a slightly peachy
look as if she had lived in the sunshine of a European
country for much of her life.

His gaze returned to the older woman, and he was
aware of feeling something that went beyond the interest of a casual observer. He had an urgent desire to
follow the woman, to know her better, but in another
moment he had suppressed the foolish thought. He had
more important things to do!

'Are you sure we should go on board, Roddy? Would
it not be better to wait for another day?' It was the older
woman who had spoken. She was, he could see now, a
beauty in her own right, though she dressed in a rather
severe if elegant manner. Now that he thought about it,

both the ladies were wearing grey—in mourning for someone, perhaps?

'If you want to attend the Belmonts' Christmas ball, we should not delay further. As I told you, the Prince of Wales, or the Regent as I should properly call him now, will be the guest of honour and invitations will be at a premium. I can wangle one for you both, but not if we leave it too late. It's an opportunity not to be missed.'

They had passed by without casting a glance towards either Ellwood or himself. Giles frowned as he wondered about the snatch of conversation he'd heard. It would be ridiculous to read too much into it, of course; all of London society must have been hoping for an invitation to the Belmonts' ball. Besides, he was looking for a French spy, a woman who would be prepared to lie and cheat for the chance to get near Belmont and mayhap the Regent himself. The Regent was known to have an eye to the ladies; it was Giles's intelligence that it had been planned to use a woman because she might have a chance of getting him alone. It would not be the first attempt on Prinny's life, though most of them had been kept private for fear of spreading panic.

'I wonder who that girl was,' Ellwood said, looking slightly dazed and a little disappointed as she and her party went on board a large ship waiting its turn to depart and disappeared below decks. 'I know him, of course, or rather I should say that we have met.'

'You knew the girl's companion?' Giles was suddenly alert.

'Sir Roderick Hazelmere, small country estate, not rich. He was in the army, sold out recently. Looking for a fortune to marry, they say.'

'I meant the older woman. Do you happen to know her at all?'

'Sorry. Hardly noticed,' Ellwood said. 'Come to think of it, she was rather attractive, well dressed too for a companion. Do you think she was the duenna?'

'I wouldn't have thought it, too much style. I feel I've met her before, though it must be a long time ago. Can't recall where. Just something that sticks in my memory, but too vague to come to mind. I don't think it was in England, abroad somewhere—could be anywhere.'

'Pity I'm not travelling on her ship,' Ellwood remarked, a rueful look in his eyes. 'Might have been interesting. I'm talking of the younger lady—dazzling, don't you know?'

'You will meet her soon enough I dare say,' Giles reassured him, a faint flicker of a smile in his eyes. 'I heard Hazelmere mention Belmont's ball.' He frowned as he remembered the rumours he'd been chasing. 'Keep an eye on her until I get back. Something has rung a warning bell.'

'You don't think that divine creature could be Boney's spy?' Ellwood was incredulous. 'Come off it, Giles! Doing it too brown by far.'

'I meant…never mind,' Giles said, dismissing the idea. Ellwood was right, it was ridiculous. 'I shall see you next week without fail.'

The passenger ship was about to clear harbour. Ellwood's captain was preparing to leave next. Giles watched as his friend went on board, remaining where he stood for a few minutes. Something was nagging at him, but he wasn't sure what—something about the companion, if that was what she was, though he didn't think it. She had style, elegance and the wealth to back it up if he was not mistaken. She seemed to have too much confidence to be unmarried so perhaps she was a widow. He was intrigued, though he wasn't sure why.

Giles found most women all too obvious; the young single ones had an eye to the title that might pass to him on his uncle's demise, while the others were often only too willing to climb into his bed. He'd had his share of mistresses, none of whom lasted more than a few months, but so far had never found a woman to whom he had the least desire to be legshackled. Marriage was a duty he owed to his family since he was the last of his direct line, but it could wait until he was ready.

Standing at the ship's bows, the wind ruffling her hair and bringing a few tendrils free of the strict confines in which it was usually constrained, Margaret wondered if the two men on the quayside had heard what she'd said to her brother just before they boarded. It had been a definite slip. Despite all she'd said to Roddy about being careful, she had forgotten the accent she intended to use in her masquerade as the widow of a French Count. Because of the time she and her aunt had spent in France she was able to speak in a creditable accent and her use of the language could not be faulted. Aunt Kate's friends had remarked on it more than once, though her uncle had merely sneered at her attempt to speak his own language.

A little shudder went through Margaret as she recalled an unpleasant incident with her uncle some months before his death. She had been little more than nineteen and they had all attended a dance at the house of some friends of his that evening.

It had been a very warm night, the air hot and sultry,

drawing her out into the gardens to cool her heated skin. She had gone walking as far as the lake, gazing down at its moonlit beauty, drinking in the peace and solitude, when her uncle had approached her. It was a moment or two before she realised that he was drunk, too late for her to leave without his making a clumsy attempt to molest her. She had struggled against his embrace, hating the feel of his wet lips on hers, his groping hands that tried to invade the bodice of her gown. It was not the first time he had shown an interest in her, but always before she had avoided situations like this and blamed herself for giving him the opportunity.

He was very strong and her struggles to throw him off might have been useless had her cries of alarm not attracted the attention of a stranger. The English voice demanding that he should unhand her had finally broken through her uncle's drunken stupor and he had come abruptly to his senses, muttering something that might have been an apology and making off before the stranger could say more.

'Are you all right?'

The gentleman's voice had been concerned, but Margaret had been unable to meet his gaze, overcome by shame at being found in such a compromising situation.

'May I be of service to you? Escort you wherever you wish to go? I think you are in some distress.'

'No…' She could not bring herself to thank him and suddenly ran off in the other direction to that which her uncle had taken.

Afterwards, she had castigated herself for her rudeness. The least she could have done was to thank him for his kindness, but she had been too upset, too shamed by the incident. It was, after all, her own fault for walking alone at night. The stranger must have thought she was meeting a lover—a meeting that had turned sour.

And she ought to have been on her guard. She had always known that her uncle was a despicable man who had caused her aunt much distress. A womaniser with a nasty temper, he had made her aunt suffer for her inability to give him a son. When he died suddenly of a heart disorder only six months later she could not grieve for him. Aunt Kate had not grieved either. Her marriage settlement provided for a large part of his estate devolving on her, though the villa in Italy had gone to a distant cousin.

'I intend that we shall enjoy ourselves now, dearest,' she told Margaret soon after she became a widow. 'Your uncle was not a kind man, but even he could not get out of the settlement—my father made certain of that before I married, and of course I have the inheritance that came to me through my mother. I have money enough to allow us a life of luxury and to make provision for you. My earnest wish is to make sure you are independent, Margaret. You shall never be put in the position I was, never forced to a marriage that can bring you only pain. If you ever marry it will be of your own choosing, I promise you.'

'You are always so generous to me, Aunt,' Margaret said. 'But I do not need so very much. Will you not provide for Caroline, too?'

'The money will be yours to do as you see fit, though I may provide Caroline with a dowry,' her aunt said. 'Her mother was treated as shamefully as I, and I am fond of the child—but you are the daughter I never had, Margaret. Everything I have is for you.'

And it was a considerable fortune. Had she been able to choose, Margaret might have wished to refuse the legacy, which had come down to her from a man she thoroughly disliked. However, without her aunt's money she would have been forced to earn a living and she knew herself to be too independent to be at the beck and call of another woman. Besides, Aunt Kate had suffered for what she had and so Margaret had reconciled the inheritance with her conscience. She would, in any case, use a part of it to see Caroline settled into the class to which she was entitled to belong.

Margaret brought her thoughts back to the present. The swell of the sea was beginning to ease now, the waves becoming less rough. For herself she had not minded, but she knew that Caroline had been feeling sick since a short time after they boarded. She had left her resting to come up for a breath of air, finding it pleasant on deck, but now she thought she ought to go below and see how her young friend was faring.

Caroline was sitting up against her pillows, a kerchief soaked in lavender water pressed to her head when Margaret entered the cabin.

'Does your poor head ache?' she asked solicitously. 'I thought you were asleep when I left you.'

'I was for a while,' Caroline admitted. 'But the vomiting left me feeling weak and, as you say, I have a headache.'

'I am so sorry, dearest,' Margaret said. 'But the swell is dying down now. It should not be too long before we are in England.'

'I have never been to England.' Caroline's slightly Italian accent was natural, having lived in Italy for the whole of her life, though she spoke English perfectly. Aunt Kate had insisted that she be taught, and by an English nun who had sought refuge in the sunshine of an Italian convent, but it had still left her with that faint accent, which was charming. 'I am not sure I shall know what to do, Magda.'

'You will behave as you always do,' Margaret told her. 'Do not let Roddy's stories of the autocratic hostesses intimidate you, Caroline. As my aunt told you many times, you have every right to mix with them. Your mother was the daughter of a gentleman, even if he did not behave in a gentlemanly fashion when he banished your mother and her duenna to the continent.'

'But I am a...bastard,' Caroline whispered and tears stood in her lovely eyes. 'Nothing can change that, Magda. If people knew the truth, I should not be accepted into polite society.'

'You are my protégée,' Margaret said and smiled, thinking how gentle and lovely the girl was, almost too obedient. Sometimes she wished for a little more spirit, but feared the nuns had crushed that out of the girl long ago. 'I shall introduce you as a distant cousin and that is enough. If a gentleman of the right kind shows interest we may tell him the truth, but in the meantime you are going to be invited everywhere and enjoy yourself.'

Caroline looked at her doubtfully. She had been quite happy in the south of France with Margaret, and there were young men who had paid her attention, young men she felt might have offered for her in time. But it was her guardian's wish that they come to England for this season of triumph and she had not liked to speak her mind too plainly. Besides, it might mean that she would see more of Roddy; of all the gentlemen she had met, he was the one she admired the most.

Sir Roderick seemed to Caroline an upstanding gentleman of good character, gentle, considerate, generous and kind. If she could choose, she thought that she

might like to be his wife, but of course she wasn't clever
or beautiful enough. He must know many other young
ladies who were far more qualified to be Lady
Hazelmere than she, and she did not suppose for one
moment that he was in love with her.

'Do you think this gentleman might not be angry
when he learns the truth?' she asked mildly. 'Will he
not feel cheated?'

'I do not see why he should,' Margaret answered with
a slight frown. 'You are Lord Monkford's daughter after
all. He did not marry your unhappy mother, but he certainly fathered you, Caroline. Your mother was the
daughter of a country squire he thought beneath his
touch, but still of good birth. And besides, you will have
ten thousand pounds when you marry and that is a not
inconsiderable sum for any gentleman to consider.'

'You should not give me so much,' Caroline said a
little unhappily.

'I can spare it without affecting my own lifestyle,'
Margaret assured her. 'I have no wish to live in London
once you are safely wed, and shall return to my villa in
France, where I shall live quietly for the rest of my
days.'

'But you will visit me sometimes?'

'Yes—or you may bring your children to visit me,'
Margaret told her. 'I have so many friends in France
that you need not fear I shall be lonely.' Even as she
spoke, Margaret recalled the restlessness that had come
over her of late. She did not welcome it or understand
it, for her mind was set on the path her own life would
follow. She had no wish for a husband, and had come
to England only for Caroline's sake.

Yet there was a tiny seed of doubt in her mind, an
acknowledgement deep down that she longed for some-

thing more—perhaps for adventure, excitement. She did not know and dismissed her thoughts with a shake of her head. Woolgathering! She was here to find a husband of the right kind for Caroline and that was all that mattered.

Chapter Two

Giles was vaguely dissatisfied as he approached Le Havre, where Lord Ellwood's own ship would be waiting to take him back to England. These past few days in Paris had brought few results in terms of actual information, though he had more or less confirmed his earlier suspicions that some kind of a plot to cause mayhem was afoot. The death of Wellington or the Regent at this crucial stage would be a huge blow against the Allies.

There was a chill breeze from off the sea despite the sun, which was trying to break through a haze of cloud. By mid-afternoon it might be warmer, but he should be on his way back to England by then, he thought, and sighed as he reflected that his efforts of late had scarcely proved profitable. He had little more to take back with him than the whisper he'd heard weeks earlier. There was to be an attempt to assassinate various members of the aristocracy close to the Prince of Wales, in particular the Duke of Belmont and perhaps Wellington himself. One man being in London, the other in Vienna, there was obviously more than one plot afoot. Wellington had insisted that Giles must go to London and do what he could to protect Belmont.

'And the Prince himself if necessary,' had been Wellington's last words. 'With him dead Napoleon would doubtless find it easier to go on the rampage once more. I have no faith in the fools who would rule in Prinny's stead, believe me.'

'I am of the same mind, sir. You may rely on me to do all I can to protect both Belmont and the Prince.'

'You have my permission to use all your resources,' Wellington said. 'Good luck, Benedict, and make damned sure you don't let me down!'

Giles had done what he could to discover more of the secret plots, but so far there was nothing much to go on, though his informant had insisted that the first assassination attempt would take place in London in the next few weeks, before Napoleon's planned return to France could take place, and that a woman would be at the centre of the affair.

'I can tell you little more than that she goes under a false name and is not what she seems,' the Frenchman had told Giles when pressed for more details. 'I would be of more help if I could...' He shrugged his shoulders expressively.

Giles had no reason to doubt the veracity of what he'd been told. His informant was a returned émigré, who had everything to gain by seeing a permanent restoration of the royal house of France and an end to Bonaparte's reign. The Marquis de Chambray hoped to win approval from the Allies and gain a position of importance amongst the ruling party.

'You have no description of this woman?' Giles questioned.

'A woman of style, perhaps, not beautiful in the common way, but attractive to men.'

It was a description that might suit a thousand women, but Giles had not pressed him further for it was clear that the Marquis knew no more. Besides, a lingering suspicion had resurfaced as he recalled the woman he'd glimpsed at Calais. Something about her had nagged at him, lingering at the back of his mind, and he was almost certain he'd seen her before in unusual circumstances. Indeed, she had invaded his dreams of late—erotic dreams, the kind he had not experienced since he was a green youth. He smiled at the memory, mocking his vulnerability to a pretty face. But, no, it was not just her face; it was the mystery, the secret allure of the woman behind the face.

He was certain he knew her from somewhere. But where? The elusive memory escaped him for the moment, but the uneasy feeling remained to tease him. Yet he had no reason to suspect her of being concerned in a plot to assassinate Wellington or anyone else, and of course she was English. Or was she? He'd thought there was a faint accent, but he could have been mistaken. Besides, Chambray had told him that the woman was not what she seemed.

He cursed himself for a fool as he went on board Ellwood's ship. If the woman was by chance the one he sought, she had gained a head start on him.

Margaret nodded her approval as Caroline pirouetted before her in a pale green silk gown they had commissioned in Paris before they left for England. It had arrived only minutes before their departure, and this was the first time Caroline had tried it on. Fortunately, the fit was perfect and there was no need to summon a seamstress.

'You look beautiful, dearest,' Margaret told her and smiled. Already the girl had attracted the attention of several gentlemen, some of whom might be eligible, others definitely not, and as yet they had been nowhere of any real importance. The ball they were to attend that evening would change everything, Margaret thought. The Duke of Belmont's ball would be a fearful crush and Caroline was bound to be a success. 'I am sure it is going to be a wonderful occasion this evening.'

'Will there be many people there?' Caroline asked a little nervously. 'Do you think…will they approve of me?'

'How could anyone disapprove of you in that dress, my love?' Margaret asked and kissed her cheek. 'Besides, you are as lovely inside as you are on the outside, and anyone who knows you must love you—as Roddy and I do, very much.'

Caroline blushed and shook her head. 'You are prejudiced in my favour, Magda, and Sir Roderick is—is very kind.'

'Nonsense,' Margaret replied firmly. 'My brother enjoys taking you out, otherwise he would not do it. Now, you should change out of that gown for he will be here to take you for a ride in his curricle in another hour and you will not want to keep him waiting.'

'Oh, no, I should not like that,' Caroline agreed and went away to ask her maid to help her out of the gorgeous evening gown and into something more suitable for a ride in the park.

Left to herself, Margaret began to consider her own attire for the evening. She looked at the expensive gown lying on the shelves of her armoire and wondered if she ought to have ordered herself a new dress in Paris, something more fitting to her role as chaperon, perhaps. The gown she intended to wear was an emerald green silk and cut quite low in the décolletage, as was the fashion. It had been ordered in Paris for a ball just before Aunt Kate's death and Margaret had never worn it. She knew it suited her to perfection and yet felt it might seem a little too stylish for the woman she was trying to become. Her mourning gowns had made her look older, but this gown would—her thoughts were interrupted by a knock at the bedroom door.

'Come in, Ellen,' she said and smiled as her personal maid entered, dropping a respectful curtsy. Having left her own servants behind in France, she had taken her on as soon as she reached London, and the girl had proved most reliable. 'Did you need me for something?'

'There is a gentleman below in the parlour, ma'am. He asked if he could see you or Miss Caroline.'

'Caroline is changing. I shall come down immediately.'

Margaret checked her reflection before going down to the small reception parlour, where uninvited guests were received before being taken to the main suite on the next floor. She had not been expecting a gentleman to call that morning, nor did she believe Caroline had issued any invitations; this being the morning of an important ball, they had decided to spend the day quietly.

'You will forgive me for calling with no warning, ma'am?' Giles frowned as her beauty struck him powerfully. She was even lovelier than he had thought when he saw her in France. Yet it was not beauty alone, but the essence of the woman that touched a chord within him, making him aware that he desired her physically.

But that was unforgivable! She was a lady, not a whore, and must be treated with respect. 'But I believe we have a mutual friend and it is on that lady's behalf that I am here.'

Margaret stared at the man who was standing before the empty fireplace, trying to recall where she had seen him. She did not think they had met recently, for she and Caroline had attended only a few small affairs at the houses of friends of her brother's, and she would have remembered such a man. He was as tall as her brother, but of a more powerful build and strong featured, attractive with dark hair and eyes that looked almost black.

Why was it that instinctively she felt that she knew him? It was as if she had known him for a long, long time, as if something inside her reached out to him.

But she was staring and she must not! She held out her hand to him, but instead of touching it briefly with his fingers, he carried it to his lips, pressing a light kiss into the palm. A tiny shiver of pleasure went through her, her cheeks slightly pink as he released her.

'Is it that we 'ave met before, sir?' Margaret asked, remembering to use the distinctive accent she had adopted for their stay in London. It made her voice husky and sensual, though she had no idea of it or the effect it had already begun to have on the men they met in company. It was not a part of her plan that she should be as much sought after as Caroline, and she would have been annoyed if she had realised that the air of mystery about her had set the town by its ears. She usually spoke in perfect English, dropping an *h* occasionally for effect, now and then using French words. 'You must forgive me, but I cannot recall your name.'

'I think we may have met somewhere, though I do

not recall it,' Giles told her truthfully. For he did not count the moment he had noticed her in France. No, they had met much earlier, though he knew not where or when, though he believed that meeting had affected him powerfully at the time. There was something important nagging at the back of his mind, but it would not come to him. 'I am Giles Benedict, Belmont's nephew, and here at the pleasure of my sister, Lady Augusta Montclair. She asked me to deliver an invitation to an evening party she is giving next week.'

'Lady Montclair...*oui*, this is correct. I believe we 'ave met at a soirée the other evening and she was kind enough to say she would send me an invitation to her own.' It had been a casual remark and Margaret had hardly expected it to be delivered so promptly and by the lady's brother. 'How good of you to come in person, *monsieur*. May I perhaps offer you some refreshment?

Her hand was reaching for the bell to summon a servant, but stayed as he refused.

'Thank you, no. I do not believe I shall stay, for this evening is an important occasion, is it not? You will no doubt be wishing me to the devil. I hope we shall have the pleasure of seeing you at the Belmonts' ball this evening, Comtesse?'

'*Oui*, Caroline and I also are, as you say, very much looking forward to it,' Margaret replied. 'It will be the first important occasion for my ward since our arrival in England. Everyone will be there, *n'est-ce pas*?'

'Ah, yes,' Giles said, looking at her with a deceptively casual manner. 'I believe my sister told me you were French, ma'am? Have you been living in France until recently?'

Margaret sensed that there was more to this casual inquiry. 'I lived in France for some years after my...

'usband died,' she said, a faint blush in her cheeks as she lied. 'Before that I lived in Italy.'

'But you are not French, I think?' Giles lifted his brows. There was a prickling sensation at the nape of his neck and he was aware of something…not quite right. 'Nor yet Italian. Would I be right in thinking you have English blood in you?'

Had he unmasked her already? Margaret knew a start of fright as she saw the grim set of his mouth—but that was not possible. She had been so sure that no one would recognise her. She had been a mere child when she left England and had never left the schoolroom. No, he could not know for certain that she was not who she claimed to be. She lifted her head, deciding to bluff it out.

'My *maman* was English,' she told him, her smile as deceptively sweet as his was casual. 'But my 'ome is in France now. I am 'ere only to give my ward a little time of 'appiness; this is a good thing, *non*?'

Giles seemed to be measuring his reply, and she guessed that he was uncertain about something, but she was not to benefit from his thoughts—before he could speak, someone came into the room.

'Ah, there you are, Mag…Magda, Comtesse, ma'am…' Roddy stumbled over his words as he realised too late his sister was not alone. 'Forgive me for bursting in on you, Comtesse. I came to inquire if Miss Hammond was ready to drive out with me and your maid told me you were in here.'

'*Mon Dieu!* You 'ave startled me, Sir Roderick,' Margaret said. 'I am, 'owever, delighted to see you so early. I believe Caroline is expecting you, though a little later this morning.'

'Yes, well, um…er, I came early to make sure the

flowers I'd ordered for this evening hadn't arrived too soon. Want them fresh, what?'

'*Oui*, certainly. You are always so thoughtful, so attentive to Caroline.' She lifted her shoulders expressively as she turned to Giles. 'It is so good to be young, is it not, Lord Benedict—but may I introduce you? Perhaps you do not know Sir Roderick Hazelmere?'

'Don't think we've met,' Roddy said, extending his hand and trying manfully to stem the tide of warm colour in his cheeks as he recovered from his blunder. 'Belmont's heir, ain't you?'

'Yes, for my sins,' Giles said, hiding his amusement at the young man's awkwardness. Clearly Hazelmere was enamoured of someone in this house and on more than the usual visiting terms, but of course he had known the ladies before this trip to London since he had accompanied them to England. And it obviously behoved Giles to be on good terms with a man who might prove a vital source of information. 'Good to meet you, sir. Perhaps we shall meet again soon.' He turned to the lady of the house once more, bowing his head. 'I must take up no more of your time, ma'am. Thank you for receiving me. I hope I may tell my sister that you will attend her evening party, though I am assured it is nothing special, just a gathering of like minds, she tells me.'

'I am 'onoured that she invites me,' Margaret told him, her voice delightfully husky, adding to the air of mystery and allure that she unwittingly exuded. Her smile seemed to invite and yet repel at the same time, and was, Giles found himself thinking, damnably attractive. He had been right to be suspicious: this woman was dangerous! He would do well to be wary of her. 'It was kind of you to come yourself, sir.'

'My sister was most insistent,' Giles replied gallantly if untruthfully. 'Hazelmere, your servant.' He bowed his head and walked from the elegant salon feeling oddly as if he had somehow been trounced, though he was not sure why. Round one to the Comtesse, he believed.

It had not been easy to get that invitation out of Augusta, much easier to discover that the Comtesse had been invited to the Belmonts' Christmas ball. Felicia had teased him unmercifully, but he usually found his uncle's delightful young wife malleable enough. She was a pretty woman, young enough to be Belmont's daughter and a surprise to the family. Giles's half-sister, Lady Augusta Montclair, declared that Belmont had done it in the hope of getting an heir in the autumn of his life.

'Depend upon it, dearest boy,' Augusta had said darkly when she met him on his return to London. 'The old rogue wants to put your nose out of joint and disappoint you.'

'Then he will be himself disappointed,' Giles had told her, his temper not one whit disturbed by the news, which had greeted him on his return from Paris, of Belmont's sudden marriage. 'If he can get himself a son I say well done to him. I do not rely on his fortune for I have made my own way in the world, and I dislike the estate. No, Gussie, don't frown at me. I haven't the least desire to be the fifth Duke. And Felicia is a delightful child. I have always liked her. I wish them every happiness together.'

'I thought you might have married her yourself,' Augusta replied with a lift of her fine brows. She was a plump handsome woman, well married with a brood of children and a considerate husband, and wanted to see her brother settled with a wife of his own. 'I'm sure our uncle did it only to spite you, Giles.'

'My only reservation is for Felicia's sake,' Giles replied. 'She is very young and Belmont is past his prime. I hope she will be happy with her choice.'

'She seems to enjoy being Lady Belmont,' Augusta said waspishly. 'But it was a bargain I should not want to make, believe me.'

Giles knew that his sister, the elder by some fifteen years, and born of his father's first wife, had always disliked their uncle, though he was not sure why. He actually quite liked the old reprobate, though Belmont's reputation was not as sweet as it might have been. He did not blame him for having one last fling and was sincere in his good wishes on learning of the marriage. For the foreseeable future his own interests lay in a military and then possibly a political career, and he had no wish to be tied to an estate that he did not even like very much. He had a house in London, which he let during the Season, preferring to stay in lodgings or at his club when he was in town. For the past ten years or more he had spent more time fighting or travelling than indulging in the delights of Society, and thought a life in the diplomatic service would probably suit him as well as any other.

Which was partly the reason he had become embroiled in this affair in the first place, Giles mused, a wry smile touching a mouth he would have been surprised to hear was thought extremely kissable by most women of his acquaintance. Wellington had selected him for more than one delicate mission in the past year or so and they had formed a bond that went beyond the bounds of mere duty. No damned woman was going to murder the commander if Giles could prevent it! Nor yet his uncle! As for the Regent, that was unthinkable but already under control. Prinny would be constantly under surveillance, both within the royal household and out of it.

His mouth settled into an expression that the polite ladies of London would not have found so seductive, but which would be familiar to the soldiers he led into battle, and to friends like Clarence Ellwood. The Comtesse—or whoever she was, for he was not convinced by her masquerade—would find she had bitten off more than she could swallow if she tried to get too close to the Regent that evening!

'What made that fellow call so early?' Roddy asked a trifle indignantly of his sister once they were certain Lord Benedict had left. 'I damned near made a slip-up there, Maggie. Ellen let me in, but the silly girl never told me you had company.'

'I shall speak to her,' Margaret said, a little frown creasing her smooth brow. Something about Lord Benedict's visit had disturbed her, though she could not say what. 'But you really must be less impulsive, dearest. People will suspect something if you are too familiar.'

'Sorry,' her brother apologised. 'Didn't think it mattered at this hour. Too damned early for visits—what did the fellow think he was up to calling like that?'

'His excuse was that he was delivering an invitation for Lady Augusta Montclair,' Margaret said. 'But there was something odd about his manner—did you not notice it?'

'Can't say I did,' he admitted. 'Too embarrassed at the start. Seemed all right, friendly enough. Perhaps he's after Caroline. Heard what a beauty she is. I dare say they'll all be after her by the end of this evening.'

'She should be able to take her choice of a husband before long, I imagine—' Margaret broke off as she heard hurried footsteps in the hall and then Caroline came in. 'So, you are ready, Caro dearest. As you see, Roddy is early.'

'I thought we'd get off early and then you will have the afternoon to rest,' he said, his eyes warm with admiration as they lingered on her lovely face. She was looking charming in a carriage gown of deep yellow trimmed with cream ribbons and wore a fairly plain but charming chip-straw bonnet tied with ribbons that matched her gown. 'Damn it, but you do look lovely, Caro. I swear you get prettier every day. I shall have to fight them off to get a dance with you this evening.'

'No, you shall not, Sir Roderick,' Caroline said and blushed a delicate rose. 'For I shall reserve as many dances for you as you request.'

'Make it three, then,' Roddy said at once. 'And I'll take you into supper if I get the chance, though ten to one they'll be in line for that honour.' He looked gloomy at the thought.

'You mustn't monopolise Caroline's time,' Margaret said, but smiled on them indulgently. They seemed to like each other well and that was good, for they were often together these days.

Left to herself after they had departed for their drive in the park, Margaret went upstairs to the first floor, to the small, intimate parlour at the back of the house that she liked best and sat down at the desk. Although rented only for a few months, it was a well-appointed house on four levels and the furniture was of good quality. Her agents had executed their commission well and she was very satisfied, both with the house itself and its position in a pleasant garden square that was fashionable, although not the most sought after.

She was glad to have a little time alone for she wanted to write some letters to friends in France, which she thought of as her home these days. England was pleasant for a visit and perhaps she would visit her brother sometimes in the future, though not in town—not after this masquerade. She would be lucky to get through even these few weeks in London without being unmasked, she realised now.

Until this morning, she had thought it was all going so well. She had been accepted by everyone, finding most people willing to be friendly, though some of the haughtier ladies had done no more than nod in passing. However, Lady Felicia, the young Duchess of Belmont, had been friendly, as had Lady Montclair—and it was good of her to send her brother to bring that invitation. Now why had she done that? Would it not have been easier to send it in the normal way?

There *had* been something odd in Lord Benedict's manner, Margaret decided, even if Roddy had not noticed it. He had looked at her in such a particular way, as if he were trying to delve into her mind and discover her secrets. And what had he said when he first introduced himself—that he thought they might have met somewhere?

She had thought that she vaguely remembered him… Yes, of course she did! All at once it came flooding back to her. He was the man she'd glimpsed standing on the harbour at Calais as she and the others had gone on board ship. She'd noticed him because…because even then he had been familiar. Yet where had she seen

him before that day? She was certain she had, for his
deep voice had stirred something in her memory.

'Oh, no! It can't be!'

Margaret suddenly recalled the incident she had
found so embarrassing some years earlier. The evening
her uncle had tried to molest her! She was almost certain that the man who had tried to help her that never-
to-be-forgotten evening had been Lord Benedict. Yes,
yes, the voice was right and the build, and the stern
manner.

Of course she hadn't known his name. She had never
known it. Indeed, she had scarcely been able to look at
him that night, which was why she had not recognised
him at once. The impression of a handsome man with
dark eyes and dark hair had lingered in her mind for
years. Indeed, he had featured in her foolish dreams!
Though always as a shadowy figure. Often in her
thoughts she had wished that she had at least taken the
time to thank him, but her distress and embarrassment
had made her flee before she dissolved into shaming
tears.

She hadn't recalled it that day at Calais, but, later,
when she was alone on the ship, she had thought about
the incident with her uncle for the first time in years,
and now she understood why. Seeing that man on the
dockside had triggered something in her mind, though
she had not realised it then. It was the particular way
he looked at her earlier that morning and something in
his voice that had brought a prickling sensation to her
nape.

Time had not changed him as much as it had her, for
he was as sternly handsome as he had been that night,
and when his mouth set in a certain way it was forbid-
ding. She thought it was that air of command that had

sent her uncle rushing away in fear of retribution, and
her in dismay. Not that she had feared him. His anger
had been all for the man who molested her, she had
known that even then, and had she not been so foolish...

There, Margaret's thoughts were suddenly suspended.
Nothing would have happened, she told herself firmly.
At the very most he would have given her a slight scold-
ing and then conducted her to her aunt. After that he
would have gone on his way and that would have been
an end to it, of course.

Besides, her plans did not include an involvement
with a man such as Lord Benedict. He was, she was
sure, the kind of man Aunt Kate had warned her of
becoming entangled with, the kind who was not to be
trusted with a woman's heart. Exactly the kind of man
she found attractive. Oh, what was she thinking of?
Foolish, foolish!

Margaret put aside her ridiculous thoughts and went
to have a lie down. She might as well have a little rest
before the evening, because she was feeling a little
tired...

She awoke from her dream to find herself drenched
in sweat. It was the old dream and the vivid pictures
were still in her head. She was in Italy and her uncle
had just tried to molest her—and then her rescuer had
come and driven him off. But this time she had not run
away. This time she had stayed to thank him, and he
had taken her into his arms, kissing her hungrily, passionately, making her tremble and cry out as she gave
herself up to his loving.

Whatever had caused her to have such a dream?
Margaret was shocked at herself. Her dreams had al-

ways, always stopped at a kiss—the romantic foolishness of a young girl. But this time she had been a
woman, responding to her lover's ardent need.

She got out of bed and went over to the window to
look out at the street. It was time for her to get ready
for their engagement that evening.

'You look beautiful,' Caroline said as she saw
Margaret that evening. She leaned forward to kiss her
cheek, taking care not to damage either of their gowns.
'You should wear things like that more often, Magda.
That gown is most becoming to you.'

'Thank you, my love. It is generous of you to say
so—but you are lovely. You will be the prettiest girl
there this evening. All the gentlemen will want to dance
with you.'

'I hope I shall not disappoint you, Magda.'

'Now why should I be disappointed?' Margaret studied her face and saw that she was nervous, but doing
her best to hide it. She reached out and took her hand.
'This visit is for you, Caroline. It is not for me. I shall
not be displeased with you if not even one gentleman
asks you to marry him—nor do I mind how many you
choose to refuse. I am merely giving you the chance
that should always have been yours, dearest. Do not
imagine that you must marry to oblige me. If you have
been thinking that, I apologise, for it was not my intention.'

Relief swept over Caroline's face. 'Is it truly so,
Magda?'

'Truly,' Margaret said and smiled. 'Silly girl! All I
want is for you to be happy. That was Aunt Kate's wish
and it is also mine.'

'I have been happy ever since your aunt took me into

your home,' Caroline said. 'She was always so kind and you have been as an elder sister to me. If I liked someone enough I think I should enjoy being married, having children—but I would not marry because the gentleman is rich or powerful. I was afraid you might want me to make a prestigious marriage, but I do not think I should be happy married to someone I cannot truly like.'

'Then I shall hope you find love,' Margaret said and was sincere in her wishes. 'Now, I think I heard Roddy arrive, and he is impatient, as you know, so we shall not keep him waiting.'

She was thoughtful as they went downstairs and watched her brother's face light up as he saw Caroline. Perhaps she had been wrong in her original plan to marry her protégée off to a gentleman from the cream of society, but all might not be lost; this visit was proving interesting, if nothing more.

The short drive to the Belmonts' magnificent house was soon accomplished and they waited in line for their turn to be received by their host and hostess for the evening. They were greeted warmly by both the Duke and Duchess and passed on into the various reception rooms to mingle with the other guests.

Since it was the middle of December now, the evening was cold outside but the rooms were crowded to overflowing and very warm, decorated with festoons of greenery tied with silk ribbons. Everyone was in merry mood and the noise of the laughter and tinkling glasses as the champagne flowed was considerable. Seeing that Caroline was a little uncomfortable in this crush, Margaret led the way through to the ballroom, which was less congested, many of the older ladies and gen-

tlemen having chosen to congregate in the main salon
to watch the newcomers enter and greet old friends.

It was a colourful scene: the ladies in ballgowns of
all hues, ranging from the pristine white to pale pastels,
such as Caroline was wearing, to the deepest blues and
crimsons for the older ladies. One dowager was dressed
head to foot in purple and gold. Jewels sparkled at the
pale throats of the ladies, and diamonds flashed from
old and young fingers, twinkling in the folds of a snowy
cravat here and there, all made brighter by the reflected
light from the glorious glass chandeliers shedding their
glow over the large room.

Margaret glanced round the room, seeing a few faces
she knew. She did not think the guest of honour had
arrived as yet, for there was bound to be a large crowd
about him. Besides, she imagined the man would have
a presence. Aunt Kate had told her the Prince of Wales
was flirtatious but charming, for she had met him somewhere when with her husband when he was a young
man, but Margaret had never had the pleasure. She
doubted she would get more than a glimpse of him that
evening, for she was not sufficiently important for her
hostess to think of introducing her.

However, her thoughts were soon diverted as the
young gentlemen began to arrive, making polite conversation with her before begging Caroline to be allowed the favour of a dance later in the evening. Some
of them came ostensibly to talk to Roddy, who was
universally liked for his easygoing manners, though
their eager eyes betrayed them and it was not long before Caroline was the centre of a lively crowd.

Several of the older gentlemen amongst them had
also asked Margaret if she would dance, but she had
declined with a smile to soften her refusal. She was

present in the guise of a chaperon that evening and thought she would be happy just to watch her young friend enjoying herself.

After some minutes she withdrew to a seat nearer the windows, thinking that she would go in search of a refreshing fruit cup in a moment or two. Caroline was clearly not going to be left a wallflower and she need not watch over her every moment for she had no fear that the girl would be careless.

'You do not dance this evening?'

Margaret was surprised as she heard the female voice and looked round as the woman sat next to her on the dainty sofa. She was a young woman, pretty, though her colouring was perhaps a little insipid beside Caroline's—but that thought was unkind and prejudiced, Margaret told herself as she smiled a welcome.

'Good evening, your Grace,' she said, her voice made husky and mysterious by just a trace of the accent she had adopted. 'I am 'ere as chaperon to my ward, as you know. I thought it best that I did not dance myself.'

'Oh, pooh, you must not call me "your Grace", it is too ageing,' the lady cried. 'I am to be called Lady Felicia or merely Felicia by my friends—and I hope we are to be friends?'

'That would be a 'onour, Lady Felicia.'

'You say you will not dance. I know it might be frowned on by some as you are here as a chaperon,' Felicia said and her eyes sparkled with mischief. 'However, you have been noticed, Comtesse. A certain person has asked me to bring you to him, and if he should ask you to dance you may not say no.'

'A certain person?' Margaret raised her fine dark brows, feeling puzzled both by the Duchess's manner and her words. 'I am not sure I—'ow you say?—I do not know who you mean…'

'Why, the Prince, of course,' Felicia said and laughed, her blonde ringlets bobbing merrily. 'Our own dear Regent, Comtesse—who else? He is the guest of honour and must have his way in all things.'

There was such a naughty look in her eyes that Margaret was betrayed into a laugh, for here after all was a woman with much the same sense of humour as her own, and that was very seldom met with in her experience.

'You should be careful when you say such things,' she warned. 'There are some ladies present who might take what you say literally.'

'There are some who would only be too willing,' Felicia quipped, her expression leaving nothing to the imagination. 'If I had not been so recently married… Prinny is a charmer to those he approves of, Comtesse, and I believe he is quite taken by you. He said he had heard of you and asked me to introduce you.' It was clear that she herself was a charming child and that she did not think before she spoke.

'Then I shall be delighted to do so,' Margaret said and rose to accompany the lively young woman into a smaller salon off the main reception rooms, where it seemed the Prince Regent had decided to receive those he perceived worthy of notice.

She was smiling as she saw the rather plump, but undeniably still attractive man she recognised immediately from descriptions she had had of him from others, though this was the first time she'd seen him in person. London was thin of company at the moment and she had attended only small, private affairs until this evening. Her smile faded as she saw the face of one of the men standing nearest to him and knew him for her visitor of the early morning. She noticed that his nose was beautifully straight and he was looking down it at her. She avoided meeting his eyes, which were once again intent on her face, as if he sought to recall something he had forgotten.

'Sir, I would like to present the Comtesse de Grenelle,' Lady Felicia said with a smile made intimate by old friendship. 'Comtesse, the Prince Regent, beloved of the ladies, young or old. I warn you to take care for he is the most terrible charmer.'

The brilliant sparkle in her eyes brought a laugh from the Regent who turned to Margaret with interest, his gaze going over her in the measuring way of a connoisseur. It was true that he had something of a reputation amongst the ladies, or so Margaret had heard, though it was also said he had married his first love, Mrs Fitzherbert, even though the marriage was morganatic and had since been officially denied. In the year 1795 the prince had been obliged to marry Caroline of Brunswick, a lady he disliked, who was presently living in Italy by mutual agreement.

'Comtesse,' he said and took the hand she offered as she dipped a slight curtsy, kissing it more lingeringly than perhaps was customary for a polite introduction. 'Come, will you not sit with me, madam, and tell me a little of yourself?'

'With pleasure, sir,' Margaret replied and sat on the chair that had been vacated by a gentleman at the ladies' approach. 'I do not know what I may tell you that will interest you. I have lived very quietly for some years now.'

'They tell me you are a widow—is that of long duration?'

'I was married only a short while,' Margaret said, a faint colour in her cheeks as she lied. Her voice was made even huskier by emotion, for her aunt's death still affected her. 'Afterwards, I lived with a…friend. She too was a widow. It was she who adopted Miss Hammond and we 'ad talked of bringing her to London for a visit, so when my friend died I decided to go ahead with our plans once our period of mourning was over. It is, you see, a very simple story, *n'est-ce pas*?'

'For which we may be grateful, else you would not have been here to grace these rooms this evening, nor the lovely Miss Hammond.' The Prince Regent's eyes seemed to hold a hint of amusement as he looked at her, which made Margaret wonder. Surely he was not thinking of making her a proposal of a nature she would be obliged to decline? 'Demme, but I'm thinking that would have been a great shame, would it not, Benedict?'

Was it her imagination, or did the Regent's words contain a laughing challenge for the man who watched her so sternly? Those eyes were almost black, she thought, but there was a hint of silver in their depths— but she was staring again! She averted her eyes, a faint colour in her cheeks as she recalled her dream. No, she would not let him overset her! If she blushed and simpered like a green girl, the wretched man would imagine she was setting her cap at him.

'Indeed, it would have been a pity if two such lovely ladies had not been here this evening, sir,' Giles answered, a tiny flicker in his cheek as he spoke but showing no other sign of emotion. He too had dreams he wished to suppress, for it was not a part of his plan to be seduced by her charms. And yet she made him instantly aware of his own need. 'Comtesse—do you dance this evening? I would be grateful for the honour of being your partner.'

'Thank you, *monsieur*,' Margaret replied, feeling her cheeks heat as she met his penetrating gaze. 'But I am 'ere as my ward's chaperon and I think it would look—'ow you English say? Not quite proper, that is it, *non*? It is not permitted for the chaperon to dance, I think?'

Unconsciously, her accent had become deeper as she spoke to him, as though needing all her defences against him. She had sensed something disapproving in his manner and felt that he disliked her—so why was he inviting her to dance?

'You must not let the tabbies deprive you of pleasure, Comtesse,' the Regent said and stood, his girth less of an intrusion now he was standing than it had seemed sitting. 'Come, you shall dance with me first and after Benedict shall have the honour. Chaperon or not, the wagging tongues will soon cease their clacking if it is seen that you dance to oblige me.'

Margaret had no option but to agree. To refuse the Regent was impossible since he was both the guest of honour and, because of his father's illness, the ruler of England. Their dance was pleasurable, for he was light on his feet despite his size, and soon over. He left her with every sign of having enjoyed himself and made an audible remark indicating that the Comtesse had obliged him to his hostess a moment or two later, which had the effect of silencing any who might have criticised her. As every lady knew, a request from the Regent was tantamount to a command that one refused at one's peril.

After their dance ended, Margaret was immediately claimed by Giles Benedict, a circumstance that did less than please her, but since the Regent had ordered it, it was unavoidable.

The nearness of Lord Benedict's powerful frame set a shiver running through her, which she immediately controlled, though she was aware of a heightened colour in her cheeks and a feeling of light-headedness. She was floating on air! How very strange. She took a deep breath to steady herself and it was as well she did. The touch of his hands at her waist sent a thrill of pleasure cascading through her entire body, making her feel slightly odd. Her heart was beating wildly and she felt her cheeks grow warm.

However, she found that he was a skilled and pleasant partner, and some of her wariness left her as he conducted a polite exchange of mere nothings. Margaret reasoned with herself. These strange feelings coursing through her were mere madness and temporary. She had only to endure a few minutes of this uncomfortably close contact and then he would leave her. Yet perversely there was a part of her that wished the dance might go on for ever.

'You dance well, sir.'

'Anyone would dance well with such a partner,' he replied, and as she gazed up at him Margaret's heart jerked. His eyes had deepened in colour and were so intent that she could not help thinking he felt much as she did, was aroused by the close proximity of their bodies. Her pulses raced as his fingers seemed to tighten about hers and she felt his heat burn into her. 'You are a very beautiful, desirable woman.' The huskiness of his voice aroused pictures in her mind—frightening, vivid pictures of herself naked in his arms. It was that wretched dream all over again and this time she was in a ballroom!

Dreams were one thing—this was reality. Margaret was almost certain that he wanted to make love to her, and, a little afraid of this strange new sensation, instinctively, she retreated, her manner becoming cool once more. 'I am flattered, sir.'

His gaze narrowed and in the next moment his expression hardened as if he had ruthlessly squashed all feeling. And then their dance was ending.

It was as he left her that something he murmured set a tingling down her spine. 'The Regent was taken with you, my lady,' he told her. 'But be warned: though some may think it, he is not a fool and neither are his friends.'

Now what did he mean by that? Margaret watched him walk to the Regent's side, feeling both bewildered and angry. Did he think she had set her cap at the Prince? That perhaps she had some idea of becoming his mistress? There were ladies who would consider this a high honour, but she was certainly not one of them! Her irritation at this misconception knew no bounds and she wished she might have demanded an explanation of his hints, but this was neither the time nor the place.

She was once again approached by gentlemen wishing to dance, and as some of them had been refused earlier she could not risk offence by doing so again, now that she had been seen willing to dance. Inwardly, she cursed the circumstance that had led to her being so obliged, but as her anger abated she began to realise it was very pleasant to dance again, and to enjoy the evening more than she would otherwise have done.

Her brother asked her for a dance just before supper, remarking mournfully that he doubted he would stand a chance of getting Caroline to himself for supper.

'Devenish has been bristling round her like a dog with a bone,' he muttered. 'And Monkford's eldest is making a cake of himself—a veritable mooncalf.'

'You need not concern yourself about Lord Monkford's son,' Margaret told him. Roddy did not know the truth, but Caroline was aware that the young man was her half-brother. 'But I saw her dance three times with Mr Rushford. I understand he has quite a large fortune. He seems a pleasant young man and it would be a good match for her.'

Sir Roderick gave her a speaking look. Indeed, he opened his mouth to speak and then shut it again, realising that he could not say such a thing to his sister and in public. But his opinion of Rushford had suddenly undergone a sea change. Instead of thinking him a decent fellow, the man had become a pompous idiot not fit to clean Caroline's boots!

'Not sure I care for that idea,' he muttered gloomily. 'She might look higher.'

'Might she?' Margaret asked, a hint of mischief in her eyes. She was not aware of it, but she looked both beautiful and a little wicked as she teased and provoked her brother, of whom she was very fond. 'I do not think we could expect an old title for her in the circumstances, do you? No, that might be too much—but Mr Rushford has no such concerns. His father left him a fortune and he is his own master...'

'Yes, well, I dare say,' Roddy muttered, his cravat feeling dashed tight all of a sudden. 'But there might be others with as good a claim to her affections as he.'

Margaret laughed and tapped his arm with her fan. 'One of them not a million miles away, I might guess? Foolish, Roddy. I merely tease you—but if you have ideas of your own it might be as well to make Caroline aware of them.'

'Bamming me, were you?' Roddy said ruefully. 'Might have known it.'

Her eyes sparkled at him, a provocative smile on her lips.

Observing Margaret from across the room, the Regent made a soft remark to his companion, which sent Giles on an errand he was loath to complete.

'Your pardon, Comtesse,' he said, his face expressionless, his eyes dark with suppressed annoyance. 'The Prince Regent asks if you will make one of his party. They are about to go into supper now.'

It was a signal honour, for a large round table had been set aside for the Regent and those he favoured to partake of the lavish supper provided by the Belmonts, and one that Margaret felt constrained to accept despite her own preferences.

'My lord,' she said, inclining her head and taking the arm he offered. 'You have campaigned with the Duke of Wellington on more than one occasion, I believe? Your sister told me that you were one of his most trusted aides.'

'It has been my honour to serve him.'

'Yes, it would be an honour. He is a brave man.'

'And sometimes reckless.'

'Truly? I had not thought it. He has had much success with his campaigns, I believe?'

'Wellington takes risks others dare not, but he bears a charmed life and usually wins through. His enemies have been confounded many times and I pray they always shall be.'

'I am relieved to hear it, sir, though I believe for the

moment he has no wars to fight? Am I right in thinking that he is at the Vienna Conference?'

'For the moment, as you say,' Giles acknowledged. His eyes narrowed suspiciously. Why did she want to know about his relationship with Wellington? And what business was it of hers where the Iron Duke was at this moment? Was she playing a deeper game than he guessed? 'But for the future—who knows?'

'Ah, this is something we may all ask,' Margaret replied and tipped her head to one side as she looked up at him, a challenge in her eyes. 'It is, 'ow you say, that none 'ave the knowledge of the future.'

Giles's gaze was intent as he looked at her. It was strange how her accent deepened whenever she spoke to him, and that her English was perfect other than when she deliberately pretended to not quite understand. He was becoming more and more sure that the so charming Comtesse de Grenelle was not what she claimed. Belmont thought he'd got hold of the wrong end of the stick, was amused by the idea that a woman like the Comtesse might be planning to assassinate him, and the Regent had brushed off the idea as nonsense. They were both enchanted with her, but Giles remained suspicious, despite being very aware of her in a physical sense. He would not deny that she was beautiful, or that there was an underlying sensuality about her that appealed to something deep down inside him.

But he must keep his mind on what was important here. The stability of Europe might depend upon it. If the assassinations of Wellington and the Prince Regent could be accomplished, it might lead to a lessening of purpose amongst the Allies. There were those who inclined to the idea that Napoleon's return could be no worse than the Bourbons, and many in France were openly speaking of their dissatisfaction.

It would do Giles no good to be distracted by the Comtesse's charm. He would swear that she was hiding something—and he was going to discover what it was, if it took him a week or a year.

It was odd that the thought of getting to know her was becoming more and more appealing every time he met her! And he was fairly certain that he would be meeting her again in his dreams that night...

Chapter Three

Margaret listened to Caroline's happy chatter on the way home, her mind only half-attending as she relaxed to the comforting clip-clop of the horses' hooves. She was well aware that the evening had been a success as far as her ward was concerned, and she was certain that the invitations would pour in for the rest of their stay in England. Caroline's dowry was not huge, but it was respectable, and her beauty was such that she would not have been friendless without a penny to her name.

At least three of the gentlemen vying for her attention that evening were in the happy possession of independent fortunes. Of the three, Mr Rushford had seemed the most particular, which was the reason for Roddy's little burst of jealousy. A secret smile touched Margaret's lips as she reflected on the possible outcome. Her sisterly affection might have prejudiced her in Roddy's favour, but she could not see that any girl in her right mind could prefer either of the other gentlemen.

She had been aware of a certain reluctance to marry on her brother's part, but he might change his mind very quickly now that several other gentlemen had shown an interest in Caroline. Margaret suspected that her brother had been toying with the idea of looking for a rich wife. His own estate was small, though quite adequate for his needs. Caroline's ten thousand would enable them to visit London when they wished and Margaret would give her brother another five thousand pounds as a wedding present. She had not told him of her intention, for she did not wish to influence him, but she could well spare it, for her own needs were modest. She intended to live very quietly on her return to France.

Parting from Caroline at the top of the stairs, Margaret went to her own room. She allowed her maid to help her out of her gown and then sent her to bed with a smile and a quiet word of appreciation.

Left alone, she brushed her glorious hair, which fell in a thick, shining curtain to her shoulders once released from its coiffeur, staring at her reflection in the pretty dressing mirror. The frame was shaped like a shield, fashioned in rich mahogany and inlaid with a stringing of light-coloured wood and had been one of many presents from her aunt, and the glass showed her an attractive woman with sad eyes.

Why was she feeling this way? It should be a night of triumph. Caroline was an undoubted success, her future surely assured. For Mr Rushford would not care a fig that she was Monkford's bastard. Lord Ellwood had also been most attentive, though Margaret believed it was less likely that he would offer, given his reputation as something of a flirt. That young man was still playing the field for the moment, as he was entitled to do, of course. No, she rather thought it would be either Mr Rushford or Roddy who won Caroline's heart. Indeed, it might already belong to Roddy, if her dawning suspicions were correct.

So why did Margaret feel so very low now that she was alone with her thoughts? It was ridiculous to feel lonely! She had many good friends who would welcome her on her return to her home—but did she want to live by herself? She could employ a companion, of course, but for some reason the life she had planned held little appeal for her at that moment. Longings and desires she had learned to suppress had somehow made themselves felt as she'd danced with *him*.

Oh, it was all the fault of that wretched man! Margaret put down her hairbrush with a little bang. Why must he look at her in such a way that it caused her heart to skitter like a leaf caught in a mischievous wind? She had done her utmost to hide her feelings as they danced, but there was no doubting that the touch of his hand, his nearness, had brought her to a new awareness of herself. She had come suddenly, tinglingly, alive in a way that she had never dreamed she could be. Then to see such disapproval in his eyes, to hear the threat in his words! Did he truly imagine she had set out to entice the Prince Regent?

Surely not! She had done absolutely nothing to bring herself to the Regent's notice, nor had she gone out of her way to attract his interest. He had laughed a few times as they spoke, seeming amused, though she had not been certain whether it was her words or his own thoughts that had brought a twinkle to his eye. He was pleasant enough as a companion, but the thought of being his mistress was abhorrent to her. Indeed, she had met few men that appealed to her senses at all—and the one who did was impossible! His touch might make her heart race, but she did not like him, no, not at all.

It was grossly unfair of Lord Benedict to suspect her of being in any way a flirt. Indeed, the last thing she wanted was to be the Prince Regent's mistress—or any man's mistress, come to that.

If an errant thought popped into Margaret's head at that moment she dismissed it instantly. She would never consider being Lord Benedict's mistress either—even if the touch of his hand did arouse such very exciting feelings. Besides, he was unlikely to ask her. It seemed that he neither approved of nor liked her very much.

Oh, be damned to the man, she thought inelegantly, and retired to bed in high dudgeon. He was not worth worrying over and she certainly did not intend to let him disturb her sleep.

Yet her sleep was again disturbed by vivid dreams that night, even though in the morning she could not quite remember them, only that they had made her toss and turn restlessly for an age. So annoying! And so foolish. Giles Benedict was nothing like the man in her foolish dreams, for that man was generous, warm and loving. He did not look at her with suspicious eyes or make comments that were meant to prick her…

Margaret might have drawn some satisfaction had she known that she was not the only one to lose sleep that night. On his return from the ball, most of which he'd spent close to the Prince's side, Giles had paced the floor of his bedchamber until the early hours.

Curse the woman! She had succeeded in getting beneath his skin despite his suspicions of her. His uncle had dismissed the suggestion that the Comtesse de Grenelle might be in the pay of Napoleon Bonaparte's friends.

'You know I value your opinion, Benedict,' he'd said. 'Your advice has proved solid in the past, but this time you are wrong. Comtesse de Grenelle is charming and quite harmless. In my opinion, neither a spy nor a potential assassin.'

'I am aware of her charm, sir—but there is something not right…something hidden.'

'I dare say there is some mystery about her,' Belmont agreed. 'Had I not recently married my darling Felicia, I might have found her irresistible. But if there is an assassin skulking somewhere, I am willing to wager it is not her.'

Giles had given way on the point, knowing it was impossible to sway Belmont once his mind was made up on the subject, but he was still uneasy. There was something wrong, he was certain of it. Something about her niggled at the back of his mind, something he ought to recall but could not.

The trouble was, he found the Comtesse too damned attractive! Dancing with her had aroused a hot coursing desire in him that had shaken him to the core. It had been unexpected, taking him off balance and requiring an iron will to control. He could not recall ever having been aroused like that simply by touching a woman's hand, and certainly not in public. Good grief, he had been tempted to spirit her away to a secluded corner and ravish her there and then! Anyone would think him a green youth instead of a man well versed in the conducting of such affairs.

It was both annoying and inconvenient to feel such desire for a woman he suspected of being a threat to the stability of England. Obviously, she was more dangerous than he had imagined at the start—but who was she really? Not who she professed to be, he would swear. And why was she here in England? His mind went round and round like a dog on a spit wheel. Why was she here?

Surely it could not be merely that she wished to find a husband for her ward? It was clear that Sir Roderick was in love with the girl. The Comtesse might have stayed at home and let matters take their own course if that was her sole purpose. No, she must certainly have another…something secret and devious.

And somehow Giles had to discover what it was before it was too late. The safety of the Regent and his own uncle might depend upon his vigilance—and he could not remain vigilant if he allowed himself to be seduced by a husky voice and a provocative smile.

To Margaret's satisfaction, several gentlemen called to leave their cards the following day, and the invitations to dinners, soirées, dances and all manner of delights began to arrive in quick succession. London society was actually quite a small closed circle, open only to the privileged, and since many of the same people were to be seen at all the large events, the Comtesse and her ward met most of their new acquaintances during the next few days. One notable exception was Lord Benedict. Not that that was of any consequence, since he had shown no interest in Caroline whatsoever.

Telling herself she was relieved not to have been forced to endure his company, Margaret still found herself looking for Lord Benedict's commanding figure when she attended Lady Montclair's musical evening. He would surely have attended his own sister's special evening?

'You are looking as lovely as ever, Miss Hammond,' Augusta Montclair said as she welcomed them to her home. 'Do go and find your friends, for I am sure they are eager to see you.' Her bright eyes went over

Margaret. 'You look beautiful. Not many women could
wear that shade of dull gold, but you can, Comtesse.
And I know that your gown could only have been made
in Paris—it has such style!'

'You are very kind to say so,' Margaret said. One
glance round the room had told her that there was no
sign of Lord Benedict. 'Your brother does not attend
this evening?'

'It is the veriest nuisance,' Augusta cried and tossed
her head in annoyance. 'He swore to me that he would
have returned from his mission by this evening, but as
you see he has not. I am cross with him and shall tell
him so when next I see him.'

'He has gone away?'

Lady Montclair looked vexed, for her brother's insis-
tence that the Comtesse and her ward must be invited
this evening had raised cherished hopes in her breast.

'To France I believe. Oh, it is always the same with
Giles. He is forever chasing off on some mission for
the Prince or mayhap Wellington, though I ought not to
say since it may be secret. He is set on a diplomatic
career, you see, and I suppose that must involve a lot
of very dull, boring work. I do not know why he does
not marry and settle down, for he is perfectly well able
to afford it. He told me that he has no interest in his
uncle's title or fortune and wished Felicia well in her
efforts to provide an heir for the family, but he might
set up his own household if he chose. His own name is
an old one and he is the last of the direct line. I have
told him to get himself an heir and come home, but he
does not listen. As it is he leaves everything to an agent,
but, conscientious as Mr Marsham is, it is not the same.
But Giles says he does not wish to settle yet and spends

his time travelling. Of course he will have to return if Belmont dies without issue.'

'I see…' Such personal information was of no interest to Margaret, of course. 'Perhaps Lord Benedict does not care for the country life?'

'Oh, I think he likes it well enough. Our families have known each other for ever, of course, since my late father's estate marches with Belmont's own, though much smaller, of course. Giles was a frequent visitor at Belmont House when he was in the schoolroom. I thought he would settle to a country life—but then he went into the army and when I next saw him he had changed. I confess that I do not know why. I suppose he grew up, though I have wondered if he was crossed in love.'

'I dare say it was just that he learned more of the world once he was in the army. I have heard that meeting with death on the battlefield is a life-changing affair.'

Augusta grimaced. 'I dare say. I know Giles has been wounded once or twice, though he made nothing of it and had recovered by the time he came home. Oh, we should not have begun this, Comtesse. Why should we discuss my wretched brother since he did not see fit to attend my party when he promised he would? And after being so particular about delivering that invitation too!' She made a little gasping sound, her face reddening as she realised what she had said. 'Not that I would not have sent it, but he was so particular.'

'I dare say he had no choice but to carry out his mission,' Margaret said and moved on, saving her hostess from further blushes.

Augusta's blurted confession had made Margaret thoughtful. It was curious that Lord Benedict should have asked his sister to provide an invitation for her and then not be at the party. Yet, if he had been sent on an important mission, it might have been beyond his power to refuse. On the other hand, why had he insisted on delivering that invitation himself?

It was a small mystery, thought provoking but impossible to solve—and she was spending far too much time thinking about the man as it was these days. She made up her mind that she would put him from her thoughts immediately.

Giles arrived back in London at an hour that was too far advanced to think of attending Augusta's soirée. His journey to France had been undertaken not at the Regent's instigation, but at his own. However, his inquiries in Paris had met with a complete blank. No one amongst those informants he trusted had even heard of the Comtesse de Grenelle. Indeed, one of them had gone so far as to declare that he believed the last legitimate holder of that title had met his death at the hands of Madame la Guillotine at the very beginning of the terror.

'Jacques de Grenelle was barely fifteen and had no wife to my knowledge,' Giles had been told. 'His parents were executed with him and there were no cousins or relatives to inherit the estate as far as I am aware. The de Grenelle chateau was destroyed by fire by the mob and the family has died out. I do not know who this lady may be, my lord, but I would swear that she is an impostor.'

If the mysterious Comtesse was masquerading under a false name she had to be dangerous, Giles reasoned. Why else would she pretend to be something she was not? She was clearly a lady and wealthy—so why play a game with Society if she did not have some nefarious purpose?

His instincts had warned him from the beginning that she was not all she seemed; that accent could not be faulted and she had clearly lived in France for some years, for when she spoke in French as she did on occasion, her command of the language was perfect. Yet he understood that she was not wholly French and nor, it seemed, was she a comtesse.

Giles was more determined than ever to get to the bottom of this mystery, but how best to proceed? He knew that he had allowed his anger to show after their dance, perhaps because she had made such an impact on his emotions. He had succeeded only in causing her to withdraw from him, to look at him with suspicion. If he continued to show her hostility, she would withdraw further and he would have no chance of gaining her confidence.

Only by getting closer to her did he stand a chance of leading her into making a mistake. Friendship and familiarity might prompt her to let something slip, but perhaps she had already taken a dislike to him? And yet he had sensed that she was as disturbed by the sensations their dance had aroused as he had been himself.

His brow furrowed in thought. She was a widow, therefore she had experienced a man's loving, had perhaps taken lovers since her husband's death. If he played the game differently, pretended to be attracted to her—to desire her as his mistress…

Giles swore as he paced the room. Damn it! He did desire her as his mistress, despite suspecting that she had a sinister purpose behind her masquerade. Would it not make perfect sense to use an attraction he believed was mutual to break down her defences and discover her secrets?

Such behaviour would be a betrayal of those values he held dear. No gentleman would seduce a lady merely to learn her secrets—and yet, if she was what he suspected, she was not worthy of his respect. She was playing a devious game and the only way to beat her might be to meet her on her own terms.

He would, he decided, take things easily, flirting with her and flattering her to gain her confidence. If they should become lovers… His mind shied away from the thought. He doubted that she was a woman to be rushed into any such affair; it would take patience and time to seduce her and if, in the meantime, he succeeded in unmasking her, he would leave her to the mercy of others and walk away.

There was no question of his being romantically entangled. The Comtesse de Grenelle—or whatever her name might be—was a beautiful woman, her voice husky and enticing, but his feelings were purely physical, nothing more.

Strangely enough, once the decision to pursue her further had been made, Giles began to relax, the agitation that had taken him over since the Belmonts' dance becoming a thing of the past. He knew exactly what he meant to do and would begin the chase the very next time they met.

In the morning he would visit Augusta and ask her when he would be most likely to next meet the Comtesse in company. Better it should seem accidental, he decided; a visit or a personal invitation might seem too obvious. No, he must take it slowly, savour the chase and his eventual victory…

* * *

Margaret was being driven around the park in her brother's curricle when she saw Lord Benedict walking towards them. He had such an imposing figure and such an air of command that her heart caught at the sight of him, especially when he doffed his hat and smiled. Roddy was reining in his horses so that they could exchange a few words.

'Good morning, Sir Roderick,' Giles said. 'Comtesse, may I compliment you on your gown? It is quite charming, but then everything you wear has its own style. I would suppose it is because you lived in France for so long.'

Why was he smiling at her like that? Margaret felt short of breath as she looked down at him; the look of hostility she had seen in those commanding eyes had completely disappeared and now there was only warmth. Now, indeed, he was the man who haunted her dreams.

'You do me too much honour, sir.' She was so taken aback that she had forgotten her accent for the moment, but corrected herself at once. 'Lady Montclair tells me you 'ave been in France, *non*?'

Giles smiled inwardly. His change of manner had shocked her and she had forgotten that charming accent, which was a pity because it was so fascinating, but clearly false. The Comtesse was playing a dangerous game and she little knew that in him she had met her equal. If she thought to fool him, she would discover her mistake!

'It was a matter of business,' he said. 'My sister scolded me for missing her party and I am exceedingly sorry for having done so—but she has allowed me to repair my fault by taking her to the Renshaws' dance this evening. I believe you and Miss Hammond mean to be there?'

'Indeed, we 'ope to attend,' Margaret replied, keeping her breathing even with difficulty. Why did this man have such an effect on her? She had never met with it in any other, but it had always been so—even that night he'd rescued her from her uncle's unwelcome attentions. His effect on her then had been so powerful that she had fled into the night rather than face his scorn, but she was older now and more able to control her emotions. 'I shall 'ope to see you there, *monsieur*.'

'Then I shall look forward to what might otherwise have been an insipid evening. Comtesse, your servant. Hazelmere, I shall be at my club this afternoon, if you care for a hand of cards?'

'Good of you to ask; don't mind obliging you, Benedict,' Roddy said, flattered by this attention from a man he believed would hardly have noticed him before this. He flicked the reins and drove on, glancing at his sister once they were out of earshot. 'And you know what that means, Maggie—the fellow's after you.'

'Please do not be foolish,' Margaret said, her stomach fluttering as if a host butterflies had invaded. 'He was merely being polite.'

'Benedict would have ignored me a few weeks ago. He mixes with Ellwood and his crowd and they're a bit high in the instep, you know. It's because he thinks I'm a friend of yours that he asked me to join his set at the club. I've been going there for years when I could, never been asked to play by any of that crowd before. He wants to pump me for information about you, depend upon it.'

'Then you must make sure not to give him any.'

'Do you take me for a fool?'

'Of course not. But be careful all the same. I do not quite trust him, though I do not know why.'

'I told you, he's after you.'

'Perhaps he is interested in Caroline.'

'Don't think she's in his line. Might be if he was looking for a wife, but can't see it, not with his uncle just wed to that young filly—no need for him to do his duty unless Belmont fails. No, he's looking for a new mistress, mark my words. I did hear that he'd broken with his last high flyer some weeks ago.'

'That is coarse, Roddy. I do not care to hear such talk.'

'It's the truth all the same, Maggie. Depend upon it, he thinks you're fair game, being a widow and all.' He glanced at her. 'Might be awkward for you, deuced awkward, if he makes you an offer of *carte blanche*.'

'Not at all.' Margaret had recovered her composure now that she was not faced with that devastating smile. 'If he should make such an offer, I shall merely refuse it. Naturally, he would not do so if he knew the truth, and so I shall excuse him and make nothing of it. There is no need to be embarrassed after all.'

Her brother glanced at her curiously. She seemed to mean what she said, but he suspected that she had been more affected by Lord Benedict than she would care to admit. She was still something of a mystery to him, for she did not often confide her thoughts to anyone, but he was fond of her in his own way.

'It's a pity he can't be brought to offer you marriage, Maggie. It would be just the thing for you.'

'Nothing of the sort! I have no wish to marry—and would not accept if he asked, which he will not, of course.'

'Can't want to live alone for the rest of your life,' her brother objected. 'I know Aunt Kate's experience wasn't a happy one, but marriage isn't always like that...' His cheerful face took on a gloomy expression. 'I had hoped I might be happy meself one day.'

'I am sure you will be, dearest,' Margaret said, making an effort to dismiss Lord Benedict once and for all from her thoughts. 'When you've finally made up your mind to settle down.'

'Think I might have,' he told her still on a gloomy note. 'Thing is, ain't sure my feelings are returned.'

'Are you not?' A naughty twinkle came to her eyes. 'And why is that, dearest? Have you spoken to the young lady of your choice?'

'Dash it all, Maggie,' he exclaimed. 'You know I haven't. The thing is, Caroline seems very taken with Rushford—driving out with him all the time, dancing with him, sitting next to him at dinner...'

'The dinner was given by his aunt,' Margaret reasoned, amused by his pique. 'Caroline sat where she was placed—and there is no reason why she should not drive out with Mr Rushford, and she must dance with someone, after all.'

'You know what I mean,' her brother said and flushed. 'I thought I stood a chance with her, but it all seems to have changed since the Belmonts' ball. Caroline ain't the same.'

'No, I have noticed that she has more confidence,' Margaret said and smiled at him, her teasing at an end. She realised that he was more upset than she had at first thought, and touched his arm in sympathy. 'But I still think she rather likes you, dearest. Caroline is trying her wings a little before she settles down. It might be that she is waiting for a sign from you.'

'Do you think so?' He looked at her uncertainly. 'I thought it might be too soon to speak. After all, you went to some expense to arrange this trip for her and she has a right to her pleasure.'

'Knowing Caroline, I think she might feel even more pleasure if she went to future dances as your fiancée— but I may be wrong, of course. I cannot speak for her. You must ask her yourself.'

'Supposing she turns me down?'

'That is a risk you must take,' Margaret told him, 'though I think it unlikely myself. Have courage, my dearest, and I believe all will be well.'

'Maybe I shall, then.' Roddy brightened and grinned at his sister. 'Turned the tables on me nicely, didn't you, Maggie, but I ain't forgotten. I've got a nose for these things and I'd wager that Benedict has it in mind to offer you *carte blanche*.'

Margaret shook her head at him, but her mouth had gone dry and she was trembling inside. Roddy must be wrong. Surely he was! Lord Benedict had seemed to dislike her at their previous meeting—unless he too had been disturbed by the startling sensations their dance had aroused. Was it possible that when he'd spoken sharply to her, he had merely tried to cover his feelings and now he had come to a decision to pursue her?

What was she to say to him if he did? Her first re-action to her brother's teasing had been to deny any interest, but in her heart she knew that that was not true. If he should smile at her, caress her, love her, as he did in her dreams, she would find him difficult to deny. But that was mere speculation.

Only time and further acquaintance would tell what Lord Benedict's intentions towards her were, however, and therefore she would do better not to dwell on such a small incident.

* * *

Margaret saw him almost as soon as she entered the
room. He had more presence than any other gentleman
present, his manner and bearing that of a man used to
command. She had been told that his army rank was a
mere captain, but also that he had refused promotion
because he wished to stay with his men at the heart of
the battle. As their eyes met across the room he smiled
and Margaret's heart seemed to stand still for one moment. In the next instant he was coming towards her,
as she had known he would.

This was the sixth night in a row that they had met
in company and each time Lord Benedict had singled
her out for special attention. Oh, it was all quite discreet, of course, nothing that could cause gossip, but he
had a way of smiling just for her. The merest brush of
his hand against hers, a lift of his brow as they shared
a joke, for it seemed that often they found amusement
in the same things; any one of these small gestures was
enough to convince her that her brother had been right.
It would appear that Lord Benedict was paying court to
her. But what were his intentions? And what should her
answer be if he made her an offer of *carte blanche*?

'Comtesse,' Giles said as he reached her, 'how delightful to see you this evening. I was not sure if you
would be here and I most particularly hoped to see you.'

'*Pour quelle raison?*' Margaret tipped her head to
one side, a gleam of mischief in her eyes that played
havoc with Giles's libido. 'You 'ave some problem, my
lord? Is it that you need my 'elp?'

Oh, God, did she have any idea what she was doing
to him? That accent and the broken English, the way
she had of pouting her lips, all drove him half-mad with
longing. Giles felt the power of her sexual magnetism,

his mouth dry as the heat in his groins intensified and he knew an urgent desire to have done with this game and take her to bed. Perhaps then he could lay these devils to rest!

'Can it be that you do not know I come to these insipid affairs merely in the hope of seeing you?' he croaked huskily. The woman was an accomplished seductress, he'd swear, and her skills had certainly had a powerful effect on him. He smiled crookedly as he remembered some plan of setting out to lure her into his web. Be damned to that, he was caught in her toils and not even struggling!

Margaret felt a spasm of something low in her abdomen that she vaguely recognised as desire. No man had ever made her feel like this, but she had dreamed of a lover as a young and innocent girl, and in her dreams she had known that love would make her feel this way. Not that she was in love, of course. It was merely the natural desire of a healthy young woman. Aunt Kate had warned her that it might happen.

'I have known desire,' her aunt had told her once towards the end of her life. They had been sitting in the warm sunshine, talking together in the garden at the villa as they often did. 'My marriage made me forget that it was possible to be young and carefree, but when I was a girl I was foolish and headstrong. The man who seduced me was not wholly to blame, though he was older and should have known better, but I was not raped, my dear. At the time I believed I was in love. Had William been suitable I might have married him, but he was a dancing master and my father would not have it. So I was packed off to marry a foreigner, who made me pay for my sin over and over again, especially after he discovered that I could not give him a child.

My experiences have led me to a dislike of men in general, but you must not think that there is never a chance for happiness with a man, Margaret—just be careful that you choose wisely before you give your heart.'

Margaret had decided then that she was unlikely ever to meet a man she could care for enough or love enough to marry, but that was before… She must not allow herself to be taken in by his sweet words.

Bringing her thoughts into line, Margaret looked into the face of the man who had just spoken, her chest tight with suppressed emotion. 'I think you flatter me, my lord.'

'You are wrong,' Giles assured her. 'I always say what I mean. This is not the kind of affair I usually attend. I have used both Felicia and Augusta shamefully to secure me invitations these past few days.'

'I am not sure I understand you…' Oh but she did, she did! Her stomach clenched as she saw the burning look in his eyes and felt its heat creep slowly through her veins. 'You cannot mean…'

'You know I do,' Giles murmured in a soft, husky voice that set her pulses racing. 'The attraction has been there from the beginning—from the moment we danced. Come admit the truth, Magda. May I call you that in private?'

'I am not sure that we shall be private together.' She was desperately trying to control the situation, feeling as if she had been swept along by a storm of emotion, like a leaf caught in a gale. She was fighting a hopeless battle, her will to resist ebbing as she gazed into his eyes and saw something that made her want to lose herself in him. '*Mon Dieu*, I think you are a man to be wary of, *monsieur*.'

'I am sure we shall find much pleasure in being private together—and the perfect opportunity has presented itself,' Giles murmured, his voice hoarse with the desire he was fighting to keep within bounds. 'You must realise that London will soon be thin of company, Comtesse. The Duke of Belmont's ball was the last important occasion of the year in town. Everyone is drifting away, to Bath or the country. Felicia has invited a party of friends to join her at Belmont for the New Year. You and Miss Hammond are to receive an invitation, I understand, also Sir Roderick and Mr Rushford.'

'And you, my lord?'

'Naturally,' he said and a distinctive gleam came to his dark eyes. 'It is a perfect opportunity to get to know each other better, do you not think so, Magda? I hope you will accept? I should be disappointed if you did not.'

'Why is that?'

'Surely you may guess?' His dark eyes seemed to caress her and his smile made her feel oddly happy for some foolish, unexplained reason.

'Perhaps…' She moved the tip of her tongue over her full bottom lip, never guessing that he thought it provocative and designed to tempt him further. 'Yes, I think it might serve…' Her eyes sought his as if trying to probe into his mind and something in them made her heart start to thump. 'I believe in my 'eart that Caroline is torn between two admirers at the moment, though she has not confided in me—Sir Roderick and Mr Rushford. A trip to the country might be useful in bringing the matter of her marriage to a 'ead.'

'It will give them more time to get to know one another,' Giles agreed, watching her intently. This was his chance and yet oddly he was loath to press his advan-

tage. 'It was for Miss Hammond's sake that you came
to London, I believe?'

'*Oui*, in part,' Margaret agreed. 'I thought it fair that
she should have a chance to meet and know the class
into which she ought to 'ave been raised, 'ad her mother
not died when she was a babe. She was adopted by my
aunt and placed with the nuns for her education—but
both her parents were English and from the gentry.'

'That is indeed a sad history, Comtesse. To lose everything so young is a terrible thing. I presume they
were a country family?'

'*Oui...*' There was something about him at that moment that made Margaret feel this was a man she could
trust and like. She had thought him her enemy, but they
seemed to have crossed some invisible line without either of them quite meaning to. She hesitated, for some
reason tempted to confide in him, the barrier she had
raised against him in her mind beginning to crumble.
Yet still there was doubt and she held back the words
that might have aroused his censure. 'I can assure you
that she comes from...good stock and is born of gen-
tlefolk. 'Owever, she has no family to provide for her
except my aunt—and now me.'

'I believe she is fortunate to have found such friends.
She might otherwise have been forced to earn her living
as a companion, which would have been a waste of such
beauty. She is a charming child and I imagine you are
fond of her?'

'Very fond. I shall miss her when she marries and I
go home,' Margaret said, betrayed into a careless moment by his sincerity.

'But you will come to London sometimes?'

'Perhaps, if it is possible after...' She realised that
she might have gone too far. She did not yet know him

and must be careful or she would betray herself. She must see Caroline safe first, and then—then she would be free to do whatever pleased her. But what would please her? Her heart was telling her one thing, her mind quite another. 'It is, 'ow you say—what will be will be.'

A little surge of excitement had started to wing its way through Margaret's body, bringing her to tingling life as she saw that perhaps she need not retire to her solitude just yet. She had long ago decided against marriage, but she was becoming more and more attracted to this man each time they met. There was a gentler side to him that she had not at first suspected, and she had begun to realise that she might enjoy being his mistress for a while. Why not indulge in playing his games? It was the kind of adventure she had planned, a passionate, consuming affair that would fulfil her dreams. She was an independent woman, wealthy in her own right and free to do as she pleased. It would be exciting and pleasurable for as long as it lasted. Time enough to return to France when it was over and live on her memories for the remainder of her life.

It was reckless and perhaps foolish of her to consider becoming this man's mistress, but, after all, why should she not? It would be a beautiful memory, something to make her smile when she was feeling lonely, which she knew she would at times when Caroline was married.

Having been the witness of her aunt's unhappiness, Margaret was sure that marriage was not for her, even if Lord Benedict were to ask her, which he would not, of course. His manner of approach was not that of a man seeking to wed the woman of his choice, and she thought that perhaps he too had chosen not to marry.

Some people were not meant for domestic bliss; she

had always felt that she was one of them, like her aunt, who had been miserable during the years of her marriage, only coming to life once she was a widow. Margaret's few encounters with gentlemen before coming to London had left her feeling it would be impossible for her to find a man she could be comfortable with. Her brief experience had taught her that often they divided into two kinds—men who used and abused, or men who thought of women as weak creatures without minds of their own. Margaret's keen mind would not allow her to be patronised or abused.

And of course she had her aunt's teachings to guide her. After the Count di Cabria died, Aunt Kate had often told Margaret that she would be quite happy to live alone with only her niece for company. She had expected that Caroline would marry, but seemed to think Margaret would choose to stay single.

'You are too independent of mind, my dear,' she had often said. 'Most men will not put up with that in a wife—though they think it a fine thing in a mistress, I believe.'

'Is there some reason why it might not be possible for you to return to London?' Giles asked, breaking into her thoughts.

Margaret had lost herself in her memories and was sharply recalled by something odd in Lord Benedict's tone. For a moment she saw a hard gleam in his eyes, a hint of hostility, as if he suspected her of some terrible secret.

'No reason,' she replied and felt coldness at her nape. What had happened to make him change his manner towards her? It was so strange. One moment he encouraged her to believe he had warm feelings for her and the next he looked at her as if he disliked her. 'Merely that I may find it preferable to stay at home.'

'I do not believe I know where you live, Comtesse. In what region of France is your home?'

Why did he wish to know?

Margaret hesitated, uncertain whether to give him a truthful reply, and then she was saved from having to make a decision by the arrival of her hostess, who had decided that the young people should dance if they wished.

'You do not object, Comtesse?' she asked. 'It is merely a little impromptu dance for the young ones and Caroline tells me you play the pianoforte rather well...'

'I should be delighted,' Margaret said and sent an apologetic smile at her companion. 'If Lord Benedict will forgive me.'

Giles watched her walk away with their hostess, cursing beneath his breath. Another few minutes and he might have begun to discover her secrets. He was sure that she had come close to confiding something in him, though he wasn't sure what it might be. Not that she had made certain plans to help in the assassination of the Duke of Belmont, of course—but perhaps his uncle was right and he had been mistaken in that matter. Belmont was certainly determined to ignore his nephew's warning—inviting her to join them at the estate was all his idea.

'If the lady wishes to kill me, best give her plenty of opportunity, what?' he'd said, a twinkle in his eye. 'Not that I think it for a moment, but better to have her where you can keep a look out, my boy, don't you agree? Give the lady her chance and catch her in the act!'

Giles had agreed. It might be foolhardy to take risks,

but at least he would be close by to keep a watchful eye on the Comtesse—if that really was her name.

There was a mystery about the Comtesse de Grenelle, he knew that without doubt, but perhaps there was another reason for her masquerade. Her accent was fascinating, but sometimes she forgot it and sometimes she seemed to him to be more English than French. He was determined to get to the bottom of the puzzle, and in the meantime he would continue to pursue her and see what happened.

Giles did not look too closely into his motives for pursuing the Comtesse, even though he was beginning to think that he might have been wrong to think her an assassin in disguise. She was beautiful, sensual and very desirable, and perhaps he need not look further for a reason as to why it was imperative that he should get to know her very much better.

Chapter Four

'It is very kind of Lady Belmont to invite us,' Caroline said when asked the next morning if she wished Margaret to accept the invitation. 'I think that I should like to stay in the country for a while—if you think we should?'

'I believe it might appear rude if we did not,' Margaret admitted. 'The Duchess has been very kind to us both, Caro. I think we must accept.' A part of her wished that she might find an excuse to escape this visit, but a restless night had provided none that would be believed. It seemed that she must face up to whatever was in store for her at Belmont. 'Besides, it will be more restful. We have hardly stopped to draw breath these past weeks—and I believe you need time to reflect, dearest?'

'You are always so kind, so understanding,' Caroline said, giving her a look of warm affection. 'I thought I knew my own heart, but…Mr Rushford has been so kind and…' She faltered and blushed. 'Oh, I do not know what to do.'

'Has Roddy spoken to you at all?'

Caroline's cheeks were pink as she shyly replied, 'He

has paid me several charming compliments, but he has not…'

'My brother is a fool at times,' Margaret said, hesitated, and then decided on a direct approach. 'Would I be wrong in thinking that at one time you had hopes of him, Caroline?'

'I thought that I should like to be married to him best of all things,' Caroline said in a muffled voice that carried a hint of the tears she was trying to suppress. 'I truly did, Magda, but…'

'Now you are not sure?'

'Mr Rushford seems to care for me,' Caroline said, her lovely face shadowed by uncertainty. 'I—I like Sir Roderick very well, but I should not want to marry him if he does not truly love me. And—and if he did he would surely have spoken before this, do you not think so? Three gentlemen have already asked leave to speak to you and I refused them as best I could without giving offence—why has Sir Roderick not—?' She floundered to an abrupt halt, blushing furiously.

'I cannot speak for my brother,' Margaret said, 'but I believe he cares for you very much.' She might have wished to say more, but could not interfere at this stage.

'Caring and being in love are very different, are they not?'

Seeing the shadows in her eyes, Margaret silently cursed her brother. What was he thinking of? Why hesitate further? If he loved Caroline, he should speak out before it was too late.

'Would you wish me to have a word with Roddy?'

'Oh, no! I beg you, please do not,' Caroline cried, alarmed. 'I should be so uncomfortable if you did that, Magda.'

'Then I shall not, of course, but sometimes gentlemen

do need a little push, my love. Could you not make my foolish brother aware that you need a sign from him?'

'Oh, no,' Caroline disclaimed, clearly distressed by the very idea. 'Please do not suggest it. I could not, for he might ask me out of a sense of duty and not truly wish it himself.'

'Then we must simply hope for the best.'

What a sad pair they were, Margaret reflected ruefully. Caroline was unsure of the man she loved and considering marriage with a man who was kind to her rather than risk being hurt. And she—she was caught in a swirling tide that would probably carry her to destruction.

The Belmont estate was huge. There were acres of parkland in which deer grazed, leading to a beautiful natural lake with a summerhouse resembling a Grecian temple and thickly wooded slopes protecting the grounds from the village and farmland beyond. The Duke was clearly a wealthy man, his classically elegant home richly furnished and filled with treasures.

Margaret had come downstairs on her first evening as a guest there and was standing alone in front of a French marquetry cabinet filled with *objets d'art* and fine porcelain, Caroline having been claimed by a party of young people who had carried her off with them. When she heard a firm tread behind her she knew without turning her head that it was Lord Benedict, for her senses had responded to his presence instinctively.

'My uncle collects rare and beautiful things. Fine porcelain is one of the interests Felicia shares with him and that set of Meissen figures was a part of her dowry, I believe. They have more in common than many thought. I believe she really cares for him.'

'Is caring the same as loving?' Caroline's words were in Margaret's mind as she turned to look at him, her heart missing a beat. He was so distinguished, so commanding, a man others would always seek out for advice. She felt a spiral of hot desire curl upwards, warming her body, bringing a becoming flush to her cheeks. 'Is fondness a reason to marry, do you think? Lady Felicia made her choice for reasons of her own and I do not seek to criticise—but I believe there should be much more in a relationship.'

'Such as?' His brows rose.

'Mutual respect, shared interests, a willingness to give understanding, to allow freedom of thought and desire. And passion, of course at the start, though this may wear itself out and when it does there must be something to take its place. A real and lasting friendship, perhaps?'

'Ah, you ask for perfection, Magda,' Giles said and smiled oddly. He was surprised by her declaration, which did not sit well with his previous opinion of her. 'Such a union is seldom achieved within marriage. I think Felicia's demands were more modest. Kindness, generosity and affection were all she asked of Belmont and I believe her well satisfied with her bargain.'

'I do not pass judgement,' Margaret told him. 'What is happiness for one person may be otherwise for another. My aunt always told me that I am too independent for marriage and I believe she was right.'

'And yet you were married?'

'We all make mistakes.' She turned her face aside, unable to bear the intent look he gave her, and, hearing a girl's happy laughter, said, 'Perhaps we should join the others?'

Giles made no move, his dark eyes intent on her. 'Your marriage was unhappy?'

She was silent for a moment, then, 'I prefer not to speak of it.'

'As you wish.' Clearly she was in no mood for sharing confidences that evening. He offered her his arm and they walked towards the large yellow drawing room where everyone had gathered in the splendour of the newly refurbished salon. 'But you cannot wish to spend your life entirely alone? It would be such a waste. You are too intelligent, too beautiful—too passionate, I think, to retire from Society altogether.'

'It was my intention once Caroline is settled.'

'But you have reconsidered? I should be sorry if our relationship were to end too soon, Magda.'

'Do we 'ave a relationship?' Her clear eyes challenged him.

'It is my sincere hope that we shall have a meaningful friendship and perhaps much more…much more.'

For one moment their eyes met and held. The smouldering heat in his eyes set off an answering heat in her. When he looked at her that way she found it difficult to breathe, and she was tempted to discard caution. Instead, she took refuge in a provocative smile.

'You 'ave a wicked way with you, my lord. I think you are a terrible man. You would 'ave your way with me, no?'

Her accent had deepened and the way she rolled the two r's in terrible was so delicious that he wanted to clasp her to him there and then. He laughed, enjoying this deliberate teasing on her part. She surely knew that every word she spoke made him more determined to have her in his bed, to know her in the most intimate way; the thought of touching that lovely body did dan-

gerous things to a certain part of his anatomy. He was
glad that the fashion for short coats no longer prevailed.
By God, he wanted her! For the moment every other
consideration was forgotten. This game begun so idly
had become a contest between them and one he had
every intention of winning.

'On the contrary, my lady,' he murmured huskily. 'I
think you are the wicked one. You have bewitched me.
What is the secret of your mystery? Who are you,
Magda? I know all is not quite as it would appear with
you. Sometimes I think you are laughing at us all.'

His words struck home, for in truth had not a part of
her determination to foist Lord Monkford's bastard
daughter on Society been because she wanted to take a
secret revenge on those same people who had cast both
Aunt Kate and Caroline's mother aside? Yet she would
not permit herself to feel guilty; it was their false pride
that made them seek to hide what they called the shame
of fallen women and so they deserved to be deceived.

'If I told you, there would be no mystery,' she said
and pouted at Giles provocatively. Even he deserved no
mercy, for was he not trying to seduce her? 'Is it not
more exciting to be a little unsure, my lord—is that not
part of the chase that you enjoy?'

'Yes—no!' he cried and laughed at the contradiction.
'You intrigue me, Magda, I admit it. There is some
mystery about you and it is a part of your fascination,
but not all. I want to solve the puzzle, but more than
that I want you, the lovely woman you are, to know
you and possess you in the most intimate of ways.
There, it is said. Not the words of a gentleman, I grant
you. I should perhaps wrap it up in clean linen, but I
have always been honest and would not deceive you. I
want to make love to you, to taste the honey of your

lips, to hold you close and feel you burn for me as I burn for you.'

'You make your feelings plain indeed, my lord.' Margaret felt almost faint, her whole body pulsing with a mixture of excitement and shock. He was speaking to a woman he believed experienced in such matters. Had he known the truth he would never have been so open about his desire to become her lover. Her body was throbbing with a passion she had not known was in her and she felt an overwhelming longing to let him carry her off and do all the things he'd promised to her willing flesh. Yet there was within her those doubts that had been planted by her aunt, stilling the reckless side of her nature. '*Mon Dieu!* You are forceful indeed, sir. You must give me a little time to consider. After all, we hardly know one another.'

'Well enough to know that we both feel the same desire—but you are right, we cannot talk further now,' Giles said, for they were about to enter the drawing room where the other guests had gathered and he was aware of curious eyes watching them. 'But please understand that I do not offer lightly. I believe that we should deal well together and that we might share a lasting friendship.'

He had for the moment cast suspicion to the wind and was sincere in his appeal. Her mystery was as deep as ever, but he knew that he had never felt this much for any other woman.

Margaret was unable to answer. She had suspected that he meant to make her an offer, but somehow she had not expected him to be so direct or so swift. It was not the first time such an offer had been made to her, but usually it had been hinted rather than spoken directly, by friends of her uncle, men she had shown the cold shoulder and avoided as much as she could. She had not wanted to make love with any of those others.

But this man was different. He had spoken of getting to know her while they were in the country, but this evening he had been urgent and she was a little nervous of the passion she sensed simmering beneath the surface. She was torn two ways, her body clamouring to know the excitement and pleasure he was offering, her mind counselling caution. Once begun, this affair might flare out of control. And yet a part of her longed for excitement, to know love and passion if only for a short time.

She was relieved when he left her to mingle with the other guests, finding it difficult at first to concentrate on the polite, but often meaningless, conversation of her dinner companions. After a while she began to recover her composure, but Giles was seated at the opposite side of the table and she was very conscious of him watching her as the evening progressed. Once she caught his eyes and his smile seemed to burn her, making her breathless. How very attractive he was!

She found herself looking at his mouth, thinking of how it might feel to be kissed by him...to be loved by him. Her fertile imagination was telling her that the touch of his hands would be sure and gentle yet firm, that he would know exactly how to bring her to a state of bliss such as she had only imagined in her wildest dreams. Yet if she allowed him to make love to her it would break down all her defences. She would have to confess the truth, to tell him her secret.

No! It was impossible. If she let him into her life she might find it too hard to bear when their affair ended, as it must in time. She would do much better to keep a distance between them. She must concentrate on what her dinner companions were saying!

'The Regent has promised to come at the weekend, just for two days,' Felicia was remarking. 'He cannot stay longer, but it will be good to have his company for a short time.'

'Prinny is coming here?' Giles frowned at Felicia. 'You did not tell me he was expected.'

'Oh, I must have forgotten,' Felicia said and turned to someone else. 'Renshaw holds his ball next weekend, I believe?'

Giles frowned, glancing across the table at the Comtesse. Had she known that the Regent was expected at the end of the week? Was that why she had made up her mind to accept the invitation? She had seemed to hesitate at first, but something had changed her mind. It would, he imagined, be easier to arrange an assassination here in the country than in town.

His doubts had returned to plague him and he had been almost ready to dismiss them. He must watch the Comtesse carefully and press ahead with his attempts to break down her defences. He was certain she was hiding something from him—from the whole of Society.

He would continue to court her, but for the moment he would not seduce her. His impatience had made him lose control earlier, but he was back in command of his senses. It would behove him to be wary. He was aware that what had begun as a game might quickly become far more. Whoever she was, Comtesse de Grenelle had found her way beneath his skin as no other woman ever had, and he would have to take the greatest care that he did not allow himself to become emotionally entangled.

*   *   *

A few days later Margaret was in the gardens, tempted out by the glorious sunshine, which was brilliant though cold. She smiled as she saw her ward walking with a small crowd of gentlemen in tow. It seemed that even here in the pleasant gardens of Belmont House, Caroline was still attracting more attention than Roddy liked, for he was scowling and looked like a surly bear with a bad head.

Turning away from the rose garden, which was a favourite place for the guests to stroll and talk, Margaret walked through an arched gate into the park. She had decided to try and reach the lake, which was some distance from the house, and perhaps sit for a while in the little summerhouse out of the breeze, which was quite bitter. It would be peaceful there and she needed solitude so that she could think.

She had been seldom alone these past three days, for the house was filled with company and often Lord Benedict sought her out, seeming to know instinctively where she could be found. He had continued to pursue her, though less urgently than that first night. She thought that perhaps he was giving her the time she had asked for, and was both glad and sorry that he was being so gallant. She thought that if he had been more insistent she might have succumbed to his advances by now, but, left to make up her own mind, she found it impossible to decide. Her own reckless nature urged her to take what happiness she could while it was offered, but her aunt's warnings lingered in her mind.

'Oh, drat the man!' she said aloud and then laughed at herself.

What did it matter? The day was pleasant, still and peaceful, disturbed only occasionally by the sound of a songbird high in the sky above her. Gradually a feeling of peace stole over her and she felt the tension fade away as she saw that she was almost at the lake. The summerhouse was closed, but when she looked inside, she saw that it was furnished much like a conservatory with Empire-style bergère furniture and green plants. She hesitated, then turned away to stroll to the edge of the lake, where she stood looking out across the rippled surface of the water, clutching her warm cloak about her.

After a few minutes, she sat down on a wooden bench, taking off her velvet bonnet and releasing her hair from the confines of the pins she had used to secure it, letting the glossy tresses fall unheeded past her shoulders. It was an age since she had felt so at peace with herself, but for a while she could almost imagine that she was back at home; in a moment her aunt would come out and tell her it was time for lunch and…

'It is a lovely day, though the wind is bitter,' a voice said, startling her. She had not been aware of his approach, for his boots had made no noise on the soft grass. She turned her head as he sat down beside her, her pulses racing at his nearness. There was a clean fresh, masculine scent about him that stirred her senses. 'You don't mind if I sit with you?'

She arched her brows. 'What would you do if I told you to go away?'

'I should wonder what I had done to upset you.'

'Then I shall not cause you to trouble yourself,' she replied and smiled. 'Providing that you do not chatter and spoil the peace.'

'A rare woman,' he murmured softly, then got up from her bench and sat on a fallen log with his back against a tree, closing his eyes. Margaret glanced down at him, amused that he had taken her so literally, half-wishing that she dare lie down beside him and let the wintry sunshine lull her to sleep as he seemed prepared to be.

She watched a pair of black swans glide silkily through the water, saw a moorhen venturing into the shallows, and then sighed. It was such an idyllic spot, but somehow she was no longer at peace.

'Did you follow me here?' she asked at last.

'I thought it too good to be true,' Giles said and opened his eyes to gaze up at her. 'A woman who did not want to talk…'

'You think so little of our sex, my lord?'

'On the contrary, I think often of one member of your sex,' Giles said and sat up. 'You have been keeping me awake at night for the past several weeks, Comtesse.'

He was alert now, looking at her, and as she got to her feet, he rose too, catching her wrist when she would have turned away. His fingers seemed to heat the delicate flesh as he swung her round to face him and she gazed into his eyes, mesmerised by what she saw there, unable to move even when she knew he was going to kiss her. Her lips parted instinctively, welcoming the firm, warm touch of his own and the tip of his tongue as it sought entry, dancing for a moment with hers as their embrace deepened.

She was swept away by a passion so consuming that she felt helpless, clinging to him as she abandoned herself to it without reserve, her body raging as if with fever. It was as if she was boneless, melting into him, becoming a part of him, losing herself entirely. She had never expected to feel this way, never known it was possible to lose oneself so completely in another, to want to become a part of that other. His mouth moved from hers, allowing her to catch her breath. But then his lips were at her throat, the feeling so deliciously sensual that she arched into him, a little mewing sound escaping her as she felt the hard burn of his arousal pressing through the thin muslin of her gown. He was pushing down the soft gathered neckline, his tongue and lips seeking the soft valley between her breasts, and then nuzzling at the rose pink tips of her breasts that had peaked for him.

He was whispering things to her now, things that made her cheeks heat for shame and yet heightened her desire, speaking softly of his need to fill her, to feel the warm honey of her sex drawing him in, to possess her. Margaret knew that she ought to stop him, she ought to confess that she was not the woman he thought her, but though his words terrified and shocked her, they also thrilled her. She was horrified to discover that she wanted to experience the things he spoke of so temptingly. She must be wanton for she felt no shame, only a fierce longing to be in his bed.

'You are so lovely,' Giles murmured huskily his lips against the white arch of her throat. 'I never meant to let you get beneath my skin the way you have. You are a dangerous woman, Magda, and I have lost all reason...'

Something almost accusing in his tone made her pull back, slightly hurt by his words. He was accusing her of having ensnared him and that was not true.

'I do not know why you should blame me, my lord,' she said and drew back, pulling the neckline of her gown into place. The moment had passed and she was in control once more. 'I am sure I have done nothing to encourage this behaviour in you.'

'Do not play the innocent with me, Magda,' Giles

said and his mouth hardened. 'Your response just now makes a mockery of false modesty. You are a woman of the world. You understand how it is between a man and a woman—and to say that you have not encouraged my advances when your every look invites me to take you to bed...'

'I do not think I like you very much,' Margaret said, angered by his attitude. Did he imagine she was a whore, his for the taking? 'For a moment I forgot myself, but I shall not permit such liberties again. Please do not follow me, my lord. I am not an opera dancer to be taken at will and discarded when you please!'

She turned away, her head high, shoulders stiff, but her cheeks were flaming. She could not entirely blame him, for she had teased him when it suited her, but his kiss had surprised her, flooding her with a hot desire that was completely unexpected. If it had not been for that note of censure in his voice, she knew that she would have allowed him to continue his lovemaking, and to revel in it.

Well, she was justly served for allowing him too much licence, she thought as she braced herself for his next onslaught. She was prepared for him to follow and try to cajole her, but thankfully he did not and she was allowed to walk alone as she returned to the house, her thoughts in turmoil.

She had been right to fear that, once begun, an affair with Giles Benedict would flare out of control. Anger had made her leave him, but already it was tempered with regret and the knowledge that it was probably too late to try and cut him out of her life; he had already taken too much of her with that kiss.

Watching her walk away, Giles stared in frustration, cursing himself for a fool. The passion and warmth of her response had thrown him, for there was an under-lying sweetness, almost innocence that had shocked him. Hers was not the practised kiss of a seductress and he'd known it even as he'd thrown those harsh words at her. It was his own feelings that had startled him, the tide of tenderness that flowed towards her, wanting to surround and protect, to sweep her up in his arms and take her somewhere private. An open-air seduction would have done very well for the woman he had thought her, but not for the woman he had discovered during that kiss. *She* was too special!

He ought to run after her and apologise, he knew it instinctively, but something held him back. His instincts told him she could not be the woman he'd first thought her, and yet he feared to be taken in by her charm. If she was planning harm to the Regent...

Yet was even that the sum of his doubts? Was there not a deeper, more personal reason why he had struck out in self-defence?

Giles frowned and turned his steps in another direction. He needed to think!

Margaret saw the Regent on her return to the house. He had just arrived and was standing in the hall, talking with his host, but on seeing her he came towards her immediately, kissing the hand she offered in greeting.

'My dear Comtesse,' he said, a twinkle in his eyes. 'How pleasant that we meet again and in such delightful surroundings. You have been walking I see. The air has brought colour to your cheeks.'

Had Margaret known it, her hair was straggling down her back despite her efforts to pin it up again, and with the roses in her cheeks she looked even more enchanting than usual, like a young girl instead of the matron she tried to appear in company.

'I like to walk when I can, sir. Especially when staying in such a beautiful place. I have been as far as the lake and it was well worth the effort.'

'Perhaps you would allow me to accompany you on your walk tomorrow morning? I enjoy a walk in good company myself—as long as you do not venture too far.'

'I should be delighted, sir,' Margaret replied and smiled, for such a request could not possibly be denied.

She went on and up the stairs, escaping to her own room to repair the damage to her appearance. Gazing at herself in the dressing mirror, she saw that her skin was glowing, though whether from exposure to the heat of the sunshine or quite another cause she was unsure.

She changed her gown, restored her hair to order and went downstairs as the gong was being sounded. Going into the smaller, informal dining parlour used for nuncheon, she saw that Caroline and Roddy were already there, standing by the buffet as they made their choice from the selection of cold meats and side dishes. There seemed to be an atmosphere between them. Caroline looked unhappy and Roddy was clearly annoyed over something.

However, Margaret was unable to ask what was wrong, as there were several more of the Belmonts' guests already gathered around the table. She was invited to sit next to one of the ladies and engaged in conversation that lasted throughout the meal.

It was not until later that Margaret was able to speak to her ward alone, when they went upstairs together to prepare themselves for the afternoon's pleasures. Some of the men had gone off to shoot pigeon in the Duke's woods, others to play billiards in the games room. However, most of the ladies preferred to stroll in the gardens or find a comfortable spot to sit with the latest offering from Miss Austen, Maria Edgeworth, or another of the romantic writers.

Having indulged herself in a good walk that morning, Margaret had decided that she would relax with a book unless Caroline needed her.

'What are your plans for the afternoon, dearest?' Margaret asked as they paused at the top of the landing.

'Some of the ladies are thinking of practising their archery,' Caroline replied with a little sigh. 'I may watch them, though Mr Rushford asked me if I would like to go for a drive about the estate in his curricle.'

'Shall you go? It is a pleasant day for a drive.'

'I wasn't going to,' Caroline admitted, 'but Sir Roderick made such a fuss about it earlier that I said I would—so I suppose I must.'

'Mr Rushford would think it odd if you cry off. Unless you have the headache, which would be a shame on an afternoon like this. I cannot think you wish to spend it lying on your bed?'

'No, I do not,' Caroline said and laughed ruefully. 'So I must keep my word and go, mustn't I?'

'Mr Rushford will not give you cause to regret it, I am sure. He seems a perfect gentleman and has the best of manners.'

'Oh, yes, I agree,' Caroline said at once. 'And very kind. The thing is, Magda, I am almost certain that he means to ask me to marry him this afternoon.'

'Ah, I see.' Margaret understood her reluctance. It could be awkward if a man spoke too soon, and must be handled carefully. And she believed that in her heart

Caroline wanted only one man, and that was not Mr Rushford. It would not do to play the heavy-handed duenna, but she would try to make things easier for Caroline if she could. 'And you are not sure how to answer him, is that it?'

'Yes.' Caroline sighed deeply. 'I am not ready to say yes, but I don't want to say no either. I haven't made up my mind yet.'

It was Caroline's choice, of course, but Margaret hoped the girl would not make a terrible mistake.

'Then simply ask for a little time, dearest. Go and enjoy yourself and do not worry. Things will work out soon between you and Roddy, I am perfectly sure of it. I shall see you at tea perhaps.'

They parted and Margaret went into her own room. She spent a few minutes tidying herself and then took her book downstairs.

She would find somewhere pleasant to sit in the garden and read her book. She walked unhurriedly in the direction of the rose arbour, but found that several others had the same idea and turned away. However, as she walked towards a secluded area she had noticed earlier that morning, she saw the Prince Regent coming towards her and stopped as he smiled at her in welcome. It was surprising to see him alone, but she thought that perhaps he had wanted a little peace for it must be wearisome to be always pursued and never alone.

'I see you have come out for a little solitude, Comtesse,' the Regent said as he saw her book. 'So I shall not...'

At that moment, Margaret caught sight of a man standing in the thick shrubbery close by and something alerted her as she saw him raise his arm and glimpsed a flash of sunlight on metal.

'Sir!' she cried and gave the Regent a great push, causing him to stumble and fall to his knees just as the ball went whistling past them, narrowly missing what must have been a prime target. 'My apologies…' she whispered, shocked both by what she had done and what had followed.

'Damnation!' the Regent cried, startled and angered by the blatant attempt on his life. 'Where is the fellow?'

'He ran off as soon as he had fired,' Margaret said, feeling shaken, though she struggled to appear calm. 'I am sorry for pushing you to the ground, sir.'

The Regent was back on his feet, not one whit the worse for his tumble, and seemingly unperturbed by his brush with death. 'Pray do not apologise, Comtesse. Your prompt action saved me from injury or death, and I can only thank you for what you did—damn it, you might have been shot yourself. It was both brave and foolhardy, ma'am.'

'It was instinctive,' Margaret said and laughed as she realised she was trembling. 'But we are wasting time. We should alert the household.'

'That is just what we must not do,' the Regent said. 'No, Comtesse, it will not serve, believe me. We should just upset Lady Felicia and to no good purpose. The fellow will have made off by now and I do not think he will risk another attempt for a while. Will you do me the greatest favour and tell no one what has occurred here this afternoon?'

'If it is your wish,' Margaret said and looked at him with respect. 'You have taken it very calmly, sir. I do not think I could dismiss something of that nature so lightly.'

'I am more accustomed to these things than you might imagine, my dear Comtesse,' he said and his eyes twinkled at her. 'Not while walking in an English garden and talking with a beautiful and mysterious young woman, I must admit—but this is not the first attempt on my life and I dare say it will not be the last.'

'I would beg you to take care, sir. England cannot afford to lose you, especially in these uncertain times.'

'Spoken like a true Englishwoman,' the Regent said and the twinkle had become a positive sparkle, for in her distress her accent had been forgotten. 'I think, perhaps, I know the answer to a part of your mystery, Comtesse, but one favour deserves another. Keep my secret and I shall keep yours.'

'It is not a very terrible one,' Margaret told him with a blush. 'My aunt met you once in London some years ago and she thought you charming and a terrible flirt, but had great respect for you, sir.'

'Should I remember the lady?'

'The Contessa di Cabria.'

'Ah, yes, I do recall—quite a formidable lady herself, I believe?'

'Some might think so,' Margaret said. They had somehow turned towards the house, walking together for all the world as if nothing untoward had occurred. Margaret was reluctant to leave him alone in the gardens, but when she saw Giles Benedict walking purposefully towards them, she turned to the Regent. 'I shall leave you to Lord Benedict now, sir. If you will excuse me.'

'Yes, of course, ma'am, and thank you.'

'It was nothing, sir.'

She walked away before Giles could reach them, not wanting to meet him too soon after the embarrassing episode of that morning.

'You could not have been more wrong about her,' the Regent said as Giles questioned him more particularly. 'Had she not acted so promptly, I might have been injured or killed.'

'Are you sure it was not just a show to make it appear that she had saved you from an assassin?'

'What purpose would be served in that?' Prinny asked. 'It was an opportunity that will not come easily again; if they wanted to kill me it was the time to do it. I shall take care not to stray so far from the house alone again—at least until we have tracked this fellow down.'

'It was a man who fired at you?'

'I never saw the fellow. Had the Comtesse not been so swift to act, he would at the very least have winged me.' The Regent frowned, his expression harsher than that he had shown Margaret. 'No, you must look elsewhere for your assassin, Benedict. I want it kept quiet, do you hear? Lady Felicia must not hear of it—but I shall speak to Belmont myself. We must question the estate workers, discover if anyone has seen a stranger lurking about.'

'I shall begin immediately,' Giles said. 'And I'll employ an agent I know to make discreet inquiries.' He would also ask some friends of his who had served under Wellington to set up a discreet surveillance, but thought it wiser to tell the Regent nothing about that particular measure.

The Regent changed the subject, determined to make light of the whole affair, and they went on into the house to be met by their hostess, who bore her honoured guest away to tea.

Giles brooded on the latest developments as he went out to set up his investigation. It was unlikely that the assassin would linger after his attempt had failed, but just in case they would make a discreet search of any outlying barns or huts where he might be hiding.

The Regent's conviction that Comtesse de Grenelle had saved his life was something else Giles must ponder. He was certain that she was not who she claimed to be, but that in itself was not a crime—though undoubtedly many in Society would not agree with him. She would be ostracised if it were known she had practised a clever deceit on them and it was not part of Giles's plan to ruin her.

However, if she was not the practised deceiver he had first thought her, and that kiss had led him to believe that he was indeed mistaken, where did that leave him and his efforts to seduce her?

Chapter Five

'May I speak to you privately?' Margaret was walking alone in the garden when Roddy came up to her. She saw at once that he was distressed, and understood his reasons.

'Yes, of course, my dear,' she said. 'But perhaps I should tell you that Caroline has already spoken to me of your quarrel.'

'I expected that she would,' he said and there was a flash of temper in his eyes. 'She is behaving like a spoiled brat.'

'Roddy, that is not a very nice thing to say.' Margaret looked at him unhappily. Her sympathy was aroused, but this was a time for plain speaking if things were to be sorted. 'You know I think you are both behaving a little foolishly here, but on the whole I blame you the most. You are old enough to know better. And as the man, you must take the lead. Why do you not tell Caroline how very much you love her? Speak to her immediately, before it is too late.'

'You have no idea of what you are asking,' he said tersely. 'It is very difficult—if not to say impossible—'

'Nothing is impossible, Roddy. I must tell you now,

my dear, that I believe you will lose her if you do nothing.'

'Oh, damn you,' Roddy muttered. 'No one asked you to interfere.'

Margaret watched her brother walk away. No doubt that streak of stubbornness in him was the mirror image of her own. She would not have taken kindly to advice from him, and could not be surprised at his reaction.

Margaret was dressing for the evening when her ward came in unannounced. It was obvious from her ravaged looks that Caroline had been crying and she was immediately concerned for her. She dismissed her maid and went to greet the girl with outstretched hands.

'What has upset you so much, dearest?'

'I've had a terrible quarrel with Sir Roderick!' A sob escaped Caroline, her shoulders heaving with her emotion.

'Oh, Caro,' Margaret said. 'Was it because you went for that drive with Mr Rushford?'

Caroline nodded and broke into a storm of weeping. It was not for several minutes that she could be comforted enough to speak of what had happened. At last her tears subsided and Margaret gave her a pretty kerchief to dry her cheeks.

'There, that is better. Would you care to tell me what was said between you?'

Caroline lifted her tear-drenched eyes. 'He—he accused me of being a heartless flirt!'

'That was unkind of him. I shall certainly take him to task for it, dearest.'

'No! No, you must not,' Caroline begged instantly. 'Besides, you may not see him this evening. He said that he'd had enough of dancing to my tune and was going home.'

'Roddy said that to you? It was very bad of him and I am most displeased.'

Margaret was astonished. Her brother was normally the mildest of men. What had got into him of late? She could only assume that he had been driven beyond bearing by his jealousy of Mr Rushford.

'What had you said to him to provoke such an attack?'

'Only that…Mr Rushford had asked me to marry him and that I had asked for time to consider.' Caroline held back a sob. 'I thought it might provoke him into asking me himself, but it merely made him angry. And then I lost my temper and told him he was impossible and unbearable and that's when he said he was going home.'

'Oh, dear,' Margaret said, looking at her sadly. 'I dare say he will calm down and beg your pardon later, dearest.'

'I do not think so. I believe he really meant to go home. He received a letter this morning from his agent asking him to return because there was some problem with the estate.'

'Ah, I see.' Margaret nodded. Her brother clearly felt he was needed at home and had blurted it out in a temper. She was a little surprised that he had not troubled to let her know of his decision, but understood that he was angry with her for her plain speaking earlier. If he had not left a letter for her, it must mean that he too was deeply upset about this situation. 'Do you feel like coming down to dinner this evening, my love? I could tell Lady Felicia that you are resting if you wish?'

'No, no, I shall go down,' Caroline said and suddenly there was a brilliant sparkle in her eyes, a determined tilt to her chin. 'And I have decided to tell Mr Rushford that I shall marry him.'

'Caroline! This is very sudden, my dear.' Margaret stared at her in concern, her amusement gone. This was serious, for it would affect the rest of Caroline's life, and she was not at all sure that her ward's choice of a husband was a good one. Mr Rushford was perfectly respectable, of course, but his manner was a little condescending at times, which she herself would find exceedingly irritating. 'Are you sure that is what you want to do, Caroline? You are not making a rash judgement because of your quarrel with Roddy?'

'Sir Roderick's unkindness has made up my mind,' Caroline said defiantly, two spots of bright colour in her cheeks. 'It is clear that he does not love me. If he did, he would not be so hurtful to me.'

'Perhaps he himself was hurt?' Margaret suggested, but she could see that the girl was not prepared to listen. 'I do not mind what you do, dearest—but I want you to be happy. I dare say Mr Rushford is a very pleasant man, but I would hate you to make a rash decision and regret it for the rest of your life. Will you not think about this for a little while—be sure what you want of life?' She was concerned for Caroline, for she believed she was making a terrible mistake. 'I would not dictate to you for the world, indeed, I have no right—but please consider carefully, dearest.'

'I shall be happy with Mr Rushford. I know he loves me and—and I am fond of him. I think we shall deal very well together.'

'It is your own decision, of course, though I would advise you to wait for a time, Caroline.' She could not forbid the girl, she had no right to do so.

'I do not wish to wait. I know my own mind.'

Margaret reserved judgement. Although she had agreed to act as her chaperon, it was not for her to tell Caroline whom she ought to marry. Besides, if Roddy had not spoken, it might be that he was undecided. She could not interfere between them even though she believed Caroline was making a mistake. Oh, what a coil it was!

Margaret felt sad that Caroline and Roddy had quarrelled for she believed that there was genuine love on both sides. Yet it was surely for them to sort themselves out. Roddy should have spoken boldly, told Caroline that he wanted to marry her. It seemed that, faced with only criticism from Roddy, Caroline had reached her own decision and there was no more to be done.

A little later that evening, Margaret watched the meeting between her ward and Mr Rushford with some misgiving, but when the young man came to her immediately after dinner and asked when he could speak to her privately she put no barrier in his way.

'Miss Hammond—Caroline—has done me the honour of agreeing to be my wife, ma'am. I am here to ask formally for your permission, and to tell you of my intentions towards her.' His manner was pompous to a degree she thought unwarranted, though she held her feelings in check and allowed him to continue.

'She mentioned her intention earlier, sir. As I have no need to ask about your feelings or your ability to provide for her, I can only wish both of you happiness.'

'You will wish to know about settlements. I propose to settle twenty thousand pounds on my wife.' He looked exceedingly pleased with himself, almost as though he believed he was doing Caroline a great favour, which set Margaret's teeth on edge. 'The income will be hers for life and the capital shall pass to her children on death. I do not approve of ladies being in charge of their capital, you understand. Most do not know how to protect it. It is our duty as their husbands to look after them.'

'Indeed?' Margaret's brows rose. 'I have always found that attitude a little hard to swallow, sir, for I think a woman as capable of most things as a man.'

Mr Rushford looked into her eyes and realised his mistake. 'Oh, I did not mean you, dear lady. You are the exception to the rule, naturally. But Caroline is such a delightful child. A pretty little butterfly to be petted and cosseted, I am sure you agree? She does not care to be troubled with business matters. Besides the income from her marriage portion, I also intend that she shall keep her own inheritance, to spend as she pleases.' He hurried out with this as though to placate her.

'That is very generous of you, Mr Rushford. Caroline is a fortunate young lady.' Yet would she be happy despite his generosity? Margaret was not sure and wished that she had done more to urge her ward to caution.

'I love her very much,' he went on and this time there was a note of sincerity in his voice. 'You must believe that I shall do all in my power to make her happy, Comtesse. I thought her affections might be engaged elsewhere, but she assures me *that* is over.'

'I see.' Margaret hesitated. She could not doubt that he cared for Caroline, and that being so perhaps her own reservations counted for nothing. Besides, it was not in her power to forbid Caroline anything, merely to advise. Although she thought of the girl as her ward, it had actually been Aunt Kate who adopted her, and there was no legal obligation on either side. 'Then, if you are happy, we shall arrange the wedding.'

'We require only a quiet wedding,' he said. 'Caroline has told me that she is the illegitimate child of a titled gentleman, but I do not care for that. I am a countryman at heart, madam, and Society in the grand manner holds little appeal. My friends will not ask who Caroline's parents are, but welcome her as my wife.'

Again, there was that hint of pomposity, of self-importance, as though he was pleased with his own magnanimity in offering marriage to a girl who was hardly worthy of him. Margaret was aware of a flicker of unease, but she quashed it. Caroline had made her choice.

'Then she has nothing to fear and everything to gain, sir. How soon would you like to marry?'

'Would five weeks be too soon?'

'Not if you both agree. Caroline has many beautiful gowns already and others can be commissioned and made in that time.'

'I see no point in long engagements and I plan to take my wife to Paris for a honeymoon. Anything she lacks may be purchased there.'

His tone struck Margaret as a little dictatorial and once again she had to smother her doubts as to the wisdom of Caroline's choice, but the die was cast now and there was no going back.

'I was thinking that we might spend a week or two in Bath when we leave here. We could journey there in less than a day. Would you wish to arrange the wedding there—or will your family expect it to be at your home, sir?'

'I have no relations to speak of other than a younger sister, who is still in the schoolroom. She can come to

Bath for the wedding. I shall send for her and she may travel with her duenna. I am certain that Sarah will adore Caroline.' He smiled, clearly well satisfied. 'It is an excellent idea, Comtesse de Grenelle. I shall visit Bath and make arrangements for the wedding and your accommodation, and then I shall go home to set everything in order for my bride. I shall return here with my sister and her chaperon in two weeks to escort you to Bath, ma'am.'

'That sounds very suitable,' Margaret said. There was no doubting that Mr Rushford was very sure of his own consequence, and that lowered her own opinion of him a little, but no matter. It was Caroline's happiness that was important here, and she seemed to have made up her mind.

Leaving the young man to go in search of his fiancée, Margaret made her way back to the main salon, but was waylaid in the hall by Giles Benedict, whose smile sent tiny shivers running down her spine. Why must he look at her like that? He seemed to give out one signal with his smiles and kisses and another with his words.

'I believe I should beg your pardon for my behaviour earlier, Magda,' he said in a voice that set her stomach churning. 'Perhaps I was too forward?'

'You take much for granted, my lord.'

'Will you not forgive me?' he said softly. 'I was perhaps too eager, too harsh in my choice of words.'

She refused to be swayed by his persuasive manner. 'You seem to imagine that I am something I am not, sir.'

'Yes, I think you are right,' Giles said and wondered if the Prince Regent had mentioned Giles's suspicion of her purpose here. But no, the Prince might dismiss the idea as foolishness, but he was no fool; he knew that it was best to keep such things close. 'Because you have been married it does not follow that you are ready to be any man's mistress. If I have offended you, may I humbly beg your pardon and ask that we begin again?'

Margaret's resolve was crumbling, her insides turning to liquid fire as she heard the pleading note in his voice. Perhaps her eager response to his lovemaking had given him the right to speak as he had—and he had let her go when she asked. Some men would not have been so obliging, nor would they have begged her pardon.

'You have not offended me,' she told him, just the faintest of accents in her voice making it husky and enchanting, inflaming the man more than she knew. 'I think we like each other, my lord, and…I believe there might be something between us. But you must give me a little time. I need to know you better—and besides, I have a wedding to arrange. Caroline and Mr Rushford are to marry in Bath in a few weeks' time. He is making the arrangements and returning here in two weeks to escort us there.'

'I should have liked that privilege myself,' Giles murmured. 'I shall leave Belmont after the weekend and go to London on business. I had intended to return here, but with your permission I shall call on you in Bath?'

'We shall be delighted to see you, sir.'

'For how long will you stay in Bath after Miss Hammond's wedding?'

'I am not sure,' Margaret said truthfully. 'I had intended to retire to my home in France almost immediately. I have a villa there. It is very pleasant, not too secluded but peaceful—and I have many friends.'

'I may have occasion to visit France myself from time to time.'

'Yes…' Margaret allowed a little secret smile to curve her mouth. 'I believe you travel quite widely, sir.'

'That is true, though I am not sure how you knew it?'

Her smile deepened, becoming provoking. 'That is something I may tell you in the future, sir. And now perhaps we should join the others in the drawing room. If we are both absent too long, it may cause some gossip.'

'If only there was reason for that gossip I would brave it,' he murmured, matching his mood to hers. 'Can I not persuade you that a walk in the gardens would be beneficial on a night such as this? I am sure the air would do us good and I would endeavour to see that you did not turn cold.'

Margaret laughed and tapped his arm playfully with her fan. 'Now you go too fast again, my lord. Have patience. If you promise to be good I shall allow you to turn the pages for me as I play the pianoforte for the Duke's guests, and later you may sit beside me and tell me something of your life.'

'Will you tell me something of yours?'

His brows lifted, bringing a ripple of laughter from her. 'I see you are too impatient, sir. You must learn to wait for what you want.'

'Patience was never my strongest virtue,' Giles replied and laughed at the way her eyes provoked him. She was an accomplished flirt, but there was something sweetly innocent beneath the sophisticated face she showed to the world, and he believed she would prove worth the waiting.

He would have her in the end, for she intrigued and haunted him, and now that he had let his suspicions go—or almost all of them—he knew that he would not rest until she agreed to be his mistress.

Margaret had dismissed her maid. She sat at her dressing chest, brushing her long hair before the mirror and staring at her reflection without seeing anything. It had been a pleasant evening, perhaps the most pleasant of her life, and that was because Giles Benedict had scarcely left her side all evening.

She had been requested to play several pieces by her hostess, as she'd known was likely, and Giles had turned her music for her. Later, they had sat and talked on a small giltwood settee in the window embrasure, a little apart from the rest of the company. Giles had spoken of his travels to Spain, Italy, France, Austria and Germany. He had fought several campaigns with Wellington on the Peninsula, but he confessed that his true ambition lay in the diplomatic world.

'I do not care for the life of a country gentleman or to idle my days away in town taking fencing lessons and gambling. I like the cut and thrust of clever minds and the constant battle against intrigue. Wellington has first call on my time and when he leaves Vienna, as he will in a few weeks, I shall join him in Paris, but when things are more settled in Europe I intend to apply for a diplomatic post somewhere abroad.'

'And have you no plans for a family, my lord?'

'For the moment, no,' Giles replied truthfully. 'If I enter the diplomatic service I could be sent anywhere— perhaps India. I saw service there when I was very young and do not believe that it is a suitable environment for a gently born lady and her children.'

'Yet there are many wives who follow their husbands

there,' Margaret replied, her gaze intent on his face. 'Is it not so 'ere as in France?'

'Yes, that is true—and some die of a fever. I knew a young lady…' For a moment the expression in his eyes became bleak and Margaret knew that she had touched on a secret sorrow.

'Do not tell me if you would rather not,' she said laying her hand on his arm. 'I did not mean to pry. It was very bad of me, *non*?'

'It was a long time ago,' Giles said and smiled, but the smile did not reach his eyes. 'Pamela was delicate and should never have been exposed to that climate. She took a fever and died…three days after we were officially engaged.'

'Oh…' Margaret felt the icy chill at the nape of her neck. His revelation was unexpected. This was indeed an intimate detail of his past and it shocked her, making her see him in a new light. 'Forgive me. I see it pains you to speak of her.' In her sympathy she had dropped her accent and spoke honestly, as she felt.

'It was such a waste of all that beauty and laughter,' Giles said. 'Of course we were in love and I thought the world had ended. I suppose I found refuge in my work, and since then I have not truly considered marriage.'

In truth he had not considered love, for once burned he had been shy of the fire, preferring shallow relationships that could not touch him. Having wandered in a wasteland of despair for some months, he did not wish to visit it again.

'Thank you for telling me,' she said. 'It helps me to understand you a little better, my lord.'

'Will you not consider calling me Giles?'

'Yes, certainly, in private,' Margaret replied and

smiled. 'I think I should tell you a little about myself
in return for your confidence, Giles. My aunt was the
Contessa di Cabria and we lived in Italy until her husband died, when she bought a villa in the south of
France—but it was in Italy that I first saw you.'

'In Italy?' His brow furrowed. 'I do not recall—
something has been at the back of my mind since I first
saw you, Magda, but I have not been able to place it.'

'It was one evening at a private villa near the lakes,'
she said. 'My uncle was drunk and he tried to molest
me. You cried out to him to stop and came to my rescue
and he went off.'

'And you ran away without a word,' Giles said, staring at her in amazement as the memory clicked into
place. 'I knew that I had seen you before! Why could
I not recall it?'

'It was such a small incident,' Margaret replied. 'I
was too embarrassed and shamed to speak to you, and
I have always regretted that I did not thank you.'

'You had no need to feel shamed.' Giles frowned.
'That brute should not have behaved so to a young girl.'

'Yet I was foolish to walk alone. It was not the first
time he had looked at me with lust, and there were other
men—his friends—who also made suggestions. I was
usually careful not to give any of them chance to find
me alone, but that night I was careless.'

'And your husband?'

'I am not ready to speak of that yet,' she said and
shook her head at him. 'An exchange of confidences,
Giles, no more.' Her voice was low and husky with
sensual undertones of which she was quite unaware.
'You are impatient, *non*? It is, 'ow you say—that you
must play the waiting game.' She had reverted to her
enchanting accent and the change was not lost on him.

'You are a very wicked lady,' he murmured. 'Do you know what those eyes and that accent do to me?'

'You must be patient,' she said. 'My first duty is to my ward. I cannot afford a breath of scandal until she is safely married—and even then I would prefer not to remain where any gossip might touch her. What I do in private hurts no one.'

'You are suggesting that I should visit you at your home in France?'

'Perhaps,' Margaret said and caught her breath as she saw the gleam in his eyes. She had almost committed herself to an affair, but not quite. She rose as she saw that her hostess was ready to retire. 'We shall see how we go on, sir. I must bid you goodnight.' She walked to where Caroline was sitting with some of the other young ladies and gentlemen. 'Come along, dearest, say goodnight to your friends. It is time that we went up.'

Now she was alone in her room, half-wishing that she had made some firmer arrangement with Giles. He would leave for London soon and when he came to Bath she would be busy with plans for the wedding, leaving her little time to be alone with him. And there was an aching need in her that cried out to be fulfilled. He was the black knight of her dreams, the only man who had ever stirred her heart. Somehow she knew that if she missed this chance she would never know love again, never understand what it was to be a woman.

She sighed, wishing that life was not so complicated. Why must there be one set of rules for men and another for young ladies?

If she had invited him to her room tonight it would not be the only such liaison taking place under this roof. Margaret knew that perhaps half of the gentlemen were having affairs with ladies staying as guests here. Some of the ladies were married and unfaithful to their husbands, who turned a blind eye and indulged themselves with a mistress of their own choosing, others were widowed ladies—like Margaret. Except that Margaret's widowhood was false.

And therein lay her greatest problem, she reflected with a sigh. What would Giles think if he knew the truth? And what would the rest of Society do and say if they learned that she had played such an audacious trick on them?

She wondered now why she had done it. Her brother had suggested that she needed no pretence and could equally well bring Caroline to London as herself, Miss Margaret Hazelmere. It would have meant engaging a companion, of course. But she had not thought her little masquerade could cause harm to anyone since she had no intention of seeking an alliance for herself. It had seemed amusing to pose as something she was not; however, she had not bargained with Giles Benedict.

How could she when she had not known that it was possible to feel this way about a man, when she had only just discovered needs and desires she had not hitherto suspected?

It was a thorny problem.

If she gave into his urging to be his mistress, she would be ruined. That did not matter in itself, because she did not wish to live in London nor to be a part of Society, but she had promised Roddy that for his sake she would not betray her true identity—and he would already be hurt and angry after Caroline's rejection.

So she needed to be cautious and discreet, and it would be better to give herself more time to know Giles before committing to him. She did not think he meant to use her lightly and throw her over after a brief affair. He had suggested something of a more enduring nature, and she rather thought that he would visit her from time to time, spending a few days or a week or so with her, then going off on his travels to return when it suited him. It was the kind of affair that might suit Margaret, she thought, for she might find marriage too confining...although with a man like Giles Benedict...but it was foolish to let her thoughts travel that road.

He had been quite honest in his approach. It was an affair he sought, even if of the lasting kind, not marriage. He did not love her, for his heart lay in India with the girl he had loved as a young man, but he did want her, to make love to her, to enjoy her company—and she knew that she wanted it too. She thought that they had much in common and would deal well together. But how to explain the truth of her situation? Ah, that was more difficult.

There was no solving the conundrum and she had brought the problem on herself. Had she appeared in Society as Miss Hazelmere Lord Benedict would never have approached her in this way. Indeed, he would have stayed well clear of her as it was obvious that he had no wish to marry.

Sighing, Margaret got to her feet and glanced out of the window. She stiffened as she saw the man lurking in the shadows. He was surely watching the house!

Remembering that the Prince Regent had been shot at earlier that day, Margaret was immediately alarmed. She had imagined that the would-be assassin must have made off as soon as his attempt failed, but it seemed that he was still here. She ought to do something! Alert someone—but who?

The Regent had sealed her to silence with a promise,

but she could not ignore what she had seen. Yet she could not go to her hostess for it would upset the Duchess and she rather thought that that lady was in a delicate condition, though it had not yet begun to show.

She must tell someone. She could not go to the Regent's room, of course, nor to her host for Felicia's sake—but there was someone. She knew which room Giles was using, for it was only at the end of her own corridor, and would take but a minute to reach.

Pulling on a heavy embroidered robe lest she be seen by anyone, Margaret looked out of her own door. There was no one about and only one small branch of candles still flickered low in their sconces. Picking them up, she went swiftly down the hall on bare feet, praying that no one would come out and see her. Her knock was answered promptly by Giles, still wearing his breeches but with his shirt opened to the waist as if he had been about to retire.

'Magda?' He stared at her in surprise and then grinned. 'My impatient love, I would have come to you had you asked.'

'Do not be foolish, sir,' Margaret said and blushed. 'I have not come to climb into your bed. I have just seen some fellow lurking in the shrubbery and—and I think he means harm to the Prince Regent. I gave my word not to say, but I have reason to believe...'

Margaret was cut short as Giles pulled her inside his room and closed the door, pressing a finger to her lips.

'Hush, I do not want anyone else to hear of this.'

'Nor did the Regent, but—' Giles silenced her with a kiss that took her breath away. She pressed her shaking hands against his chest, holding him at bay.

'You could not have heard what I said—there is someone skulking in the bushes outside.'

'He is there to protect Prinny,' Giles said and smiled, reaching out to touch her hair that was falling about her shoulders in glorious disarray. 'On my orders, Magda. I have known there might be an attempt on his life; after it was made, I called in men I trust to guard him until he leaves here. He was being constantly shadowed in London, but I did not know he intended to come here and my men had no instructions to follow.'

'He told you…' She was bewildered.

'We are very close in such matters,' Giles said. 'Perhaps I should have told you, but Prinny hates a fuss. He is lampooned as a fool in the newspapers, but is actually a rather brave and intelligent man, though sometimes excessive in his tastes. He will take no more foolish risks in a hurry, believe me.'

'Then I am a fool to have disturbed you—'

She was cut off again as he caught her to him, kissing her with such hunger that she felt herself dizzy with desire and clung to him breathlessly, wanting to surrender herself to him.

'Giles, I…'

'We shall talk later,' he murmured huskily as he swept her off her feet and carried her to his bed.

Margaret made no demur as he set her on her feet once more, one mobile brow arched questioningly. And then the time for speaking out had passed as he began to kiss her—such hungry, tantalising kisses that set her pulses racing and she had no will or wish to deny him. Instead, she gave herself up to the thrill of discovery as his tongue invaded her mouth with little teasing flicks, arousing her so that she felt a surge of white-hot fire welling up from inside her. She whimpered with pleasure as he undid the fastenings of her embroidered robe and helped him to ease it over her shoulders so that it slid to the floor in a whisper. Her fine silk nightgown followed it to the floor, leaving her naked to his devouring gaze.

Even as she felt shyness at being looked at so intently by a man for the first time it was forgotten in a new pulsating sensation, for now Giles was murmuring the kind of compliments that set her tingling with newly discovered desire; he praised her beauty, the milky whiteness of her skin, speaking of his admiration and desire, and then he was kissing her, touching her, loving her with his mouth and tongue. Her breasts were achingly aware of need, a need his laving tongue went some way to assuage, but then the need moved further down to the very centre of her femininity. She gasped as he knelt before her, kissing and licking his way down her flat stomach, down to the mass of dark curls that covered her mound of Venus. He buried his face in the silken moistness, breathing in the scent of her sex, his hand moving between her thighs to seek out…just the right place. She moaned in ecstasy as his finger stroked firmly but softly, making her tremble with the force of her need.

'You're so wet, Magda, hot and wet,' he murmured. 'I want to feel your heat as you take me inside you, my angel. You drive me wild with desire. Forgive me, I must have you…'

Margaret had moved beyond all recognition of right or wrong. She was aware only of the throbbing need between her thighs, so impatient herself for something she hardly understood but knew must be that the sight of his naked body and the evidence of his erection only thrilled her more. She was swept away on a tide of reckless excitement, prepared to live for the moment, to let the future take care of itself.

'Giles, please,' she whispered throatily as he lifted her to the bed and lay beside her, his eyes moving over her with hot intent, 'I want you to love me now. I want you inside me, deep inside me…'

His flesh burned hers as he pulled her closer, his mouth taking hers in a passionate kiss that swept her breath away, moving down to her throat, her breasts, his tongue laving the rose-dark nipples, moving down again to that most intimate part of her that cried out for his attention. She gasped and writhed as he brought her to a swift, incredible explosion of feeling, and then, even as she cried his name, her nails clawing at his back, he moved across her and she felt the hard nudge of his throbbing maleness. With a groan he thrust into her, stilled momentarily as he felt the impediment and then thrust again, breaking through her maidenhead.

For a moment the pain was sharp, but it was not sufficient to make her draw back and within seconds her hips were grinding against his as she strove to be a part of him, one with his flesh, moving urgently together. She heard his groan of release and then a curse of frustration as he spilled his seed inside her and lay with his face pressed against the fragrance of her hair.

'I waited too long,' he muttered. 'But you didn't tell me…'

Margaret was glad that she did not have to look into his eyes as she answered, 'I did not know how to. Besides, I did not expect this to happen just yet. I thought we would take things slowly and then I would have told you, when we knew each other a little better.'

Giles raised his head to look down at her. 'No, don't turn away. I'm not angry, Magda, just surprised and sorry. Had I known it was your first time I might have made it easier on you.'

'You only hurt me a very little,' Margaret whispered, feeling shy but trying not to show it. He hadn't intended to deflower a virgin and she was afraid that he might feel cheated because of her lack of experience. 'It—it was what I wanted. You have no need to be sorry, for I promise you I am not.'

'You are not angry with me?'

'No, of course not,' she said and sat up. 'There is always a first time, is there not?' Her accent had deepened, her smile become provocative.

'Who are you, Magda?' Giles asked. He rolled away from her, pulling on his dressing robe as he left the bed and handed her nightgown to her. 'Was there a Comte de Grenelle?'

Margaret dressed, her mind searching for the right answer and finding none that would serve.

'I shall tell you everything very soon,' she said at last. 'For the moment I ask for your patience, Giles. My secret is not shameful, but I wish to keep it a little longer—just until Caroline is wed.'

'You will not trust me?' His brows arched.

'Forgive me, please? Once Caroline is safe I shall tell you all, I promise.'

'And in the meantime? You wish to keep me at a distance?'

'Oh, no,' she said and gave him her naughtiest smile, reverting to the broken English and accent she knew he found fascinating. 'You 'ave seduced me, my lord, but I confess that I like it—and I 'ope you will not tire of our—friendship too soon. Please come to me in Bath as you intended and who knows…'

Giles laughed. She was enchanting, a delightful blend of innocence and wanton abandon that had given him more pleasure than he had felt in the arms of any other woman he had taken to his bed. Her eyes gleamed with mischief, her smile so provoking that he felt himself growing hard once more.

'You make me want to return very quickly, Magda,' he murmured. 'Since you were virgin until this evening I shall not indulge my own need again just yet, but do not expect such forbearance when I return.'

'I shall not expect or ask for it,' she replied. 'You will forgive me if I return to my own room now, Giles. I must be discreet for Caroline's sake. I would do nothing that might compromise her happiness.'

'I could consign Caroline to perdition most willingly, my love,' Giles murmured huskily. 'But I shall allow you to go.'

'Thank you.'

Margaret moved to go past him, but he caught her wrist, his dark gaze seeking hers. 'I am forgiven? You will not shut me out of your life? You will tell me everything?'

'*Oui*, it is a promise—*n'est-ce pas*? I hope you will forgive me when I have made my confession, which is a little naughty but not so very terrible, I think.'

She rolled her r's, making him laugh as he released her.

'I am not certain who was the seducer here, Magda.'

'Who can say, my lord? Perhaps neither of us could have resisted at such a moment—*non*?'

And then she was gone, leaving behind the scent of her perfume and Giles to stare after her in frustration. She had bewitched him and he was not sure he would ever be the same man again!

Chapter Six

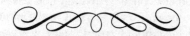

Would this tedious journey never be over? Margaret's head was aching, and she felt out of sorts with herself as Mr Rushford danced round them like a broody hen when they alighted from the carriage. His manner had become increasingly pompous throughout the day and she had grown weary of his fussing over small things. In his company constantly these past hours, listening to the way he spoke to Caroline, which to her mind seemed to belittle her ward's intelligence, it had begun to seem that he was one of those gentlemen who imagined that females were vapid, weak creatures who could do little or nothing for themselves. And his behaviour towards his sister was little short of tyrannical.

Margaret had not thought him so irritating before this, but then she had never spent so much time with him in a confined space. But at last they were in Bath and she would be able to send him packing very shortly.

'I hope this will suit your consequence, Comtesse?' Mr Rushford asked, looking mightily pleased with himself as he indicated the house. It was indeed a fine example of the new building that had taken place in recent years, being one of several terraced houses that were designed in the shape of a crescent. 'I promise you it was not the first I looked at and quite the best I was shown.'

'It will do very well,' Margaret replied for she could do no other, though for her own taste she would have preferred something smaller. 'It was very good of you to escort us here yourself, sir—but I believe you must have many other concerns. We do not want to monopolise your time and shall see you in the morning. This evening I believe both Caroline and I will want to rest.'

'But I…' He gave her a look that was somewhere between outrage and disbelief, but, meeting an implacable one from Margaret, was forced to bow his head. 'Yes, of course. I would not want to tire either of you. I shall see you tomorrow, dearest Caroline. Indeed, you do look a little pale. Yes, I shall leave you to rest this evening. Comtesse, your servant.'

Caroline sighed as she went inside and took off her bonnet. Several of their own people had gone on ahead to prepare for their coming and she smiled a little wearily as they were greeted by friendly faces. Margaret was receiving a report on the house and its permanent staff from her personal dresser, and Caroline ran on ahead to the room where her own maid was waiting to help her ease away the strains of the journey.

Margaret noticed the sigh and long face, but did not follow immediately for she wanted to meet the housekeeper and discuss the household arrangements, which Mr Rushford had insisted on making for her. It was necessary to make a few changes, but she had no real fault to find with his choice of a house and went up to her own room feeling more in tune with herself than she had on arrival.

She was just wondering whether she would bother to

change her gown for dinner, which would be served she had been told in an hour, when Caroline tapped at her door and asked if she could come in.

'Yes, of course, dearest,' Margaret said. 'I was just considering whether or not I ought to change my gown, but I do not expect company and we shall dine quietly together.'

'I came to tell you that I am not hungry,' Caroline said and gave another deep sigh. 'My head aches and I would rather just rest in my room—if you won't think me a terrible grouch?'

'Is your head very bad?' Margaret asked, looking at her in concern. 'I am so sorry. Shall I make you a tisane and bring it to you when you are in bed?' She declined to mention her own headache, reserving all her sympathy for her ward.

Caroline hesitated, and then agreed. 'It began aching some time ago and now it is throbbing. I did not want to say anything earlier because Mr Rushford makes so much fuss…' She blushed as she realised what she had said. 'I know he means well and is concerned only for my comfort, but…'

'I know exactly what you mean,' Margaret said and smiled. 'Some gentlemen do seem to imagine we ladies are poor creatures who need looking after every moment, when all we really want is a little peace—especially when we have the headache.'

Caroline's frown lightened. 'I knew you would understand. Poor John is so kind and generous, but he does fuss so. I dare say he will grow out of it in time.'

'Yes, I dare say,' Margaret agreed, though she doubted it. Men like John Rushford were prone to worship their own consequence and expected a certain conformity from their wives. He would drive Margaret to distraction within a week—but she did not have to marry him. 'As you say, he is both kind and generous.'

Margaret hesitated, wondering whether she ought to say what was in her mind. If Caroline had changed her mind about the marriage she would support her, take her back to France and hope that another, happier match presented itself when the scandal had died. However, as yet Caroline had said only that she had a headache and to put doubts in her mind might cause friction between them. The girl surely knew that she would support her in any decision she might make, so there was no need to say more at the moment.

Caroline went away to her room, and Margaret, not in the least tired, her headache easing now, went down to partake of the excellent supper their cook had prepared for them. She ate it alone, then made a tour of the house before retiring, armed with a book by Sir Walter Scott that she had been wanting to read. The book had been loaned to her by Lady Felicia, who had promised to retrieve it when she visited Bath for the wedding.

The wedding list had grown somewhat since congratulations and cards had poured in and several friends had already sent gifts. Margaret reflected that that might not altogether suit Mr Rushford, but since the expense was hers he really had little say in the matter. Caroline had added several names herself, and Margaret was anxious that her ward should be happy with the arrangements.

As she sat before her dressing mirror, gazing at her reflection in the mirror, Margaret's thoughts turned towards her own future. Lady Felicia had invited her to visit them again after her confinement, and several other friends had offered kind invitations. She could if she chose remain in Bath until the spring and then take a house in London... A smile touched her lips as she thought of the letter she had received from Giles just before she left the Belmonts' home. In it he had said he was impatient to see her again and would be with her in Bath within a day or so of her own arrival.

Much of her own plans depended on his, she realised, feeling a flush of warmth spread through her body. She would, after all, be Giles's mistress, at least for the immediate future. How shocking that was! She knew that she had stepped beyond the bounds of acceptable behaviour for a young woman of her class by going so willingly to her lover's arms, and yet she could not regret it. However, it did mean that she must keep up her masquerade, for already Felicia had begun to suspect there was something between them, and though she might smile and condone it in a widow she would think it unpardonable in a single woman. Indeed, she would probably be ordered to cut Margaret. Lord Belmont would certainly not think her a suitable companion for his wife if he guessed how shockingly she had behaved.

Margaret got up and went to bed, opening her book and beginning to read, but finding it difficult to concentrate even on Sir Walter's incomparable lines. She had wondered what might happen if she were to conceive a child, but of course the answer was simple. She would go home to France, where she would live quietly, receiving those friends who wished to call, but content with her child and her memories.

Nothing would make her give up this brief time of happiness, which had been offered so unexpectedly. She had been a little shocked when she reflected on what she had done that night at Belmont, but a short time of contemplation had settled her mind. She was past the first flush of her youth and had no wish to make the kind of marriage Caroline had chosen, even if it was offered her. No, it would suit her to remain independent and to receive Giles as her lover when he chose to visit. She suspected that she might find it painful when their affair ended, as it would in time, but she had made up her mind not to think too much about that.

She would take what she could from life from now on, she decided, and, smiling, blew out her candle and closed her eyes. Very shortly she was sleeping, at peace with herself and the world.

Giles frowned over the letter that had reached him when he returned to his lodgings in London that evening. Wellington had written in confidence that an attempt had been made on his life, and by a French woman and her male accomplice.

It was well that you warned me, Giles, Wellington had written, *I was suspicious of the lady from the start and when she fainted at my feet I called an attendant instead of hastening to her assistance myself. I was therefore able to fight off the assassin who tried to stab me in the back. I know I have no need to warn you to keep this to yourself, but the pair have been arrested and will be held accountable. I am glad to hear that an attack on a certain person was prevented; though that may have a different source, as you know. I believe my own life is no longer at risk, but you would do well to remain vigilant.*

It seemed that Giles had misjudged the Comtesse de Grenelle from the start. His information had been correct, but he had picked the wrong quarry. He was relieved that the attempt on Wellington had been thwarted. Particularly as he had only that evening re-

ceived word from his agents that the attempt to shoot
the Regent had been by a known agitator, who had published inflammatory material about the Prince and was
even now being sought by the runners from Bow Street.

Magda was not the scheming assassin he had suspected; Giles realised that he had wronged her and felt
the sting of shame. His feelings towards her were far
from clearly established in his mind, for he knew that
she affected him powerfully, in a way no other woman
ever had. She had agreed to be his mistress, but even
in that there was shame, for he had given her little
choice, his forceful seduction sweeping away her resistance.

And she had been a virgin. He was frustrated by her
refusal to tell him her story, and what could only be her
lack of trust in him. Nor could he blame her, for he had
in his own opinion treated her shamefully, his determined assault on her resulting in reactions and feelings
he had not dreamed of. What if she should deny him—
refuse to allow him near her? Giles discovered that he
would find that more painful than he could ever have
imagined previously, and wondered at himself.

What were his feelings for Magda exactly? And who
was she? Could she be brought to trust him sufficiently
to tell him her story?

'What is the matter, dearest?' Margaret asked, looking at Caroline's unhappy expression one morning.
They had been in Bath for some days and she had noticed her ward was looking less than happy of late. 'Is
something troubling you?'

'Oh, no,' Caroline said and sighed. 'It is just
that...Mr Rushford did not like the way I behaved at

the assembly last night. He said I was too forward with one of my partners, and that people had noticed.'

'I did not notice anything untoward.'

'No, nor would anyone with an ounce of sense,' Caroline said angrily and then blushed. 'Oh, I should not have said that. It was very rude of me.'

'I would not expect you to speak of the gentleman you mean to marry in such terms, dearest.'

'I wish I were more like you,' Caroline said. 'You are so kind to me that I feel as if we are related, but I am not at all like you.'

'You are more like me than you realise,' Margaret said with a smile. 'I believe you have more spirit than most believe.' Including Mr Rushford, who might be in for a surprise after they married. 'I have been called stubborn, and I think you too have that trait.'

'I am all mixed up…' Caroline sighed. 'It might have been better had I listened to your advice, rather than ignoring it.'

'Are you regretting your decision to marry Mr Rushford?'

'No…I do not think so,' Caroline said, looking doubtful. 'At least, only sometimes. He can be unbearably irritating at times…'

'Yes, I have observed it,' Margaret said, hesitated, and then, 'If you should change your mind, my love, you have only to say.'

'You are so good to me,' Caroline said and hugged her. 'You are like the mother I never knew, my sister and my friend all in one.'

'Well, put your bonnet and shawl on, dearest, and we shall go shopping. I always find that the best cure for the blue devils…'

* * *

Margaret saw the gentleman's hat on the stand in the hall as she and Caroline returned from a shopping trip on which they had been joined by Mr Rushford for most of the morning. Politeness had made her offer him a light nuncheon, but he had taken himself off, claiming a prior engagement and promised to escort them to the Assembly that evening.

'A gentleman has called?' she asked when the parlour maid came to take her pelisse and scarves.

'It is Sir Roderick Hazelmere,' the girl said. 'I did tell him you were out, ma'am, but he insisted he would wait.'

'Yes, that is perfectly all right,' Margaret said. She had heard the smothered gasp from Caroline, but ignored it. 'Shall you greet Roddy and get it over, my dear—or would you rather take your parcels to your room?'

'May I go up first and come down in a moment? I— I should like to apologise, but I need a moment...'

'Yes, of course,' Margaret said and smiled at her. The girl looked pale and nervous, but she must be wondering how Roddy would take the news of her engagement.

Margaret walked into the small rear parlour where her brother was standing with his back to her, staring out into the garden. His shoulders looked stiff and straight and she guessed that it had cost him something to come to them that morning.

'Roddy, my dearest,' she said as he turned and saw her. 'I am delighted you could come. I was worried about you when you disappeared like that with no word.'

'That was wrong of me,' he said, a dark colour flooding his cheeks. 'I flew into a temper and stormed off and I have repented of it ever since—especially when I read that notice in *The Times*. I have no one to blame but myself. Caroline had every right to make her own choice.'

'She has made her choice,' Margaret said. 'I am not sure that it was a wise one, nor that she would have made it if you had spoken of your own feelings, Roddy. I did advise you to speak to her, my dear.'

'I couldn't, Maggie,' he said in a strangled voice. 'I had no right. Rushford can give her so much more than I...'

'I am sure your own estate is adequate, Roddy.'

'You don't understand,' her brother replied, looking wretched. 'I've been a fool—gambled more than I could afford. It happened in London just before we went down to the Belmonts'. I lost five thousand guineas in one night and have had to mortgage some of the land to pay the debt.'

'Oh, Roddy,' Margaret said, feeling shocked as she saw the despair in his face. 'Why on earth did you not come to me, my dearest? You must have known I would pay the debt for you. I was going to give you five thousand pounds as a wedding present, and I could manage a bit more if you need it.'

'Dash it all, Maggie, I can't sponge off you,' Roddy said and ran his fingers through his hair. 'I'm ashamed of myself for being such a fool.'

'I have far more than I need,' Margaret assured him, 'and I shall give you a draft on my bank immediately so that you can settle your debts. Would six thousand guineas cover all you need?'

'More than enough,' he said, his colour deepening. 'I'm such a fool, Maggie. I couldn't cope with seeing Caroline with that damned prig and took myself off in a temper when all I wanted was to beg her to marry me. I should have listened to you, but I was too proud. I love her so much…I'm not sure that I can bear to stay for the wedding. To see her marry that fellow would tear the heart out of me.'

'Roddy—' Margaret broke off as she heard a gasp, and she turned her head towards the door to see Caroline standing there, her face ashen. It was obvious that she had heard at least some of what he had been saying. 'Caroline, my dear.'

'Sir Roderick…' Caroline's eyes were huge in her pale face as she walked into the room. She looked like someone moving in a dream, clearly stunned, disbelieving. 'Did you mean…?'

'Caroline!' He strode to meet her, his face working with the emotion he was striving to control and failing. 'I beg you to forgive me for the wicked things I said to you. I was mad with jealousy and angry with myself for not being able to offer you marriage.'

'But I have my ten thousand,' Caroline whispered, her voice little more than a croak. 'I could have paid your debt.'

'I could not have taken that!'

'But it was yours if you'd asked. I would have given you…done anything.' She stared at him, the glitter of tears in her lovely eyes. 'I did not think you cared at all.' A sob rose in her throat as he seized her hands and pressed them to his lips. 'You seemed angry all the time and…'

'Only because I was jealous of all the others,' Roddy said. 'That damned prig Rushford more than any of them. He isn't worthy of you, Caro. He may have a fortune, but he's a pompous ass and I'm certain he won't make you happy.'

'But…I've promised to marry him,' Caroline faltered, a tear trickling from the corner of her eye. 'It is all arranged, announced in *The Times*…'

'You can tell him it's off,' Roddy growled. 'Or I shall for you. You cannot marry that damned fellow, Caro my darling. You will be miserable.'

She looked a picture of misery as it was, her eyes dark with the tears she struggled to hold back. 'I don't know,' she choked. 'Oh, I can't…I can't talk about this now…' Giving a cry of despair, she turned and fled from the room.

Roddy started to go after her, but Margaret called him back.

'Leave her for the moment, Roddy.'

'But she is upset. She doesn't want to marry him. I know she doesn't.'

'If that is her decision, she will make it herself,' Margaret told him. 'Let her have time to think this through, dearest. A decision like this bears heavy consequences for her—for you both. I shall talk to her myself shortly and then we'll decide what to do for the best. You ought not to get involved. Mr Rushford would be within his rights to sue you for enticement. No, you must have patience. If Caroline breaks off her engagement, I shall take her home to France and you may come to her in a few weeks. We shall arrange a wedding when sufficient time has passed—for both your sakes.'

'Damn it, Maggie! I love her. I want to comfort her.' He glared at her, clearly frustrated by her counsel. 'She needs me…'

'You must be guided by me in this,' Margaret said. 'Of course I understand your feelings, my dear. However, you have both been foolish and impulsive and that is why you are in this predicament. There will be such a scandal. You could lose much more than five

thousand pounds if Mr Rushford chose to sue, Roddy.'
She moved towards him, laying a hand on his arm, then
taking his face between her hands and smiling up at
him. 'You know that I want you to be happy, my dearest…'

'Lord Benedict…' a maid announced from the doorway and Giles walked in as Roddy bent his head to kiss
her cheek.

'Forgive me if I come at a bad moment.'

'Giles…' Margaret was struck by the icy tone of his
voice and then immediately realised what had caused it.
'You 'ave not come at a bad time, my lord. I 'ave been
comforting my foolish friend. I fear he is suffering from
the pangs of frustrated love. I would tell you in confidence that Caroline's marriage to Mr Rushford may be
cancelled…'

'Come to her senses, has she?' Giles asked, a faint
flicker of humour in his dark eyes as he realised he had
once again jumped to conclusions regarding Magda.
'That's a tricky situation for you, Hazelmere. Rushford
is a pompous ass, but dangerous. You'll have to go
carefully or you may find yourself caught up in expensive litigation—men like that have a habit of standing
on their rights.'

Roddy's face was a dark brick red. 'I know I've been
a damned fool,' he muttered. 'Maggie has spelled that
out for me, believe me. I should have come to her in
the first place instead of rushing off the way I did.'

'Matter of a gambling debt, was it?' Giles nodded
wisely. 'I did hear something. Are you in need of a
loan? Glad to be of help if you're bothered.'

'Maggie has sorted that for me,' Roddy said, completely forgetting that his sister was supposed to be
merely an acquaintance. 'Didn't want to ask her, of

course, but should have known she'd stump up—always does when I need her.'

'Oh, Roddy,' Margaret said, and sighed. She raised her brows at Giles, a rueful smile on her lips. 'Well, I suppose there's no hiding it now—this forgetful gentleman is my brother. I am Margaret Hazelmere, and I must beg you to keep my secret for the moment, Giles.'

'*Miss* Margaret Hazelmere?' Giles looked at her intently. 'Would I be correct in thinking that there was no Comte de Grenelle?'

'I believe that the last holder of that title was executed during the Terror,' Margaret admitted ruefully. 'It was merely a little subterfuge that I believed could harm no one. My brother begged me to enter Society as myself, but the thought of a duenna irked me beyond bearing. I have been accustomed to being my own mistress, you see, and since I had no desire to marry...'

'So it was merely a little masquerade?'

'I told her it would provoke a scandal if it got out,' Roddy said. 'But she wouldn't listen. She is too independent and contrary for her own good sometimes—but it's my fault she's been found out. Sorry, Maggie.'

'It will not go beyond this room,' Giles promised, a gleam of amusement in his eyes. The sheer audacity of her masquerade appealed to him, though he knew the consequences if she were unmasked. 'I assure you I can be the soul of discretion when I choose.'

'Glad to hear it,' Roddy said. 'We're going to be in enough trouble when this thing breaks as it is—and that's my fault as well.'

'I think I shall ask Mr Rushford to call,' Margaret said as Giles remained silent. 'I shall explain that Caroline has decided she needs more time and...'

'You might do better to plead illness,' Giles said,

looking thoughtful. 'If you take her away somewhere quiet and let the whole thing blow over that might be best. She could write to Rushford and tell him that she has decided, after a period of reflection, that they are not suited. I believe he may cause you a deal of trouble if he feels his consequence has been slighted.'

'I think I should deal with the fellow,' Roddy said, his face assuming a stubborn look.

'You would be unwise to do so at this stage,' Giles replied with a considering look. 'My advice would be for you to leave Bath rather than give Mr Rushford cause for suspicion.'

'I'm not going without talking to Caroline.' Roddy's hands clenched. All this advice was very well, but damned interfering! 'I shan't just give her up—no matter the consequences.'

'No one has suggested that, my dear.'

'It sounds suspiciously that way to me, Maggie.'

'Will you take Roddy away with you, my lord, and try to talk some sense into his head?' Margaret begged, meeting Giles's eyes in desperation. 'I shall discuss this quietly with Caroline and try to discover what she really wants—and then I'll let you know, Roddy. If she wants to see you, you may come this afternoon and talk to her alone. It is not one of our at-home days and you will not be disturbed.'

'You need not let me know. I shall be here at three o'clock,' Roddy said, his mouth set determinedly. In that moment he looked very like his sister and Giles wondered that he had not noticed the resemblance before. 'I shan't be kept from her, Maggie. I know she can't want to marry that fellow—'

'Go away, Roddy!'

'Yes, bear me company,' Giles said. 'I have a horse to see and I would value your opinion, Hazelmere.'

'Really?' Roddy was so struck by the signal honour that had been bestowed on him that he allowed himself to be ushered from the room and out of the house. 'Well, that's damned good of you, Benedict. Always fancied myself a judge of horseflesh, you know.'

Margaret breathed deeply as she heard the front door close behind them. Her secret was out and she could not let herself think what might happen next. Giles would surely think her a scheming minx for playing such a trick on Society as a whole, and on him in particular. He would also think her fast and without shame—and she had given him good reason!

But she could not worry about that just at the moment. The matter of Caroline's wishes in all this must be her first priority. Squaring her shoulders, she walked up the stairs and knocked at the girl's door.

'May I come in, dearest?'

There was a moment's pause, then, 'Yes,' in a muffled voice. Caroline was lying on her bed, her face red from weeping, but she sat up when Margaret came to her and handed her a kerchief. 'You must think me very foolish? I have behaved very badly, have I not?'

'You have been a little misguided and impulsive,' Margaret said. 'It is awkward, but the situation is not irretrievable, dearest. What is important is what you want to do.'

'I—I love Roddy. I always have,' Caroline said and blew her nose on the kerchief. She brushed the back of her hand across her face. 'I should never have encouraged Mr Rushford. I—I do not truly like him very much. I think I accepted him out of a desire to spite Roddy...to make him suffer for being so horrid to me.'

'Ah…' Margaret nodded her understanding. 'You have discovered that Mr Rushford is not quite as pleasant as he first seemed?'

'He thinks that I should be guided by him in all things, that I am foolish and have no opinions worth listening to,' Caroline cried, a spark of indignation bringing back the spirit to her eyes and banishing the tears. 'Roddy is never like that—is he?'

'No, he isn't,' Margaret agreed. 'He is probably too easygoing for his own good and you will have him eating out of your hand when you are married. He can be impatient and sometimes thoughtless, and stubborn, too, but I have always thought him exceedingly affable. His behaviour towards you at Belmont was out of character and brought on by jealousy.'

'But…how can we be married?' Caroline stared at her miserably. 'I have promised to marry Mr Rushford and I don't see how I can get out of it. It would be a terrible scandal.'

'Yes, there will be a scandal,' Margaret agreed. 'I must admit that things will be difficult for you and Roddy in the coming months. It may be that you will never be admitted to the best circles again here in England.'

'I do not care for that,' Caroline said. 'I would much prefer to live in the country with…' She gulped back a sob. 'Only I think it will be very difficult to tell Mr Rushford.'

'Roddy is calling at three this afternoon,' Margaret told her. 'Do you wish to talk to him alone?'

'Yes, please, if I may?'

'I shall leave you to talk, but you must promise to be patient and not do anything reckless, my love. I think I shall speak to Mr Rushford myself and explain that you are not feeling quite the thing. I shall ask that the wedding is postponed. We shall go away, perhaps to France, and then in a week or two you will write to him and tell him that you cannot marry him.'

Caroline looked at her doubtfully. 'Supposing he will not agree to a postponement?'

'Then I shall tell him that you are too ill to be married for the time being.' Margaret frowned for a moment. 'I could tell him that you have an hereditary weakness of the chest from your mother and that your doctor has advised sea air.'

'Magda!' Caroline stared at her. 'That would be a lie.'

'Not the first I've told,' Margaret said and smiled oddly. 'I would prefer to tell the truth and shame the devil, as the saying goes, but for your sake I am prepared to tell a few white lies if necessary. We shall see how things go, dearest. Now wash your face and I shall send a light lunch up to you. I shall tell any callers that you are not well, and you may come down when Roddy calls.'

'What about the Assembly this evening?'

'I think we must cancel our appointments for the next few days,' Margaret said. 'It would be awkward if you were to meet either Mr Rushford or his sister in company.'

'Sarah will be upset,' Caroline said, who had come to like Mr Rushford's sister in the short time she had known her. 'I think she was hoping that she would have more freedom when her brother married.'

'Yes, well, that is not your problem,' Margaret said, though she too felt a little sorry for Miss Rushford, who she had met on several occasions since her brother had brought her to Bath. She thought Sarah seemed a plain shy creature much under her brother's domination. 'Try to rest now, Caroline, and do not worry too much. I shall do my best to smooth things over with Mr Rushford.'

'Thank you. I am sorry to be so much trouble to you.' Caroline looked a little ashamed of herself. 'I should have listened when you told me to wait and consider. I knew almost at once that I had acted unwisely.'

'You made a mistake, but that was my brother's fault as much as yours,' Margaret said. 'Now wash your face and eat your lunch when it comes, and then you will be fit to see Roddy.'

She left Caroline to reflect on what she had said, and went to her own room to tidy her gown. She did not look forward to the interview with Mr Rushford, whom she suspected might be difficult to deal with on such a matter, but it must be done. Caroline could clearly not face such an ordeal in her present state, and it would be best to confine her to her room for a while rather than let her be exposed to any unpleasantness.

It was all such a coil, she thought and sighed, for there was her own problem to be considered when Caroline's was solved.

Margaret sent a letter to Mr Rushford almost immediately, telling him that they were forced to cancel their engagements for a few days due to Caroline's having taken a little chill. She begged him not to call, telling him that the girl was not able to see anyone for the moment, and that she would write as soon as it was possible for him to see his fiancée.

When Roddy was announced she took him into the small back parlour and left him there. Caroline had heard and was swift to come downstairs. Before the door closed behind her, Margaret heard their cries of endearment and knew that they had flown to each other's arms.

Now why could they not have done that weeks ago?

She shook her head over it, but left them to their private conversation.

However, it was not a half an hour later that the front door knocker was rapped imperiously and when the housekeeper went to open it, she heard the loud, demanding tones of Mr Rushford.

'I wish to see Miss Hammond or the Comtesse de Grenelle.'

'They are not at home to visitors, sir.'

'I am not a visitor. I am Miss Hammond's fiancé.'

'I am sorry, sir. Madame told me no one was allowed in this afternoon.'

'You are impertinent. Fetch your mistress to me at once!'

'I cannot, sir. I have my orders.'

Margaret went out into the hall. 'I will see Mr Rushford for a moment,' she said. 'I am sorry to disoblige you, sir, but we may 'ave a contagious disease in the 'ouse. You will forgive me if I do not come too near you.' She coughed slightly. 'I do not wish to give you this putrid cough.'

'Contagious?' He looked at her in alarm. 'I did not realise. I thought it just a chill...'

'I did not wish to alarm you, but the doctor fears it may be something worse...diphtheria or...' She had said enough and Mr Rushford's face turned pale as he took a step backwards. 'Of course it may be just a chill, but it would be best if you wait until I send for you. You understand, *non*?'

'Yes, yes, of course,' he said. 'I did not perfectly understand…'

'I am so sorry you 'ave 'ad a wasted journey,' Margaret said, breathing a sigh of relief. For a moment she had feared that he would refuse to leave the house without seeing Caroline. 'Please, I beg you will not worry too much. I shall write to you very soon, I dare say.'

He tipped his hat to her, turned on the doorstep and went off at a pace that made Margaret smile inwardly. She felt no remorse for having deceived him, for he deserved no sympathy. Had he demanded to see Caroline and been distraught with worry she might have felt otherwise, but his manner had made it clear that he was more concerned for his own health than his fiancée's.

She returned to her own sitting room and was engaged in writing a letter to some friends when Roddy and Caroline entered the room together. They were holding hands and it was clear from their faces that they had settled their differences.

'So, you have made up your quarrel, then?'

'It was so silly of me,' Caroline said and blushed. 'We both want to apologise to you, Margaret. We have caused you a great deal of trouble.'

'I do not mind for myself,' Margaret replied.

'As you know, I have no wish to live in England, and shall return to France as soon as it may be arranged. I think it best if you come with me as I suggested, Caroline. As I said, you may write to Mr Rushford in a few weeks. I shall speak to him before we leave, but you need not be here. I will arrange for you to go on before me.'

'We want to be together,' Roddy said his cheeks

heated, a stubborn light in his eyes. 'Let Rushford do his damnedest. In heaven's name, he can't force Caro to marry him if she does not wish to.'

'No, but he could make things very uncomfortable for you both,' Margaret warned and smothered a sigh. Roddy's worst fault had always been his impatience. 'It would surely be best for you to let him down lightly, Caroline. In fact, I must insist that you do things my way. I cannot be a party to any other arrangement. You must at least have the decency to consider Mr Rushford's pride, if nothing else.'

'We don't want to wait weeks and weeks to be married,' Caroline said, a tearful note in her voice. She looked at Roddy as if begging him to help her. 'We love each other and we want to marry as soon as possible.'

'Nevertheless, you must leave a reasonable period between jilting one man and wedding another,' Margaret said, feeling like an ogress, but knowing she had no choice for their own sakes. 'Otherwise you will make me regret my decision to give you this time in England, and you will seriously displease me—that goes for you too, Roddy.'

'Dash it all, Maggie! You don't understand how we feel.'

'I understand more than you imagine,' she replied. 'However, I must ask you to give me your word that you will do nothing reckless.'

'I would never do anything to hurt you,' Caroline said and a tear trickled down her cheek. 'But I will not meet Mr Rushford and I do not see how I can stay in my room all the time—especially if he comes looking for me.'

'You may leave me to deal with that,' Margaret replied. 'I shall arrange for a carriage to take you back to our house in London. There you will wait for me, and we shall travel on to France together. Once you are safely on your way, I shall tell Mr Rushford that you are ill and cannot marry him for the moment. I think that by the time you write to him from home he will have accepted the inevitable, and then we may think about arranging a wedding for you and Roddy.'

'Dash it all, Maggie! You take too much on yourself. This is between Caro and I.' Roddy looked stubborn, clearly prepared to fight for his love and Margaret smiled inwardly, though she gave no sign of it.

'I am asking you to do this for my sake, if not your own.'

'Please go,' Caroline whispered, looking at him with tear-blinded eyes. 'We have to do what your sister says.'

'I don't see that at all,' he protested, but as she made a little choking sound he cursed beneath his breath. 'Oh, very well. I'll be sensible since you ask it of me, Caro— but I insist on escorting you to London, and I shall accompany you both to France.'

'As you wish,' Margaret said, feeling unable to continue the argument. 'Please go now, Roddy. I took a risk letting you come here in the first place. Mr Rushford was refused, and if he should hear you spent the afternoon here he would become suspicious.'

'I'll be here in the morning without fail,' Roddy said, looking mutinous. 'And I shall escort Caroline to London. You may do as you please, Maggie, but if I stay here any longer I shall knock that damned fellow's head off his shoulders.'

Caroline looked horrified as he went out, clearly in high dudgeon.

'He is angry with me, not you,' Margaret reassured her. 'I am only imposing these restrictions for your own benefit, Caroline. You and Roddy will be living in England when you are married, and even in the country it is uncomfortable to live beneath the shadow of scandal. You would not be happy if your neighbours decided they could not know you.'

'I know you are right,' Caroline admitted on a sigh. 'But you won't make us wait too long?'

'No longer than necessary,' Margaret promised. 'Go up to your room now, my love. It will be best to keep up the pretence of your illness if we are to deceive poor Mr Rushford. I do not care for the man myself, but there is no doubt that he has suffered a slight from your change of heart.'

'Oh, dear,' Caroline said. 'It is so very bad of me but I cannot—I really cannot marry him.'

'No, my dear, of course you cannot,' Margaret said and smiled. 'I wouldn't allow it, but we must let him down as kindly and as discreetly as possible, do you not agree?'

'Yes, of course,' Caroline said. 'Roddy is so impatient and when he is with me…nothing else but being his wife seems to matter. Yet I know you are right, Maggie.'

'The sooner it is done the better,' Margaret said. 'We shall have your trunks packed and you may be on your way first thing in the morning. After that I shall speak to Mr Rushford.'

Chapter Seven

'Have there been any more callers?' Margaret asked later that evening when she was served a simple supper of soup, fresh bread and a little cold chicken on a tray in the back parlour. 'No one asking for me?'

'No, ma'am. Two ladies called and left their cards, but I told them Miss Hammond was not well and that you were not at home.'

'Lord Benedict did not call?'

'No, ma'am. No one else.'

Margaret was left to eat her supper alone, for Caroline was busy supervising her packing and had requested only some tea and cake in her room, as she had no time for more. It had been decided that she would take just a bag and her small trunk with her. Everything else would follow later with Margaret's own things.

'I may as well have everything sent home to France,' Margaret said. 'We shall stay in London for a few days to close up the house and pay the staff, but then we shall leave. I shall feel more comfortable once we are at home. Besides, it will not do for you to be seen in town since you are supposed to be ill.'

Caroline had pulled a face at this, but made no further

comment, apparently resigned to her fate for the time being.

Margaret did not relish her own role in this sorry affair. Even though she did not particularly like Mr Rushford, she could not but feel that he had been badly used. It would have been better if Caroline could have faced him to apologise in person, but she knew that that was beyond her ward. Besides, she suspected that there might be an unpleasant side to Mr Rushford when he felt himself slighted. She would give Caroline and Roddy a day's start, then she would tell him that the wedding must be postponed. It was perhaps a little deceitful of her, but no worse than she had done before by pretending to be other than she was—something that had given her several pangs of conscience since she had discovered that she actually liked many of the people she had expected to despise.

Having settled her mind on this point, she allowed herself to think about Giles Benedict. She had expected he might call later in the afternoon to see her and was a little uncomfortable with her thoughts. It must have been a great surprise to him to discover the truth of her identity. She had planned to tell him once they knew each other a little better. He might have understood her reasons for behaving as she had by then, but coming so suddenly upon her secret would have been shocking indeed. Young, single ladies of good family did not take lovers, and on the rare occasion when such a thing did happen it was frowned upon and hidden away as a shameful secret. He was bound to think the less of her and to suspect that she meant to trap him into marriage.

Of course! Margaret's cheeks flamed as she realised why Giles had not called. He was considering his position. As a gentleman he would probably feel that he had compromised her. Indeed, if the truth were known, she was ruined. She would be cast out as a fallen woman, shunned by the ladies who had welcomed her as friends.

She would mind being cut by some ladies—Felicia Belmont for one—but others would not cause her grief. Yet she thought she could bear even that if only Giles did not turn from her. She was afraid that he would either end the affair at once—or, worse still, insist on marrying her.

Marriage to Giles might have been pleasant under other circumstances, Margaret reflected, but not if he felt obliged to offer for her because of what had happened between them. Oh, damn Roddy and his loose tongue! Had he not blurted it all out like that she might have enjoyed a comfortable relationship with Giles for some months. Now it seemed that all was changed. Quite clearly he was holding back for the moment, and perhaps he was angry with her.

Finding that she had lost her appetite, Margaret left her chicken untouched and went upstairs to see what she could do to help Caroline with her packing and think about beginning her own.

Roddy helped Caroline into the carriage the next morning, then turned to take his leave of his sister. She accepted his kisses, waving as he mounted his horse to ride beside the smart travelling chaise. Caroline had her own maid and one other with her for propriety's sake, and Roddy would accompany them on horseback.

If they had been seen leaving in a carriage together all sorts of rumours might have started, and Margaret hoped to brush through the sorry affair with as little scandal as possible.

She wrote a few letters cancelling engagements for the next few days, and letting friends know that Caroline was unwell. It left a bad taste in her mouth for she did not enjoy deceiving people who had been kind to them like this, but it seemed the best way. At noon she had a simple nuncheon and then set out for the lending library, returning some books Caroline had borrowed. She met several ladies and gentlemen, who inquired after her ward, and was forced to repeat her tale of Caroline's illness.

'We heard that she had diphtheria,' one lady said and kept her distance from Margaret as if she feared that she too carried the dread disease.

'No, no, it was nothing of the kind,' Margaret replied. 'I did not want to say—but I believe it may be an 'ereditary weakness she 'as from her poor dear mother.'

'Oh, how sad,' the lady said, looking relieved. 'I know these things do run in families and that they can be very bad. I am so sorry. Will the wedding have to be cancelled?'

'I fear it may be.'

'Well, that is a shame. Tell me—was it Dr Morrison or Dr Boland that you called?'

'I...' Margaret coughed. 'Oh, please excuse me. I must not stand in this chill wind. I am used to a warmer climate, you understand, *non*?'

She hurried away, feeling wretched and wishing that she had never begun this masquerade. If only she had come to England as herself—and if only she had insisted Caroline wait for a while before becoming engaged to Mr Rushford. The blame was hers, she decided. She had made two ill-considered decisions and now she was regretting them.

She felt the sting of further regret when she returned

to the house and discovered that there had been no message from Giles. It seemed clear that he had decided their affair was best ended, and Margaret was aware of an ache in her heart. How foolish she had been to allow her own desires to sweep away all caution and surrender to his loving that night. He had lost all respect for her and wanted nothing more to do with her, it seemed. Well, it served her right! She had begun that foolish masquerade and had no one but herself to blame for the consequences.

Margaret wrote to Mr Rushford that evening, telling him that the wedding must be postponed for a while, and had the letter delivered to his lodgings immediately. She had also told him that Caroline wished for no visitors and that they were returning to France as soon as possible.

We shall, of course, write to you when there is any news, and beg your pardon for any disappointment you may have suffered at this delay. Caroline begs for your forgiveness and your forbearance, but cannot bring herself to see you at the moment.

It was best to keep it short, Margaret decided after several attempts at what was perhaps the hardest letter she had ever written in her life. She would have liked to write to Giles as well, but since he had not furnished her with his address in Bath she was unable to do so and laid down her pen.

She had decided to leave Bath in the morning. There was nothing more for her to do here and she had begun to feel that she would not be able to compose her emotions until she was at home once more.

She had foolishly allowed herself to dream and now the dream had ended, and she was punished for it. A wry smile touched her mouth as she reflected how right Aunt Kate had been to warn her of the perils of loving unwisely.

Giles had seemed to be a man she could deal with, a man who would not bore her or fuss over her or try to wrap her in chains of duty—but a man like that was clearly not the kind to relish being deceived and trapped. Since he had not come to see her, he must suspect that she had set out to trap him, but instead of offering her marriage as she'd feared, he had decided to ignore her altogether.

Margaret thought that of the two, she preferred the course he had chosen. It would have been too painful to be offered marriage as a duty—but how much sweeter it would have been if he could have accepted what she offered as it had been intended. A love that asked for no favours and no strings. Hers was a free spirit, independent and strong, and the affair she had envisaged with Giles could have been all that she desired, but she had believed he was different, and now it seemed that he was after all a man of his age. Hemmed about by convention and a sense of what was proper, he had failed to see the uniqueness of their love. Unlike the black knight of her childish dreams, he would not sweep her before him on his horse and ride into the sunset.

But perhaps he had not felt the completeness that Margaret had experienced in his arms? She had been merely a challenge, a woman he found amusing for a while, and he could not accept the unconventionality of their relationship.

She felt saddened and hurt by his failure to understand her nature, but there was no bitterness, no regret. He had not seduced her, for she had responded willingly to his lovemaking, and she would remember that night for the rest of her life.

It was a brief moment to last her a lifetime, Margaret reflected, for she doubted that she would ever trust enough to love again. But she would not let her disappointment sour her. She had friends, and there would be Roddy and Caroline's children to love and spoil. Besides, she might travel, for it had always been her desire to see more of the world. She thought that she might like to see the wonders of China and India, to become one of those intrepid ladies who stepped out of their world and found a new one beyond the confines of the narrow life they had been born to.

Her mood lifted at the thought, her head raised as she contemplated a lifetime of learning and discovery. At least she would not die without having tasted the sweetness of love.

Margaret had her carriage brought round early the next morning. She saw no reason to delay, for she did not particularly wish for a difficult interview with Mr Rushford should he call, and the roads would be quieter at this hour. The sooner she was in London, the sooner she could begin her preparations to return to France.

Her journey was without incident and quickly accomplished since she travelled post and changed horses frequently, and it was early evening on the following day that she was welcomed into her London house by the housekeeper she had employed on her arrival.

'It is good to have you back, ma'am,' the woman said and curtsied. 'Your room is ready for you and a meal will be prepared shortly. Had we known you were coming, it would have been sooner.'

'But surely Miss Hammond told you that I would be here within a day or two?'

'Miss Hammond, ma'am? Is she not with you?' The housekeeper looked surprised.

'No—no, she is not,' Margaret said and frowned as the icy finger trailed down her spine. 'Perhaps I misunderstood her. She may be staying with friends.'

'Yes, ma'am. It's an exciting time before a wedding, isn't it?'

'Yes. You have not seen Sir Roderick Hazelmere, I suppose?' At the woman's puzzled look she smiled easily. 'No matter. Excuse me, I shall want a tray of tea in the parlour—and some bread and butter and cold meat will do very well for my supper, thank you. I must go up and refresh myself after the journey.'

Where could Caroline and Roddy be? Margaret's mind wrestled with the problem even as she accepted the answer. They had deceived her and eloped together. She had no doubt who the instigator of the change of plan must be. Her brother had been determined he would not wait to make Caroline his bride, and had merely seemed to accept her stipulations until he had Caroline away from her.

She was furious with them. How could they play such a scurvy trick on her? It was beyond anything! She had trusted them, and they had given their word to behave decently—at least Caroline had, she remembered. Roddy had merely grunted and looked stubborn. She had been naïve to trust him! Yet she had expected better of him than this, but perhaps he considered that all was fair in love as in war.

It was all very well, but she would have to deal with the consequences. The circumstance of their disappearance was bound to get out and then there would be a terrible scandal.

How could she have been fool enough to let them go off alone like that? She ought to have left Bath with them, and sent her letters later. Yet she had never dreamed that they would behave so badly towards her. It was hurtful and unpleasant—and might result in serious consequences. Litigation could ruin a man and Roddy was now very much to blame for Mr Rushford's loss of a bride. It was not unknown for such cases to come to court, though many preferred to accept being jilted and brush over the scandal as best they could. Caroline would be ruined socially, of course, and Roddy might be ruined financially if Mr Rushford decided to press for damages.

Margaret felt close to tears, but anger prevented them from falling. Why should she bother her head over the ungrateful pair? She had done her best for them and this was the outside of enough.

An hour or more spent pacing the parlour left her no nearer finding a solution to her problem. She could not chase after the errant pair, nor did it seem worthwhile since nothing could be gained by preventing the marriage, and that might not in actual fact be possible. Caroline was not truly her ward but Aunt Kate's and it was doubtful whether Margaret had the authority to stop the wedding. Roddy knew that, of course, and had no doubt taken it into consideration.

Well, they had made their bed and they would just have to lie on it, Margaret thought angrily. There was nothing she could do for the moment, rack her brain as she might for a way out of this dilemma.

The best thing she could do was to close the house in London as quickly as possible and return to France.

Feeling as she did now, she was not sure that she wanted to see either her brother or Caroline again!

In the morning Margaret's anger had abated somewhat, but was replaced by anxiety. It really was very foolish of the pair to behave so badly, but she could do nothing about it now.

She spent the day seeing to her affairs in London, giving her staff notice and paying them their wages to the end of the period for which she had engaged them. The keys must be returned to the agent's office, and she could safely leave that to her housekeeper after she had departed for France.

'I shall be sorry to see you go, ma'am. I thought you might stay for a few months.'

'My plans 'ave always been loose,' Margaret replied with a little shrug. 'Who knows, perhaps I shall come 'ere again.'

She knew it was doubtful that she would visit London for some years. Perhaps one day when the Comtesse of Grenelle had been long forgotten she might risk it, but not in the near future.

Most of her possessions had already been sent on ahead, but she spent the last evening finding books and packing small items that had been forgotten. Discovering the book that the Duchess of Belmont had loaned her, Margaret packed it neatly and wrote a letter to thank Felicia for her kindness. She had already written to say the wedding had been cancelled and made no further mention of it or her own plans.

It was as she was on the verge of retiring to bed that a loud knocking at the front door made her pause at the foot of the stairs.

'Now who can that be at this hour?' the housekeeper asked as she went to answer it.

Margaret said nothing, but was not in the least surprised when she heard Mr Rushford asking angrily for her or Miss Hammond.

'Ah, Mr Rushford,' Margaret said and smiled pleasantly. 'Will you please come into the parlour? I fear you 'ave made a long journey for nothing.'

'I demand to see Caroline,' he said as soon as the door was closed behind him. 'I do not know why you have spirited her away like this, madam, but I shall not stand for it. I have my rights. Miss Hammond promised to marry me and I have been to a great deal of expense for her sake.'

'I am sorry if you 'ave spent money that you would not have done otherwise,' Margaret said. 'The ring you gave Miss Hammond will be returned, of course, and any other gifts you may 'ave made her—though I think there was none of any particular value?'

'I intended to give her jewels when we were married,' he retorted, his face purple. 'I meant expense at my estate in preparation for her coming.'

'Ah…' Margaret nodded. 'I thought that must be your meaning, sir. You will lose little by it since it is for your own benefit as well as your wife's—and of course you may marry…'

'Not good enough, madam!' he cried, clearly furious. 'I am not deceived by your lies. Caroline was seen driving away from Bath in a closed carriage, accompanied by Sir Roderick Hazelmere—and everyone knows that you encouraged the match between them. You have cheated me and I intend to be repaid.'

'You are holding me personally responsible?' Margaret

stared at him in disbelief. 'If—and I say *if*—Miss Hammond has chosen not to marry you, that is her affair. You cannot 'old me accountable, sir.'

'You were her guardian and you signed the marriage contract,' he said and his expression was what she could only think exceedingly nasty. 'Everyone knows Hazelmere has mortgaged his estate to pay a gambling debt—but you are a wealthy woman. The choice is yours, madam—either you restore my fiancée to me or face a law suit.'

'That is ridiculous,' Margaret replied. 'No court would find for you in such a case.'

'There is precedent,' he said triumphantly. 'Lord Rawlish withdrew his permission for his daughter to wed after the contract was signed and he was forced to pay damages of fifteen thousand pounds. I shall ask for ten—which was the sum of Caroline's inheritance.'

'But you were to allow her to keep it.'

'That was before this shameful seduction, which you have connived at from the start!'

'I 'ave done nothing of the sort,' Margaret replied, struggling to keep up her accent.

'Then why was Hazelmere always here at any hour of the day or night?' he demanded. 'He was at the house when I called the other afternoon in Bath—and do not lie, for I have it on good authority and a witness I may call at will. You agreed to this elopement and lied to me about Caroline's health—deny it if you can.'

'No, I shall not deny it,' Margaret said, anger stripping her of all caution. 'If you must have your pound of flesh, sir—sue and be damned to you. The truth is that Sir Roderick is my brother and that is why he was allowed entry whenever he chose—and why I entrusted her to his care.'

Rushford's mouth fell open. 'I don't believe you—Hazelmere doesn't have a sister.'

'Clearly you have not done your research properly,' Margaret said, a deadly smile on her lips. Now she no longer made any pretence, speaking crisply in her most English voice. 'If you intend to press for damages I would advise you to do so, sir. My lawyers in London will pass on any documents that come from yours—and now I must ask you to leave. I have nothing more to say to you.'

'You will not yield Caroline?'

'No, I most certainly shall not,' Margaret said. 'Had I guessed at the nasty set of your mind I should never have allowed her to accept your proposal in the first place, and I think she is well rid of you. Goodbye, Mr Rushford. I think there is no need for us to meet again as our lawyers may do the business for us. Please leave now, or I shall have my servants throw you in the gutter.'

Rushford opened his mouth and shut it again. It was unlikely that he had ever met with such open defiance from a woman before and he was clearly at a loss. Margaret smiled as he turned on his heel and walked away without another word.

He was fortunate that she was a woman for she would have liked to take a horsewhip to him, she reflected and turned away to pour herself a glass of brandy. Her hand was trembling slightly and she spilled a few drops before managing to take a sip.

'Hitting the bottle, Magda?'

She almost dropped the glass as she heard the voice

close behind her, whirling round in disbelief. 'Giles—
how did you get here?'

'I rode my horse,' he replied and gave her a mocking
smile. 'More to the point, perhaps, is why Mr Rushford
has just departed in such a foul mood?'

'He is going to sue me because Caroline has jilted
him,' Margaret said. 'He says that I connived at it and
broke my promise—the promise I made when I signed
his marriage contract.'

'The man is a fool,' Giles said arching his brows. 'I
take it that Sir Hothead wouldn't listen and carried off
the lovely Miss Hammond against your advice?'

Margaret gave a strangled laugh. 'My poor brother
was determined to have his way. I was furious with
them when I realised they had not come here as I asked,
but fled to the border. There will be the most terrible
scandal, and Mr Rushford intends to ask for ten thousand pounds.'

'I hope you told him to sue and be damned?'

'Yes, I did,' she said. 'It rather took the wind out of
his sails, I'm afraid.'

'He hasn't a hope of succeeding,' Giles said and
walked over to take the brandy glass from her hand,
setting it down on one of the little tables. 'I am certain
his lawyers will tell him that at once, but he does have
rather more of a chance of success against your brother.'

'Yes, I know,' Margaret said. 'I would rather he sued
me than poor Roddy or Caroline.'

'If he managed to make you pay he might still have
a case against your brother. Better to limit the damage
as much as possible—could you afford to pay him if he
won that sum?'

'Yes, just about,' Margaret replied with a slight
frown. 'I am a little low on funds after the expense of

this trip and the wedding—and Roddy needed to repay that stupid mortgage. I have money tied up that I could release in time. It wouldn't ruin me—just make things awkward for a while.'

'I rather think I might be able to handle this better for you, Magda. Would you trust me to do that for you?'

'Yes, of course,' she said and then looked him in the eyes. 'If you will not think it too much of an imposition?'

'Do you imagine I would offer if I did?'

'No…' She smiled oddly and tipped her head to one side, reverting to the accent, which had been sadly lacking. 'I think you are a man who must 'ave his way, my lord—*non*?'

'Whenever possible,' he riposted, a twinkle in his dark eyes. 'Why did you run away from me?'

'I wasn't running from you,' she said and yet even as she spoke she knew that wasn't quite true. A part of the reason for her hasty departure was because she did not want to meet Giles by accident. 'I expected Caroline and Roddy to be here—and I was trying to avoid a scene with Mr Rushford.'

'Was that all your reason, Magda?'

'No, not quite,' she admitted meeting his intent gaze honestly. 'I think you must guess that I was a little…anxious about facing you after my shocking secret had been revealed so abruptly.'

'Not so very shocking,' Giles murmured, his voice husky, his eyes moving over her in a way that started little wavelets of desire crashing through her. 'The situation is unconventional, I shall give you that, but not shocking. After all, I distinctly recall that you told me you did not wish to marry—that your aunt had decided you were too independent of spirit.'

'Yes…' Margaret caught her breath. The look in his eyes was making her tingle with desire, rousing a need in her that she knew could be slaked only one way. 'Are you saying that you are prepared to continue our… relationship?'

'Come, let us not mince words, my love,' Giles said and his eyes gleamed with sheer mischief. 'We are lovers. This is an *affaire*—a passionate, emotional involvement that I for one believe will last for many years, until we part by mutual agreement. To remain lifelong friends, I hope and believe.'

'You truly feel that way?' Margaret looked at him dawning hope in her eyes as she realised he was describing what would be for her a perfect arrangement. 'You do not think me a wanton, lost to all shame?'

'You may be slightly wanton, Magda my sweet, but all the great lovers in history must have shared that tendency—do you not think so? Do you not think the Queen of Sheba and Helen of Troy must have been born in your image? Cleopatra caused the Romans to fight amongst themselves and Helen launched a thousand ships. While I hope you do not intend to play havoc with my life, I certainly feel you bring to it a spice that has been sadly lacking.'

Margaret's laughter rang out joyously. 'Oh, Giles! When you did not come to the house I thought you had decided to cut the connection. I have been planning to become an intrepid explorer to fill the emptiness in my life.'

'Now that is very interesting,' Giles said. 'For I am bound to say that it might be awkward if you were not prepared to travel. My own life is almost certain to be in the diplomatic service and I shall need to come and go—and since I do not wish to be parted from you for years at a time I thought it might suit us for you to accompany me. In England there are no doubt some who frown upon the idea of a mistress, but abroad it is more openly accepted. We shall need to keep up the idea of a departed husband if you are to have the entrée into certain circles; you must be known as Magda for the moment, but that is a matter of mere discretion.'

'Oh, Giles,' Margaret said. 'I am afraid that Mr Rushford knows the truth. I lost my temper when he questioned why Roddy was allowed to visit when he chose.'

'Have I not told you that I shall deal with that gentleman?'

'Yes.' She laughed as he raised his brows. 'Very well, I shall say no more. I look forward to a life of adventure at your side, my lord.'

'You were not planning to chase after your brother and Caroline?'

'I saw little point in it. Her reputation is gone—besides, they are determined to be married, and who am I to deny them? I can hardly preach morality at them, can I?'

'No, perhaps not,' Giles murmured, a husky note in his voice. 'Besides, it would be a waste of time, do you not think so—when we might be better employed?'

'Oh, certainly,' she agreed breathlessly. 'I do agree, Giles…'

She got no further for she was in his arms, being kissed so thoroughly that words were clearly a wasted effort. She smiled when he released her, holding out her hand to him invitingly.

'I can see you are determined to 'ave your way with me, my lord.'

'Do you have any idea of what that does to me?'

Giles demanded and then shouted with laughter as he saw the mischief in her eyes. 'But of course you do, my wicked lady. You know very well that it drives me wild with longing.'

'Then come to bed,' Margaret invited and led him from the room and up the stairs. 'It has been too long, Giles.'

'Far too long,' he agreed and suddenly swept her up in his arms. She gave a shriek of laughter, which was answered by a low growling in his throat. 'My sweet seductress. I adore you. I swear I shall never have enough of you.'

Giles proved his words time after time as they loved that night, taking her fiercely and tenderly in turns, the hot desire raging between them as they came to know each other's bodies so intimately that not one crevice remained unexplored and thoroughly kissed.

'You are the loveliest woman I have ever known,' Giles whispered against the creamy pale skin of her throat. 'And the most exciting. You have enslaved me, my darling. I am yours to command.'

'Then promise me you will tell me when you are tired of me,' Margaret said. 'Promise me we shall never hate each other or bore each other, but that if the fire burns itself out we shall part as friends.'

'The fire inside me when I look at you is unquenchable,' Giles murmured and drew her hand down the bed to discover the swelling hardness that her touch had aroused. 'Perhaps one day, when we are old, you will tire of me—but I shall never have enough of my wicked lady.'

Margaret laughed and began to kiss him, little pecking kisses that followed the arrow of dark hair on his flat abdomen, down to the evidence of his burning desire to be one with her again. She flicked at him delicately with her tongue, making him quiver and cry out at the bittersweet torment. But he would not allow her to unman him in that fashion and rolled her over on to her back, thrusting into her suddenly and with such hunger that she gasped and writhed beneath him, her body arching to meet the onslaught of his with equal urgency. Their coming together that time was an explosion of feeling that made them both scream the other's name aloud, Margaret's nails raking his shoulders in her abandon.

'You are mine, darling Magda,' he muttered fiercely against the soft curve of her belly, moving up to kiss her lips once more and clasp her to him possessively. 'Never doubt that you are mine and I shall not relinquish you, no matter what.'

Margaret smiled in the darkness. Had she not dreamed of something like this as a young girl? A knight in black armour who would sweep her up on his charger and ride off with her to his impenetrable fortress, there to make her a prisoner of love.

It was a foolish dream of course, one that most young girls might experience, though most would have chosen the White Knight and marriage. Margaret had always thought the Black Knight more romantic, and after his timely interruption that night in Italy her bold seducer had always worn this man's face.

It was a girl's dream come true—but for how long could it last?

Giles was gone before Margaret was awake. She found a note on the pillow beside her and held it to her lips, smiling as she inhaled the scent of him and recalled the passionate night that had just gone. It was as well that they had agreed she should leave as planned this morning, Margaret thought, for the servants would know he had spent the night in her bed and she thought they might be shocked.

However, there was no sign that anything had changed when Margaret took her leave that morning. She gave them all a small gift of money, thanked them for looking after her and went out to the chaise that had been hired to take her to Dover.

She would wait there at the Seagull Inn for Giles to come to her. He had some business in London that would take him a few hours, and then they would travel to her home in France.

'Wellington has had news,' Giles told her as they lay side by side in the aftermath of their loving the previous night. 'Napoleon Bonaparte is on the move and we expect him to land in France—perhaps by the beginning of next month. He will try to raise an army and take France back into his hands, and it is likely that he will succeed.'

'I met Napoleon once some years ago,' Margaret said. 'Or at least I made my curtsy and he glared at me as he passed. His history has been both glorious and sad, do you not think so?'

'Perhaps—though he has caused havoc in Europe. You cannot think that glorious?'

'No, I suppose not,' Margaret agreed. 'But he was an adventurer and he made his own destiny. I admire him for that at least. You have to excuse some bad behaviour in men like that, do you not?'

'Not to the degree that I would allow him to be set loose again. He will be stopped, Magda. Wellington means to finish it once and for all.'

'Yes, I dare say it must be,' Margaret agreed, though she thought that without such men history might have been less interesting, the world a little duller. 'But I know you are right. I do not wish to see Europe torn apart by war. Besides, I do not wish you to fight, Giles. I expect you will go to your general when the call comes?'

'I must,' he confirmed. 'But you shall be there with me before—and be waiting for me after. You will be there, Magda?'

'You know that I shall,' she said and gave him a loving smile. 'I am not ashamed to admit that I love you, Giles. I did not think I should ever truly mean that—my aunt convinced me that love was a myth— but it is in my heart and I would have you know it.'

'Then I am content,' he said. 'For the moment I could ask no more.'

There was something a little odd in his look at that moment, but it was gone so swiftly that she might have imagined it.

'What did you mean, *for the moment*?'

'Nothing,' he murmured. 'But I am a greedy creature, Magda. When I want something I want it all and I never let go, believe me. You are mine and I am yours. Do not think to leave me, for I should not let you go easily.'

She shook her head at him as his hand began to move amongst the moist curls at her mound of Venus, surrendering herself to the pleasure of his touch. She was happy at this moment, happier than she had ever expected to be—why think of the future until it was necessary?

'Your home is very beautiful,' Giles murmured as they stood together, looking down at the deep turquoise sea glistening in a pale sun. The hillside was covered in greenery that became a wash of colour in the spring and summer, while behind them the mellowed pink brick walls of the villa had a warm, comforting appeal. 'I can see why you might want to stay here—why you might be reluctant to leave it.'

'It is beautiful,' Margaret agreed, for the villa had the charm of age and nestled into the hills softly like a bird, rather than looking garishly conspicuous like some of the newer houses. 'But I have often thought I should like to see more of the world. I am looking forward to travelling with you, Giles.'

'A lady after my own heart,' Giles said and smiled oddly, as if amused by some secondary meaning. 'Wellington has left Vienna and is en route to Paris, where he will take command of the British army—such as it is. So many of our best troops have been sent elsewhere that we shall be hard put to it to raise a decent fighting force.' His words were mild when compared to those his commander was reported to have uttered, calling the men left to him an infamous army made up of the scum and dregs of his troops. Reaching out to touch her cheek, Giles gazed earnestly into her eyes. 'You are still willing to come with me—you have not changed your mind? You would not prefer to stay here until I am able to come to you again?'

After leaving England they had gone first to Margaret's home in the vague hope of finding Roddy and Caroline there, but there was no sign of the errant pair nor yet a message.

Margaret had not truly expected it, but their careless behaviour saddened her. Yet she could understand her brother's rebellion. He had come close to losing the woman he loved and was making certain of her, prepared to take the consequences whatever the outcome. His attitude showed spirit and determination and Margaret found that she admired that in him despite all. Giles had told her that his lawyers would deal with Mr Rushford in his absence and she felt that she must trust in him and allow the future to take its course.

Her relationship with Giles had filled a need in her that she had not been aware of until they became lovers. It was not only the pleasure and completeness that she found in his arms in the dark reaches of the night, it was the discovery of so much more.

They shared a similar sense of the ridiculous and Margaret laughed more when they were together than she had since she was a carefree child at her parents' home. Their interests were varied, sometimes shared, sometimes opposite, and they argued eagerly over the merits of Byron's poetry, Shelley, and Sir Walter Scott's novels, of which Giles had none too high an opinion. Margaret, an avid reader, had delighted in *Waverley* and they argued fiercely for and against its merits as a literary work. But they were in complete accord on the worth of Shakespeare, Coleridge, Wordsworth—and, surprisingly to Margaret, Miss Austen's novels.

'Now there is a modern novelist I do admire,' Giles told her. 'And I know that Prinny also enjoys her books.'

Their arguments always led to laughter and then to kisses. Giles appeared to relish her independence and never deliberately put her down or patronised her, seeming to value her opinions as highly as if they came from another man.

His conversation was a delight to her, his keen intelligence instantly understanding her meaning when others might have stared at her with bovine dullness. Even Roddy and Aunt Kate had sometimes been slow to grasp a point she was making, while Caroline could never match her for intellect. Giles was often ahead of her, putting her on her mettle so that she was spurred to meet his laughing challenge—but in bed they were equals, both transported to a paradise beyond anything that she had previously imagined.

It was as perfect as any relationship could be. So perfect that Margaret knew moments of fear when she wondered how long such happiness could last. She loved with all her heart, her soul, her mind and body, and yet feared that something would happen to snatch her happiness away.

Now she turned to him as the sun began to set over the sea turning it flame coloured instead of blue, the provocative smile that had first intrigued him on her lips.

'But of course I wish to be with you, my lord. I 'ave not yet begun to weary of this…friendship.'

Giles shouted with laughter, drawing her close, the throb of his urgent need evident in the swelling hardness pressed against her thigh. 'You are enchanting,' he murmured huskily into the silken white arch of her throat. 'Come to bed, my love, or it will be all up with me before I can take my fill of you.'

'Willingly,' she said and took his hand.

Chapter Eight

'The news is not good,' Giles told Margaret as he came in that evening. He had been out scouting for Wellington, picking up information across the border in France for several days, and she had been on thorns lest he should come to harm. 'They are sealing the borders and our spies will be hard put to it to discover anything of true worth, but I know that Boney is up to his old tricks again. He thinks that we are isolated and will try to surprise us and cut us off from Blücher if he can.'

As expected by those with experience of Napoleon Bonaparte from the past, the French troops sent to capture the emperor returned from exile had gone over to his side and he had marched triumphantly on Paris the day after the Bourbons had fled to Brussels. It was here that Wellington had gathered his infamous army and was already pledged the support of Blücher's troops.

'You have been expecting this for a while, have you not?' Margaret asked as he kissed her, the hunger in his embrace telling her that he had felt as bereft as she during their separation. 'Is Wellington going to attack first or wait for Napoleon to come to him?'

'That is the question the French would gladly pay a

million *livres* to have answered, my sweet,' Giles said
and grinned at her. 'But Old Hookey plays things close
to his chest. We must be prepared for Napoleon to strike
first, I think, for he must know the longer he waits the
more tenuous his position becomes. If Wellington's allies are given a chance to regroup in force, the French
will be outmanoeuvred at every turn. I believe this sealing of the borders is the signal that Bonaparte is preparing to attack.'

'But it is rumoured that Bonaparte has a great army,
and some say the British are vulnerable until the Allied
forces join them. Can Wellington hope to prevail
against such odds?'

'Do not be anxious, sweetheart. The Iron Duke is not
so named for nothing, believe me.'

Once her questions would have aroused his suspicion,
but he knew her too well, knew her spirit and her sweetness, each moment spent together all the more precious
since he accepted that there was a danger it might be
their last. The battle when it came would be bloody, for
Bonaparte knew this was his last chance to regain the
power he craved and would either crush the opposition
forces or be crushed by them. Giles smiled at her, aware
how precious life had become to him these past months.

It was the beginning of June and they had been in
Brussels for some weeks now, spending all the time that
was available to them together. Margaret had continued
her masquerade as the Comtesse de Grenelle, but her
liaison with Giles was an accepted thing amongst his
friends. Lord Ellwood was one of their constant visitors
at the house they had hired in Margaret's assumed
name, dining with them some evenings, joining the
lively supper parties they gave for gentlemen and their
ladies. And where he went his set followed, for he was

a known friend and confidant to the Regent himself, and popular with the younger fellows.

For the most part Margaret was accepted into the same circles she had been during her stay in London, for many of the younger set had gathered in Brussels to await the coming struggle with Napoleon. The atmosphere here was more relaxed than in England, and she knew that if she were to return there, she might not be invited to certain houses where the stricter hostesses held sway. But that did not worry her as long as Giles was content, and it seemed that his closest friends were only too happy to know her.

They had found it impossible to hide their affair, nor had they tried very hard. It was generally accepted that gentlemen had their mistresses, and, in a case where the lady was of the quality, most were prepared to turn a blind eye. Providing they were discreet about their arrangements, nothing was said to indicate that their relationship was known, though on occasion Margaret received a frosty stare from one of the stricter matrons. However, Giles was constantly at her side at any social gathering, and she knew that it was because he was generally respected that she had been accepted so easily. If their affair ended, she might find life more difficult…but if that happened she would want only solitude and could retire to her villa. Or perhaps travel as she had always intended, exploring regions of the world where reputation hardly mattered.

'You think it will begin soon, don't you?' Margaret looked at him anxiously now, sensing things he would not tell her. 'How soon, Giles?'

'You will be safe enough in Brussels,' Giles told her and understood her anxiety. 'We shall not let the French break through, my darling.'

'You know I do not worry for myself.' There was a spark in her eyes that made him smile.

'I have fought many a battle and survived to tell the tale,' Giles said. 'But away with these frowns and pouts, Magda. I have to tell you that you have been invited to the Duchess of Richmond's ball next week—and this evening we are bidden to Ellwood's supper party.'

'Would you rather not rest quietly here this evening?' Margaret asked, noticing the lines of weariness about his eyes. 'You have been riding hard these past days, I dare say?'

'My work is over for the moment,' Giles said, raising his brows. 'You like Ellwood and the others, don't you? I thought it pleased you to go out in company?'

'Yes, of course I like your friends. Lord Ellwood is a particular favourite, as you know,' she said. Some of the young lord's friends were on occasion a little forward, but that was only to be expected. Gentlemen considered it good sport to try and steal each other's mistress, and she was well able to parry their compliments and their hints. Giles was held in enough respect and awe that no attempt to do more than flirt with her had been made as yet. 'I was merely thinking of you, Giles. You look tired, my love.'

'It is nothing. We shall have a few days together now, I promise you,' he said and bent his head to kiss her softly on the lips. 'Tomorrow I am going to take you shopping. It occurs to me that I have given you nothing of any particular value, Magda, and I want you to have something pretty.'

To remember him by?

Margaret did not fear that Giles meant to leave her, for his loving had become even more tender as their time together became increasingly meaningful. Their lives fit together in perfect harmony, and there was no reason for her to doubt his steadfastness. If he wanted her to have a special gift, it must mean that he too was very aware that their happiness could end all too soon.

Suddenly, she understood why he and his friends filled their spare time with gaiety. War was a bloody reality to those who had campaigned with Wellington on the Spanish peninsula and they had lost too many comrades to dismiss it as the young recruits might as a jolly lark.

'What shall you buy me?' she asked teasingly. 'A diamond pin for my 'air or a new gown?'

'We shall see,' Giles said and smiled at her. 'Look at me like that, Magda, and I shall take you to bed and forget that I have not washed off the filth of three days on the road.'

'I shall 'ave a bath prepared for you, my lord,' she said with a distinct sparkle in her eye. 'And then I shall come and scrub your back myself.'

'Now that sounds promising,' Giles murmured, an answering gleam in his own eyes. 'I see that you are intending to have your wicked way with me, my lady, choose how.'

'But you know that I am a terrible woman,' Margaret said, rolling her r's and laughing huskily. When they were alone together she often abandoned her accent completely, but she knew it amused him, and used it to tease him now and then. 'But we waste time and there are only three hours before Lord Ellwood's supper party.'

Ellwood had chosen to give his party at a superior hotel in the best part of Brussels, commandeering the banqueting hall and the services of the manager and his

best staff. He was a man of some wealth and consequence, and the heir to a rich earldom. Most young men
in his position would not have chosen to rejoin the army
and risk all, but, like so many of those young officers
who had served with Wellington before, he was devoted
to his general.

His party was well attended by young men of like
minds, many of whom were accompanied by their mistresses. Yet there was no rowdiness, for it was an un-
written code that respect should be accorded to these
ladies. A few had brought their wives, and two of those
ladies had been their husband's mistress before a change
in circumstance had brought about their new status.

'I was married to a man I detested when I was sev-
enteen,' Kitty, Lady Russell, told Margaret in confidence. 'I gave my husband two sons and considered my
duty done. When I met Freddie we became lovers almost at once, and my daughter Clara is his child. When
my husband died we were able to marry and Freddie
has acknowledged his daughter. We hope for a son, of
course.' She patted her stomach complacently, for she
was five months with child. 'But Freddie says it does
not matter to him whether I give him a son or not. He
has a nephew who may inherit the title after all.'

'I think it was very brave of you to come out with
Lord Russell,' Margaret told her, for Kitty was one of
the ladies amongst their set that she liked best.

'I would rather be here than waiting at home,' Kitty
said. 'Lord! Why should I sit at home and miss all the
fun just because I'm increasing?'

'No reason if you do not wish it,' Margaret said and
laughed at her expression. 'I imagine waiting would
drive you wild with impatience, ma'am.'

'Kitty! You will not stand on ceremony with me, if

you please, Magda,' Kitty said, her eyes sparkling. 'I believe we are friends, are we not?'

'I 'ope so,' Margaret replied, a delicate flush in her cheeks. She thought that Kitty might have divined her secret, which was so new and so terrifying that she had kept it to herself for the moment. She had after all been sick only once or twice and was not certain that she had fallen for a child. 'I should like that, Kitty.'

'Well, we must certainly stick together,' Kitty said and patted her hand. 'Things may get a little difficult in the next few weeks, Magda. My sweet Freddie keeps telling me that it is going to be a picnic and will be over before Boney gets near us, but I am not sure it will be as painless as that. I have a friend who followed her lover to the Spanish peninsula, and she experienced war at first hand, which I may tell you is not at all glorious despite how history may make it. Poor Selina saw things that give her nightmares to this day. I dare say we shall not see so very much of it here, but our men will not be so lucky.'

'No…' Magda clamped her teeth on her bottom lip as a ripple of fear went through her. 'Giles says they will beat the French before ever they get near us, but I fear there will be fierce fighting until that is accomplished. Our soldiers will be much at risk…'

'We shall comfort each other,' Kitty promised her and took her hand. 'Now, my dear, I had a letter from England today, and I fear I have sad news for you. I have heard that the Duchess of Belmont has miscarried her child. Her husband is distraught, they say, though more over his wife's health apparently than the loss of the child—which is rumoured to have been a girl.'

'Oh, no!' Margaret cried, feeling distressed by the

news. 'I am so sorry. Felicia was so happy to be carrying her husband's child, and the Duke was overjoyed at the possibility of an heir.'

'Yes, it is very sad for them,' Kitty said. 'Of course it means that if the Duchess cannot carry full term, then Giles will probably be his uncle's heir after all—a wretched nuisance for him since he will have to marry and provide a male line himself in time.'

'Yes...I suppose he will,' Margaret said, feeling oddly cold at the prospect. Would Giles change his plans for the future when he heard the news? Perhaps not immediately, but in time he might be forced to reconsider his future.

'Well, it need not affect your relationship,' Kitty went on blithely. 'Giles is head over heels in love with you, Magda. No wife is going to interfere with that.'

'These things are all subject to change,' Margaret replied, outwardly much calmer than she felt. 'At the moment we think only of the next hour, the next day.'

'How wise you are to do so,' Kitty replied approvingly. 'I have been in your position, Magda, and I know it can be uncomfortable at times—but I shall always remain your friend. Please remember that should you ever need help.'

Margaret promised that she would and they moved on to greet other friends. Kitty had given her thoughts an uneasy turn, but she tried not to let them spoil her evening. Everyone was in high spirits, perhaps because the sense of danger had heightened their awareness. For some of the young men gathered at Lord Ellwood's party that evening, time was running short. Margaret could only pray that Giles was not amongst their number.

* * *

The evening passed off well, and it was not until they were leaving that one of the gentlemen asked her if she had seen Caroline Hammond recently.

'Of course she is Lady Hazelmere now,' Edward Marshall said and pulled a face. 'Rushford is as mad as fire, I dare say—but I doubt we shall see him here. He will not venture abroad until things are settled.'

'You have seen Caroline and Sir Roderick here in Brussels?'

'Why, yes, only this morning,' he replied. 'He has rejoined his old regiment, I dare say, as many of us have. Got to answer the call to the Iron Duke, don't you know? Can't send him out alone with that rabble they are pleased to call the army.'

'Have you any idea of their lodgings?' Margaret asked. 'I should like to see Caroline, to make sure she is well and 'appy.'

'Not much doubt of that, ma'am. She looked blooming from what I could see, and Sir Roderick is like a dog with two tails. A pity that Rushford is determined to sue, but it may all brush over—a few thousand guineas and the matter is settled.'

'Yes, perhaps,' Margaret replied feeling anxious. It seemed that Giles's lawyers had not been able to settle the matter as he'd hoped. 'Thank you for telling me. I was not aware they 'ad arrived.'

'Thought you'd be pleased with the news,' he said. 'May I say you are looking particularly lovely this evening, Comtesse. Benedict is a lucky fellow—always happy to oblige you if you should wish for a change, Magda. Always admired you from a distance, you know.'

'You are very kind,' Margaret said and smiled at him,

for he was young, eager and inoffensive, his offer made
rather wistfully as if he knew he had no chance of winning the prize.

Margaret mentioned her conversation with Edward
Marshall when she was alone with Giles later that evening. He frowned when she told him that Mr Rushford
was still intent on his pound of flesh.

'I shall write to my lawyers with further instructions,'
he said. 'I knew he would not be easily dealt with, for
he has a vindictive streak. We may have to pay, though
I shall see what can be done to reduce the amount. But
for the moment that is not so important. What shall you
do about Caroline and your brother?'

'I intend to call on them. I would mend the breach if
it is possible, Giles.'

'You are very forgiving.'

'They are my only family. Besides, I believe Caroline
will be wretched until she has seen me.'

Giles nodded. 'Well, we are going shopping tomorrow morning, but you may call on them later if you
wish, my love. You know the address of their lodgings?'

'Mr Marshall was able to help me there. I believe I
shall find them easily enough.'

She gave no hint of her uncertainty, for it would not
be easy to meet her brother in new circumstances. He
would be bound to feel defensive over his own behaviour and might chide her for her own.

Putting such doubts to one side, Margaret went willingly into her lover's arms. She had decided to say nothing for the moment of her suspicions concerning a child.
Giles would of course have to be told as soon as she
was certain. She prayed that it would not change things

between them, for these past months had been such a happy time, for them both, she believed.

His kisses were as hungry and as sweet as ever, his tender loving bringing her to a satisfying climax that swept her away on a tide of pleasure. And afterwards they slept, limbs entwined, hearts beating almost as one.

Giles seemed intent on making her happy. The next morning he took her to an exclusive jeweller's shop and bought her a beautiful diamond pendant on a rope of huge, creamy pearls, and matching eardrops. He also insisted on buying her a gold bangle set with pearls in a design of a crescent moon with a diamond star at its centre.

'That means you are special,' the jeweller told her with a smile. 'In the language of jewellery it tells you that you mean both the moon and the stars to the person who buys it for you—and one presumes the whole world as well.'

'Or simply that it is a beautiful object,' Giles murmured drily. 'Fit for a beautiful lady.'

Margaret laughed, for he was actually looking as if the jeweller's words had embarrassed him. 'I am interested in the language of jewellery,' Margaret said and the man beamed at her, explaining that in some of the items the first letters of the stones spelt a message.

'This is Regard,' he said. 'Ruby, emerald, garnet, agate, ruby and diamond.'

'Ah, yes,' Margaret cried as she picked up a brooch with different coloured stones. 'And this, I think, spells Dearest.'

He congratulated her on her quick grasp of the idea and when his assistant presented the neatly wrapped packages bowed them to the door.

'I shall hope to see you again, *madame*. My good wishes for the future.'

Margaret thanked him and smiled. Giles gave her a wry look.

'There is a man with an eye to business if ever I met one.'

'Yes, certainly. But it was interesting to discover there is a secret message attached to some gifts. I shall take more interest in future when someone displays a new ring, for it may also mean a new lover. It is certainly a fascinating idea.'

Giles arched his brows at her mockingly. 'I would not have thought you interested in such romantic notions, Magda. Can this be the same woman who consigned marriage to the devil in favour of a sensible relationship?'

There was something odd in the way he looked at her then that caused a prickling of unease at her nape. Margaret could not decide if he was teasing her or asking something important. Her breath quickened and it was on the tip of her tongue to ask him to explain when she saw Caroline and Roddy coming towards them.

For a moment they all stared at one another awkwardly, and then Margaret smiled and took a few steps forward, her hands outstretched in welcome.

'Caroline, my dear...'

'Oh, Maggie!' Caroline cried. 'I have been so nervous of meeting you.'

'Did you think I would be angry with you?' Margaret embraced her warmly, kissing her cheeks and then drawing back to look at her. 'Tell me, dearest—are you well and happy?'

'Oh, yes, very much so. As long as you do not hate

me? I could not bear that after all your kindness. I thought you would be terribly angry with us, Maggie.'

'I could never hate you, though I was angry for a time.' Margaret turned to her brother, her manner slightly less warm. 'And you, Roddy—what have you to say?'

'You blame me for what happened, of course,' he said, looking rather ashamed and yet unwilling to admit it. 'And you are right. I persuaded Caro to elope with me. She was not happy about deceiving you.'

'I had no doubt of it,' Margaret replied. 'And I was angry at first. Hurt and upset that you had not considered my feelings, but also anxious. I could not know for certain that you had eloped and I wondered if there had been an accident. You might have sent me a note to tell me you were all right, Roddy.'

'Well, I could not at first,' he said. 'You were right and we did have a small accident after we left London. A wheel came off the chaise I was driving and it almost overturned. In fact, we had more trouble with the whole business than I had imagined and then we thought we would visit you instead of sending a letter, but you were not at home. Your servants would not reveal your whereabouts and we had no idea where you were until we heard you were here in Brussels.'

He was frowning at her and Margaret realised that he did not approve of what she had done in taking Giles as her lover. Well, she had expected that and would not let it distress her.

'As you see, we are indeed here,' she replied, her head high. She met her brother's cool stare unflinchingly. 'Giles's place is with Wellington and I came with him. We have an understanding and you will please respect that, Roddy. Indeed, you must do so if we are to remain friends.'

'Sir Roderick and I will discuss this at another time, more privately,' Giles spoke for the first time. 'For now I think we should repair to a decent inn and bespeak our nuncheon. Tell me, sir, which troop have you been assigned to?'

Giles skilfully drew him on, leaving the ladies to follow a few steps behind. Caroline looked at her shyly.

'We heard…are you Lord Benedict's friend, Maggie? Or should I still call you Magda?'

'Magda is better for the moment. And, yes, we are lovers. I suppose some would call me Giles's mistress, though that would not be a true description. We are friends certainly and lovers, but also equals. There is no master or mistress in our relationship.'

'Oh…' Caroline digested that in silence. 'I love Roddy very much, but I would not call myself his equal. He—he looks after me and is everything I could desire in a husband, but though he always consults my wishes, I know that his is the stronger will. I am not as quick and clever as Roddy—or you. I think you ought to have been born a man, Magda.'

'Once I would have agreed with you,' Margaret replied and laughed. 'But things have changed for me. I no longer wish to be anything other than I am now. However, I see no reason why a woman should not be the equal of a man if she can truthfully lay claim to it. Yet I know many ladies who would not only disagree, but shriek with horror at the very idea. They prefer to be pampered and petted, as Felicia does, and if that is their choice then it is not for me to say they are wrong. However, it would not do for me—which is why I was never interested in making an attachment until I met Giles.'

Caroline nodded her understanding and then looked sad. 'Have you heard that the Duchess of Belmont has lost her child? They say she was quite ill because of it and may not be able to bear another child. Is that not sad for her?'

'Yes, very. I am truly sorry. I wrote to wish her well. God willing she may yet recover enough to give her husband his heir.'

'They say he has renounced all thought of it. Apparently, his wife is of paramount importance in his eyes. He adores her.'

'Then they may still be happy together.'

'Yes…but children are important.' Caroline's voice held a wistful note. 'I had hoped by now…'

'It is early yet,' Margaret reassured her. 'Besides, Roddy will be in no hurry to share his wife with a babe. I trust all is well with you both—you have no problems that I may help you with, anything you wish to ask?'

Caroline blushed a delicate pink. 'Oh, no, no problems. We are well suited in that respect and very happy. I do truly love him, Magda, and I know that he loves me.'

'Then you must be patient for a little longer, dearest. It will happen in time. For some it happens quickly, with others a year or two may pass and still there is no need to worry.'

'Roddy says he wants only me—but I should like children.'

'I am sure you will have them. Now, tell me, are you invited to the Duchess of Richmond's ball?'

The subject was changed, though it lingered on in Margaret's mind. She had experienced nausea again that morning. So far she had managed to hide her sickness from Giles, but could not do so forever. Besides, it would be foolish to wait too long. Yet she knew he had much on his mind at the moment and did not wish him to be anxious for her sake.

War was creeping closer. Margaret knew that Giles was expecting something to happen soon. No, she decided, she would not burden him with more worry at this moment. She would know when the right time had come. Until then she would keep her suspicions to herself.

It was about eleven o'clock the next morning when Margaret's housekeeper came into the parlour to tell her that Sir Roderick Hazelmere had called to see her. Giles was not at home, having been summoned to a meeting with Wellington, and Margaret's heart sank as her brother was asked to come in. His expression was grim and she knew at once that he had come to pull caps with her.

'I suppose you know that you have ruined yourself?' he said without preamble. 'No decent man would marry you now.'

Margaret raised her head, giving him a direct look. 'Since I have no wish to marry that is of little interest to me, Roddy. And I hardly think your own behaviour has been exemplary of late. Please do not presume to lecture me about mine.'

'How could you do it, Maggie? You preached to me about propriety and scandal—a fine scandal there would be if your true identity were known. Caroline has enough to bear without that, and I should not care for it much. Some of our friends make nothing of what happened, but others…she has recently been cut in the street by one lady she thought her friend.'

'I am sorry about that, but it will pass in time and you will know your true friends.'

'If there is another scandal, we shall be ostracised altogether.' He glared at her as if the whole sorry business was her fault.

'I am sorry if you think I have let you down,' Margaret replied, hiding her hurt at his harsh tones. 'But I shall not reveal my identity to anyone, and there is really no need for you to do so, my dear. You have my permission to cut me in public, if you prefer.'

'Don't be such a damned fool! As if I would do that. I am your brother and I care for you.'

'Then be glad for me that I have found happiness.'

'That's all very well, Maggie—but people would think you shameless if they knew you had never been married.'

'Then do not mention that I am your sister to anyone.'

'You may depend on it that I shall not own to it,' he said, clearly still angry with her. 'But that is not my only concern. I am anxious for you, Maggie. What is to become of you when he loses interest in you?'

'Are you so sure that he will?'

Roddy had the grace to blush. 'Well, your arrangement is hardly permanent, is it? These things are by nature merely temporary—otherwise he would marry you.'

'I was not aware that either of us had discussed that with you.'

'No, well, that's beside the point—these things always end in time. That, after all, is why a caring father insists on a decent marriage for his daughter—as I would have done for you if you had consulted me.'

'You have become as tedious as Mr Rushford, Roddy,' Margaret said. 'If this is what marriage has done for you, I do not care for it.'

'I am your brother and the head of the family!'

'And I am well past the age when I would allow anyone to dictate to me,' she reminded him coolly. 'If that is all you have to say to me, Roddy, I wish you will go away.'

'Well, do not come running to me when he throws you out!'

'He is hardly likely to do so since the house is in my own name and I paid the lease myself. Giles is my lover, Roddy, not my protector. We are equals and I am as likely to leave him as he to leave me.'

'You will not be told,' Roddy said and glared at her. 'I'm sorry for you, Maggie, and that's the truth of it. I never thought you would be such a fool as to let a man use you this way.'

'Please leave now, before I say something I shall regret. You may bring Caroline to see me when you have reconsidered your rudeness.'

His brow furrowed angrily but he said no more, simply turning on his heel and walking out on her, the door closing behind him with a little bang. Margaret frowned. For some unaccountable reason she was close to tears, but she had no intention of letting her brother reduce her to that state. She had been prepared to forgive him, but it seemed that he was not ready to do the same for her.

Oh, damn him! She was not going to cry and she was not going to let him spoil things for her. She would go and visit Kitty and talk about new dresses and bonnets and forget all the rest.

* * *

Margaret wore the beautiful jewellery Giles had given her for the first time on the evening of the Duchess of Richmond's ball. She had a new gown of dark green silk with a high waistline tied with a wide sash of a paler shade and trimmed at the hem with delicate embroidery. She had purchased the gown and matching slippers herself, as she did most things she wanted. While she was prepared to accept gifts and allowed Giles to buy their wine, she was not a kept woman. She had made it clear at the start that she would not accept *carte blanche*, and Giles had not offended her by offering. They played the game by unspoken rules and he seemed to understand her almost better than she knew herself.

There had been times these past few days, especially since her quarrel with Roddy, which had not yet been made up, when she was plagued by irrational doubts and fears. She had been tempted to tell Giles that she suspected she might be with child, but something had made her hold back. She was not sure if it was fear that their relationship would change or whether she was merely concerned not to place the burden of knowledge on his shoulders.

However, as their carriage conveyed them to the ball that evening, Margaret had nothing on her mind but an evening of pleasure. She was looking forward to meeting the Duke of Wellington, of whom she had heard so much, and to dancing with Giles.

They did not arrive until the first couples were already dancing, having been somehow delayed by an urge to make love when they ought to have been dressing. It had been sweet and hungry, almost as urgent as the first time they had ever lain together, but more satisfying.

Giles had laughingly apologised for his impatience.

'Forgive me, my darling,' he whispered afterwards as he helped her to fasten the necklace he had given her. 'I do not know how it is that you look even more lovely lately. It seems that I cannot keep from touching you, wanting to love you.'

'For that you need never apologise,' she said and laughed huskily. 'I think love must be a drug, Giles, for it becomes addictive. No matter how much we have of each other we want more.'

'Like those poor wretches bound to their opium pipes in China?' Giles teased. 'Yes, perhaps you are right, Magda. Whatever the reason, I find I can never have enough of you—and if you look at me like that we shall not go to the ball at all.'

His threats made her laugh, but there was no danger of his denying her the treat. It was important for her to be accepted socially, and Giles was aware that this honour might not have come her way had Wellington not insisted on it himself.

The Duke knew well that Giles would not attend without her and had made his wishes known. It was his particular desire to meet the Comtesse de Grenelle, he told his hostess. At this hour of destiny his word was law; had the Duchess not issued the invitation, she might perhaps have found herself without two of her most important guests.

Margaret had no idea of this, naturally, for Giles could keep a secret as well as she. Had she but known much of what was in his mind, her thoughts might have been very different that night, so perhaps it was as well that he was what Wellington termed a born diplomat and the soul of discretion.

Finding herself welcomed warmly by the Duchess of Richmond and then by the Iron Duke himself, Margaret was prepared to enjoy herself. She understood at once why the thin-faced man with the rather hooked nose and steely eyes inspired such respect amongst his men, and when she caught a glimpse of something akin to amusement in his eyes knew why he was loved by many of his closest aides.

Giles danced with her first, but at the end of the set they were joined by a group of their friends who challenged him to give her up to them. Laughing, Giles allowed Ellwood's claim and went off to join Wellington, who had received some disturbing news earlier and was waiting for confirmation.

Later he claimed priority, whisking Margaret away from under the nose of a young lieutenant and leading her on to the dance floor for a waltz.

'Are you enjoying yourself, my darling?' he asked as he held her close, whirling her around the floor so fast that for a moment she was breathless.

'You know that I am. Our friends are all here. Kitty was wild with jealousy over my bracelet. She knew what it meant immediately—or at least, what the jewellers claim it to mean.'

'Kitty is a charming lady,' Giles said and she felt the pressure of his hand a little firmer in the small of her back. 'I think she would be a good friend to you— should you need one in the near future.'

Margaret felt a warning chill at her nape, but kept her tone steady as she said, 'You have news?'

'It is expected,' Giles said and glanced across the room as someone he knew as a trusted aide whispered in Wellington's ear. 'I believe it may have arrived. If it is as I think, I must leave you shortly.' He looked down at her, eyes suddenly dark with some deep emotion. 'Come outside, Magda. I have something I must say.'

She let him draw her from the brilliantly lit ballroom where an atmosphere of pleasure had suddenly become tense with expectation, noticing that that several young officers had slipped away or were talking earnestly to their dear ones. In the garden Giles did not immediately embrace her, gazing into her face in way that made her heart skip a few beats.

'I do not need to tell you that I care deeply for you, Magda?'

'As I do for you, Giles. I—'

'Hush,' he cautioned and placed a finger to her lips. 'This ought perhaps to have been said earlier, but I did not wish to spoil things. I have made certain arrangements for you—and for any eventuality of our relationship. No, do not protest, Magda. You have meant more to me than any woman I have known. I know that you have money of your own, but you also have a headstrong brother and I could not have rested easily had I not done what I could to protect you.'

'There was no need,' she said, her throat tight, for such talk could only mean that he had prepared for his death. 'Oh, do not speak of such matters, I beg you! I want only you, Giles. The rest means naught.'

'It means something to me. In the event of my death, my lawyers will contact you, but do not look so distraught, my love. I assure you that I have no intention of dying just yet. It is merely a precaution out of my regard for you.'

'Giles, I love you.' Her lashes were wet with the tears she was fighting to hold back. Still she did not speak of the child, could not at this final moment of their parting. If he worried so much for her sake, it would simply cause him more anxiety. He must not think of her in the heat of battle, only of himself. Oh, pray God he would come back safe to her!

'As I you. Now I must leave you, Magda. My duty is to Wellington and the army.'

'Yes, of course.' She could not delay him though her heart cried out for one more hour, one more day.

Oh, my love, my love, her heart called to him, but no words passed her lips as he gazed down at her, though she knew he had heard her silent message as she was hearing his.

He bent his head and kissed her, so much pain and passion in that kiss that it tore the heart from her as he broke free, striding off without a backward glance, as if to look back would unman him.

'Oh, Giles,' she whispered as a sob rose in her throat. 'Come back to me, my love. I do not think that I could bear to live without you now.'

Such a fool! Such a fool to have given all of herself.

Margaret ruefully recalled the woman she had been. Oh, Aunt Kate had been right after all! Love was something that denied all sense, overcame all reason. She had believed she could limit her commitment, walk away from their affair when it cooled and still find some kind of a life for herself. Never had she dreamed that her feelings for this man would be so all consuming, so powerful that without him she would be only half-alive.

She knew without a shadow of a doubt that had he asked her to be his wife before he left she would have given him her promise. Where was her fine independence now? Margaret laughed inwardly as she recalled her careless words to Caroline a few days earlier.

No master, indeed! Giles possessed her body and soul. She admitted it now and the humour of her total surrender brought a return of courage.

This wicked, wicked war! How she hated it, hated that it must be. Like every other woman whose man must fight, she resented the need. Why must men fight to settle their differences?

Men must die and women weep. Who had said that? She neither knew nor cared. Her heart was ripped apart, her tears burning with the tears that gathered. Yet there was something in her that would not let her give way to this terrible grief. Her head came up, her face proud.

She must not weep too soon. Prayers might help, but in truth all she could do was wait and hope that Giles would come back to her.

Chapter Nine

The worst part was the waiting, Giles thought. In the quiet of early morning before battle was due to commence, when it was impossible for men to sleep and yet too soon to rise, that was when your personal devils came to haunt you. Her face haunted him when he slept. That teasing smile and the magical laughter that had bewitched him; her accent that she often allowed to slip these days, unless she wished to tease him: all had combined to ensnare his heart. How he longed for her, to tell her what was in his heart, to lie in the quiet hours whispering together. Yet he must not think of her, for he had his duty and in a few hours he would need all his wits about him.

The situation on the ground was not good. Napoleon Bonaparte's swift action had surprised even Wellington, who had believed that the attack was more likely to come from the rear. Cleverly, Bonaparte had made demonstrations of force towards the coast of France, as if planning to cut off the British from their supply route, when all the time he had another bolder plan in mind.

His commanders were Ney, Grouchy, and Soult, men of stature and popular with the ranks. From the first week in June all the frontiers had had been sealed, as Giles had reported, and the French corps, Imperial cavalry and Reserve guard had begun to converge towards the area Bonaparte had designated, concentrated around Beaumont. The French presence there in such large numbers so close to the borders threatened the safety of Brussels itself.

His action had surprised the Allies and Wellington had smartly ordered his army to move west of Brussels towards Mons, believing that the French might go for his right flank. Blücher, suspecting something, had ordered his army towards Fleurus, thus blocking the path of the French right wing. The effect had been to cut the Allies in two, which suited the French.

Wellington had now realized that Bonaparte's aim was to control the road through Quatre Bras to Sombeffe, cutting the Allies off from each other completely. However, when on the fifteenth of June Ney was in sight of his objective, a small Allied force, who had not immediately obeyed the order to move west, gave the French general pause. He had halted—something Giles was sure was due to the mistaken belief on his part that Wellington's main army was waiting out of sight to pounce.

It was during the ball that the Iron Duke had realized he'd been duped and ordered his army toward Quatre Bras, but as he had said to Giles in confidence, 'We shall be damned fortunate if we can muster enough men in time to fend Ney off.'

'General Picton's Fifth Division is still at Brussels, sir, and we've word from Blücher that he will support us.'

Giles had been out scouting all day on the sixteenth, Wellington declaring that he was of more use as a courier for the moment. The overall picture was thus: there had been two battles about seven miles apart. The Emperor and Grouchy were in action against Blücher's forces of some eighty-odd thousand men and Ney attacked at somewhere around two o'clock that afternoon. As Wellington was reported to say to one of his lieutenants, 'It seems our luck is in, for the fool delays when he might have caught us with our boots off.'

Bonaparte had needed reinforcements against the Prussians and Giles had learned that orders had been sent to bring Ney to him, but for some reason there was a misunderstanding and an important corps did not take part in either battle.

As Giles reported to his general that evening, 'There was a time when I thought it was all up with Blücher, sir. Had Ney sent reinforcements, they might have crushed the right flank.'

Since the muddle Bonaparte's generals had made of the day's work had enabled Blücher to hold out and Wellington to gain the upper hand as more of his own troops arrived, the situation had changed in favour of the Allies.

'Tomorrow will see the beginning of the end,' Wellington told Giles. 'What happens then will decide our fate, I think.'

'Yes, sir. I believe that you are right.'

With his commander's words ringing in his ears it was hardly likely that Giles would find it easy to sleep that night, though he had snatched a few hours wrapped in his cloak, but he was awake now and knew that he would not sleep again.

He began to walk about the camp, exchanging words with men who could not rest either, aware that their minds must be divided between thoughts of their loved ones and the coming battle. Already there had been men wounded and killed, and some of them had been transported back to Brussels, away from the front line—but only the seriously injured were relieved of duty; all others would fight on.

Giles stopped to talk to men he knew, men he had fought with in the past, speaking of trivialities and saying nothing of what was truly in their minds. He came upon Lord Ellwood staring at a wood not too far distant and asked if something had disturbed him.

'You look as if you expect trouble from that quarter?'

'No...' Ellwood shook his head and smiled ruefully. 'It was merely that I was thinking... It is at times like this that you wonder who will remember you, Giles. I have not considered marriage seriously for it seemed that there was plenty of time, but now I think of the son I might have had.'

'And will have,' Giles said and squeezed his shoulder. 'You have fought the French before and survived, my friend. I have no doubt that you will do so again.'

'Yes, of course.' Ellwood grinned at him. 'It's this damned waiting. Once we begin I think of nothing but winning my way through whatever is in front of me— but I can't stand the dark hours, Giles.'

'I believe we are all much the same,' Giles said, for his words had echoed those that had been running through his mind all night.

Damned fool that he was! Why the hell had he not spoken the truth to Magda a week ago, told her what was in his mind and heart? She might have consented to be married quietly before the war began—it was what he wanted, what he had wanted for months. Yet he had held back from speaking. At first it had amused him that she was determined to carry her masquerade through, but then the desire to have her as his wife had become stronger and stronger.

He knew now without a shadow of a doubt that he loved her. At the start he had confused love with lust; mistaking her for something that she was not had led him astray. He smiled ruefully as he realised that he had done everything wrong from the beginning.

Magda had told him she did not wish to marry, but he should have courted her, made her see that marriage did not necessarily mean the end of freedom. Oh, of course with some men it would mean exactly that, and Giles had often frowned over the behaviour of men he knew and liked, wondering at the way they changed after marriage. A wife belonged to her husband, as did her property, but there were ways to make it a good arrangement, as there were things that might be done to ensure that a woman did not have to ask for every penny she spent.

It was damned uncivilised the way some men expected their wives to be at their beck and call, and he would never dream of treating Magda like that. Not that she would let him! Giles smiled to himself as he thought of her fiery independence. It was her spirit that made her such an exciting lover, and these past months had been both thrilling and satisfying—satisfying to a point, that was. He thought that he might be willing to sacrifice some of the excitement to have her as his own.

This freedom thing was a two-edged sword, damn it! While he was free to thank Magda and walk away from the relationship, so was she—and there were several others only too willing to oblige her. She might take her pick of a dozen gentleman if she chose.

Over his dead body!

Giles had the uneasy feeling that she had been hiding

something from him recently. He was not certain what it was, but he had seen a certain expression in her eyes...

She could not be tiring of him!

'Ah, Benedict,' a voice hailed him and he turned to see Sir Roderick approaching him. 'I hoped I might see you.'

'Hazelmere—what may I do for you?'

'It's awkward. Not really the thing to bring it up at this time—but it might be my only chance, if you see what I mean?'

'Speak out, sir. No other time will be better for what you have to say.'

'No, don't suppose it will. Two things really—would you mind telling me what you intend towards my sister in the future?'

'Normally I would tell you to go to hell,' Giles said. 'But I shall give you the truth as neither of us may live beyond the day—if she will have me, I shall marry her.'

'Damn me if Caro wasn't right,' Roddy ejaculated, looking stunned. 'She told me she was sure you would marry Maggie, but that she was the one holding off. I may tell you that I reprimanded my sister for being so careless of her virtue, but if your intention is to marry her—'

'Exactly.' Giles clenched his fists. If it had not been a few hours before an important battle, he would have done his best to knock Hazelmere's head from his shoulders, but that would be a waste of effort and could result in them both being shot as troublemakers. 'If you breathe one word of this to your sister, I shall see that you regret it, sir!'

'No, no,' Roddy said at once. 'Leave it to you, Benedict. Know your own business best. Maggie would only bite my head off again. Caroline said it served me right.' He paused, then said hesitantly, 'I wanted to ask—if anything should happen to me…'

'I shall see that your wife is not left stranded in Brussels,' Giles said at once. 'Not that she would be alone, for I know that Magda is very fond of her.'

'Yes, I know.' Roddy had the grace to look a little ashamed. 'Made a bit of a cake of meself, haven't I?'

'Shall we forget and start again?' Giles asked and extended his hand. 'No point in quarrelling at a time like this.'

'No!' Roddy said with feeling. 'It's this damned waiting—that's what made me seek you out. Don't mind when we get started, don't you know. Can't stand this time in the morning.'

Giles smiled. 'Everyone feels the same,' he said. 'Think how it must be for our ladies. They can do nothing but wait…'

It was just before the dawn that she found herself lying awake, her thoughts reaching out to Giles as if to draw him to her. Where was he and what was he doing? Had he seen action—had he been wounded? But, no, she felt that she would know if his life were in danger.

Sometimes as she lay halfway between sleeping and waking she almost believed she could hear his voice talking to her, telling her he loved her, asking her to wait for him.

'Of course I shall wait for you, my love,' Margaret whispered. 'I could never love anyone as I love you.'

She wished that there was something she might do to ease the anxiety of simply waiting. If only she could be of some use in some way!

* * *

'Do you really think you ought to in your condition, Kitty?' Magda asked her as she told her what she was going to do. 'Freddie would be furious with you.'

'I can't stand the waiting,' Kitty said and pulled a face at her. 'The not knowing what is going on out there…'

'Yes, I know what you mean—but sometimes I feel that it is almost better when there is no news.'

'But at least if you know…' Kitty shivered and closed her arms over herself for a moment. 'When I saw that wagonload of wounded come in and realised they had nowhere left to put them, I knew we had to do something, Magda. I've commandeered a public hall and asked everyone I know what they are willing to contribute to help our men.'

'You know I shall give money for medical supplies and food,' Margaret said. 'But like you I find it difficult to wait at such a time. If you can provide me with something useful to do, I am only too willing to help.'

'The hospitals are already stretched,' Kitty told her. 'I've been told that there has been heavy fighting for two days, and, God help us, some are saying that the French will break through our lines today—someone came in this morning to say that yesterday Wellington was forced to retreat to somewhere called Mont-Saint-Jean…'

Margaret's face paled as she heard the news. She took a deep breath. Her fear was not for herself, but for Giles and the other young men who had ridden out so bravely to confront the enemy.

'Tell me what you want me to do.'

'Some of the ladies are willing to roll bandages and keep records, that sort of thing—but I need nurses. I thought you might feel able to do that, though I know some would disapprove of you for doing it. Particularly as the men are of all ranks, not just officers.'

'They were all wounded fighting for their country and for us,' Margaret said. 'Of course I shall come, and at once.' She stood up and rang the bell for her house-keeper, explaining that she wanted money from her strongbox and her shawl as she was going out and did not know when she would be returning.

'They say that the French army will break through by evening, *madame*,' the woman said, looking fright-ened. 'Are you leaving Brussels?'

'No, I am not,' Margaret replied. 'I do not fear such a thing and those fools who are fleeing Brussels will find more danger on the road than here in the city. I am going to help with nursing the wounded—and you may tell any of my servants that they are at liberty to come and help. They will not be accused of deserting their posts if they have been nursing the sick.'

The woman looked relieved. 'I thought you were leaving us.'

'No, not at all,' Margaret said. 'Come and help me nurse our men, Madame Hellier, and I shall reward you for your trouble.'

'I shall certainly come with you, Madame la Comtesse, for the streets are full of the rough element, they say, those who will take the chance to steal and loot while the city is in uproar.'

Margaret knew that for the past several days many of the shops had boarded up their windows and doors to keep out the French army and looters alike. From her window she had seen the panic on the streets as many tried to flee the city, but she had given no thought to the idea.

Each day she had been on a tour of the hospitals,

checking the list of wounded and feeling terrified until she saw that the names she dreaded to find had not been added to the tally. So far she had seen only one fatality listed that she knew personally, though Edward Marshall had been slightly wounded in the first battle.

She had visited him for a few minutes and found him fretful. He was in pain from the slash to his arm by the sword of a French hussar, but otherwise seemed in reasonable shape.

'It seems I am lucky,' he had told her. 'I have no fever and wish that I could be back with my comrades.'

'You would not be much help to them at the moment,' she had comforted him. 'You have done your share, sir.'

Later, when she had done what she could at the hospital Kitty had set up, she would visit him again, Margaret thought. But for now she was at last going to be able to do something useful.

If she worked until she was too tired to think, perhaps it would make this time of waiting easier to bear.

Wellington's ploy of retreating to Mont-Saint-Jean had fooled the French as much as those left behind in Brussels. In fact, it was not a retreat but a regrouping, enabling the general to spread his troops more thinly and wait for Blücher to come up to him again. His position was strong, and his force was posted in three places of strategic importance: La Haie Sainte in the centre, Hougoumont Chateau to the right, Papelotte on the left.

There were sixty-eight thousand British and Allied troops under his command and he had a large contingent of heavy guns. As he had mentioned to Giles earlier, his only hope was to hang on to his position for all he was worth until Blücher could come up to him.

It had rained all the previous night, a circumstance that might explain why Bonaparte had delayed over-long. Indeed, the morning wore away and still there was no attack from the French.

'What do you think he gains from this?' Wellington asked when Giles came up to him with a message. 'The fool should have come at me earlier. By this delay he gives us an advantage.'

'I have heard whispers that he is not well,' Giles said. 'Our scouts took some prisoners last night and I under-stand that one of them was persuaded to talk. He com-plained that the emperor was not the man he had been; there were too many muddled orders, too much coun-termanding of orders—and this may be what is causing the delay.'

'Whatever, it is damned convenient for us!'

Giles smiled inwardly. He had not added that the cap-tured French had said Bonaparte openly scorned his en-emy as 'a damned Sepoy general'!

'You may go and see where Blücher is, if you will,' Wellington said carelessly, as if he were asking Giles to play a hand of cards and not to ride through enemy lines. 'Report back when you can—and take a couple of trusted men with you.'

'Yes, sir,' Giles said. 'I'll bring you news of Blücher as soon as I can find him.'

'You'd better pray the French don't find him first!'

Giles grinned and walked away from his general. He summoned two stalwarts from the ranks and then turned to find Ellwood at his side.

'May I be of assistance to you, Giles?'

'We're looking for the Prussians,' Giles said. 'They

should be somewhere in the vicinity of the Blois de Paris. Come if you care to, Ellwood, and take one of these men with you. We'll take two different routes and hope that one of us finds Blücher. If you spot him, your duty is to get back with the news. Remember that, all of you! The Duke is relying on Blücher. If one of you falls wounded, you leave him where he lies and ride all the harder. Victory may depend on your success.'

'Good luck to you, Giles,' Ellwood said and took his hand briefly before turning away. He mounted his horse and rode off, one of the soldiers following him. Giles motioned to his own escort, mounted and rode off in a slightly different direction. They knew which way the Prussians ought to be approaching from earlier messages, but it was a case of determining when Blücher could get to them.

Rumours were flying about the city. Some said Wellington was retreating towards Brussels, the French in hot pursuit, others that the rout was so complete the Allied forces were in disarray, still others that it was no such thing and the French were being held. It was impossible to be sure of anything—except that the fighting was fierce and might go either way.

Not until late in the evening did quite different stories begin to trickle into the city. Now they were told it was the French who had suffered setback after setback, but still the outcome was not certain. One thing that was indisputable was the numbers of dead and wounded on both sides.

Margaret had never before understood the reality of war, had never understood how it might smell or taste or look. It was something she would never forget and yet she knew that she had been right to respond to

Kitty's plea. There could be no doubt that she and other ladies who had answered the call were needed, even if they could do no more than hold a soldier's hand as he died or stroke a fevered brow.

The situation was desperate. More and more wounded men were coming in, though theirs was only one of many emergency stations set up to cope with the injured. Margaret was too busy to think of anything other than the constant need for fresh bandages, water and bedding. Her fears for Giles and her brother were constantly at the back of her mind, but the cries of those in terrible pain prevented her from dwelling on her own fears too much.

She and others took turns to rest throughout the long night, but none of them went home. Their own comfort was the farthest from their thoughts, the reality of un-bearable pain stripping away all pretence of normality. It was an odd existence: fine ladies who would never have thought of dirtying their hands in their own houses were willingly carrying water or rolling bandages, help-ing where they could and working side by side with their humbler sisters.

Every time a new batch of wounded came in, Margaret's heart caught with fear. She prayed desper-ately that Giles would not be amongst the wounded or dead.

She was there when Lord Ellwood was brought in on a stretcher, a bloody bandage round his head. One of the doctors called to her to assist him.

'This man is badly wounded, nurse. I need to operate at once or he will die.'

'I am not a nurse, sir, but I shall willingly do what I can to help.'

He frowned at her. 'You seemed so efficient I thought

you must be one of our few trained helpers. Well, you are all I've got, so you will have to do. Don't faint at the sight of blood, do you?'

'I hope not, sir. I am here to help, not hinder you.'

He gave her an approving nod and proceeded to outline what he meant to do. It seemed that the head wound was the least of Lord Ellwood's problems. He had a badly torn leg, which had to come off for it would not mend.

'Is there no way of saving it?' Margaret asked, a wrench of pity clawing at her heart for the man she knew as Giles's closest friend.

'None or I should not waste my time in taking it off.'

He outlined what he was going to do and her part in it. Margaret felt the sickness swirl in her stomach, but did as she was bid. The awful sound of a saw cutting through a man's leg just below his knee was one that she thought might haunt her the rest of her life. However, she neither fainted nor vomited, standing her ground as she was passed the bloody remains and told to dispose of it while he patched the man up.

'Come back as soon as you've done,' the surgeon told her. 'If you aren't a nurse yet, you should consider it. You're a damned fine woman.'

Night had become day and day night, a constant blur of pain and misery as she made her rounds of the beds where injured soldiers lay weeping, begging for help she could not give them. There was hardly any medication and what there was they saved for amputation cases; the lesser injuries were left to heal themselves. Once a man was bandaged there was little Margaret could do for him other than offer a cup of water and a soothing hand on his brow.

'Oh, God,' she prayed constantly as the tears caught at her throat. 'Do not let this happen to Giles. Please do not let him suffer this…'

She would rather he had a clean death, she thought. Her eyes were gritty with tiredness and red rimmed, but she could not think of leaving while she was needed here.

Somewhere—in some lonely field hospital—Giles might be calling for her as these men called for their loved ones. She prayed that a gentle woman would do what she could to help him in his agony.

But no! She would not let herself think like that. Giles was strong and clever. He would live and he would return to her. She must believe it or her heart would break.

For two more days Margaret stayed at the makeshift hospital, snatching an hour's rest when she could, but on the third day Doctor Morgan sent her home.

'You will take a few hours for yourself, ma'am. Come back to me when you feel rested. You'll be no good to me if you fall asleep at your post.'

'It is a bath I need more than anything,' Margaret said. 'But I shall not desert you for long, sir.'

'I am glad to hear it.'

Returning to her house, Margaret was welcomed by her housekeeper, who clucked over her like a brooding hen and ordered the bath she needed so desperately and a change of clothing.

'Just a plain dark gown, if you please. This one is ruined, I am afraid.'

'You are never going back there again, *madame*? You have surely done your share? Let someone else take your place.'

'Certainly I shall return. I have given my word. Besides, there is still much to do and we do not have so many volunteers as at the start.'

It was not surprising. Men were limping home all the time, some of them the lesser wounded who had walked all the way back to Brussels, to loved ones and the comfort of their homes and lodgings. Many of the women who had helped out at the start had their own men to care for now that it seemed the war was over.

Margaret was not sure where she had heard it, for the past few days had passed in a blur, but bells had rung from the churches in triumph and the word was on everyone's lips that Wellington had routed the French. She had few details of battles, defeats or victories, for her time had been devoted to nursing the sick and dying and she had scarcely been able to take in the news, but it seemed certain that it was all over bar the mopping up.

At the back of her mind her fear for Giles hovered like a bird of prey waiting to strike. She had held it back while she washed and dressed sorely injured men, but now it came to torment her with images of Giles lying somewhere in a makeshift bed, crying out for her as others cried for their loved ones.

'Are there any letters for me, Madame Hellier?' she asked the housekeeper after seeing that the salver in the hall was empty.

'Yes, three. I left them in your room, *madame*.'

'Thank you. I shall find them.'

Margaret went wearily upstairs. She could hear the maids preparing her bath in the dressing room as she picked up her letters. She was almost too tired to read them, but she saw the first was from Kitty, thanking her for her help. She laid it aside and briefly scanned one from Caroline asking if she might call, then looked at the third. Her heart missed a beat as she realised that it was Giles's hand. Not quite as clear and strong as usual, but still his. Her hands trembled and her eyes stung as she tore it open, unable to see at first for the tears blinding her.

Beloved, Giles had written. *I write this on the morning of the 19th to tell you that I am well. I received a slight wound to my shoulder in the fighting at Hougoumont yesterday, but was fortunate to escape with no worse. I have been treated at a field hospital and feel sore, but otherwise in spirits. I wish that I might come to you personally but this business must be finished and there is still much work to be done. The French are retreating, but we must follow. Bonaparte must not be allowed to escape for there has already been enough bloodshed.*

I cannot tell when I shall see you again, my love, and would advise you to seek a way of returning to your home in the near future. It may be some weeks, perhaps a month or two, before I can come to you, but be sure I shall do so as soon as possible.

Margaret sank down on to the edge of the bed, tears of relief coursing down her cheeks. Giles had survived. He was wounded, but not sufficiently to be released from his duties. Praise be to God! Her prayers had been answered.

'*Madame*…' Her housekeeper faltered as she paused in the doorway. 'Have you had bad news?'

'No.' Her smile was brilliant. 'It was foolish of me to weep. The news is the best, the very best. Lord Benedict is alive.'

'That is good news indeed, *madame*. I understand

why you weep, it has been a terrible time for you. I came to tell you that your bath is ready.'

'Thank you. I shall enjoy it all the more now.'

Giles was alive! He was alive. After the strain of the past days it was almost too much to take in and she felt the relief overwhelm her. Only her strength of will prevented her from giving vent to the storm of tears that had built inside her.

Madame Hellier hesitated on the threshold, seeming unwilling to intrude at this time. 'Lady Hazelmere called again. I told her you would see her in an hour. Was that sufficient time, *madame*?'

'Caroline called again?' Margaret's brow furrowed. 'Caroline's letter had not seemed urgent, but she would not have come unless she had good reason. 'Yes, thank you, *madame*. I should be ready to see her by then.'

She had hoped to sleep for a while before returning to the hospital, but she would feel better after her bath.

'Oh, Maggie,' Caroline cried when she saw her. 'They told me every time I called that you were at the hospital and I did not like to disturb you there. I am so worried. I have heard nothing of Roddy. His name is not on any of the lists of the—' She choked and could not continue.

'He has sent no word to you at all?'

'No,' Caroline said, her face white with strain. 'He would do so if he could, I am sure of it.'

Margaret was sure of it too. 'You have been to all the hospitals?'

'Yes, all that I know of. I thought you might know of others I did not.' She bit her lips, tears trembling on her thick lashes.

'I have been told that some of the injured are being

treated in field hospitals, dearest. Others may have found shelter for themselves. The lists are not always conclusive. You must be brave and try not to worry too much just yet. As long as Roddy is not listed as dead there is still hope.'

'Yes, I know, but it is so hard. I do not know what I shall do if—' She broke off on a sob, clearly beside herself with worry. 'But I am selfish. You must be tired and anxious yourself.'

'I am tired,' Margaret admitted. 'But I have heard from Giles. He is injured, but safe. Merely a flesh wound that does not keep him from his duty.'

'He did not mention Roddy?'

'Had he done so I should have told you at once.'

'Of course. It was foolish of me to ask. I should not have bothered you when you have so much to do.'

'Now you *are* foolish. You know that I shall help you as much as I can, dearest. I am returning to the hospital station later and will make what inquiries I can. Have you spoken to Kitty?'

'She has heard nothing of him.' Caroline could not prevent a sob escaping. 'They say there are rows of dead soldiers lying on the road to Brussels, the French and our men side by side... If Roddy is one of them I shall not be able to bear it.'

'Now this will not do!' Margaret said sharply. She had heard the stories herself, but it did not serve to dwell on them. 'Stay and have something to eat with me, and then we shall go to the hospital together. We may ask there if anyone has heard anything.'

'I do not think I could eat a morsel.'

'It will not help Roddy if you make yourself ill, dearest. Have a croissant and honey with me, and a bowl of coffee. I dare say you have been neglecting yourself.'

Caroline gave her a wan smile and admitted that she had. 'Perhaps I shall try to eat a little to please you.'

'It would please me very much.' Margaret smiled at her. 'I have a feeling that my brother will turn up, Caroline. Do not despair just yet.'

Margaret made her usual round of the dimly lit room. Groans and the sound of muffled weeping came from the men lying in their hard cots, for these were the most seriously ill of all her patients and there was little she could do for them but offer water and kindness. Most were not expected to survive. She paused to glance down at a man who had lain unconscious since the desperate operation to remove his leg and saw to her surprise that his eyes were open and focusing on her.

'Lord Ellwood?'

'Water…' he croaked and gulped eagerly as she held a cup to his lips.

'Not too much at first. You have been in a fever some days, my lord.'

'Magda?' He blinked at her, clearly bewildered but recognising her. 'Where am I?'

'At one of the receiving stations we set up during the emergency. You have been here more than a week, sir.'

Many of the others who had come in at the same time had been transferred, to private accommodation if their relatives claimed them, or to the hospitals, but he had been considered too ill to move—and no one had come to claim him.

'Have you been nursing me?'

'Yes. Some of the time.'

'You have cool hands.' He offered a faint smile. 'I think I must thank you for my life.'

'Doctor Morgan saved your life, sir.' She took a deep breath. 'I am sorry, but he could not save your leg.'

He closed his eyes, his face working as he fought to accept the dreadful news, but then he opened them and looked at her again. 'I'm damned lucky to be here. We rode straight into an ambush and I was caught in the full blast of the guns. Giles instructed us all that we must go on, but the trooper with me must have disobeyed orders and brought me in. Have you heard from Giles?'

'He is safe.' She laid a hand on his brow. 'Hush now. You will tire yourself. Rest and sleep if you can. I shall come to you again when I am able.'

'Giles is a lucky fellow. Told him at the start you couldn't be the spy he was looking for. Too beautiful to be an assassin...' His eyes rolled upwards as he spoke and he made an odd gasping sound that Margaret had learned to know only too well.

'No!' she cried, his last words forgotten as she bent over him. 'Oh, please, no. Don't die now...don't die.'

Suddenly the tears were trickling down her cheeks. She reached out and closed his staring eyes, then bent down to kiss him softly on the mouth.

'God protect and keep you, dear friend.'

She walked away blindly, overset by a storm of emotion that had stayed inside too long and was stopped by a pair of strong arms and a concerned exclamation from Dr Morgan.

'Who was it?' he asked, recognising the signs of exhaustion turning to grief.

'Lord Ellwood. He had recovered consciousness. I thought he had turned the corner. There was no fever...I should have called you.'

'I am not God. Like you, I do what I can.'

'You have been wonderful,' Margaret told him, wiping her face with the back of her hand. 'I count it a privilege to have helped in whatever way I have.'

He smiled at her. 'The men call you "the angel",' you know,' he said. 'And you have been a good brave girl, but now you must go home, take up your life again and try to forget the nightmare you have endured here—if that is possible.'

'But there is still so much to do. I cannot desert you.'

'This station is being closed down,' Doctor Morgan told her. 'It was a temporary measure, and as you know we have patched most of our patients up and sent them on. They will collect the others later and take them to the hospitals and I shall go back to my regular work.'

'You work in private practice as a rule, I believe?'

'That is so,' he told her. 'But when I was young I trained as a surgeon and I knew that I would be needed during the crisis. Now I shall go back to treating wealthy ladies with a nervous complaint or gentlemen who have the gout.'

'You have been a hero, sir.'

'I have done what I could, as we all have. In times like these we must do what is right—and my duty is to send you back to your loved ones, Magda.'

'You know my name?'

'I know everything about you,' he said and the smile came from deep inside him. 'And may I say it has been a privilege to know you, Madame de Grenelle.'

'I am not a Comtesse,' Margaret replied, for she felt compelled to speak the truth to this man with whom she had shared so many terrible hours. 'My name is Margaret Hazelmere and I am unmarried.'

'You are a brave lady and one I shall never forget,' he said and then bent his head to kiss her briefly on the mouth. 'God be with you, ma'am.'

'And with you, sir.'

Chapter Ten

Margaret had just risen the next morning when one of the maids came up to tell her that Lady Hazelmere had arrived.

'She says it is urgent, *madame*.'

'Please ask Caroline to come up,' Margaret said. 'We can talk as I finish dressing.'

It was apparent as soon as Caroline entered the room that she was in great distress. She looked pale and shaken, clearly unable to cope with whatever was causing her distress.

'You have heard something?'

'One of Roddy's friends came to tell me half an hour ago. He was missing for several days, but he has been found and brought to Brussels for treatment.'

'That is surely good news?'

'Yes, but...' Caroline caught back a sob. 'There was an explosion where he was standing and his head was wounded as he fell and...he cannot see.'

'He has been blinded?' Margaret felt the nausea rise in her throat, but fought against it. For a moment all she could see was her brother as a young boy, and then wearing his uniform when he was first commissioned,

any unpleasantness that had been between them quite
forgotten. 'Were his eyes badly damaged? What do the
doctors say?'

'I am going to the hospital now,' Caroline said and
dabbed a kerchief to her eyes. 'But I do not wish to go
there alone. I know he was awful to you over Lord
Benedict, but—'

'Of course I shall come with you,' Margaret confirmed at once. 'I would not dream of letting you go
alone. Besides, Roddy did not mean all those unpleasant
things, I dare say, and it is forgotten. He is my brother,
Caroline, and I must do whatever I can to help him and
you through this thing.'

'Oh, Maggie,' Caroline cried on a jerky sob, 'I do
not think I could bear this if you were not here to support me.'

'Well, I am here and we shall face this together,
Caroline. Perhaps it may not be as bad as it seems, and
blindness is not the end of the world. At least he is
alive. So many of our friends have died—Lord Ellwood
only yesterday as I was talking to him…'

He had said something strange just before he died.
Margaret had not taken it in properly at the time because of the shock of his death, but it had come back
to her later, making her wonder what he could have
meant. Something about Giles having been wrong to
think her a spy and her being too beautiful to be an
assassin—now what could that mean? No, she must
have mistaken his words or more likely he was wandering in his mind. In either case she had no time to
think about it now.

'How very sad,' Caroline said and wiped her face on
the kerchief Margaret handed her. 'I believe he had no

family to speak of—or at least only a distant cousin who will now inherit the title, I suppose.'

'Yes, it was sad. But I am ready now and we must delay no longer.' She looked at Caroline's white face. 'Courage, dearest. You love your husband and must be prepared to accept whatever comes with courage.'

'Yes, I shall, I am determined on it—but you will help me? You will not leave me?'

'You know that I shall do all I can for you, and I shall stay with you until you have come to terms with whatever you must face.'

Margaret had been considering leaving Brussels for her home in France in a few days, but she could not think of it now. She must obviously stay with Caroline while she needed her.

'The wound to Sir Roderick's head is superficial,' the doctor told them a little later that morning. 'He should be able to leave hospital within a few days, but his eyes are another matter. To tell you the truth, *madame*, I do not know what has caused the loss of sight.'

'His eyes were not burned by the flash or entered by splinters?'

'No.' He looked at Margaret thoughtfully. 'You have had experience of such injuries?'

'I helped a very little at one of the temporary receiving stations. I saw cases of burns and shrapnel wounds—and men blinded by them. They were in terrible pain. My brother...'

'Ah...' He nodded. 'Well, you may rest easy, *madame*. Sir Roderick was merely knocked off his feet by the blast and cracked his head against the wheel of a wagon as he fell. He was one of the lucky ones. There is no disfigurement or visible damage, and only slight headaches now and then.' He spread his hands. 'As I told you, I do not know why he cannot see.'

'Thank you for explaining so carefully.' Margaret glanced at Caroline, who was weeping softly into her kerchief. 'May we visit him, please?'

'Yes, of course. He is with others who no longer need nursing care in our conservatory. They gather there to talk and take exercise. You may make arrangements to take him home at the end of the week.'

Margaret thanked him and Caroline added a few tearful phrases.

'Try to stop crying now, dearest,' Margaret said as they left the doctor. 'You must not let Roddy know how this has overset you. You must try to be cheerful for his sake.'

'Yes, I know,' Caroline said and lifted her head, a determined jut to her chin. 'I shall think of his needs rather than my own.'

They saw Roddy sitting in a wing chair by an open window, through which the powerful scent of flowers was wafting. He was staring rigidly ahead of him, his expression so dejected that Margaret's heart caught with pity. Such a cruel blow to a man just married to a beautiful wife. Pray God the blindness would not be permanent.

'Roddy! Oh, Roddy, my darling,' Caroline cried and ran towards him. 'My dearest love. How glad I am to see you.'

Margaret hung back, watching as the girl dropped to her knees and put her arms about her husband in a loving embrace. He seemed to hesitate for a moment, then hugged her to him in a desperate, crushing embrace that told of his torment. It was clearly a very emotional meeting for them and Margaret gave them several minutes to themselves before she joined them. When she did she saw that Caroline had lost that air of nervousness and seemed remarkably calm.

'Roddy wants us to take him home, Maggie.'

'Is that you, Maggie?' Roddy raised his head as if trying to see her. Apart from a small dressing at his temple he seemed to be in perfect health—other than his lack of vision. 'Get me home, will you?'

'The doctor says you may leave in two days.'

'I don't mean just out of here. I want to go home to England. Will you help us, Maggie? I'm too much trouble for Caro to manage alone.'

'You want to go to your estate? You wouldn't rather come to the villa for a while?'

His answer was unequivocal. 'I want to go home to Hazelmere.'

'Very well,' Margaret said. 'If you can wait for two more days, I shall make the necessary arrangements. I dare say you will feel better there.'

'I'll be safe at home and so will Caro. There are people I can trust to look after her.'

'You look after me,' Caroline said. 'You always do.'

'In future you will have to look after me,' Roddy said, a note of bitterness in his voice. 'I am a helpless cripple now—no damn use to anyone.'

'That's not true! I love you.' Caroline looked at Margaret, her eyes filled with tears. 'Tell him it isn't true, Maggie.'

'You do not know that it is a permanent condition,' Margaret said. 'Your eyes were not burned or pierced.'

'Then why can I not see?'

'I do not know—but I shall consult with a doctor who might. It is possible that he can shed some light on this mystery.'

'I doubt it,' Roddy said. 'I've seen it happen to others in battle. I doubt there's a miracle cure.'

Margaret thought he might be right, but was determined to discover what she could.

'I have heard of such things,' Dr Morgan said when she called on him the next morning. 'You are certain that your brother's eyes are not physically damaged?'

'They show no sign of it. I am as sure as I can be for the moment.'

'Then it may be the blow to the head or simply the shock of witnessing so many of his colleagues killed violently. I am not an expert in this field, ma'am, but I can recommend someone in London your brother might care to visit. Of course the blindness may be temporary and go as suddenly as it came.'

Margaret accepted the address he had given her, tucking it inside her reticule. 'Thank you for your help, sir. I can at least give my brother some hope.'

'I wish I could offer more. You leave for England soon?'

'I have arranged passage for us all in three days' time.'

'Then I wish you a safe journey and hope the news will be better soon.'

Margaret thanked him and left. He had refused a fee for the consultation, telling her that he was glad to be of what help he could.

After leaving his consulting room, Margaret decided to visit Kitty and tell her she was returning to England.

'We are to follow Wellington to Paris,' Kitty said, smiling contentedly, for Freddie had come back to her unscathed. 'For there will be much to do setting this wretched business to rights.'

'It all seems such a terrible waste. So many killed and injured, but there were acts of immense bravery too. I heard that the Old Guard covered the flight of the rest of the French army and were saluted by our men for their courage.'

'They fought bravely and soldiers respect that,' Kitty replied. 'As for the future—Bonaparte has no choice but to abdicate, though he will try to rally support if he can. Indeed, I believe he may be on the verge of doing so, though I understand there is still some fighting outside Paris. However, it cannot last and will be settled soon enough.'

'It is to be expected that the Emperor will receive harsher terms this time,' Margaret said. 'In the past I admired him, but I cannot find it in my heart to pity him now—this was all so unnecessary and has caused so many deaths. You have heard about Lord Ellwood?'

'His commanding officer told me at dinner last evening. I was sad to hear that he has no close family to grieve for him.'

'I shall grieve, and so will Giles when he hears,' Margaret said. She took a sealed packet from her reticule. 'Would you give this letter to Giles for me when you see him? He will be with Wellington. It is merely to tell him that I am to accompany Sir Roderick and Lady Hazelmere to their home in England.'

'Your poor brother,' Kitty said for they had grown close during the war, and after Roddy's injury, Margaret had confided the sad news to her, breaking her silence and telling her the truth of her situation. Kitty, herself a victim of gossip, appreciated the confidence, assuring her that it would remain a secret. 'I had guessed there was some secret, my dear friend, and I had noticed that your accent was stronger at times than others, but I am glad to be in your confidence. Be assured that my feelings towards you have not changed. As for your poor brother, I wish him well, my dear—and I shall make sure that Giles receives your letter at the earliest opportunity.'

'Thank you.' Margaret hesitated, then, 'Lord Ellwood said something odd to me just before he died—something about me being a spy...that Giles may have thought so at one time.'

'The poor man must have been wandering in his mind,' Kitty said and shook her head over it. 'I do know that Giles sometimes does secret work for Wellington and that he may have been searching for a suspected assassin last year, but as for thinking...no, that is too foolish for words. You cannot believe it, Magda?'

'No, not truly,' Margaret said and laughed at herself for having raised such a nonsensical quibble. 'I dare say you are right. Lord Ellwood was in some considerable pain and clearly did not know what he was saying.'

'Giles adores you. You can have no doubt of that?'

'No, I do not doubt that he cares for me,' Margaret replied. 'It was mere nonsense as you say. I shall put it out of my head at once. I wish Giles were here so that I could tell him of his friend's death. He seemed quite peaceful and the end came suddenly.'

'If one must die...' Kitty shrugged expressively. 'We shall be in Paris for the next few weeks, I dare say, but then Freddie insists I must return home. He wants his son born in England at his ancestral seat, so I suppose I must oblige.'

'Certainly you must,' Margaret said with a smile. 'He wants to take care of you—and why not?'

'Oh, I do not care for too much fuss,' Kitty replied. 'But I know he is right.' She hesitated for a moment, then, 'Have you told Giles—about the baby?'

Margaret blushed a delicate pink. 'I thought you might have guessed. No, I have not told him yet. I did not want to worry him before he went away. I shall talk to him as soon as I see him again.'

'Yes, do so,' Kitty said. 'It is always better to speak of these things than to write—or I would advise you to write now, Magda.'

'Oh—why do you say that?'

'You have not heard the news from England then?'

'I have heard nothing much for days. I was at the hospital night and day for a week and since then I have been concerned for Caroline and my brother.'

'Giles's uncle has died quite suddenly. In his sleep, they say.'

'The Duke of Belmont?' Margaret stared at her in dismay. 'But that is terrible. No one could have expected it, surely?' She felt a pang of sadness as she thought of his wife, that lovely, lively girl who had lost first her child and now her husband. 'Poor Felicia. She must be distraught, of course. I cannot think how she must be suffering.'

'Yes, one can only guess at her feelings—to lose everything that way. It happened during the fighting, so Giles would not have been able to go home to pay his respects, of course. I dare say he will do so as soon as Wellington sees fit to release him from duty. I am sure the lawyers will be anxious to see him.'

'Yes. I suppose he will have duties to his estate now.'

'Oh, certainly,' Kitty said. 'An estate of that size bears heavy responsibility. Giles has always left his own to the care of agents when he was away, but Belmont is a different matter. I dare say Giles will have to resign his commission and devote himself to the estate.'

'It was what he feared,' Margaret said. 'He had hoped that Felicia would give her husband a male child—and he will be devastated by this news, for he was fond of the Duke.'

'Yes, I have heard him say it. Others would be over-joyed to inherit such wealth, but Giles is not like other men. This will be awkward for him.'

'I think he will do his duty, no matter what it costs him.'

'Yes,' Kitty said. 'The future may not be as you had hoped, Magda. But always remember what I have told you: I am your friend no matter what.'

Margaret thanked her and took her leave soon after. She knew that Kitty was trying to be kind in breaking the news gently to her, but it was clear that she did not think Giles would marry her. It was his duty to care for the estate now—and to marry and produce heirs, of course.

Kitty clearly thought that she would not be consid-ered a suitable wife for a man of Giles's new conse-quence. And of course she was perfectly right. The Duke of Belmont could not marry his mistress. It was unthinkable!

Driving back to the house in her carriage, Margaret felt cold all over. They had planned such a wonderful future together. She had feared that things might change once Giles knew she was increasing—but what would happen when he discovered that he was now the Duke of Belmont?

She wanted to believe that it would make no difference and their lives could continue much as before, but the niggling doubts had begun to creep in.

The journey to England was an anxious one for both Margaret and Caroline, though in actual fact it went quite smoothly. To their surprise they had discovered that Edward Marshall was to travel home on the same ship and he insisted on doing all in his power to help them.

'I am completely recovered as you see,' he told Margaret when she expressed concern for his own health. 'All that ails me is a sense of guilt that I was wounded so early in the war and unable to be of more service to my country and my comrades. It would make me feel very much better if I could be of some use to you.'

Margaret could not refuse such an offer and she was glad of his company, for she found him both intelligent and kind. He helped with overseeing the transfer of her luggage on board ship and with settling Sir Roderick in his cabin.

Afterwards, he and Margaret spent some time on deck together. They were not the only English nationals to be returning home and Margaret was subjected to a frosty stare from a lady she thought she might have met before. As she could not recall the lady's name, and it was clear that she did not approve of Margaret, she neither spoke to her nor mentioned her to Edward Marshall.

When they left the ship at Dover he secured a comfortable chaise for them and made arrangements for their trunks to follow in a baggage coach, before taking his leave of Margaret.

'My parents will be anxious to see me or I would escort you to your home, Magda. If you need me, I shall send them word and do so, of course.'

'You have already been more than kind. We are quite able to manage now, thank you. I am grateful for your company and all that you have done.'

'It was a pleasure to me,' he told her truthfully. 'Perhaps I may call in a few weeks to see how you are all settling in?'

Margaret would have refused him, but she felt obliged to smile and say that he would be welcome. After he had taken his leave she wished that she had been firmer. There was no point in offering him the slightest encouragement, for he could never take Giles's place in her life. No man would ever do that!

If Giles should wish to end their relationship...but, no, it would not happen. It was wrong of her to doubt his love. Indeed, she did not truly, but she knew that he might consider it his duty to marry and provide an heir. He would almost certainly feel that way, and then...she would have to end their affair.

Margaret could never consider continuing their relationship if he were to marry. It would seem too sordid, and be too cruel and unfair to his wife, whoever that lady might be.

She had thought of Giles as her lover, seeing their break with convention as brave and freethinking, an adventure. He had linked her with Helen of Troy and other great lovers of history, and that was how she had seen them, as passionate lovers, glorious and untouched by sordid reality—but now she realised that unless she wished to spoil her memories she would have to let him go.

The thought was so heartbreaking that she felt dizzy

and ill from the crushing pain in her chest as she fought the rush of denial. She could not bear it! She could not stand aside and see him wed another. Yet she must! Giles might not want to give her up—but she would not be his mistress once he married.

'Are you all right, Maggie? Roddy is wondering why you do not come.'

'Oh…' Margaret blinked at her sister-in-law. 'I had not realised you were ready. Forgive me.'

'Are you quite well? You look a little pale.'

'It is nothing,' Margaret said. 'I am ready to leave now.'

Once settled in the carriage, she tried to make light conversation with Caroline. She knew that her sister-in-law was anxious because Roddy was so quiet, but there was little she could say that would ease Caroline. Roddy had become very moody and unpredictable. One moment he seemed cheerful, telling them that he was looking forward to returning home and beginning again, the next he was reserved, sunk into himself—sullen. Margaret was almost as worried as Caroline, but she was careful not to show it.

'I have not been to Hazelmere for many years,' she said. 'It will be interesting to see the changes.'

'At least you can see them,' Roddy muttered. 'God damn it! I should have been better off if that blast had blown my head apart.'

'Oh, Roddy!' Caroline cried. 'Please do not say such things.'

'Feeling sorry for yourself will not help matters,' Margaret said. 'We may seek help from the doctor I told you of—and we can pray.'

'Prayers are useless. They did not help the men who died in battle, nor those who lay weeping on the field, their bodies torn apart by the French artillery. God does not listen to you sing his praises or your pleas for help.'

'No,' Margaret agreed. 'Sometimes it seems that He is not listening to our prayers, and there was undoubtedly too much loss of life—thousands on both sides, they say—but you were spared to us. You should thank God for that, Roddy, and make the best of what you still have.'

'Damn you!' he muttered. 'I'll not be preached at by either of you.'

'Oh, Maggie…' Caroline looked at her tearfully, but she shook her head, putting a finger to her lips.

'I think I shall try to sleep for a while. If I were you, I should do the same, Caroline. We shall be some hours on the road before we are home.'

Closing her eyes, Margaret tried not to let Roddy's angry outburst hurt her. It was not directed at her, but at the cruel hand Fate had dealt him. Pity made her heart wrench with pain for him and for Caroline, who must suffer for him. She was not sure how much of this her sister-in-law could bear. Only time would tell.

Giles stifled a yawn. Would the diplomatic wrangling never cease? The war was over, but it seemed that the peace had yet to be won.

Wellington had been appointed generalissimo of the Allied armies of occupation after Bonaparte's exile. The defeated emperor had departed for his island prison and would find St Helena harder to bear than his former home in exile on Elba. In his heart Giles could find some sympathy for the man who had lost so much, though he would never forgive the deaths of so many friends. Word had reached him of Lord Ellwood's death and he'd cursed himself for accepting his friend's offer of help that fateful morning. If he had not done so, Ellwood might still be alive.

The meeting was coming to an end at last. Wellington made a discreet signal to Giles to stay behind, turning to him with a snarl of frustration once the door was firmly closed.

'I swear there are times when I would sooner be in the field with Bonaparte again!'

'My feelings exactly, sir.'

'Greedy dogs fighting over the bones of Europe—but that is not why I asked you to stay, Giles. I need you to take a confidential message to the Regent. Besides, you asked for leave to visit your uncle's widow.'

'She will not know how to go on. I ought to settle things. My lawyers have the business in hand, but I should like to see her—and Magda.'

'Ah, yes. May I ask what your intentions are in that direction?' His brows arched. 'You have my permission to send me to the devil if you choose.'

'As it happens you are not the first to ask, and my intentions have not changed.'

'Discretion as always. Let me ask you another question then—are you still intent on a life in the diplomatic service?'

'That depends on several things,' Giles replied. 'I have a duty to the estate, though I may find a way round that. I must discuss the future with someone else before I can answer you, sir. I shall report back shortly and then you may have my answer.'

'Well, you must do as you think best, but I am likely to be in Paris for some time to come and I would have you in my service, Giles. I need men about me that I can trust. In my opinion, it will be a waste if you give

it all up too soon, but you must do your duty as you
see fit.'

'Exactly, sir.'

'You will leave in the morning. You have one week's
leave after you have delivered my message and then
you will return. You have not been given your discharge
yet!'

Giles saluted smartly and went out, the important letter tucked inside his coat. Kitty had given him Magda's
brief note some days earlier. So he knew that she was
not in France, but staying with her brother and his wife.

Giles frowned over that for he had heard that Sir
Roderick had been blinded in a blast of the French can-
non and believed that he would not be an easy patient.
He doubted that Lady Hazelmere would know how to
manage her husband and she would be bound to cling
to her sister-in-law. If he was plagued by the need to
do his duty, Magda would be no less conscious of her
own towards her brother.

Sir Roderick had apologised that morning in the waiting hours before battle, but he was in Giles's opinion
rather a selfish young man, and might consider it his
sister's duty to devote her life to him and his wife.

'Oh, Maggie,' Caroline wept, holding a lace kerchief
to her eyes. 'How long must this go on for? We have
been at home some weeks now and there is no improve-
ment in his mood. I thought that once we were here he
would be content.'

'It is very difficult for him,' Margaret said, though in
her heart she sometimes lost patience with her brother.
He was always snapping at her or Caroline, seemingly
so caught up in his own misery that he had no feelings
for others. 'If we might persuade him to visit the doctor

in London, there might be a chance of discovering something. I wrote to Sir Denis, as I told you, and his letter was quite encouraging. He says that it may be no more than shock and that in time, when Roddy begins to forget the horrors he saw, his sight could come back to him.'

'He does not believe that,' Caroline said and sniffed. 'Sometimes, when I can persuade him to walk with me he seems happy enough, but at other times he sinks into a black despair and I do not know what to do to comfort him.'

'I know how painful it must be for you, dearest,' Margaret said. 'I can only say that you must try to be patient and not to let his attitude hurt you. Remember, he is angry with what has happened to him, not with you.'

'Oh, I do know that,' Caroline replied. 'And I know that underneath it all he is still the man I love. Sometimes he clings to me and he is so frightened, Maggie. I try to comfort him, but I am frightened too.'

'In time he will grow more accustomed.'

'If he does not…' Caroline caught her breath. 'He spoke of throwing himself into the river…'

'Such foolish talk! And unkind to upset you. Would you like me to talk to him?'

'No, for he will only be angry with me for telling you.' Caroline lifted her head, her face blotched with tears. 'You will not leave me, Maggie? You will not go away?'

'I had hoped to return to France once you were settled.' Margaret placed her hands on the gentle swell of her belly. She had told her brother and Caroline that she was increasing before their return to England, but everyone else would be aware of it before long. 'It will soon be apparent to all that I am increasing. Are you sure you wish for me to stay, Caroline? There is bound to be scandal, you know. Too many people here know me as Margaret Hazelmere. In London I was able to play out my little masquerade, but I fear the truth may soon become known. I was foolish enough to confess it to Mr Rushford—and I have had a letter from my lawyers. I think he means to make trouble for us.'

'Oh, Maggie!' Caroline's eyes widened with anxiety. 'As if we did not have enough to worry us. That dreadful man is not still trying to sue us, is he?'

'My lawyers tell me that he has demanded another meeting with me. He knows I am staying here and I dare say he means to force you to speak to him, perhaps demand an apology.'

'I shall never apologise,' Caroline said and lifted her head proudly. 'If he wants my ten thousand he may have it. I do not regret that I married Roddy—only that I ever quarrelled with him. It is because of that that he distrusts me now. He thinks that I shall grow tired of looking after him and look for a way out of our marriage.'

'It is his fear talking,' Margaret replied sadly. 'You must try not to be hurt by the things he says. I am sure he does not mean them.'

'I know he does not mean to hurt me; sometimes when he makes me cry he apologises and then we kiss and forgive each other—but it does hurt, Maggie. It hurts very much.'

'I know how you feel,' Margaret said and her lovely face clouded with sadness. 'I had thought that Giles might write in reply to my letter, but he has not and...' She could not finish for her thoughts were not to be shared.

Giles must have much to consider and she was perhaps just a woman he had loved for a while and decided to forget now that he had his duty to think of.

Oh, but to speculate was foolish. She could not know his thoughts and was tortured by her own. Giles was not the kind of man to desert her without a word. If he once made up his mind he would come to her and tell her, and until then she could only wait.

Besides, even if he had come to her she would not have been able to leave her brother and sister-in-law in the lurch at this time. Roddy's moods did not seem to improve and Caroline was constantly on the verge of tears.

Oh, what a coil it all was! Margaret sighed. She had known happiness for such a brief time, and now it seemed that it might have to last her for the rest of her life.

Giles embraced Felicia briefly, then looked at her pale face. Widow's weeds did not become her, and her grief had left its mark on her. She had grown up too fast these past months and his heart wrenched with pity for her.

'I am so glad you have come,' she said on a sob. 'I was afraid you might be killed and then I should be all alone. You will not desert me, Giles? If you return to France I must stay here in this mausoleum for a year—unless you wish me to retire to the dower house?'

'No, I do not require that,' Giles said and looked at her carefully. 'As I have told you before, I had no desire to inherit the title, Felicia. I had hoped it would be otherwise, but it is useless to say more and I do not wish to make your grief worse.'

'My child was a girl. You would still have been the heir.'

'For the moment. Had my uncle lived you might have had another child—a son next time.'

'They told me it was unlikely,' Felicia said. 'And now I shall never know, shall I?'

'You are young. Belmont left you well provided for. I dare say you will marry again.'

'Perhaps.' Felicia smiled oddly. 'I think that the worst thing is that everyone keeps announcing me as the Dowager Duchess...and I do not feel like a dowager, Giles!'

He was glad to see a spark of rebellion in her eyes. 'You do not look like a dowager, Felicia.'

'Black makes me look like a positive hag!'

'You need only wear it for six months. After that you may go into pale greys and lilac, which will suit you very much better.'

'May I tell everyone that those were your instructions?' she asked, a faint smile in her eyes.

'You have my permission to do so as the head of the family. Indeed, it is your duty to obey me, Felicia.'

His smile made her gurgle with laughter. 'I think I should have married you, Giles.'

'I should not have spoiled you shamefully as he did.'

'No—and he did love me,' she replied. 'Everyone believes I married him for the money and the title, but I cared for him very much. I am not sure that I would wish to marry again.'

'It is natural that you should feel that way for the moment. I am sure that you will begin to feel better when you can go into company again.'

'It is so boring, all this mourning. My dear one would not have wished to see me like this. Dressed like a crow, and so many things I may not do.' She pouted at him. 'You must stay with me a few days, Giles dearest. Please say you will. I have been so miserable.'

'I have some instructions for my uncle's agents, and people to visit,' Giles replied. 'I can stay two days, but I have to return to France at the end of the week and there is someone else I must see first.'

'Do you mean the Comtesse de Grenelle?' Felicia frowned. 'I thought you had parted from her, Giles. I knew that you were…friends, of course, but I had a letter from Annis Crosby. Do you remember her at all?'

'Yes. I never liked that particular lady. She set her cap at me all one summer, but I am afraid I was rather rude to her.'

'Well, perhaps that was why she took such delight in letting me know that Magda has a new protector.'

'What do you mean?' Giles grabbed her by the shoulders, his fingers biting deeply into her shoulders. 'I never heard such wicked lies. How dare you repeat such a tale to me?'

'You are hurting me, Giles! I am only telling you what Annis wrote to me. She returned to England on the same ship as Magda and Edward Marshall and she saw them laughing together. She assumed that they were having an affair. If you say it is not so, I believe you.'

'It is a scurrilous lie!'

'Yes, of course. If you say so, Giles.'

Felicia looked at him accusingly as she rubbed at her shoulders.

'Forgive me if I hurt you. I was angry. You should not repeat gossip.'

'I did not know it was a lie. Why was she on the ship with him?'

'Magda came to be with her former ward and Sir Roderick. He was blinded in the fighting near Waterloo and Lady Hazelmere cannot cope with it alone. If Edward Marshall was there it was a coincidence, no more.'

'Forgive me, Giles,' Felicia said. 'I would not have hurt you or made you angry for the world.'

'You are forgiven, but you will please not repeat such scurrilous gossip in future.'

'No, I would not dream of it. I like Magda.'

'I hope you do—I intend to marry her,' Giles said. 'She will be living here if I take up residence and you will need to make friends with her if you wish to continue my friend.'

And with that he turned on his heel and walked swiftly from the room. He did not believe that Magda had taken another lover without at least telling him that their affair was over, but Felicia's careless words had distressed him more than he could say. It was clearly time that he asked Magda to be his wife!

Margaret and Caroline were sitting together in the green salon when the butler entered to announce that they had a visitor.

'Were you expecting someone?' Magda asked and Caroline shook her head. 'You said it was a gentleman, Burrows?'

'A Mr Rushford, ma'am.'

'Oh, Maggie!' Caroline exclaimed and jumped to her feet. 'I cannot see him. I really cannot.'

'I am with you,' Margaret said and smiled calmly. 'There is nothing he can do to harm you, dearest. And I believe you do owe him some sort of an apology— even if it is only for the inconvenience you caused him.'

'Yes, I know you are right.' Caroline breathed deeply. She clearly did not wish for the interview, but Margaret had left her little choice. 'Very well, Burrows, you may show the gentleman in.' She looked at Margaret nervously as the butler went away. 'You must not leave me alone with him!'

'Nothing could persuade me to do so,' Margaret said. 'I am not afraid of Mr Rushford and neither must you be. You are Lady Hazelmere now and nothing can change that.'

'No…' Caroline smiled, but her smile wavered as the butler announced their visitor, her face turning pale as he came in.

'Madame la Comtesse. Lady Hazelmere…' He bowed stiffly to them, seeming to be suffering a mixture of feelings at seeing Caroline again. 'Thank you for seeing me at such a time.'

'You allowed us little choice, sir,' Margaret said. 'I gave my lawyer instructions that I had no wish to talk to you in person.'

'It was really to Lady Hazelmere that I wished to speak,' he replied, his face like a board. 'I believe I was unwise to threaten you with action when we last met, ma'am. My lawyers have made it plain to me that I have no claim on you.'

'I did not imagine you had,' Margaret replied. 'However, I was more than willing to meet you in court had you persisted.'

'Well, I have decided not to do so…however, I do have a claim on Lord Hazelmere for enticement. I have suffered a loss and he was at fault. He must be made to pay for his actions…' He hesitated and looked at Caroline, an appeal for understanding in his eyes. 'You must understand that I am not by nature a vindictive man. It was the shock of learning that you had run off with Sir Roderick without a word to me that made me decide on this course of action.'

Had he really come here to explain his actions expecting understanding? The nerve of the man! Margaret was in two minds whether to throw him out or give him the rough edge of her tongue, but decided to do neither. His answer would be better if it came from Caroline.

'That was wrong of me,' Caroline said, her lips white. 'I should have been brave enough to see you and tell you face to face, but I could not. I meant to write to you from France, but then...'

'You were persuaded to run off with your lover?'

'Roddy was not my lover,' Caroline replied, a spark of pride in her eyes now as she looked at him. 'You insult both my husband and me, sir. Sir Roderick is a gentleman. He did not attempt to lay a finger on me until we were married.'

Bravo, Caroline! Margaret silently applauded.

There was something like regret mixed with jealousy in Rushford's eyes. 'If that is so I am glad to hear it, though it makes little difference. Your reputation was lost once you left Bath alone with him.'

'I had two maids with me, both of them dragons, who slept in my room and guarded me as fiercely as any duenna!' Caroline was very angry now. She got to her feet, glaring at him. 'You are the rogue, sir. To insult me and threaten my husband when you know that he has been wounded in the service of his country. He is brave and honourable and kind and I love him more than my own life. I am glad that I married him. I know now that I should have been miserable if I had married you. If I have only the first few months of my marriage to treasure, I am glad that I took my chance of happiness when I did. One hour with Roddy is worth a lifetime with you or any other man! Take my inheritance if you must. I would rather live in a hovel with Roddy than in a palace with you!'

'Caroline....' Everyone turned to look towards the doorway as Roddy spoke and it was plain to see that he had heard every word of Caroline's tempestuous speech. 'My brave darling...' He opened his arms and she went running to him as he gathered her in a hungry embrace. 'I don't deserve that you should love me so much. I have been such a growly bear these past weeks.'

'I do not care how much you growl. I love you.'

Mr Rushford was staring at them, a mixture of stunned dismay and deep disappointment on his face. Watching him taking in every word the husband and wife said to each other, Margaret realised that he must have come in the hope that he would see her regretful and wishing that she had married him. She was not sure whether he had come to gloat or in the hope that she might run off with him, but whatever had been his reason he was disappointed with the result.

'I think you have your answer, sir,' she told him as he stood there clearly undecided. 'It might be better if you left. Any further business may be conducted through your lawyers.'

'Madam,' he said and his eyes swept over her with contempt. 'You may be certain that your brother and his wife will be hearing from me soon.'

Detestable man! Margaret thought that she would like to strike him, but refrained.

She did not give him the satisfaction of an answer. She remained silent until he had gone, watching from a distance as Roddy and Caroline whispered together. Then, after a few moments, they came towards her, hand in hand. She felt a shadow lift from her as she saw that they had settled things between them.

Caroline gave her a tentative smile. 'Roddy has something to say to you, Maggie.'

'I am listening. But first of all, I would like to second what my brother told you—you were very brave, Caroline. I applaud you for standing up to Rushford and I quite agree. You would have been miserable married to him.'

'I thought she must be miserable married to me the way I am—but it is not so, apparently,' Roddy said and smiled for the first time in weeks. 'It seems that Caro still loves me and wants only to be with me—whether I can see or not.'

'Of course she does,' Margaret said. 'Have we not tried to tell you that all along?'

'I was not listening,' he said. 'I want to apologise to you, Maggie—and to say that I am ready to visit the doctor you told me of whenever you can arrange it.'

'That is wonderful news,' Margaret said and went to kiss first him and then Caroline. She had not hoped to see this day so soon, fearing that her brother would slip into a decline. 'I suggest that we leave for London first thing in the morning. Sir Denis may not be able to offer you a cure, Roddy, but at least we shall know his opinion.'

'If I am permanently blind, I must accept it,' Roddy said. 'I am beginning to come to terms with it and to find it is possible to do certain things for myself—but it was thinking that Caro would tire of me that made me so desperate. Now that I know…' He gave a laugh that might have been a sob. 'I have been such a damned fool!'

'Yes, perhaps,' Margaret said and smiled as she saw Caroline's adoring look at her husband. 'But we shall forgive you, dearest. And we shall all pray that the news will be good when we speak to Sir Denis.'

Chapter Eleven

'I have come to see the Comtesse de Grenelle,' Giles said and then, as the servant began to deny him, 'Perhaps she is using her maiden name here—Miss Margaret Hazelmere.'

'Oh, Miss Margaret,' the girl said, nodding her head as the penny dropped. 'Yes, sir—I mean, no, sir. You can't see her. She is not at home.'

'What do you mean, not at home?' Giles demanded, nostrils flaring. His temper, which had been on a short rein for the past several days, was close to erupting. 'Explain yourself, girl!'

'Very well, Fanny, that will do,' a voice said and a rather dignified man dressed in severe black came into the hall. 'Please come in, sir. Forgive us for allowing the girl to answer the door. It is not her place, but I was busy in the pantry and she happened to be here, I dare say. How may I help you, sir?' Burrows knew Quality when he saw it, and he could tell when a gentleman was near to losing his temper.

Giles stepped inside the large hallway, which was airy and light, furnished with a clutter of well-polished furniture and smelling faintly of lavender and rose, but

with a welcoming atmosphere. It was a country home
for a gentleman of the Quality, not grand or imposing
but pleasantly appointed.

'I am Belmont,' Giles replied. He had been schooling
himself to use the title for a while now and knew that
it would have the butler jumping to attention. 'I came
to see Miss Hazelmere—or Lady Hazelmere, if Magda
is not at home.'

'Your Grace, it is an honour to welcome you to
Hazelmere. The family is away, sir. They left the day
before yesterday for town, all of them together. Sir
Roderick is to visit an eminent doctor while they are
there, I understand.'

'Ah, yes, how is your master? I had heard the sad
news of his injury.'

Burrows looked grave. 'He was very poorly, sir, very
poorly—in his spirit, you know. However, I am glad to
say that his condition took a turn for the better three
days ago and he seems much more like himself now.'

'I am glad to hear it,' Giles said and frowned. It
would take him a day of hard riding to reach London
and that meant that he would have little of his leave to
spend with Magda. 'Thank you for your information,
sir. If you could furnish me with Miss Hazelmere's address?'

'I believe she left it here, sir.' The butler reached for
a small pile of cards. 'Ah, yes, this is where they will
be staying for the moment. These have come in useful.
Mr Marshall was here only yesterday. He was returning
to London after a visit to his parents and called to see
Miss Margaret. He asked for the address too.'

'Mr Edward Marshall, was that?' Giles's mouth drew
into a thin line as the man agreed. 'I see—thank you
for your help. Good day.'

'Good day to you, your Grace.'

Giles winced at the obsequious tone and left, his mood blacker than a thundercloud. It seemed that Felicia might have been right after all. And yet he could not believe that the woman he loved could behave in such a callous fashion.

He had written to her twice since hearing she was with her brother and sister-in-law in England. No replies had come from her, but he knew that it was possible his letters might have gone astray.

As he began his journey to town, his thoughts were gloomy. He had waited to speak to Magda, firstly because he felt she was not ready for marriage, and then because of the war, but now he realised that perhaps he had waited too long.

Margaret rose from her seat in Sir Denis's reception room as her brother and Caroline came out of his surgery. She had chosen to remain here while they went in, believing that it was time they came to rely on her less heavily, and she could see from their faces that the news was not conclusive.

'What did he say?' she asked.

'There has been no physical damage to the eyes or the nerves as far as Sir Denis can tell,' Caroline said. 'He thought he detected a flicker of reaction when he held a match close to Roddy's eyes and he says he believes the vision is not impaired and that it may return at any time—just as you have said all along, Maggie.'

'But nothing more conclusive?'

'He does not know why Roddy cannot see, but believes it may be something to do with what happened out there—the shock of seeing such awful things.'

'The man is a fool,' Roddy muttered and Margaret's

heart sank as she saw that his black mood had returned. 'I've seen men killed before. I'm not a coward to fail at the sight of a little blood.'

'I am sure he did not mean to imply that you were,' Margaret said. 'However, we must just be patient and wait for a while. You have so much to be thankful for, Roddy.'

'Yes…' His frown cleared. 'I suppose that I have. Besides, it is my duty to look after Caro and the estate. I can still talk and listen so I suppose that all is not lost.'

Margaret drew a breath of relief. He was naturally disappointed that the doctor had not been more positive, but it seemed he had made up his mind to accept things for the moment. She had been afraid that her brother was about to sink back into his mood of despondency, but it seemed that he had turned a corner in his mind.

'Well, I believe I shall leave you to return home together,' she told them. 'I have certain purchases I want to make and will find my own way home later.'

'You do whatever you want,' Caroline said. 'We are able to manage now, thank you, Maggie. You have been good to us these past weeks, but we must not expect you to give all your time to us.'

Margaret noticed the new confidence in her sister-in-law and smiled. Clearly, she would soon be able to leave them and return to France, and that would be a good thing. As yet her condition was not obvious, but it could not be much longer before it became so.

One of the reasons she had decided to go shopping alone was that she wanted to make arrangements to see another doctor, for herself this time.

* * *

She spent the first two hours shopping and then visited the consulting rooms of a doctor known for specialising in advising on maternity problems, and delivering the babies of the aristocracy. After a brief consultation and an even briefer examination, he told her that she was indeed with child.

'I should imagine you are nearer four months than three, madam,' he said. 'You seem in good health and I would think you should have no particular problem in giving birth to a healthy child.'

'Thank you for your reassurance, sir. I hope to be in France when the child is born. Is there by chance a doctor you could recommend for the confinement?'

'Yes, certainly,' he said and took up his pen. 'One of my patients was confined while in France a short time ago and she recommended this gentleman highly. I think you could place your confidence in him, madam. He lives in Paris and you would need to be prepared to take up residence there for a period prior to the birth, I imagine.'

'Thank you, that is kind of you.' Margaret placed the paper in her reticule, asked for his account to be sent to her lawyers and took her leave.

'Don't hesitate to call on me nearer the time if you are in London, ma'am.'

'I do not expect to be,' Margaret replied. 'But should that be the case, I would ask if you could be present at my confinement.'

They parted on excellent terms and she emerged into a pleasantly warm day, almost bumping into a passing gentleman as she stepped down into the street. He put out a hand to steady her and then exclaimed as he recognised her.

'Oh, I beg your pardon,' she apologised and then

laughed as he did the same. 'Mr Marshall! How odd that it should be you.'

'Magda,' he said, his face lighting with pleasure. 'I called at Sir Roderick's country house some days ago, but was told you were in London. I had intended to visit this afternoon—but now that we have met perhaps I may escort you home?'

'That is thoughtful of you, sir.'

'I have my curricle close by and would be delighted to take you for a drive in the park first should you care for it.'

'How kind of you,' Margaret said. 'It is such a pleasant day—why not? I was thinking of finding a cab to take me home, but there is no hurry, I think. I believe I should enjoy a little drive in the park, *non*?'

He doffed his hat to her and offered his arm. Margaret took it, thinking it was pleasant to have cheerful company again after weeks of being confined to her brother's house with only gloomy faces.

'You were coming from the doctor's house, I think,' Edward Marshall said. 'Forgive me if it was a private matter, but I do hope that you are not unwell?'

'No, I am in perfect health,' she said and smiled as he handed her into his carriage, telling his groom to stand away as he took the reins himself.

'I shall see you at home, Griggs.'

'Yessir!'

Margaret wondered what the young man would think if he knew that she had been consulting the doctor about the birth of her child, but hoped that he would never need to know. She had made up her mind to return to France as soon as she could make the arrangements. Caroline and Roddy no longer needed her, at least not as much as they had at the beginning, and she believed that it would not be good for them to rely on her too much.

She had no intention of remaining at Hazelmere to become a prop to her sister-in-law, though she was not truly certain what she wished to do with the rest of her life. She had looked for a letter for Giles every day for weeks, but so far nothing had come. He must be very busy, with his work in Paris and the cares of a large estate. Yet she would have hoped that he would come to say goodbye to her, to tell her that he had decided their affair must end—as she was sure it must. The Duke of Belmont needed a wife, and the woman who had been his mistress was not suitable to fill that important position.

Oh, how it hurt to know that she had thrown away all chance of marriage to the man she loved! Had she not been so willing to be his mistress…but it was foolish to allow herself such thoughts. A childish dream, no more.

Sometimes she dreamed of him, of the last time they had made love, when he had seemed almost desperate in his loving—and of that emotional farewell. Surely he could not have deserted her without a word? Letters from abroad were often known to go astray. She could not even be sure that Kitty had passed on her own.

'You were great friends with Kitty Russell in France, were you not?'

Margaret brought her attention back to what Edward Marshall was saying. '*Oui*, that is so. Indeed, we were very close. I have written to her since I returned to England and received one reply from her.'

'I hear that she was brought to bed of a son a few days ago,' Edward told her. 'I imagine Lord Russell must be overjoyed at the news.'

'*Oui*, I am certain of it,' Margaret said. 'It is wonderful news and I must buy a gift for her before we return home. She gave me her address in Yorkshire, which is her husband's ancestral seat.'

'Talking of which…' Edward said and glanced at her. 'I heard that Belmont is home at last. I do not know how long he means to stay for Wellington will have need of him yet. However, that estate can hardly be left to manage itself for long. It is a heavy responsibility for any man. I have always been glad that my own is smaller and that I do not expect a title. Not that I am unable to support a wife, of course.'

'I am sure you are perfectly able to give the lady of your choice a pleasant home and a comfortable life,' Margaret said. 'I believe you told me you have an elder brother, Edward?'

'Yes—but I have my own small estate in Oxfordshire.' He hesitated for a moment. 'I had no thought of marriage, but war sharpens the mind. I was fortunate to be so slightly wounded, even though my arm is still not free of pain—but it has not impaired me. I have begun to think more of marriage of late, Magda.'

'I am sure you would make a kind husband, sir, for the young lady of your choice.'

'I do not care for very young ladies,' he replied, an assumed air of innocence about him. 'They are often very silly. I prefer a woman with a little experience of life—a woman of compassion, who can make sensible conversation and be relied upon in an emergency.'

His expression was so studied that Margaret smiled inwardly.

'Ah, yes. I suppose there are advantages to such a marriage—but would you not grow tired of the lady in time? An older woman might perhaps want to rule the roost too much, Edward. With a young bride you would be master in your own home. And just think—she would lose her looks all too soon and you would be put to the trouble of finding a pretty mistress, *non*?'

He risked a glance at her. She had put on a very French accent, tipping her head to one side, her eyes very bright. 'I think you are teasing me, Magda!' he said a little indignantly.

She gave a gurgle of soft laughter. '*Oui*, just a trifle, *mon ami*. I thank you for those pretty compliments, but it really would not do, you know.' She did not pretend to misunderstand his meaning for it had been plain enough and she wanted to be honest with him. 'I like you very much as a friend, Edward, but I do not love you as I believe a woman ought to love the man she marries.'

'I suppose you still care for Belmont?'

'I am very much a one-man woman, Edward. I do not wish to find a new protector or to marry anyone else.'

'I was asking you to marry me.'

'Yes, I know you were, and I am not unmindful of the compliment you have paid me, but it would not serve. Your parents could not approve of me, Edward.'

'I am sure they would come to love you.'

'Not once they realised—and this is in confidence, Edward—not once they knew that I had given birth to another man's child.'

He drew the curricle to a halt and looked at her, startled by the admission. Instead of shocking him, he found that he admired her all the more for her honesty. She was an exceptional woman and he wished that she had fallen in love with him, even though in his heart he thought her far above him. 'I thought when I saw where you had been just now…but I imagined it might be for your sister-in-law.'

'No, for myself. Caroline and Sir Roderick are aware of the situation, and Kitty Russell has guessed, but I have told no one else. I intend to return to France before it becomes apparent—and I would ask for your word that you will not speak of this to anyone.'

'You have my word as a gentleman,' he replied earnestly. 'But are you sure you will not change your mind and take me, Magda? It would be so much more comfortable for you in the circumstances. I should not reproach you with it, I promise you, and the child would be treated no differently from my own—should we have them.'

'It is very good of you to ask again, knowing the truth,' she said. 'You are indeed a generous and honourable man, Edward—but I must decline. I thank you, but my answer remains as it was.'

'Forgive me if I intrude, but do you have hopes of Belmont?'

'I think not,' she said and for a moment her voice was husky with emotion. It was painful to put her thoughts into words and yet comforting to speak to someone who would not condemn her. 'He is Belmont now and must get himself an heir, I dare say. A marriage between us would not be suitable, and I could not consent to an affair once he is married.'

'It was thought he might marry Felicia once,' Edward said. 'Some say she married his uncle out of pique because he did not ask her—but I do not know if that is true.'

'I believe she truly loved her husband.'

'Well, she is a widow now, and available, though she

lost her first child—and Belmont must be certain of getting an heir. If you were to tell him that—'

'No,' Margaret said firmly. 'I shall not do so and I should be seriously displeased if you were to speak of it to him, sir.'

'I have given you my word,' he said and gave her a smile of rare sweetness, reaching across to kiss her on the cheek. 'I do truly care for you, Magda, and would wed you in a tick if you would have me.'

She laughed and shook her head at him, and neither of them saw the man staring at them from the window of a passing cab.

'Are there any letters for me?' Margaret asked of their housekeeper when Edward Marshall had left her at the front door an hour or so later.

'None that I've seen, ma'am,' the housekeeper said, helping her off with her shawl. 'There were a few cards left earlier, but Lady Hazelmere took those with her when she went up to change.'

'We had callers when we were out?'

'Yes, ma'am. I did not answer the door every time, but there were two ladies and a gentleman, I believe, but I do not know their names.'

'Very well, I shall ask Caroline,' she said and went up the stairs to the first floor parlour where she found her sister-in-law embroidering a pretty cushion cover. 'Were there any messages for me?'

'No, none at all,' Caroline said, holding out the tapestry for her to see. 'Do you not think this is delightful, Margaret?' It was a design of black swans on a silver lake and very fine.

'Yes, very pretty,' she replied. 'We had some callers while we were out, I believe?'

'Oh, two or three,' Caroline said carelessly. 'The cards are over there on the table. No one of any consequence. There is one invitation to dine, but it is for next week and we shall be home by then, I expect.'

'Well, I dare say London is thin of company just now,' Margaret said, struggling to hide her disappointment. She had hoped that there might be a message from Giles since he was in England, but perhaps there would be a letter waiting for her when they returned to Hazelmere. Surely he would at least write to say goodbye! She had not thought him cruel enough to leave her without a word.

Caroline was a little quiet, but Margaret took it for disappointment that there had not been more invitations, and, after promising to come down for tea in a few minutes, she left her to her sewing and went upstairs to look over her purchases. She had bought several bolts of cloth suitable for a child's first raiment and some more to make new gowns for herself. She would need to buy much more for the baby, of course, but she could do that when she visited Paris to make arrangements for the birth.

She realised that she had begun to look forward to returning to her own home. She had given Caroline support when she most needed it, but unless she was prepared to stay with Roddy and his wife for ever, she must make the break soon. Otherwise she would find herself in the position of a maiden aunt, expected to be at the beck and call of her family.

Looking through her purchases again, she took up a book with illustrations of flowers into which the perfumes of some of them had somehow been impregnated. It was a little gift to her brother, which she thought might please him. She had a new tapestry and silks for Caroline, and she intended them to be her farewell gifts.

She would say nothing until they were settled at Hazelmere again. Perhaps in a few weeks she would leave them. Unless she heard from Giles in the meantime, of course, but it did not seem that he intended to get in touch with her. Margaret smothered a sigh and blocked out the wave of unhappiness that threatened to overwhelm her. He could surely have left her some kind of message by this time if he was in England?

Giles felt the ugly prick of jealousy. The smile on Edward Marshall's face and the way she had looked at him! It had made him grind his teeth and taken all his strength of will to stop himself going after them in the street and causing a scene.

He had never thought himself a jealous man. In Paris he had watched in amusement as his friends fell over themselves to flirt with Magda. She had shown no interest in succumbing to their blandishments then— though she had seemed a little reserved in the last week or so before the war.

Had she tired of him? He was some years older and it might be that she was amused by the attentions of a younger man. Giles had known that Marshall was besotted with her in France, but he had thought Magda merely tolerated him out of kindness.

It was his own damned fault if he had lost her! Giles cursed himself a thousand times for not having made sure of her months ago. At the start he had been uncertain of his feelings, but once they became lovers he had realised that no other woman fulfilled him in the same way—no other could again.

He loved her so much that life without her seemed a

barren wasteland, stretching on and on into eternity. Yet he could hardly snatch her up and make off with her if she had decided to end their affair.

Felicia had seemed to think Edward Marshall was her new lover. Even after his angry denial he had known that she was still doubtful—or should that be hopeful? Giles knew well that his uncle's wife had enjoyed being the Duchess and would not care for having another woman in her shoes too soon.

He did not think she was malicious—but she might have been tempted to make more of the incident as reported to her than need be. She might have hopes of him, perhaps, though it was the furthest thing from his mind. Felicia was amusing, but she could not hold a candle to Magda in his estimation and he would not consider such a match.

Giles supposed that he would have to try and get himself an heir one day, though he was not sure that that was possible. As far as he knew none of the ladies he'd had intimate relationships with had given birth to his child, and it might be that he would not be able to father a child.

He knew that some of the ladies he'd had affairs were knowledgeable in these things and might have taken precautions of their own to ensure that it did not happen—but he thought Magda had not.

Her manner in that last week had been odd, but there had been no restraint or change in her when it came to their loving. Was it possible that she…? He frowned as he began to see that there might be a reason why she had not replied to his letters. If she was carrying a child it might be that she felt awkward about her situation, for she would not wish to take what she saw as an advantage.

He had called earlier in the day at Hazelmere's house and left his card, but he would return and ask to see her, and if she was not at home he would leave another letter for her before he left for Paris.

'Did I hear the door knocker?' Margaret asked as she came down to dinner that evening. 'I thought I heard something just as I was dressing.'

She was wearing a pale grey gown that had the understated elegance that only the best French seamstresses knew how to achieve, and her long hair was wound in a sleek chignon at her nape. She looked beautiful, though there were shadows in her eyes.

'I believe someone Roddy knows called,' Caroline said. 'I asked him to come back tomorrow and he said he would.'

'Oh, I see.' She smiled at her sister-in-law. 'You are looking very pretty this evening, dearest, but then you always do. Roddy is very fortunate to have you as his wife. I have every confidence that you will give him all the care he needs and I shall not feel terrible when I leave you.'

'I wish you would not talk of leaving,' Caroline said. She was wearing a gown of straw silk trimmed with chocolate brown ribbons, her hair dressed in ringlets. 'We cannot spare you yet, Maggie. Roddy is better than he was, but we need you with us for a little longer.'

'Perhaps a few weeks,' Margaret promised. 'But then I really must go home. I want my child to be born at my home, Caroline, and I am going to make the arrangements for my confinement with a doctor I have been told of in Paris.'

'But you could live with us,' Caroline said, a sulky downturn to her pretty mouth. 'I should love to have both you and the child, Maggie. You know I want children and I—I may not be able to have them myself. If you were with us, I should have the pleasure of your child.'

'That is nonsense, dearest,' Margaret said. 'You are young and healthy and there is no reason why you should not conceive in time. You are too impatient.'

'You are increasing and you were not with Lord Benedict for long.'

'It is not the same for everyone.'

'Please change your mind,' Caroline pleaded. 'Stay with us, Maggie. I wish you would not think of leaving.'

'I shall stay for a little longer,' Margaret said, but she knew that she ought not to give into Caroline's pleading. In the hall the longcase clock was chiming the hour, and Margaret felt as if it was warning her. Caroline was becoming too dependent. It was clearly time they went their separate ways.

Sitting at her dressing chest later that evening, Margaret stared at her reflection without seeing herself. For a moment when she'd heard voices in the hall earlier she had thought it was Giles, come at last to see her and she had been filled with an irrational hope that had all too soon been dashed by Caroline's explanation.

It had not been Giles she'd heard at all, just her imagination playing tricks on her. She knew a sharp pang of loss, a creeping despair as she realised that she must let her dreams go. If Giles had not taken his opportunity to see her, it must mean that he wished their affair to end.

'Oh, Giles…my love, my love,' she whispered brokenly, every fibre of her body reaching out to him, longing for him, for him to come and take her in his arms and carry her to their bed. 'I miss you so…'

The days and weeks ahead seemed empty, as did the years when she must learn to live with only her memories. But she must manage, for she had no choice but to go on.

Remembering her child, she placed a hand tenderly on her swollen belly and smiled. At least she had her child and that must be enough.

It was mid September now and the nights were becoming colder. Margaret shivered as she returned from walking in the grounds of Hazelmere. It was pleasant enough to live here and the trees were beautiful as the leaves caught fire with the colours of autumn, but this was not her home.

Caroline was happy enough in her own way, very much the mistress here in her home. She had begun to take Margaret for granted and she had noticed that she was expected to take on the duties that the mistress of the house would normally assign to a dependent relative. It irked Margaret a little—she stayed at Hazelmere only out of concern for her brother and his wife, and was growing bored with being a guest in their house.

She had been patient long enough, she decided, as she walked upstairs. She would tell Roddy and Caroline this evening that she would leave at the end of the week. It would not please Caroline, but she believed that Roddy might actually be relieved. He was a little embarrassed by her condition, which was becoming more noticeable and would soon be impossible to keep a secret.

Yes, she would tell them this evening. It was pointless to delay further when the parting must come sooner or later.

'I have had news,' Roddy announced as Margaret went down for dinner that evening. 'My agent read a letter to me today from the lawyers. After long discussions, Mr Rushford has decided to settle for four thousand pounds. I think I shall pay him and put an end to it, Maggie.'

'It is despicable that that man should be able to take our money from us like this!' Caroline cried. 'I cannot believe that I ever considered marrying him.'

'How will you find the money, Roddy?' Margaret asked, looking at him anxiously.

'I can take a mortgage on some of the land, I suppose.'

'No, do not do that,' Margaret said. 'I have made some arrangements to release funds, Roddy, and I shall let your bank have a draft on mine.'

'Can't take it, Maggie. You've done too much for us already. Besides, you may need it for yourself…with the child…' He looked slightly awkward, as if embarrassed at the need to mention her condition.

'I have enough for my needs and my child,' Margaret said. 'It may leave me a little short for a while, but I can manage. It will be my parting gift to you. I have decided to go home at the end of the week.'

'This is your home!' Caroline cried looking distressed. 'You can't leave us. Roddy, tell her she can't go. This is her home. You have no need to leave, Maggie.'

'I am sorry, but I have made up my mind.'

'No! Please, Maggie. Do not leave us—not if you care for us.'

'Roddy is getting better all the time,' Margaret said. 'And you are very capable of looking after both him and yourself, Caroline. You think you need me, but you really do not, dearest. It is time I left you to stand alone, for I do not care to live here with you both for the rest of my life. There, it is said, though I do not mean it harshly and I hope we shall see each other every now and then.'

'Oh, how cruel you are,' Caroline said and tears started to her eyes. 'If you cared for me, you would not leave me, Maggie. You know how I was looking forward to seeing the baby...' She gave way to her emotion and dissolving into tears, ran from the room.

'I am so sorry,' Margaret said as she saw the concern on her brother's face. 'I did not want to upset her—but it is best that I go. This is your home and Caroline's. It is not mine.'

'I agree with you,' he said and she was not truly surprised. 'At the start I wanted you to help her, but she is quite capable of running things herself. Besides, it might be awkward for you in a few months' time.'

'And for you too, Roddy?'

He had the grace to look ashamed. 'Yes, well, you know I don't like the idea of scandal. There's been enough of it already and we shall have to live it down. We've good friends in the country and I want to make a life here.'

'Yes, of course. Besides, I want to go home.'

'You haven't heard from him?'

'No...'

'Bit rotten of him,' Roddy said. 'Thought more of him than that, Maggie. He told me...still, less said the better in the circumstances. I expect he needs to make a good marriage. Owes it to the family name, I dare say.'

'Yes.' She hesitated, then, 'You will be all right— you yourself, I mean? I know things can't be easy for you...'

'I'm not sure...' Roddy hesitated in his turn. 'Caroline doesn't know yet, but I've started to get flashes of light sometimes, Maggie. I don't want to tell her in case it doesn't happen, but I think my sight might be coming back. Your face is just a blur at the moment, but in the strong sunlight this morning...I could see just for a few seconds and then it was gone.'

'Oh, my dearest brother,' Margaret said on a rush of emotion. 'I shall be so happy for you if it happens.'

'Well, I haven't set my heart on it,' he said. 'It's the damnedest thing, Maggie. If the eyes were damaged I would know what was wrong and accept that I was blind—and maybe I'm imagining it, but I think it may be starting to happen.'

'I pray that it will,' she said and kissed his cheek.

'You will say nothing to Caroline?'

'Of course not,' she promised. 'That must be for you—but it makes me feel easier about leaving you.'

'I thought it might,' he said and grinned at her in his old way. 'I haven't been the best of brothers, Maggie— but I know you need your own life. It wouldn't be fair to keep you here against your will. Go back to France and find what happiness you can. And I wish you luck for the future. Who knows, you might find someone who wants to marry you one day.'

Margaret smiled. She did not tell him that she had recently turned down a proposal of marriage from Edward Marshall, for he would think her foolish to have refused him—and perhaps she was. Yet to marry without love would be to betray all that she felt in her heart.

'Thank you,' she said. 'Caroline is upset about my leaving just at the moment, but she will soon realise that she does not truly need me here. Indeed, I think she will enjoy being the complete mistress of her own home.'

'I think it's because of the baby,' he said. 'If she could fall herself, she would not care two hoots.'

And that was the truth of the matter, Margaret knew. Her brother's honesty could be devastating at times, but she preferred it to half-truths and pretence.

Caroline avoided her as much as possible for the next two days, giving her reproachful looks every time they met. Margaret was a little hurt by her manner, but smiled and talked as if nothing was wrong. She could not stay for ever and believed it was best to make the break now before it was too late.

It was on the morning of her departure, after she had given Roddy and Caroline the small gifts she'd bought for them in London, that Caroline brought her a neatly wrapped package, pressing it into her hands.

'Thank you, dearest,' she said and began to open it.

'No, not now,' Caroline said hastily and looked oddly guilty. 'Open it when you get home, Maggie. Promise you won't do so before that?'

'Very well, if that is your wish.'

Margaret put the little package into her smallest trunk, and then went to take her sister-in-law by the hands.

'You will visit me sometimes, I hope?'

'Yes, of course. If you want me to.'

'Of course I shall,' Margaret said and kissed her. 'Take care of yourself, Caroline, and be happy.'

'Yes. I am happy. I would like a child, but Roddy says it will happen one day and I must believe him.'

Margaret nodded but said no more. The footman had come to take her trunk downstairs and she was ready to leave.

Margaret put a hand to her back, feeling the strain of the journey. She had never minded travelling before, but she was now four and a half months pregnant as near as she could tell, and it was tiring for her. She had planned to visit Paris in the near future and make an appointment with the doctor for her confinement, but she would spend a week or two at home first resting.

She glanced at her trunks, which had been brought up, and which a maid was busily unpacking. 'Leave the contents of that small trunk for the moment, Lisette,' she said. 'I shall unpack that myself when I am ready.'

'*Oui, madame,*' the girl said and curtsied to her. 'We are so pleased that you have come home. We thought that you might stay in England…after the troubles.'

'You mean the war, of course?' Lisette nodded and then sighed. 'It was sad that it had to happen, but it did not much affect you here on the coast—besides, I like it at the villa. It is so peaceful.'

'And *madame* needs to rest,' Lisette said.

'Yes, I need to rest,' Margaret said and looked longingly at the bed. 'Indeed, I think I shall do so just for an hour or two.'

When the maid had gone she lay down and closed her eyes, drifting into a troubled sleep in which Giles appeared to look at her with accusing eyes.

* * *

'But it was you who deserted me...'

The words were on her lips as she woke and realised it was early morning. She had slept for hours and her servants had allowed her to rest. They had seen her tiredness, and her swelling belly must have given them the reason for her unusual fatigue.

Margaret got up, feeling restless. She had expected that her unhappiness would melt away once she was at home, but after so many months of absence it did not feel quite the same, and she realised that it would take her a while to settle. After all, she had expected Giles to be with her when she stayed here in future. But she must put all such dreams aside and think of herself and the child now.

She poured herself a glass of wine and ate one of the little almond comfits that had been placed beside her bed in a small porcelain box. Then she walked over to her dressing table and bent down to open her small trunk, taking out some of the treasures that were always carried in it for safety's sake.

Her pearls and the diamond pendant that Giles had bought for her in Brussels—and the bracelet that had seemed to tell her of his love, with its design of a crescent moon and star.

'Oh, Giles, my darling,' she whispered, glancing at herself in the mirror, the candleglow making her look pale. 'Giles—why did you stop loving me?'

Laying the jewel box on the dressing chest, she reached for something else and found the small package Caroline had given her. It was so odd that her sister-in law should have requested that she open it only after she was home in France.

Untying the strings, she stared in surprise as she saw

it contained three letters and a calling card—Giles's card, and, she knew immediately, the letters were all from him. How had they come to be in Caroline's possession?

'Oh, no!' she exclaimed as she realised what the girl had done. 'Caroline, how could you?' Her sister-in-law had been afraid that Giles meant to take her from them and had concealed the letters all this time, giving them to her only when she knew that Margaret was finally leaving.

Opening the letters, she saw that one had been written almost three months ago, just before Napoleon Bonaparte left for St Helena.

I write in haste, dearest, Giles had scrawled. *The Emperor has gone, but we have endless meetings and it seems that they will never be finished. I can make you no promises for the future, for I am not certain how long I shall be tied up here, but I want you to know that you are always in my thoughts.*

Though brief, it ended with his love and was just as she had imagined it might be were she to receive a letter from him, telling of his frustration with delays and problems that he could not solve.

The second was longer.

My darling Magda. I have received word that Belmont has died and I have inherited the estate and the responsibilities that go with it. As you may imagine, it is a burden I did not want and I am not sure how you may feel about this. The future cannot now be entirely as we had planned it, for at some time I must do my duty, even though I may find ways to put it off for a while. Eventually I must succumb to convention, my love, annoying as it may be for us both. However, this will not make any difference to the way I feel for you and I hope you will find it in yourself to forgive me for what must be. You know you have my heart as always. Your own Giles, Duke of Belmont. Oh, how I hate that title!

The third had been written just a few weeks earlier in London.

Someone has told me your news. I wish you all happiness, my dear, but I am sad that you did not see fit to tell me about Edward Marshall yourself. I shall not bother you again. I remain your friend if you should need me, Giles.

The stark message of his words stunned her after the loving letters that had preceded it. Even the scrawled note on the back of his card said that he longed to see her before his return to France.

What could have changed him?

Margaret sat down on the edge of the bed, reading the letters through again and again until she knew them by heart.

What did his second letter mean exactly? He talked of his duty and the changes it must mean eventually—yet at this time he had thought to continue their relationship. That part at least was plain to her.

So what had made him write those harsh words?

He had been in London during their own visit to Sir Denis. Suddenly, Margaret recalled the chance meeting with Edward Marshall. They had gone for a drive in the park—and he had kissed her briefly on the cheek after she had refused his offer of marriage. Could Giles have seen them? Surely not!

She glanced at the letter again. Someone had told Giles her news? What did that mean? Had someone seen her with Edward and told him that she had transferred her affections to the younger man?

Surely Giles would not believe such a thing? Margaret puzzled over it, but unless he had happened to see her that afternoon himself he could not have thought any such thing. Even Caroline would not have told him such a terrible lie—would she?

Margaret felt heartsore at the thought, but then she dismissed it. Whatever Caroline had done in the past, she had returned the letters to her now—which meant that Margaret must make her own decision.

She could write to Giles at the embassy in Paris. Alternatively, she could call to see him when she went there herself—or she could wait and do nothing.

If Giles could believe such a thing of her, he could not love her as she loved him. Surely he must know she was not the kind of woman who would discard one lover and fall straight into the arms of another? And if he did not, was it worth trying to repair their relationship?

Perhaps he had accepted the lie because it was easier?

Margaret looked at his second letter once more. He had written that the future could not be entirely as they had planned it—perhaps his plans no longer included a mistress who would travel with him as he moved about the world. Perhaps he wanted a respectable lady for his wife, a lady who would consider it her duty to stay at home and provide him with a string of heirs for the dukedom.

She had no objection to providing the string of heirs if that is what he truly wanted, of course, or to living in that beautiful house—but she was a fallen woman. She had been his mistress and could not expect him to offer her marriage.

Kitty, Lady Russell, had married her lover, but that did not happen often. Kitty had tried to warn her when they were in Brussels, but Margaret had not wanted to listen. She had believed that Giles would want to continue their affair—as he had at the beginning of the war. His first letters had seemed to promise so much.

So why had he changed his mind? Perhaps he had met someone else? They had been apart for some months. It might be that he had forgotten her.

The thought was so painful that she wanted to dismiss it, but it lingered in her mind. Giles must know that their relationship could not continue once he married, and perhaps that was why he had written her such a harsh letter. It might have seemed easier to make the break that way.

A part of her longed to leave for Paris immediately and seek him out, but in her heart she knew that she could not do that. If Giles wanted their affair to continue, he must come to her.

She would do as she had planned on her return, rest here for a week or so until her strength was back to normal and then travel to Paris to make an appointment with the doctor and buy the things she would need for the birth of her child.

Chapter Twelve

'So it is settled then,' Wellington said. 'You leave for Vienna in the morning, Giles. This message is urgent and I must have a reply—you understand me?'

'Yes, sir, of course.'

Giles was thoughtful as he left the room. He had regretted the harsh words he had written to Magda in that last letter. Jealousy was an ugly emotion and it had been strong in him when he returned to his lodgings after seeing her with Edward Marshall. However, had she not refused to see him it might have stayed in his pocket and been torn up. It was Lady Hazelmere's direct speaking that had decided him. However, since then he had had time to think and regret.

Would Magda really have left orders that she did not wish to speak to him? It did not sound like the woman he remembered, the woman who had surrendered so sweetly to his loving, who even now possessed him in his dreams, haunting him every waking hour. It sounded like a rather petulant, spoiled young lady—which perhaps fitted Caroline Hazelmere rather better than her sister-in-law.

If that were the case…it was entirely possible that

Magda had received none of the letters that he had sent her.

Surely Caroline could not be that vindictive? She must have known how hurtful it would be for Magda if she believed he had abandoned her. Giles frowned over the thought. He had been hurt and angry because of rumours and that little scene he'd witnessed by chance between Magda and Edward Marshall—but if Magda believed he had deserted her without a word…she might perhaps have turned to another man in her despair.

The anger boiled over in him and it took all his strength not to post off to England immediately and consign his duty to hell. Only the knowledge that Wellington would then be within his rights to court-martial him kept him from rushing to find Magda and demand that she speak to him in person. Yet he could not allow others to dictate to them, on that much he was determined. He must do his duty, but after that he would see Magda, even if it meant resigning his commission.

In the meantime, he would write to her at her home in France. There was just a chance that she might have returned there and that this time she would receive it. But, no, he would not again put his faith in letters. He would visit her on his return, no matter what!

'I shall be delighted to attend you at your accouchement, *madame*,' the eminent doctor told Magda. 'It will be a pleasure to advise a sensible lady like yourself, *n'est-ce pas?*

'Thank you,' Magda said and smiled. 'I feel very much better for having talked to you, *monsieur*.'

Margaret was smiling as she left his consulting rooms. The sun was shining and she felt very much more relaxed than she had when she arrived back in France three weeks earlier.

She had made arrangements to stay at a small, discreet hotel that she and Aunt Kate had used once or twice on their visits to Paris in the past. The most important appointment had been with Monsieur Delvalle, and now that that was over she had nothing to do but enjoy herself.

It was pleasant to stroll along the wide boulevards in the gentle autumn sunshine and to sit and drink coffee at an open-air café. Even at this time of year the scent of flowers was everywhere, filling the air, mingling with the smell of hot pastries and fragrant coffee. She was aware of feeling a slight pang of envy as she watched a pair of lovers strolling hand in hand by the river, but she fought down any tendency to self-pity. She had so much to be thankful for and now that she had had time to consider, she had promised herself that she would not regret anything.

Nor did she regret her affair for one moment, only that it had ended too soon. She had known happiness far beyond her expectations and she was to have her lover's child; that was more than she had thought she would ever have at one time, and she had decided that she would not allow the bitterness to creep in and spoil her memories. Not many women had experienced a love affair as exciting and satisfying as hers, and that must sustain her for the rest of her life. She had promised herself that she would look forward, not back in regret.

To that end, she had written to Caroline and told her that she had forgiven her for her deceit.

I know that you were upset and frightened at the time, she had written. *I am hurt that you did not care for my feelings over this, but I have decided that it will not come between us. We shall forget it and go on as if it had never happened.*

And if she was prepared to forgive Caroline, then she must be prepared to give Giles the answers he deserved, Margaret had decided. She had made up her mind to call at the embassy that very morning and leave a message for Giles, telling him where she might be found, and if he were not there then she would send a letter to his estate in England.

She would tell him that she understood his position had changed, and that while she could not consider being his mistress after he married, she would be happy to welcome him as a friend—but she would not tell him she was carrying his child. If he chose to visit her, her condition would be only too apparent.

Her inquiries at the embassy were met with politeness, but little more. The Duke of Belmont was not in Paris at the moment, and, no, they were not able to contact him—but if she cared to leave a letter he would receive it on his return.

Margaret was disappointed, but she had known that his work entailed a deal of travelling, and had been prepared for this eventuality. She thanked the junior official who had taken the time to see her, left her letter with him and went back out into the sunshine. She would spend the few days in Paris that she had planned, enjoy the shopping, the atmosphere, and perhaps even a visit to the theatre, and then she would go home to the solitude of her villa.

Yes, there were days when she was lonely, nights when her dreams of Giles were so vivid that she woke up with his name on her lips, but she was strong. She would take things quietly until after the birth of her child and then…

'Magda!' She turned as she heard the voice calling to her and stared in surprise as she saw the lady leaning out of the door of a smart equipage that had pulled up in the sunlit square. 'I was told that you had returned to France. How fortunate that we should meet this way.'

'Felicia…' Margaret stared at her in astonishment, for the late duke's widow was the last person she had ever expected to see here at this time. Surely her period of mourning was not yet finished? As she crossed the road to speak to her, Felicia got down and she could see that she was wearing a very fetching gown of pale lilac silk, a pretty bonnet with curling grey feathers perched at a jaunty angle on her head. 'It is lovely to see you.'

'You are surprised,' Felicia said and bobbed her fair curls, which cascaded from beneath the bonnet. 'But I really could not stay cooped up at Belmont another moment. Some friends of mine were coming to Paris and I persuaded them to let me accompany them—and here I am. Please do not scold me for breaking all the rules. I know it is very naughty of me, but Belmont always said rules were made to be broken. He would not care a fig, believe me.'

'I do not reproach you,' Margaret assured her. 'As you say, your husband was not a narrow-minded man.'

'Oh, no, not at all, or I should not have married him,' Felicia said and laughed. 'I considered Giles once, you know—but he can be a little stuffy sometimes. He was so angry with me when I told him I thought you had found a new lover. La! You should have seen his face, Magda. It was vastly amusing. Of course, I know I was wrong to repeat gossip—and Annis Crosby is very spiteful sometimes. I am sorry if it made trouble between you for a while, though Giles said he intended to

call and see you as soon as his business was finished.
Is he here in Paris at the moment?'

'He is away,' Margaret replied, feeling chilly all of
a sudden. 'What did you tell Giles, Felicia?'

'I had a letter from Annis. She had seen you with
Edward Marshall on a ship returning from France. She
assumed you were lovers and I asked Giles if it was
over between you—that was when I was very firmly put
in my place, I can tell you.'

'It was not true. Mr Marshall was merely being kind
to Sir Roderick, his wife and myself. There has never
been anything but friendship between us.'

'Giles would have it so, but then he is in love with
you,' Felicia said and laughed gaily, her eyes sparkling
with confidence. 'Men are such fools when they are in
love. It is so easy to twist them around one's little finger, is it not?'

'Perhaps.' Margaret knew that Felicia was not malicious and did not resent the inference. 'Are you staying
in Paris long?'

'Oh, for a week or two, I dare say,' Felicia gurgled
at her. 'You have no idea why I said that about men
being foolish, have you?'

'No, I must have missed your meaning.'

'Well, I thought Giles must have told you—what he
thought at the start. You recall the attempt on the
Regent's life? They kept it from me at the time, but I
wormed it out of Bel later—and that is what is so funny,
Magda. At the start Giles thought you might be a French
spy working for Bonaparte. He knew that there might
be an assassination attempt against the Prince Regent,
Belmont or Wellington, and of course there was. Only
you saved the prince and Wellington saved himself, and
my poor darling Bel was perfectly safe all the time.'

'Giles thought I might be an assassin?'

'You really did not know?' Felicia pealed with laughter, her ringlets bobbing. 'That is what I thought so amusing. He set out to seduce you to learn your secrets, of course, and ended up falling in love with you.'

Margaret felt sick. Her head was whirling and for one moment she thought she might faint, but Felicia clutched at her arm, steadying her.

'Oh, are you feeling faint? I am so sorry. It happened to me several times when I was carrying. I hope I didn't upset you? I did not mean to hurt you, Magda. Please do not think that. Giles realised he was wrong long ago, of course, and I know he adores you because he told me so. He thought I might have hopes of him when my mourning was over, but of course it was no such thing. I prefer to be spoiled and Giles is far too stern to suit me.'

Margaret had recovered her balance. It took a little longer to recover her composure, but within a few seconds she had managed it.

'How foolish of me to turn faint,' she said. 'It is my condition as you said, *n'est-ce pas*? You are very right, men can be fools—but I fear we are often just as bad for we love them too well.'

'Oh, pooh, as to that...' Felicia shrugged her shoulders expressively. 'I was fond of Bel, but not in love. I do not think I wish to be in love; it is too painful from what I have seen of it. I much prefer to have a man fuss over me, that is why I am determined to marry a man of Bel's age next time—so much easier, don't you think? A few smiles and dimples and pretty looks and they ask for little more. Young men are so demanding. I prefer an older man every time.'

'Your choice entirely,' Margaret said. She wondered

how much more of Felicia's chattering she must endure, for her head was still swimming, and was glad when the young woman started waving at a couple across the street.

'My friends have finished their shopping,' Felicia said. 'It was lovely to see you again. You must ask Giles to bring you to visit me one day when you are in England. I am still at Belmont, though I think I shall take a house in Bath, for that will suit me very much better.' She darted a kiss at Margaret's cheek and went back to her carriage just as her friends came up to her.'

Margaret inclined her head to the couple, who were not known to her, crossed the road to a small café and sat down at the nearest table. She needed a glass of wine and a moment to clear her head.

An artist asked if she would have her likeness taken, but she shook her head, unable to smile for him as was her usual wont. Felicia's revelations had been a severe shock to her and she was struggling to come to terms with the knowledge of Giles's betrayal.

If she had met Felicia before she visited the embassy, she would not have left that letter for Giles. She had wondered for a moment when Lord Ellwood mentioned something of the kind, but believed it was just the muddled ramblings of a dying man—but now she knew the truth. Felicia had made everything more than plain.

Had she not known the young woman was an empty-headed charmer who never thought before she spoke and was not capable of being malicious, she would have thought it had been said to poison her relationship with Giles. However, she did not suspect Felicia of making mischief deliberately, merely of blurting out what she thought was amusing.

Magda did not find it so amusing. Giles had deliberately set out to seduce her, that much she had not needed telling. At the beginning of their acquaintance she had thought it merely an attempt at seduction, but then she had fallen deeply in love and she believed he had also—but now...

How could she believe anything any more? That he should think her a spy—even worse, an assassin! It was hurtful beyond anything that had happened to her so far.

Sipping the good Burgundy wine from the glass in front of her, Magda felt its warmth spread through her veins, giving her back the life that she had felt draining out of her as she listened to Felicia gaily shatter all her illusions: Giles had never loved her. He had merely used her.

She wished that she had never met him, never given her foolish heart to a man who did not deserve it. Her pleasure in being in Paris was destroyed, but she decided to stay despite that. She would need things for her child... For a moment she wished that she could tear it from her body, but then the thought was crushed. Her child was an innocent. She could not blame the father's perfidy on her unborn baby.

But she could and did blame Giles. She wished with all her heart that she had not left that letter for him, but if he came to see her—and he probably would not—she would simply refuse to see him.

Giles returned to Paris a few days after Magda had left. He had made all speed and for once had not been kept kicking his heels for longer than a day. He reported immediately to Wellington and requested leave for a week, which was grudgingly given with the admonition not to expect it again too soon if he wished to remain in the service.

At this moment, Giles was not at all certain that he did. For years he had believed the life would suit him, that he would prefer it to the life of ease that would be his if he took up the reins of his estate and settled down.

He had installed three good agents he knew to be loyal to him to run things at Belmont for the moment, and it had been in his mind to give the service a couple of years more, and then perhaps go home—but it depended on Magda.

Of paramount importance was the need to talk to her and settle things between them. His thoughts had made uneasy bedfellows these past few days and he blamed himself for giving up too easily in London. When Caroline Hazelmere told him that Magda did not want to see him, he should have stood his ground and demanded an interview—and he would have, had it not been for that little scene he had witnessed.

But that could have been innocent, as he well knew. Marshall was besotted with her and would have taken any opportunity to kiss her—and thinking about it calmly, it had been more a kiss of friendship than of passion. Such things happened for all kinds of reasons, and normally he would have waited for her to tell him of the incident, which she would have done had they still been together.

He would go to England, discover where Magda was living and then find her. Somehow he would make her listen to him, sort this thing out between them once and for all. Until he knew for certain how things lay between them, he would know no peace.

It was as he was about to leave the building that the young clerk ran after him.

'Your Grace,' he panted, holding out a sealed package. 'I almost missed you. This came for you when you were away, sir.'

'Thank you,' Giles took it, intending to put it in his pocket and read it later; then something in the clerk's expression made him pause. He caught a hint of perfume and held it to his nose, his senses immediately assaulted by overwhelming memories. It was *her* perfume! He could not be mistaken, for it carried the essence of her and no other. 'Was this delivered by a lady?'

'Yes, your Grace—a very beautiful lady.'

Giles nodded and thanked him. 'Your name is?'

'Samuels, sir.'

'Then I shall remember you, Samuels. If you look for a better position, come to me when I return to Paris in a week's time. I need enterprising men in my employ.'

'I should like to work for you, sir.'

'Then I shall not forget.'

Samuels glowed, but Giles hardly noticed. He was tearing open the letter as he strode away, his heart racing as he perused it, swiftly, greedily at first like a man dying of thirst, and then more slowly.

Now what on earth did she mean by that? She would not consider being his mistress after he married—surely she could not imagine that he would marry anyone else?

He had told her in every way he could that she was important to him, showing his love not only when he took her in his arms, but in other countless ways, down to telling her to put on a cloak when it was cold and the wind was biting. Surely his letter had been plain enough? He could not quite recall what he had written, but it had been meant to be an apology that their amus-

ing game had come to an end and they must settle for
the convention of marriage.

Was it possible that Magda had not realised that he
was asking her to be his wife? He swore beneath his
breath, but loudly enough to startle a passer-by. Why
had he not spoken that night at the ball, asked her to
wait for him?

How often he had regretted his hesitation. But there
would be no more of it. Magda had explained that his
letters had been delayed, but she had received them in
the end and that meant she would have read the last.
Yet she had still left this for him, which must surely
mean that she had decided to give him one last chance.

If he wanted her, which he assuredly did, he must
make the most of it.

Margaret wandered over to the furthest edge of the
garden and stood looking down at the sea. It was a deep
midnight blue that evening, for the sky had been over-
cast all day and it seemed that they might have a storm
before morning.

A sigh escaped her—the air was heavy and she was
feeling oppressed, perhaps because of her condition,
which was beginning to become irksome at times. She
had not been ill since the sickness had stopped, but she
did tire more easily and sometimes her back ached, as
it did today.

Her housekeeper had told her that she ought to rest
more, but she hated to be shut in the house and preferred to walk when the weather was fine.

Even though it was December it was much milder
here than it would be in England now, she thought, and
despite Caroline's abject letter of apology, which had
reached her that morning, she was glad she had come

home. It would not have suited her to reside in her brother's house too long. She needed her independence and the freedom to think and act, as she felt right. Perhaps her aunt had been right all along, and what had happened was for the best. At least she had her memories. But no, she did not really believe that. She longed for Giles with all her heart despite the anger that still lodged like a stone in her breast, refusing to leave her in peace.

She was not sure how long she stood looking down at the restless sea, feeling in tune with its endless movement. Why were her nerves on edge? Was she waiting for Giles to react to her letter? Surely she had decided that she could never forgive him? But perhaps there would be no need...he might just ignore it.

'Magda...' Had she conjured his voice up out of thin air? She turned to look at him, hardly believing her eyes as she saw him striding towards her. He was just as he had always been, tall, powerful, assured and a little stern, but, oh, so attractive! Her heart raced and she felt the usual rush of love for him, but fought it down. She remained perfectly still where she stood right at the edge of the cliff, not trusting herself to speak as he came up to her. His expression was a mixture of annoyance and relief as if some strong emotion worked within him. 'At last! I looked for you at Hazelmere and in London—and it seems I missed you in Paris...' His eyes went over her, taking in the stage of her pregnancy, calculating the months, though he had no need, for he knew that she was carrying his child. 'Why did you not tell me? You must have known before I left you.'

'I was not certain...either that I was with child or that you would wish to know,' she said and she was in control, her voice flat, cold, and expressionless. 'After all, it is not always the most welcome news to a gentleman. Many would prefer not to know.'

'Damn you, Magda! I have not deserved that from you.' He grabbed hold of her arms, his fingers digging into the tender flesh and making her wince. He released her instantly. 'Forgive me, I do not mean to hurt you. You know—you must know that I adore you!'

'I know that you desired me,' she replied and turned away her face to gaze over the sea once more, her heart beating so fast that she felt breathless. It would be so easy to melt into his arms, to give herself up to this raging desire inside her—but did she dare to trust him? 'I imagine a man may desire many women in his life, but he will not want to be responsible for their children.'

'That is unpardonable! You will take that back, Magda. You know that I would never have deserted you. My duty took me from you. I wrote to you as soon as I was able. I do not know what happened to delay my letters, but…' Giles was furious, his lips white with temper, nostrils flaring as his hands clenched at his sides. For the moment he did not trust himself to touch her.

'Caroline kept them from me,' she said, turning to look at him once more. He wondered at the reproach in her eyes. What had he done to make her look at him like that? 'I imagine she was afraid of being alone with Roddy at the start. He was so moody—so desperate— that she thought he might try to take his own life. It was unfortunate, but she gave them to me when I left Hazelmere, though I did not read them until I reached France. She begged me not to. I think she was ashamed of what she had done.'

'I am sorry for your brother's trouble,' Giles said. 'It

cannot be pleasant for either of them and I dare say she was distressed. But that does not excuse what she did.'

'No, it does not,' Margaret agreed. 'I was glad to have your letters, Giles. It hurt me that you had not written. I had thought you would tell me that you must end our relationship in person—and perhaps that was your intention when you tried to see me?'

His expression hardened, becoming angry once more. 'No, it was not. I have no intention of ending it—even less now that I know a child is expected.'

Her head went up, her expression proud, unreadable. 'I do not want you to continue our affair just because of the child, Giles. I have money enough for our needs. You have no need to feel responsible—for me or my child.'

'Be damned to the money!' He glared at her, frustrated by his inability to break down this barrier between them. 'If you were not in that condition I would shake you, damn it! How can you say that to me after all that was between us? I would not have believed you could so misunderstand me. I thought my letter plain enough.'

'I was not certain of your meaning. You seemed to say that you wished to continue our relationship, but that your duty was to marry. I could not be a party to such a relationship, Giles. It would be grossly unfair to your wife.'

'Not if you were my wife.'

'That is impossible.'

A sigh of exasperation escaped him. 'For pity's sake! I know you had this foolish notion that you did not wish to marry, that you wished to be free—but damn it all, Magda, I'm not going to lock you into a chastity belt every time I go away. Nor shall I belittle you at every opportunity or ride roughshod over your opinions.'

'You would find a chastity belt difficult to administer at the moment,' she allowed, a tiny smile on her lips as she saw his frustration. 'But that was not my meaning ever and...' She had been about to confess her change of heart, but then she remembered why she was so very angry with him. 'Oh, how can I believe anything you say? It was all a lie from the very beginning.'

'What are you talking about? I have not lied about my feelings for you. I love you and I want to marry you, not for the child, not for duty, but because it is what I have wanted in my heart since the first time we made love.'

'But you lied to me at the start,' she accused him. 'Perhaps not in words, for you never pretended to mean more than an affair—but in your mind. You thought me a spy and an assassin...'

She saw by the look in his eyes that it was true. He looked shocked, devastated by her words, and unable to deny that she spoke truly.

'I was a fool,' he managed at last. 'I admit that I was working on information I had received and you did seem to be a prime suspect, but that all changed once I kissed you. I knew then that you were not the sophisticated, ruthless woman I had believed you might be. Besides, if you had not pretended to be other than you were, I should never have suspected you in the first place.'

'So it was my fault?' She stared at him angrily. Felicia's words had stung! 'Because of my harmless little masquerade I had to be a spy and a murderess?'

'No, no, of course not. But you will admit that you

were masquerading under a false name, and that I had cause for suspicion?'

'I admit that it was foolish of me.'

'Why did you really do it?'

'I do not know,' she said honestly. 'I was bored, restless; I wanted an adventure, I suppose. Aunt Kate had filled my head with her stories. I thought all the fine ladies and gentlemen in London were decadent, selfish creatures and deserved to be taught a lesson. It was just a little jest, nothing more, a way of repaying my aunt for all she had given me—and she had promised Caroline a Season. Also, I wanted to be in control of my affairs, not hampered by convention...' She smiled ruefully. 'When I met people who welcomed me warmly to their homes, good, honest people who were kind to me, I felt ashamed of what I had done and wished I had not deceived them. I have often wished that I had been honest with you from the start, Giles.'

'I would never have tried to seduce you if I'd known the truth, Magda. You must know that?'

'I dare say you would hardly have noticed me,' she said and her smile was softer now. 'I would just have been another spinster past her last prayers.'

'Now that is the most foolish thing I have ever heard you say,' Giles murmured and reached out to take hold of her arm as she tried to move away. 'You know that I was caught from the first, Magda.'

'By who you thought I was,' she said and her eyes flashed fire at him. 'It was the accent, the mystery that intrigued you, Giles. Miss Hazelmere and her duenna and ward would not have taken your interest—and perhaps that might have been for the best.'

'Never!' He pulled her towards him, holding her in his arms as he bent his head and kissed her softly on the lips, and then with a little groan, passionately. 'Will you never learn, my stubborn love? I want you more than any woman I have known.'

She gazed up at him, her lustrous eyes wide and questing. 'Wanting is not loving, Giles.'

'Have I not told you in every way possible that I adore you? Even that foolish jeweller knew why I had bought that bracelet for you—because you were the moon and stars to me, and all the world. How can I make you see what you mean to me if you will not listen?'

'Oh, Giles…' She felt the tears prick behind her eyes. 'I am afraid to believe you.'

'I swear that I shall never intentionally hurt you, Magda. This parting was not of my making, as you well know. I want you to marry me—but if you will not I shall never marry. If you insist that we carry on as before, I shall renounce my title in favour of some distant cousin, and we shall go on with our plans.'

'Giles, you cannot. I cannot allow you to make such a sacrifice. Besides…' She was about to tell him that she wanted to be his wife when he took a sudden step backwards without noticing where he put his foot and the next moment she felt him slipping. 'Giles! The edge is not safe!'

He let go of her as he lost his balance and she saw that a small chunk of the cliff had given way beneath his feet. She screamed as he slid over the edge, clawing desperately as he tried to get a hold to save himself. For a moment as he disappeared from sight, she was terrified, convinced that he had slid all the way down, but then she heard his voice call to her and knelt to look down at him. Her heart seemed to stop as she saw how precarious his situation was and knew that only the merest chance had prevented him from plunging into the sea. His coat had caught on a tuft of coarse grass protruding from the cliff face, his feet balancing on a precarious ledge, a sheer drop beneath him to the jutting rocks below, while he sought for a firmer grip.

'Get help,' he said. 'I can hold for a while—don't try to pull me back yourself. You couldn't manage it in your condition…'

'Don't you dare tell me what I can manage, Giles Benedict!' she cried. She was frightened almost out of her wits, but she knew that there were only seconds to spare. His hold was tenuous and before she could fetch help he might slide all the way down to the bottom and be shattered by the rocks. 'For once in your life you will do as I tell you.'

Margaret had been wearing a separate skirt and bodice over her petticoat and she whipped off her skirt, tying it into a knot with her shawl to make a makeshift rope. Behind her there was a stubby bush that looked secure enough to take his weight, and fastening one end of her rope to the bush with three knots, she threw the other down to him.

'Tie that around your wrist,' she instructed as he caught it instantly. 'It is secured to a bush. You can use it to climb back up. I shall help to steady you and pull as much as I can. You have to do it, Giles. That grass won't hold much longer; it is already giving way. Trust me, the bush will take your weight!'

'God help me if it doesn't,' he muttered, but he wound the material about his wrist, before freeing his coat, and then pulled sharply on the rope she had made, testing it before putting his full weight on it.

As soon as Margaret saw he was trying to haul himself up, she went to the other end and put her weight before the bush, giving him what assistance she could, though it was of scarce help to him. However, he had powerful shoulders and strong arms, and gradually he was hauling himself over the edge. She saw first his head and then his shoulders appear above the edge. Letting go of the rope, she ran to tug at his coat as he lay half-suspended over the edge, and then in that moment a shout came from behind them and all at once her gardener was there, adding his strength to hers. In seconds Giles was lying on his face, safely away from the edge.

Margaret fell to her knees, exhausted by the effort she had made, unable to move or speak for several seconds. It took Giles a moment longer to catch his breath before he looked up at her, his expression unreadable.

'I shall expect better obedience from my wife in future, Magda. If you ever risk your life so unnecessarily again, I shall break your neck myself.'

'That is a ridiculous contradiction, Giles,' she said and, rising to her feet, turned to thank the gardener effusively in French. He grinned at her, pulled at his forelock and then ambled off, chuckling to himself. Margaret turned to Giles once more. 'If you are not going to lie there all night, you had better come up to the house.'

'As long as you don't intend to throw me out as soon as you've assured yourself that I am fit to travel.' He stood up and looked at her, one eyebrow quirked. '*Madame*, you are hardly decent to be congratulating your gardener in that state. It is no wonder that he was laughing as he walked away.'

Margaret glared at him. 'Sir, I do not give a damn what I look like! Had I not acted as I did, you would even now be lying on those rocks down there. I have no wish to have your death on my conscience—even if you are a stubborn, bad-tempered, impossible man!'

His eyes gleamed. 'You are a stubborn, wilful woman, and you deserve I should put you across my knee and administer a spanking.'

'Sir, I am turning cold. Will you not give me your coat? If you intend to stand here all night in useless conversation, I may well catch my death.'

'Oh, Magda,' he said and glanced back towards the cliff edge as if only then realising how close he had come to death. 'What am I going to do with you?'

'Do you think you could give me your coat—and then kiss me?' she said, her voice husky with emotion. A shiver went through her as she realised what might have happened. 'Or perhaps…'

His arms went round her and she felt the shudder run through him seconds before he bent his head to kiss her on the lips, softly at first and then with increasing demand.

'Damn it,' he muttered as he looked down at her. 'I am not sure how to treat you, my love. I have been starved of the sight of you and now I am half-afraid to touch you.'

'Well, you need not be. I shall not break if you touch me,' she said and smiled at him, the glitter of tears in her eyes. She had come so close to losing him for ever that she dare not even think about it. 'Do you truly love me so much? I have been afraid that I would never see you again. And I was not sure of your heart once I learned the truth of your behaviour at the start of our affair.'

'Who told you that I was once foolish enough to think you an assassin and a spy?' He asked, raising his brows.

'Lord Ellwood said something to me just before he died, but I took it for the rambling of a dying man. It was Felicia who told me the whole story. I saw her in Paris when I visited a few days ago. Belmont told her the whole before he became ill, I suppose.'

'Damn her for her interference! If she was meddling…'

'No, no, my dearest,' Margaret said and placed a finger to his lips. 'She hasn't a malicious bone in her body. She just doesn't think before she speaks.'

'She has the brain of a peahen.' Giles said crossly. 'She enjoyed being the duchess, but if she imagines I am interested…'

'You flatter yourself,' Margaret teased. 'Felicia thinks you too stern and cross. She prefers an older man to fuss over her—someone she can twist around her little finger.'

'Am I too stern?' He looked genuinely surprised and Margaret laughed.

'Sometimes, just a little. I thought so at the start.'

'I suppose I have always taken life seriously. But when I was with you I think we laughed a great deal?' He raised his brows at her. 'You are going to marry me, aren't you, my darling?'

'We shall go up to the 'ouse and discuss it,' she told him, tipping her head to one side, her accent for his benefit alone. 'I think that I shall 'ave to consider very carefully, my lord. I 'ope you are intending to make up for lost time? I 'ave not been kissed for too long…' She laughed huskily as he reached out for her. 'I have been so very alone without you, Giles—and I thought I should never know how it felt to be kissed again.'

Giles reminded her immediately, and, putting his coat and his arm about her, they turned as one and began to walk back towards the house.

Chapter Thirteen

'I cannot believe we are really here together like this,' Giles said and reached out, drawing her closer to him in the bed. Somehow she managed to nestle into his body despite the awkwardness of hers. 'Are you going to marry me, my darling?'

'Of course I want to be your wife,' she said and touched his face, stroking the slight roughness of the shadow of beard on his cheek and feeling the deep shudder that went through him. She could never have guessed that it meant so much to him to have her for his wife. 'I have known that for months, Giles. I was such a fool to believe that it would be impossible to find happiness with a man.

'Aunt Kate was unlucky in her husband, as was Caroline's mother in her family, but I have learned that it does not always have to be like that. I love you and I know that I should be miserable without you.' She smiled and kissed him. 'I discovered that when I saw men dying of their wounds and knew that you might have been one of them.'

'I heard how brave and good you were to our men.

It must have been a terrible experience for you, my darling.'

'It was hard to see their suffering,' she admitted. 'But how could I do otherwise, knowing that you might be in like case? I used to pray that if you were injured a gentle woman would tend your hurts. And I was terrified that you might die and I not be with you.'

'Did I not promise to return?'

'But promises may be broken. Until I had your letter I was on thorns, my love.'

'Oh, Magda, how I have missed this, lying close to you, just talking, being alone with you. You are so lovely. It is no wonder that without you life no longer holds the zest it once did,' Giles admitted, his hand smoothing the little hollow at the small of her back. He kissed her softly on her lips and then on the tip of her nose. 'Since I thought you lost to me I have not known what I want to do with my life, Magda. Nothing seemed to appeal without you, my love.'

'For me the years ahead seemed empty, though I would have had some compensation in your child,' she said and stroked the soft hair on his chest and sighed, recalling her unhappiness these past months. 'But the future must be for you to decide, Giles. I shall be happy anywhere as long as I am your wife and we are together.'

'The estate is in good hands for the moment, though at some time I dare say we shall make it our home—but Wellington says he needs me here for the foreseeable future. I dare say it may take two or even three years to settle everything to his satisfaction. We should be based in Paris until then, though we could take a small house out of town—and we could stay here when we have a few days to ourselves. I should have to travel to Vienna or perhaps Rome sometimes, and once the child is born I should like you to come with me—if that is your wish?'

'You know that it is,' she said and lifted her face for his kiss. 'For the moment it would suit me to live here in France, and, indeed, in Paris itself, for it is a city I love. One day we shall go back to England so that our children know that it is their home, but I am happy to travel where you will, Giles. I have often had a fancy to see more exotic lands.'

'We shall see,' he promised. 'The climate of certain countries can be harsh for some, but particularly ladies and small children, and I would not want you to suffer ill health because of it.'

'You are thinking of the girl you loved and lost when you were young?' She raised herself on one elbow to look at him, her hair falling forward like a scented curtain across her face. He brushed it back, his hand lingering on her cheek as she gazed down at him. 'That was so sad and hard for you to bear, Giles, but you must not worry. I am very strong and seldom ill.'

'Pamela was too young and fragile to be exposed to the rigours of such a climate and the fever that ended her life was virulent. I think she took it from a native girl she had befriended, but I was devastated by her death.'

'I understand, my love. She was your first love and you will never quite forget her.'

'Only because it was such a waste of life,' Giles said and put out his hand to tangle his fingers in Margaret's hair. The scent of her was tantalising, making him aware of the burning need inside him. 'But she was not right for me, Magda. We should have grown apart as the years passed—I need a woman like you, a woman who can share my thoughts and feelings in a way that would have been beyond Pamela.' Margaret laughed softly and he stared at her. 'What is funny about that?'

'Nothing you meant to say,' she told him and explained about Edward Marshall's proposal. 'He was so sweet and generous, Giles. And I believe he would have married me had I accepted him.'

His eyes were dark, intent on her face. 'If you believed I had deserted you, why did you not accept his offer?'

'I would rather live alone than be married to another man. Surely you know that? No one could ever take your place in my heart and I will not compromise, Giles. I meant it when I told you I had no particular desire to marry. If I had not met you, I dare say I should have remained single all my life.'

'But you have promised to wed me and I shall not let you escape now,' he murmured huskily against her throat. 'Do you know the agony I suffered when I thought I had left it too late?'

'Foolish one,' she said and stroked his dark head as it nestled against her breast. 'Can you not feel the pounding of my heart? I do not want to escape you ever. Marriage to you will be the fulfilment of all my foolish dreams. Do you know that I used to dream of a knight on a black horse who came to ride off with me into the sunset?'

He lifted his head to look at her in amazement. 'That sounds unlike you, my love—far too romantic.' He gave her a mock scowl. 'What did this knight look like? Have I a rival after all?'

'He looked very like you and should—since the dreams did not begin until after the night you rescued me from my uncle.'

Giles chuckled deep in his throat, clearly delighted with this revelation. 'I see that I have not yet truly begun to know you, my wicked lady,' he murmured huskily.

'Ah, yes, we had not finished that particular discussion,' Margaret said and frowned at him. 'How could you imagine that I might be an assassin, Giles? A spy—now, perhaps I might just have been that…but an assassin?'

'It was very foolish of me,' he said and smiled down at her, knowing that she was merely teasing him, that their love was strong enough to surmount any such hurts. 'Yet a woman and her accomplice did make an attempt to kill Wellington, though that is a secret and must not be repeated.'

'And there was an attempt on the Regent's life,' Margaret said. 'Though I believe I am right in thinking that that was nothing to do with Bonaparte, but an act of revenge on the part of a dangerous political activist?'

'Yes, that is correct,' he agreed. 'It was not the first attempt and I dare say will not be the last—though these things are hushed up as much as possible. But you were very brave that day, my love. Prinny is your devoted admirer. He is firmly convinced you saved his life and told me recently, when I saw him, that he expects an invitation to our wedding.'

'Are we going to have a large wedding?' Margaret smiled at him and placed his hand on her swollen belly. 'Do you not think that inappropriate in the circumstances? It is bad enough that the Duke of Belmont is to wed his mistress, but to flaunt my condition before the eyes of polite society as a whole when we might marry here quietly…'

'Be damned to them all,' Giles said fiercely. 'It is my

intention to marry you with as much pomp and ceremony as is due to my duchess, Magda. Those who wish
to remain my friends will attend, and those who do not
may please themselves. We shall be married in London
as soon as I can arrange leave and return to France
almost at once. Wellington will not be best pleased that
I shall ask for more leave, but I hope to persuade him
by promising to remain in his service while he needs
me.'

'You must ask him to be godfather to our child,'
Margaret said. 'That should soften his heart a little, do
you not think so?'

'I think it might if you were to ask him yourself, my
darling.' Giles leaned over and kissed her lips. 'Much
as I want and love our child, my beloved, I cannot help
thinking he is a little in the way just at the moment. I
want so much to make love to you, but I am afraid of
hurting you and him.'

'You are so sure it will be a boy?'

'I do not mind whether we have a son or a daughter,
but you have referred to *him* several times, Magda.'

'Yes. I have always thought of *him* as a son,' she
replied, a little smile curving her mouth. 'But if you are
careful you need not treat me like Sèvres porcelain,
Giles. I am still the woman who loves you. At least we
can kiss and touch each other, if no more.'

Giles stroked her hair. 'I shall be content with that,'
he murmured. 'It is enough to have you near.'

Margaret laughed huskily and reached up to draw
him close, whispering of her own feelings as they lay
together in a gentle embrace.

Margaret looked at herself in the mirror and pulled a
face at Caroline, who was her chief maid of honour.

Kitty and Felicia had insisted that they also wanted to stand up with her on her wedding day, and they were elsewhere in the room busying themselves with her bouquet and various accoutrements.

'I am afraid that there is no disguising the fact that Giles's son is almost ready to be born,' she said ruefully. Her gown of ivory lace and satin had been cut flatteringly full in the front, but her condition must be plain to all. 'Wellington kept us dallying too long in Paris and I think we should be there now if Giles had not told him the wedding could not wait another week.'

'Surely it does not matter?' Caroline said. 'Everyone knew of your affair, after all. If they did not condemn you then, they cannot now that you are to be married—and I dare say you do not care for the opinion of those few who have decided to cut you?'

'Giles says they are the losers, not us, and to be honest, Caroline, I do not mind. We have so many friends in Paris that I should be happy to stay there for ever if Giles did not have to return eventually. He will of course assume his duties toward the estate one day, but for the moment we prefer the life we lead in Paris.'

'I hope you will visit us sometimes,' Caroline said and blushed a delicate pink. 'I have not told you my news, but I am certain now that I am to have a child—and I told Roddy last night.'

'Oh, Caroline,' Margaret said and hugged her. It was awkward and they laughed together. 'That is wonderful news. I am so pleased for both of you.'

'You know that Roddy can see a little now, don't you?'

'He did tell me that he saw flashes of light sometimes.'

'It is more than that now,' Caroline said and her face

lit up with happiness. 'In a good light he can see my face. We visited Sir Denis again and he says that he thinks Roddy will regain his sight completely in time.'

'Then I shall have nothing more to wish for,' Margaret said and kissed her cheek. 'And now I think we had better leave for the church or my impatient one may decide to dispense with the ceremony—and I do not mean Giles!'

'Oh, Maggie,' Caroline said and giggled. 'Wouldn't it be awful if you started to give birth walking down the aisle?'

'Unthinkable!' Margaret said. 'Do not put it into my head, dearest. I am concentrating on getting through to-day without mishap.'

'Of course you will,' Kitty said, hearing the last few words. 'Just make up your mind to it, Magda, and you'll manage perfectly.'

'I wish I had your confidence,' Margaret said. 'Keep your fingers crossed all of you!'

It was a cold winter day but the sun put in a reluctant appearance as the bride walked into church to join her groom—or *waddled*, as she described it mischievously later when they were alone. However, she managed to survive the church service and the glittering reception that followed without mishap.

If there were some ladies who tittered behind their fans and whispered that the bride was a disgrace, most were happy to see her glowing smiles. She was a favourite with the Regent, who claimed the privilege of kissing the bride with every evidence of pleasure.

Edward Marshall congratulated Giles at the reception. 'You are a lucky man, sir. Magda is truly lovely, not just in looks but in all the ways that a man might desire.'

'I know that I am fortunate,' Giles said. 'She tells me that you have been kind to her and for that I thank you, sir.'

The two men shook hands and Margaret smiled to see them, for she knew that Giles had conquered his jealousy and would not need to feel it again.

Her son was born in the early hours of the following morning, in the comfort of Kitty's best guest chamber in London. Lord Russell had offered his home for their brief honeymoon, and it had been arranged that Margaret would stay for a week or two until she was recovered from the birth, when Kitty and her husband would accompany her to Paris.

'I was afraid I might have to return to Paris before he was born,' Giles said as he proudly nursed the child later that day and smiled down at Margaret as she lay resting against piles of soft pillows. 'But you have given me the greatest gift a man could ask and I shall never be able to tell you how much I love you both.'

'I am only thankful that it did not happen in church. I was terrified that my waters would break during the ceremony and shame us all,' Margaret said and laughed. Only with this one man could she dare to speak of such things openly. With any other gentleman the details of childbirth would be inexpressible. Oh, how lucky she was that they had met! 'So I may take it that you are pleased with your son, my lord?'

'Oh, yes,' he said softly and returned the child to its nurse. He sat on the edge of the bed as the door closed behind the girl and they were alone. Giles reached for her hand, then bent to kiss her. 'He is beautiful, my darling, and very like his mother.'

'I think he has your eyes, Giles,' she said and smiled at him as he reached out to stroke her hair back from her face. 'And I am glad that you are pleased with him.'

'I am pleased with you,' he said and took out a pretty little velvet box, handing it to her with an odd smile. 'It is merely a little gift to mark the occasion.'

Opening it, she saw that it was an exquisitely painted miniature of Giles on ivory set in silver and mounted with various coloured stones, the first letters of which spelled 'dearest'.

'Oh, Giles,' she said and smiled up at him, understanding so much more than she had when he had given her the gold bangle set with pearls in the shape of the crescent moon and a star. 'It is beautiful. I shall always treasure it.' Tears stung her eyes because she knew how much thought had gone into the gift, which had been commissioned just for her.

His hand caressed her cheek and he bent to kiss her once more. 'I am glad it pleases you,' he murmured softly. 'I wish that I did not have to leave you here, my darling, but Wellington was reluctant to have me leave Paris even for these few days.'

'You must do your duty,' she said. 'I shall join you in a few weeks, Giles.'

'Yes, I know,' he said. 'But I shall miss you.'

'I am always with you in my 'eart,' she whispered, her voice soft and husky. 'I 'ave no lovers but you, my lord, and I 'ope you know that in your 'eart. I am always yours, *n'est-ce pas*?'

'My own wicked lady,' Giles said and laughed as he saw the mischief in her eyes. 'To others you may become Margaret Duchess of Belmont, to your family you have always been Maggie, but for me you will always be Magda—the beautiful seductress who stole my heart.'

'You 'ave no cause to accuse me of seduction,' Margaret said. 'For it was you who would not be denied, my lord—you who set out to seduce me. Is that not so?' But her mouth was provocative and smiling, begging for his kisses, which he instantly supplied.

'I hate us to be apart even for this short time, but I must leave you, my darling. I cannot wait for the time to pass, but I shall trust you to be good, though if I hear that you have been driving in the park with Edward Marshall I shall come to fetch you back myself!'

'And you 'ave my permission to spank me,' she said, giving him a look that promised much. 'But for the moment I must rest and sleep—and if you do not mind so very much, my love, in a little while I shall have to feed your son.'

Win a luxury midweek break at Champneys!

To give you a special treat this Mother's Day, we have teamed up with Champneys to offer one lucky winner a special midweek mother and daughter break.

This fabulous prize includes two nights' accommodation for two people, all meals and unlimited use of the facilities — together with a massage and facial for each person.

As a family-run business, Champneys prides itself on offering exceptional standards in beauty, fitness, nutrition and well-being – so you can be assured that you'll be getting nothing but the best!

You can choose to take your break at one of four top resorts around the UK: Champneys Henlow in Bedfordshire, Champneys Forest Mere in Hampshire, Champneys Springs in Leicestershire or Champneys Tring in Hertfordshire.

To complement your relaxing break, we will also send you a complete month's supply of your favourite Mills & Boon® or Silhouette® series romance books absolutely FREE!

For more information on Champneys visit www.champneys.co.uk or phone 08703 300 300.

YOUR JOURNEY TO SPA HEAVEN STARTS HERE...

For your chance to win, simply fill in your details below:

Name _____

Address _____

_____ Post code _____

Telephone no. _____

Your preferred prize for a month's supply of series books:

Mills & Boon® ❑

8 Modern Romance™, 4 Sensual Romance™, 2 Blaze™, 4 Tender Romance™,
6 Medical Romance™, 3 Historical Romance™, 1 Super Historical Romance™

Silhouette® ❑

6 Special Edition™, 3 Desire™ 2 in 1, 6 Sensation™, 4 Intrigue™, 3 Superromance™

Please send your completed entry form to:

Mother's Day Promotion, Harlequin Mills & Boon Ltd., PO Box 676, Richmond, Surrey TW9 1WU.

Closing date for entries is 30th April 2005

Terms and Conditions

1. To enter, follow the directions above or to obtain an entry form, please write to the above address. All requests for entry forms must be received by 31st March 2005. One entry per household only. 2. Draw open to all residents of the UK and Eire aged 18 and over. Employees and immediate family members of Harlequin Mills & Boon Ltd and Champneys are not eligible. 3. To be eligible, all entries must be received by 30th April 2005. No responsibility can be accepted for entries that are lost, delayed or damaged in the post. Proof of postage cannot be accepted as proof of delivery. 4. The offer is for two nights' accommodation for two people sharing a standard twin room with all meals, unlimited use of the facilities (swimming pool with whirlpool, sauna/steam, gymnasium and complete programme of exercise and relaxation classes) and a massage and facial per person included. This is available at Champneys Henlow in Bedfordshire, Champneys Forest Mere in Hampshire, Champneys Springs in Leicestershire or Champneys Tring in Hertfordshire. Prize must be taken within 12 months. No alternatives to the prize will be offered. 5. Travel to and from venues is not included. 6. Winners will be determined in a random and independently supervised draw from all eligible entries received. 7. Prize winner notification will be made no later than 14 days after the deadline for entry. Winners will be obligated to sign and return a Release of Liability within 15 days of attempted notification. In the event of noncompliance within this time period or if any prize or prize notification is returned as undeliverable, an alternative winner will be drawn from eligible entries. 8. Names of winners and full terms and conditions are available on request. 9. As a result of this application you may receive offers from Harlequin Mills & Boon Ltd. If you do not wish to share in this opportunity, please write to the data manager at the address shown above.

MILLS & BOON®

Volume 10 on sale from 2nd April 2005

Lynne Graham

International Playboys

Bond of Hatred

Available at most branches of WHSmith, Tesco, Martins, Borders, Eason, Sainsbury's and all good paperback bookshops.